"Every story in *The Human Alchemy* is a finely-wrought tapestry, containing many shades of darkness and light. Michael Griffin deftly weaves together threads of loss, mysticism, and creeping fear to create a truly remarkable collection. His tales usher the reader through the familiar world, then reveals to them the infinite."

—Richard Gavin, author of *Sylvan Dread*

"Griffin's characters often live in the aftermath of loss and, deeply wounded, they search for something to make them whole or to make them feel the world is not an arbitrary place. From cult followers awaiting enlightenment, to believers in mystical texts, to a mathematician who tries to formulate the structure of the world, to a woman who thinks she's entering a threesome but ends up getting (and losing) so much more, Griffin's characters pursue the lure of enlightenment into places that are very dark indeed—and once they're inside, chances are they won't be able to get out. A strong collection that makes us understand the weird in a powerful new way."

—Brian Evenson, author of *A Collapse of Horses*

"Michael Griffin's *The Human Alchemy* is fine art dripping slime from another dimension. This is cool, strange, creepy, elegant fiction. Think Iceberg Slim in a tailor-made Italian suit channeling the best of Lovecraft while dragging it, kicking and screaming, into our time. Throw in crackling dialogue and an Escher-like ability to bend time and space while forging new realities and what you have is a collection that cements Griffin as one of the most stylish, unique, and entertaining voices in contemporary weird fiction."

—Gabino Iglesias, author of *Zero Saints*

"Michael Griffin's *The Human Alchemy* reveals a multifoliatedly arcane world hidden beneath the surface of our own mundane one, riddling it with hell-holes, quicksand and potential ecstatic ruin. His stories snag and drown readers by degrees, fast or slow, every sequence a new section of reef lying in wait for unwary navigators, especially those trained to expect the usual horror tropes. In other words, damn this stuff is Weird."

—Gemma Files, author of *Experimental Film*

Praise for Michael Griffin's *The Lure of Devouring Light*

"Mike Griffin skillfully works the rich seams of quiet horror and contemporary weird. *The Lure of Devouring Light* is a superb selection of strange stories. It's the kind of debut that should command attention from genre fans and critics."

—Laird Barron, author of *The Beautiful Thing that Awaits Us All*

"Michael Griffin's fiction is sleekly poetic, disorienting, light and fierce. With this debut collection, Griffin establishes himself as a writer of already matured sensibilities, fiercely dedicated to the exploration of pain. Merciless."

—Michael Cisco, author of *Animal Money*

"Often, Mike Griffin's stories isolate an extraordinary dynamic between individuals who can only sustain the strange world they inhabit, secretly and together, with abject devotion to it. Anything short of passion will cause a rift in the narrative they've created, disclosing uncertainty, selfishness, ambition. Opening old wounds, or asking new questions. (For example, is love worthwhile or even possible set against a natural environment we've degraded beyond recognition? Or, what kind of integrity will we maintain if the monsters come for us?) At his finest moments Griffin achieves either a luminous grace or a breathtaking plummet into the unknown. In both cases the shock is earned by the tale that precedes it, and the stakes are as high as they can get. What I admire most (and there is plenty to admire in his writing) is an unforced, elegant ability to make his characters matter to us, in all their preening desire and almost magical expressions, like people we've known, loved, and left behind when all the bad shit happened—but with deep regret."

—S.P. Miskowski, author of the Skillute Cycle

"The focus in these stories is often on relationships that cause the characters to analyze how they intersect with the lives of others, and to contemplate their lives as individual beings—these examinations reflected outwardly in an environment of nightmarish disorientation and dreamlike transformation. This is dark fiction of a rare literary refinement, crystalline and poetic, that never sacrifices the frisson of the weird and horrifying. A highly impressive collection."

—Jeffrey Thomas, author of *Punktown*

THE HUMAN ALCHEMY

Other books by Michael Griffin

Far from Streets
The Lure of Devouring Light
Heiroglyphs of Blood and Bone

THE HUMAN ALCHEMY

MICHAEL GRIFFIN

WORD HORDE
PETALUMA, CA

TABLE OF CONTENTS

Introduction by S.P. Miskowski xi

Firedancing 1

The Smoke Lodge 21

Everyone Gathers at Haystack Rock 43

The Slipping of Stones 67

The Tidal Pull of Salt and Sand 85

Delirium Sings at the Maelstrom Window 109

An Ideal Retreat 127

Endure Within a Dying Frame 227

The Only Way Out Is Down 247

The Insomniac Who Slept Forever 271

The Human Alchemy 287

Publication History 321

To my mother, Kathleen Griffin, who always made me believe I absolutely could.

INTRODUCTION

S.P. MISKOWSKI

Among the notably talented writers currently testing the boundaries of weird fiction, the usual literary classifications still apply. There are prose stylists known primarily for beautiful language and haunting atmosphere; experimentalists playing with the limitations of structure and characterization; and authors who accentuate action to demonstrate or reinforce a theme. Some of these writers are strongly influenced by H. P. Lovecraft, others more obviously by Edgar Allan Poe. Some follow a subtle and narrow path established by Shirley Jackson or Robert Aickman in pursuit of mundane or domestic horrors. Others are more profoundly affected by the work of Karl Edward Wagner and Charles L. Grant, inspired by folk horror and modern psychology.

I'll go out on a limb to say the most compelling and original weird fiction I've encountered combines all or most of the above. Furthermore, it is both intensely personal and objectively philosophical, considering both experience and context within the same works. In such fiction the atmosphere reflects theme, and theme supports the psychological underpinnings of the story, creating a seamless, multi-layered narrative.

When I think of weird fiction of this caliber, synthesizing the most arresting elements of the weird tradition while discovering new or relatively uncharted territory, I think of Mike Griffin's fierce and gracefully delineated stories. He is familiar with the work of past masters of horror and fantasy but unlike devotees who adhere to the perceived 'rules' of legendary genre writers, Griffin understands that literature is not a vault filled with tattered, precious relics. Its substance is more akin to a garden where strange and fascinating hybrids keep emerging. The only important rules are those the writer selects for a given story.

On the surface, the stories in this volume—Griffin's second, following and building upon his 2016 collection, *The Lure of Devouring Light*—are about isolation and communion, ritual and sacrifice. We understand from the start that something must be given up or given over in the natural pursuit of harmony, even if that harmony is elusive or impossible. The suspense comes from not knowing the severity of the sacrifice, or the exact form it might take.

In "The Smoke Lodge" an emotional exchange between natural and supernatural beings seems at first glance benign. Early on a character among the cheerful ensemble of writers compares their gathering to *The Big Chill*. Later when these old friends conjure the restless spirit of a dead mentor their actions might be merely a heartfelt tribute. Yet the means of communication between the living and the dead is a book of arcane knowledge that might have powers not fully understood by those who employ it for this macabre reunion. By the end of a booze-, drug-, and magic-induced communion with the oracle they take to be their dead friend, we feel a dark-edged undercurrent to the proceedings. There is both sadness and an intuition that what was conjured might have been better left untouched.

Often Griffin's tales of longing and loss express a dangerous duality, one life observed and another just out of reach, perhaps mirroring one another or existing in a kind of echo or reverberation within the same space. This is true of the houses in "An Ideal Retreat" and "The Only Way Out Is Down." These locations offer what we would ordinarily take to be comfort and privacy. Yet the characters attached to them are not comfortable. They are plagued by a sense of alternate spaces, shadows and shapes that keep shifting—and not only with the light. A quiet madness pervades these stories, forcing the protagonists to explore every crevice until they can locate a border, a parallel, or a door leading to something that cannot exist in the world we know.

In "The Insomniac Who Slept Forever," first published in *The Madness of Dr. Caligari* edited by Joseph S. Pulver, Sr., a man seeks only the relaxation and solace of restful sleep. In the hands of a strange doctor at a special clinic he undergoes a cure for his chronic insomnia, one involving extraordinary mechanics and physical constraints. The result is not freedom from insomnia but rather a melding of the worst aspects of dreaming and wakefulness. The two sides of his dilemma merge into a singular and terrifying awareness of the present as an ongoing nightmare.

The title of the collection is drawn from its final tale. Originally appearing in the anthology *Eternal Frankenstein* edited by Ross E. Lockhart, "The Human Alchemy" is the ultimate story in more ways than one. This bright gem perfectly brings together certain ideas with which Griffin is often preoccupied—male and female duality, the nature of passion, and the merging of art and science.

Two extraordinary individuals, married doctors, attempt to create a system of never-ending renewal in order to avoid the gradual wearing away of their desire for one another. To accomplish this, they must first make a confidante of an attractive younger acquaintance. As their plans unfold before the young woman, uneasiness gives way to a crazy kind of logic. The couple's beauty and allure are undeniable, perhaps irresistible. Their plans begin to make a terrible kind of sense. And the final reveal is one of those moments Griffin constructs so well, a breathtaking and surprising embodiment of everything that precedes it, all of it underscored by the fear that none of this can possibly turn out well.

The worlds created within a Mike Griffin story are like that—gorgeous to the eye and ear, charged with an erotic current that makes us long to simply revel in the moment. Yet all around are signs that mortality may not be the only price to pay for indulging in all of this natural and unnatural beauty. By the time our worst suspicions are confirmed, we are lost. But is being lost in such beauty really the worst way to go?

— S.P. Miskowski

"The secret is that only that which can destroy itself is truly alive."
—C.G. Jung, *Psychology and Alchemy*

"The common matter of all things is the Great Mystery."
—Paracelsus, *Liber Primus*

FIREDANCING

Bay wakes on the living room floor amid mounded clothing pulled from the bedroom closet. The house stripped of furniture, the kitchen lacks food. Even after a night spent endlessly slow-falling through black tar, Bay aches to retreat into sleep, to face the intolerable panic moment before death.

The new reality won't be blinked away. Sunlight blazes through bare windows, reflects on glossy hardwoods. Everything Bay owns, aside from the pile of shirts and jeans on which he slept, leans against the wall. Twenty large canvases, tortured visions in black, umber and gray. Bins of crushed and depleted tubes of oil paint. Jars of solvent, thinner, a few brushes. The room in which he painted, until yesterday, stands empty as the rest.

He contemplates a fresh canvas, mixing pigments, trying to organize color into some sort of clarification. Lately his painting's been work-for-hire, no time left for himself. The job's finished. Annie's gone. His future is nothing, a vacant expanse.

Taking everything, shutting off power, that's Annie's message. He hears her voice.

All you need is art, so I'll take the rest. See how you do, just you, your ratty jeans and boots, and your fucking art.

She's right. He's stuck. A house he can't pay for, a wardrobe more suited to a college kid than a man almost forty, and a pile of what Annie calls *your primal scream paintings.* The only thing left is her note.

Just go. Our accounts are all closed. I'm with him now.

Art always trumped everything, an all-important matter of depth and complexity amid life's shallower trivialities. Now Bay feels embarrassment at this self-indulgent conceit. Art, a child's game. What's it ever gotten him? Three gallery shows, twelve canvases sold. No options, no hirable skills, no money for a new place. Nothing to eat. Worse than hunger is the shame. Even if he had somewhere to land, he can't drive. Collecting the money owed him by the theater would mean facing the man who took his wife.

Bay sees her point now. A man's able to take care of himself, his wife. If he can't do those things, he's just a child. Worse, a joke.

Hopelessness, a gaping chasm. Recognition of his future, a dawning chill. Like blood slow-trickling from a vein, life's warm pulse replaced by icy fear. Bay envisions the bridges of Northeast Portland, questioning his own seriousness even as the thoughts occur. Would he really go there?

The bridges aren't high enough. He laughs. So lame, predictable. What options are left? He shivers.

From his pocket, the cell phone rings. He's forgotten it, assuming she'd cancel the service. The only numbers programmed in are the last two people he'd ever call. The incoming number seems familiar. 541, somewhere south.

Bay presses a button. "Hello?"

"Hi ho, Buckaroo. Been a while."

"Petersson..." Bay trails off, calculating years. Wondering, *Why now?*

"Bad time?" Petersson sounds like he's anticipating a joke. "Sorry it's been so long. You know the grind, buying wood, selling wood. Thing is, Minerva called out of the blue, told me to invite you—"

"Called you? Did I miss—"

"Divorced, yeah. Both of us traveling. One time, she didn't come back. Anyway, hill party's this weekend. Minerva says, make sure you come."

"Shit, my wife too. She just..." Bay stops, changes his mind.

"What?"

How to say the words? If Minerva left, Petersson will understand. "What's the hill party?"

"Shit, Minerva said something's up with you." Petersson's tone shifts.

"She always said, if just once I'd believe... Anyway, listen, I'm driving up. You still at that bungalow in Irvington? Get your ass ready."

"When?"

"Right now, Hoss. Fucking Hill Party, capital H, capital P."

"I heard, but what's the Hill Party?"

"You visited Roseburg how many times, you missed every Mallard Hill Party? I'll be there in three hours."

The call disconnects. Petersson's coming.

Bay's hands tremble, as if in recognition of something averted.

2.

"Thoughtful of you." Bay tips back the Jim Beam fifth. The bottle knocks the ceiling inside Petersson's posh gentleman's pickup. "I was gone just a few hours. She managed to empty the place. Must've hired—"

"I said, don't talk about that. Don't think about that." Petersson's driving, I5 South. Three hours to Roseburg. "Lesson I learned after Minerva skipped. Obsessively sifting back, through everything, that ain't what you need."

"What do I need?"

"Mental reboot." He grins. "Puke your troubles away at a two-day party."

"So this Mallard Hill place, it's where Erik and Minerva grew up?"

"Mmm. Fifteen miles outside Roseburg."

"Speaking of Minerva."

Petersson's grip flexes on the wheel.

Bay tries again. "The worst thing about Annie leaving, I finally did what she wanted. Took a commission, murals for Cinema 21, that's an art theater in Northwest."

"I know, dummy. Film major, remember? You took us there." He exhales. "*Seven Samurai*. Me and Minerva."

"Lumber baron with a film degree, that's funny. Most of us liberal arts guys..." Bay stops. Another swig. "Annie set it up, knew the owner. They kept showing up, checking on me. Arrive together, leave together."

"We weren't going to talk about that."

Bay thinks, *What else?* "So Erik grew up on this hill, but won't attend the big drunk-fest?"

"Nah, he stopped that recovery shit. After he withdrew from us, his sponsor tried to make him cut off Minerva." Petersson shrugs. "Erik only drinks beer now. Lives on the edge of the Mallard tract, a cabin overlooking the South Umpqua. Started some river guide thing. Fishing, rafting." His face clouds. "Minerva's in the main house. Stopover from the endless touring."

"So much land, Erik gets his own corner." Bay resists redirecting toward Minerva. Petersson's breakup makes him feel less awful.

"Might be the most impressive parcel in Douglas County. Everyone thinks Old Mallard got rich in lumber, but Minerva let slip he returned from the Merchant Marines, World War II, a millionaire at nineteen."

"Merchant Marines, is that still a thing? Maybe they'd let me—"

"He climbs aboard the post-war lumber boom, builds Mallard Hill. Meets a woman up in Washington, on business near Olympic Forest. This first wife starts him jetting around, blowing millions in Mexico. Spends the sixties and seventies financing films, legendary stuff by Buñuel and Jodorowsky."

"Lest I forget that film degree."

Petersson makes an undignified snort. "Always trekking the wilds of Mexico, South America, Antarctica, returning rejuvenated, trailing new wives to replace ones who die of typhus or malaria. Finally disappears, the Chilean Andes. Erik and Minerva, living under Old Mallard's tutors and housekeepers, assume they're orphaned a second time. Everyone gives up hope."

"But..."

"He reappears, head shaved, silent as a mystic. No explanation where he's been ten months, what happened to wife number six, seven, whatever. Thereafter, no more film production or travel. Grabs another wife to replace the one rumored frozen to death. Further expands the house. His only indulgences are these parties, and the visiting artists, visionaries and occult weirdos. Some remain months, years at a time. Old Mallard, he's like fucking Tom Bombadil. Erik grew up thinking the man's his grandfather, later learns, no, it's *great*-grandfather."

Bay stifles envy at such a life. "One part Dos Equis' Most Interesting Man in the World, one part Kwai Chang Caine."

3.

The lower hillside is dotted with stainless RVs, psychedelic buses, cars, trucks, motorcycles. Tents fill the slope nearest the towering house. The ground floor sprawls, annexed with rock-walled gardens, greenhouse, picnic areas with fire pits, and a concert stage beneath a log pavilion. The upper levels narrow like a mountain coming to a peak. Windowed surfaces reflect afternoon sun.

"You never said..." Bay marvels. "What a structure!"

"We've got motorcycle stunts, costumed freaks, and topless hippie girl volleyball." Petersson points. "But you, you're into architecture."

"Boys!" Erik approaches, grinning and newly bearded, carrying a belled half-yard glass of mealy brown beer. "You staying all weekend? Let's kayak the Umpqua Sunday. I've got kayaks."

Bay indicates Erik's beer. "I'm just glad our friendship's no longer *regrettably over*."

Erik smacks Bay's shoulder, leads them toward the pavilion. "We all gotta be stupid sometimes. Anyway, there's no sober at the Hill party." He offers a taste.

Bay sips. "What the hell is it? An oatmeal stout, or something?"

"Belgian dark. Minerva's friend makes it. Nuts, chocolate, who knows what. Like eating a slice of cake."

Under the pavilion stand six old refrigerators with taps through the doors. Erik fills plastic cups. "So, you want to meet Old Mallard before things get ridiculous?"

The atmosphere beyond the door is rustic as a lodge, and smells of smoking game meat. A black walnut stairway climbs.

Imagining glass-walled brightness above, Bay starts toward the stairs.

Erik pulls him back. "Sorry, off limits. Old Mallard's rules."

"Such incredible design," Bay says. "Unbelievable, something like this hidden out in the trees. I'd pay to go up—"

The stairs creak under the barefoot descent of a silver-stubbled man in black robes, followed by two older men and three women, all in black outfits of striking expense and formality, considering the setting. Each carries identical luggage, glossy black leather and chrome.

Bay, Erik and Petersson stand aside.

The six, despite lined skin and silver or gray hair, are all tan, vigorous and trim. Watching their goodbye embraces, Bay wonders at identities, connections. The last, an Asian man younger than the rest and standing apart, bows and turns to depart.

"Here, Toshi." The robed one, certainly Old Mallard, pulls Toshi into a warm hug.

Old Mallard closes the door behind the others, turns with the stable grace of a judoka, and places a familiar hand on Bay's shoulder. "One party ends, another begins. Members of my circle. Octobers we gather to hunt Roosevelt elk, have done since…" His gesture suggests many repetitions. "This fall, they'll expedition six months in Chile, so we hunted early. Splendid success."

"Expedition, those…" Bay stops.

"You mean, at their age?" Old Mallard assesses Bay, turns to Erik. "Finally, you bring someone who appreciates my architecture."

Erik smirks. "You never let anybody upstairs."

"Or downstairs," Old Mallard allows. "This main floor, called Earthwide, it's for everyone. A few see the second floor. If you do, I tell you its name."

"Each level has a name?" Bay asks.

"Why not? Blackshard, Subterrain, Earthwide, Attainment, Lightpulse. Now I've told." Old Mallard smiles. "You crave a look upstairs?"

"I didn't mean…" Bay stammers. "I'm just intrigued. I studied architecture briefly, before changing to a more lucrative major."

Old Mallard turns to Erik, questioning.

"Bayard's joking," Erik explains. "Fine art degree. Financially, he's fucked."

Old Mallard laughs, touches Bay's arm. "Bayard Lane, Minerva mentioned you. If you're still upright later, come. I'll show you Attainment."

Petersson shoots Erik a look.

4.

Bay and Petersson emerge, confronted by sunlight, and a cluster of bikers speed-drinking Jack Daniel's, swigging and passing. Another group of bikinied girls and shirtless boys smoke pungent weed from punctured beer cans and kick hacky-sacks.

Petersson heads uphill. "Let's dodge the crowds a bit."

Bay sees something's wrong. "What?"

"I've been coming since high school, shit, I was married to Minerva eighteen years. I've never been upstairs. Didn't even know there were basements." Creases bracket Petersson's mouth. "Anyway, you're going upstairs later. Good for you."

A barefoot twentyish girl approaches, face painted green with yellow flowers. "You look sad. Don't be sad." She digs in pockets of short-shorts cut from camo pants. Grass-stained palms cup two red and white capsules.

"Tylenol?" Petersson asks.

She grins. "No, it's Molly." Her eyes widen, excited with a secret. "My uncle, he's a chemistry prof in Eugene."

"Why the hell not?" Petersson pops one. "Wipe the slate."

"Molly, that's X in kiddie-speak?" Bay swallows the other. "Terrible decisions are sometimes best."

The flower girl, fragrant of marijuana and pumpkin bread, kisses Bay's cheek. As she skips away, he feels a flutter of desire.

"Homebrew," Petersson says. "This place. One big experiment."

They circle the upper field, and at the top slip through a gap in the perimeter wall of blackberry vines. Crowd noise fades.

Bay stumbles over a hippy couple fucking in the grass.

Petersson laughs. "I don't think they want you joining in!"

Bay waits until the couple are well behind. "Tell me something about you and Minerva. So I'll feel better about my shit."

As he climbs, breathing hard, Petersson appears to be pondering the question, not ignoring it. "Turns out Minerva's poly."

"Polly what?"

"Polyamorous. Not the best thing to learn, post-marriage." Petersson gestures at thickening forest. "This goes miles. Doubt anyone's surveyed all ten thousand acres." He turns, walks backward. "Fuck, now you've got me remembering. At Minerva's place. On drugs."

"Right now, I don't feel so bad," Bay says. "But I keep feeling like I want to talk about it."

"No, don't talk. Just climb."

Steel blue sky deepens into evening. The tractor-notched trail arcs, old growth looming on the upper slope.

Petersson stops at a cultivated viewpoint, overlooking the house, surrounding fields full of vehicles and tents, and the river beyond.

"You can almost…" Bay steps out, compelled toward the edge. How far would he fall? Vision flashes, inexplicable memories of motionlessness. A tar-stuck insect wriggling. A frozen moment. Inertia stored before a crash.

"All it would take…" Bay leans forward, starts to tip. Sickness rises in his gut. He reins himself in, starts to sit back. "I better sit."

"No, not here!" Petersson grabs Bay's arm. "This hill's one big ant colony."

Bay looks down, trying to figure. "Bullshit."

Petersson crouches, snatches something up. Grinning, he pops the wriggling ant into his mouth.

5.

They descend to fields illuminated by flickering bonfires and the volleyball court's stand-mounted event lamps. Sludge metal slurs on the pavilion stage for an audience of bearded heavies in leather boots and vests.

Bay almost mentions the twitching, teeth-grinding tension, until he sees Petersson's shirt soaked, his forehead dripping sweat.

As they near the gravel lot, a girl with a black bob shouts. "Bayard Lane! Hey, fucker." She weaves side to side, blocking Bay from sidestepping to keep up with Petersson. "Don't fucking go past me."

He remembers: a long-ago ex, from college weekends visiting Roseburg with Petersson. "Sorry, didn't recognize you, Rachel. Someone gave us ecstasy."

"I used to love X. Definitely more fun." She raises a bottle of lime snow cone syrup. "Had to quit vodka. Now I'm addicted to sugar." She drinks. "You're in Portland, right? What do you do in Portland?"

"Nothing." Bay looks for Petersson.

"Got to have a job, make money. Otherwise why go to college?"

The sky overhead churns, gray winged outlines against black. Vast gaping mouths.

Bay slips hands into pockets. "I paint a little. It's just, there's no money in it."

"Creativity, that's awesome, you know I have my radio show, plus drive a cab. I had this idea, broadcast my show from the cab, kind of kill two birds. Also, did you know about my kid? I had this idea I could save on babysitters, take him with me. My fares get a kick out of it, watching me breastfeed, plus the radio audience calling in, wanting to ask him questions, saying are you really driving a cab around Roseburg, carrying your baby?"

"Shit, Rachel," Bay says. "I forgot you were crazy."

She smiles. "He's seventeen now. Not really a baby."

Bay doesn't really trust his own math. *Ninety-four? No, ninety-five?*

"I see you figuring. Not yours, not quite. Got kids, Bayard?" She points at his ring. "See you're married."

Clouds seethe, emitting sparks. The moon's potent gravity pulls. Invisible gases drift.

"Don't know. Yeah."

"What's that mean?" She flashes white teeth. "Tell me something tasty."

"Yesterday, my wife emptied the house. Took all our stuff, all the money. Her money, really. Didn't have my own."

"Wow, truth. I don't drive a cab, that's stupid. I wait tables in Riddle Diner."

Down the hill, a bonfire roars. So huge, Bay wonders if it's hallucination.

"I need to look for Petersson."

He breaks away, drifts downhill, carried by a current. He looks back. Rachel's eyes change. Black coal pits burn, glowing fire, spewing smoke.

6.

Nearer, Bay decides the fire near the pavilion is real. Several bikers chest-bump and gesture. It seems like posturing, until real fighting starts. Motorcycles circle, revving an overpowering roar.

A burly gray-beard intervenes, embracing one fighter, who pushes him away, then clutching the other. Knives appear. The peacemaker continues, heedless of swinging blades. Others rush in, some trying to keep peace, others bringing the fight. The swarm spills dangerously near the fire.

A biker lobs something sizzling, like a huge firecracker. It explodes. Bare-chested men scramble, fall, hands over ears.

The only sound, bright ringing.

A mirrorshaded Lemmy lookalike staggers, right eye streaming blood.

Knowing he should stay back, Bay approaches. Out of the flames, an arm extends, pulls Bay near. Radiant heat, so intense. Bay pulls back against the sweat-slick hand, breaks free. He runs clear, shirttail smoldering.

A wild-eyed tiger girl, naked body painted orange with black stripes, runs into the fight. Those nearest freeze.

"Stop, you assholes. They're about to start the firedancing!"

7.

Pavilion loudspeakers emit subtle percussive loops. The bonfire crowd quiets, listening. Sonic layers accumulate, suggestive of impending drama.

Onstage, Minerva Mallard leads the troupe of twelve women and men in loose white shirts and black short tights. They stride barefoot, confident, descend steps and slip through the crowd. They form a uniform line, impossibly near the flames. All are dark-haired, and even the Caucasians are so tanned, the troupe appears uniformly chestnut-skinned.

The dancers follow the music's lead, building a kinetic, multi-layered churn, a blending of world influences. Sweat glistens, despite seeming effortlessness. All appear ageless, though Minerva is Bay's age, nearly forty. Movements express natural joy, like a smile of the whole body. The pace quickens.

The fire wall flickers, coloring dancers and watchers red-orange. Even standing back, Bay feels a warm, luminous glow, a sensation of youthful energy and potential he can't explain. For the first time since Annie's note, he feels buoyed, capable of imagining a future. Life continues. He may encounter pain, but he'll survive.

Darkening music, a new dance. The horizon shifts. In the soundscape, crisp metallic ticking snare offsets a black sea. Clouds swirl, darkly churning. The ground rumbles. Flames leap and roar.

Thoughts veer sideways, out of control. What happened to possibility, to hope? Bay sees Annie, laughing. The bastard cinema owner flicks his tongue. Bay wants to kill. From self-pity to hope, sidelong to potent rage. He feels energized, lifted. An inward surge, a brew of anger and lust, propels him nearer the crowd. Strength surges in his muscles, a hot surging wave of testosterone. Vitality, danger. Bay wants to drink it in.

The throng moves in rhythm, rising, falling. Movement is handed off by touch. Each contact conveys from one to next the knowledge and timing of impending shifts.

Minerva's eyes are fierce, her body sweat-slick. She leads the dancers, pulling white shirts overhead to reveal naked torsos. Every body is tattooed on shoulders, arms or breasts. The tattoos themselves are alive, their flow distinct from the motions of bodies. Ink churns, spreading across hands, rising over faces like a devouring virus. As rhythm conveys from dancer to audience, lines of ink intertwine and extend, travel body to body. The audience nearest the troupe transforms, dark figures swimming outward in a wave of seeping black. Patterns move, carriers oblivious to their infection. The dance intensifies, quickens.

Bay wants to approach. Whatever this is, he'll surrender, let it take him. He's willing to forget, to wade in and submerge himself.

As he reaches the crowd's perimeter, those nearest the fire start to fall. They drop without protest, overcome. The troupe halts, motionless as mannequins, apparently unsurprised. The music continues, slowing. The audience's movements don't halt, but diminish with the rhythm. Those upright begin to disperse, sweat-drenched, murmuring satisfaction.

The collapsed are few. An opening widens around them. Others seem not to notice. Dark faceless figures in black hoods descend and drag away five motionless fallen.

Bay remains separate from the crowd, never quite joined.

Music stops. Bay wonders what he saw. Maybe he imagined black ciphers dragging bodies inked with contagion.

From the crowd, someone beckons. Minerva, in the white shirt again. She skips toward him, weightless. Her embrace is damp with the sweat of exertion. Her heart pounds against his chest.

"I'm so glad Petersson brought—" She backs up, pointing. "Oh Bay, you're hurt."

The front of his shirt is cut, blood-soaked. "The fight."

Minerva pulls his hand. "Come in, I'll get you something."

8.

Inside the house, a tranquil oasis. Minerva vanishes into darkness behind the stairwell, returns holding a jar.

"Come up." She starts upstairs.

One hand pressing his wound, Bay follows into the dark void. Halfway, he bumps into Minerva.

"Hold still," she says. "I'll fix you."

His shirt lifts.

Minerva smears cold, astringent balm. "How's that feel?"

"No pain," Bay says.

"There's always pain." She turns, resumes climbing. "Old Mallard keeps asking about you."

The room is a broad, many-windowed hexagon packed with hand-built variants on musical instruments: a horizontal long-stringed harp like an oversized bodiless piano; squares of metal plate hung like gongs; panels of knobs, vacuum tubes and tangled wire.

"Welcome to Attainment." Old Mallard speaks without looking up from a tray of water-filled glass bowls. Delicately he strokes the rims, sounding vibrations which shimmer high and light.

A Miles Davis lookalike clad only in white tennis shorts perches on a piano stool before a plywood harpsichord beside a stand of DIY electronics, horned speakers and arcane analog circuitry. A microphone cable dead-ends in acid-smelling yellow liquid in a Pyrex dish from which a second cable-end emerges into a mixing board. Tall speakers emanate thrumming drone.

Minerva leads Bay to a pair of Mies Van der Rohe lounge chairs. Both sit, listen.

Old Mallard and not-Miles improvise a slow-shifting ambience interspersed with rhythmic bursts verging on jazz. Patterns of insistent repetition underpin chiming drones. The mood tilts into a a slant, euphoria fraught with digressions into panic.

Bay's stomach goes queasy. Nerves jitter. Maybe the pill he took?

"Ecstasy these days," Old Mallard intones, "mostly amphetamine, I'm afraid." He steps away from the bowls. The drone continues, sustained in feedback of loops overlapping. He slides a subwoofer across the floor, takes Bay's hand, places it flat upon the low bass cabinet. "You need to slow down. Feel this."

Old Mallard drifts away, turning knobs, tweaking circuits, plucking at hacked-together string instruments.

Bay's teeth ache, a taste like radio static. The bass makes his head wobble as if barely attached. Thoughts split into nonsense, then cohere again. He fears he's missing time, phasing in and out of reality, or consciousness.

In panic, realizing he's alone, Bay jolts upright. "Where is she?"

Minerva lies reclining beside him, eyes closed, face pleasantly relaxed.

Bay tries to stand.

Old Mallard approaches. "Stop looking. Close your eyes."

"You reminded me of The Necks," Bay says. "They're an Australian avant—"

"I know them," Old Mallard says. "They've performed in this room."

Bay wants to express what he imagines to be his own transformation. The walk in the trees, the firedancing, this world of sound. Something within feels loosened. "I need to…" He trails off, urgency extinguished.

"You've been imprinted, like light-struck film." Old Mallard lifts an eyebrow. "Development awaits… some impetus."

"Why am I here?" Bay asks. "Why not Petersson, or Erik?"

Old Mallard looks to Minerva. "The way is closed by default."

Minerva's eyes remain closed. "Even me, Grandfather only accepted me when I returned, already initiated. Many possibilities opened, but that ended things with Petersson."

At the same moment, both Minerva and Old Mallard turn, looking to a dark corner. There stands a figure, costumed and hooded in black, like those who retrieved the fallen firedancers.

"Soon," the figure turns, disappears.

Old Mallard stands. "To Lightpulse."

Bay expects Minerva to guide him downstairs. Old Mallard gives her a look.

"This way." Minerva leads Bay to another stairway, hidden in darkness.

9.

Lightpulse is smaller than Attainment, glass walls transparent to night. Hexagonal sides merge in steel pillars hung with massive photographs and dark paintings.

"Witkin, that photo. Joel-Peter Witkin." Bay turns, stops, unable to believe. "That's... you have a Francis Bacon!"

"Bacon created this," Old Mallard says calmly, "tormented at his love's dying."

Bay scans memory, trying to place the image. It resembles the Black Triptychs, brushwork looser, more organic. "Is that *Misperceptions of Broken Philosophers*?" Immediately he regrets the suggestion. "It's considered lost."

"Lost?" Old Mallard shrugs, palms up. "Some may consider it so. Lost to the world of buyable critics, dollar-focused museums. But truly lost?" He points. "It's right there, on my wall."

Bay approaches the next pillar, hungry to discover new wonders.

He stops.

In a window seat beyond the reach of halogen spotlights, a cloth-draped human shape reclines.

"Bayard," Old Mallard asks behind, "have you recently imagined dying?"

"I dreamed...." Bay backs up, turns. "Who is this?"

"Thoughts of death brought you here," Old Mallard insists. "Tolstoy said, Life is indestructible; it is beyond time and space, therefore death can only change its form, arrest its manifestation in this world."

Bay returns, scrutinizes the figure. Must be a sculpture. Some art piece, like a full-body death mask. "What did you say?"

"Death."

"I dreamed falling. The moment before the end extended forever."

Beneath the drapery, the figure moves.

"You want to postpone death." Old Mallard steps nearer.

The figure breathes. The head turns, the drapery slips. A woman's face, chalk white.

"Lightpulse is her favorite place. She chose to remain here tonight. Listening, waiting."

Bay doesn't realize he's reaching to touch the wrinkled face until Old Mallard stops his hand.

"My wife, Maia." Old Mallard turns her like an inanimate object. "She will be gone soon. Tonight."

Her eyes flick open, vibrantly alive. Such vivid green, Bay can't believe she's dying.

Old Mallard turns to Bay. "You're almost ready. But first..." He extends an open palm, offering a white flower petal, dry and powdery as Maia's face. "From Chile, in the Andes where I was initiated to the Six Sided Circle. The wise have utilized it for millennia, perhaps eons. There hidden, sight turned inward, they shrug off our culture's pallid temptations for ancient truths. Such is only attainable..." He looks down, as if remembering. "...through deep time."

Bay accepts the flower, places it on his tongue.

Old Mallard's smile is so subtle, almost not a smile. "Tolstoy again, *The Death of Ivan Ilyich.* 'He sought his former accustomed fear of death and did not find it. Where is it? What death? There was no fear because there was no death. In place of death there was light.'"

He bends, lifts Maia as if she weighs nothing.

"Come." He carries his wife in his arms.

10.

Bay follows quietly, mind reeling in a way distinct from the afternoon's ecstasy trip. His vision brightens, even in the dark stairwells.

They pass Earthwise, the main floor, and continue down.

A room hexagonal like the others, but smaller. Dark stone floors. Around the perimeter, six classical statues, white marble figures.

"Subterrain," Minerva whispers.

Old Mallard places Maia, face uncovered, on a granite platform. He mutters words, like an incantation. Rhyme, poetic meter.

Time speeds past, a blur of obscure ceremony. From hallucination into clarity, back again.

Is it still night? Fear tickles the back of Bay's mind. What does Old Mallard want, and Minerva? It was her idea Petersson invite him. Now she leans against him, clutches his shoulder, his hand. So much is uncertain. Bay keeps expecting Old Mallard to reveal some surprise, or Maia to spring the joke. To sit up, laughing.

They're all looking at him. Even Maia's green eyes.

"The long view means watching many shorter lives end." Old Mallard's voice is steady, grave. He lifts his wife again. "Soon Maia will go. There will be no laughing."

"Down," Minerva whispers.

Bay follows through another doorway, hidden until it's seen.

11.

Strange atmosphere, basement smell. Floor of dusty, hard-packed earth, walls grown with fungus or ferment. Bay doesn't remember the bottommost level's name until Minerva speaks it.

"Blackshard."

Here, no artistic wonders to rival Lightpulse's Witkin and Bacon. None of Attainment's otherworldly sounds, Subterrain's statues. Colored lights shine on twelve books, ancient black leather, each displayed within locked glass cases.

Bay recalls the story Petersson told. Is this a burial chamber for ten previous wives?

"Nine," Old Mallard says. "Maia is ninth." He pulls back the cloth to fully reveal her body. Her face, hands and feet are perfectly white, strangely chalky, but the rest of her body is pink and vital, decades younger than Bay guessed.

"Her breasts, still round as the earth," Old Mallard says, "soft as clouds." Lightly he touches her nipple. The skin hardens. "You see, and her sex, still pink and moist." Gently, reverently, he touches the cleft between her legs. "Why should she die? Because she accepts this end. Cancer beckons, she follows."

Maia lets out a breath. Bay jumps, startled, then realizes it's an ordinary sigh.

"Teaching the Six Sided Circle must wait. Maia won't last, nor the others. I offer this, to prepare you for what comes." Old Mallard's voice deepens. "The existence of *huitzitzili* is cyclical, like a tree. Vibrant and motile in summer, in winter motionless, shed of adornment. Waiting through cold for rebirth."

"What is?" Bay asks, breathless.

"*Huitzitzili*, the hummingbird. It defies physics, gravity, death. In winter it attaches to a tree trunk, remains frozen there, dry and featherless, lacking heartbeat. Spring thaw, it twitches to life, regrows feathers. It flies again, blue and weightless, a tiny god."

Minerva nods.

"I'm sorry for Maia," Bay says. "But what does this mean to me? And you, and Minerva?"

"I'm telling you there's no need to ride the train to the end of the line." He looks down, covers his wife in her wrap. "I will lie down with Maia, and others. I'll take from them, then wake strengthened."

"Even if that's possible, you can't live like that," Bay protests. "Always borrowing. There are only so many people..."

Old Mallard raises an eyebrow. "Such consumables are never in short supply." He bends, lifts Maia.

"Where next?" Bay asks. "We're at the bottom."

Minerva approaches his side, cautious, as if afraid he might spook.

"There's another, deeper, unnamed," Old Mallard says. "There had to be six."

12.

Through a curtain, down a sloping dirt ramp. Bay imagines the bottom-most room a circle. Eyes adjust, discern flat walls. Six sides.

The floor slopes to a central pit, wider and shallower than a grave, moist soil crawling with worms. Five bodies are arrayed around the hollow, skin seething ink-black. All lie twitching, sweaty and open-eyed, life stories re-written in creeping lines of ink.

This nameless room, so different from the rest. No art, no music or books. Just dying bodies and damp earth.

Old Mallard places Maia among the firedancing's fallen. She makes the sixth.

He turns, brushes Minerva's mouth with his thumb, then grasps Bay's elbow. "I'll take their deaths. I'll return. Distilled and clarified."

Bay realizes others are present, watching. Shrouded in black, they blend into walls. Bay recognizes the humming, throaty intonations, reminiscent of the music upstairs.

Old Mallard takes his place beside Maia.

Bay's mind spins, uncertain what he's seeing, what he's been offered. Membership in some circle? A creative life, empowered by agelessness. He can't imagine. The dead-end he fled already seems far away. Memory of Annie's face, the words in her note. All of it, another man's problem.

The tomb chills, the singing fades. The watchers vanish.

All that remains is the quiet stillness of death.

"Clarified," Bay whispers, sifting hints.

The emptiness of his life gives him freedom. If he found another Annie, he'd forget himself.

Minerva takes one step toward the bodies, then turns to Bay. He hopes she'll explain. She cut Petersson away, freed herself to enable her own pursuits. She knows how to live, unencumbered. Perfect, weightless freedom.

Bay remembers falling, stuck in black pitch. Extended anticipation of death. The agony of perpetual imminence.

Minerva's hand reaches.

Not a relationship beginning. Something else.

She glances to where her guardian lies clarifying in the shallow pit, then to Bay.

Her hand opens, reaching for his open shirt, grasping for his wound. Black lines on her palm elongate. Streaks of ink form vines and leaves, black fruit, wild faces. New forms creep outward, spreading to cover his chest, his arms.

Hot skin trembles. The bones of her hand reflect his heartbeat.

THE SMOKE LODGE

Creamy mist followed Robert Doret and his friends in from the beach, dampening their jackets and hair like rain, though no drops fell. As the six approached the blackened restaurant shell, Robert told them about the night the Moby Schooner burned.

"We'd arrived that evening, just Milla and me," Robert said. "The commotion brought us outside, through all this thick smoke, toward shouting and sirens and orange glow. The firefighters couldn't stop it. Wind whipped the inferno into such heat, it vaporized water sprayed at it. Sparks streamed into the black sky like outpourings from some occult ceremony."

Robert realized he'd conveyed how the fire had looked, but omitted how he'd felt.

"What was this place?" Jack Irons asked. Only thirty, Jack was younger than the others by a decade or two, and accustomed to needing explanations for all he'd missed.

"An old fish and chips place, always packed. Best chowder in town." Robert stood looking over charred foundation and beams. As far back as boyhood, he'd eaten here whenever his family visited Lincoln City. It was more than just the vanishing of the only restaurant in the Road's End area. The real sting was lost tradition, another familiar comfort gone too soon. Worse, a reminder everything and everyone was under that same threat, might vanish before its time.

"Been a year, why haven't they rebuilt?" Paulsen asked, habitually stroking the bushy mustache portion of his beard.

"The neighborhood's zoned residential now," Robert said. "Moby Schooner was grandfathered in, now they can't rebuild, at least not here. They're moving up to Highway 101, but it won't be the same."

Robert knew his friends, all fiction writers and editors, understood well enough notions like memory and loss. This group shared history, overlapping lists of places and events, yet crucial aspects of memory couldn't be shared. Robert remembered too much, some of which pained him. He wanted to get back to the house, to eat and drink and search out more pleasurable reminiscences.

"So here you have five writers," Paulsen said, "though in the case of the pup Jack Irons, such an appellation may be too generous. Some of us, even award-winning." He slapped Robert's shoulder.

The day before, at the 96th World Horror Conference in Portland, Robert Doret's latest novel *At Midnight the Demon Sings Morning* had won the H.P. Lovecraft Award for Best Novel, beating among others, Jon Paulsen's *The Harlot Oracle*. The award was Robert's sixth HPL, would've been Paulsen's third. None of the other writers on this post-convention trip, Jack Irons, Michael Standish or his wife Agni, had ever won.

Paulsen insisted each should declaim what story they'd tell of the burning of an oceanside restaurant, and himself suggested a ghost story in aftermath of fire, the rebuilt place haunted by the spirit of a waitress who burned to death.

Though Robert declined to offer his own story, he was glad for Paulsen's carrying on, and the time it granted him to control his emotions. Memories of fire always got to him.

Jack Irons proposed a curse brought back to land by a trawler that delved into a cove where long ago fishermen killed natives.

"A fish curse?" Paulsen roared. "The halibut filet terror? Alright, pup. What about Standishes?"

Dr. Agni Standish spoke of folklore, campfire tales handed down over generations.

"Bzzzt, gong!" Paulsen said. "Sounds boring. What of your estimable husband, the lesser doctor?"

Michael Standish's idea involved an angry husband, forced out by his wife who's divorcing him, and keeping the restaurant they co-own. If he can't have the restaurant, she can't either. He chains the doors, burns everyone alive inside.

The five walked beneath a sky already darkening. Surf roared, distant.

Robert smelled smoke, though the Moby Schooner was blocks behind. Maybe fireplaces in neighborhood vacation homes? More than just smell, a whole array of senses. The pop and sizzle of firehose spray hitting hot timbers. Steam rising, while something glided along behind and overhead. Ghosts of memory silent and invisible, yet personified.

From the crest of Keel Street, the Doret house came into view. Upstairs windows glowed, where two women moved cooperatively in the kitchen: Milla, Robert's wife of two decades, and their partner Lisa, a recent addition to what had always been a monogamous pair.

"Back to the wives," Paulsen said. "Good wives, making supper."

"Hey, I'm here!" Agni Standish protested. "A wife, not making anybody supper."

"And we're glad you're not," Paulsen said. "I'm just trying to nudge the award-winning Robert Doret into explaining his new domestic triangle."

Robert unlocked the front door. "Maybe later."

In the entry hall they banged sand from shoes, hung jackets, and shivered off the damp October chill. Upstairs, a fire burned. Robert went to his blond women, kissed short-haired Milla first, then younger, longer-haired Lisa. Always this ritual, both women, never just one, and always in this order. He felt eyes upon him, knew they watched and wondered, but he didn't mind. Observation of human behavior and relationships, especially the unconventional, was universal among writers. Study from life yielded crucial details which might someday lend characters or scenes more interesting shading.

Those who had been outside drifted toward the fireplace.

"I heard rumors of good single malt," Michael Standish said.

"Better be more than rumor." Paulsen patted his belly. "It's the sole reason I let myself be dragged to this hell of tangible mist."

"I picked up a Lagavulin 16-year," Robert said. "Thought it was time."

Michael Standish's head turned. His expression shifted, surprise to wistfulness.

Paulsen smiled sadly.

"What's this?" Jack Irons asked. "Another tradition unknown to the new guy?"

"Karlring," Robert said.

Agni Standish was apparently more able to compartmentalize this emotional subject than the others. "It was the favored dram of Edward Karlring. He brought a bottle to every convention, even when he couldn't afford it."

Robert went to the kitchen, returned with the bottle and seven glasses on a tray. While the rest sat by the window, or stood overlooking the sunset, he poured. As Milla and Lisa started in from the kitchen to join them, Robert asked them to bring another glass.

"An eighth?" Jack Irons asked.

"If it's time for Lagavulin 16," Paulsen said, "Karlring needs one."

"I sense him." Robert raised his glass. "Especially here. He loved the coast."

"For me, he haunts the HPL awards," Paulsen added.

"He won plenty, I know." Irons phrased it like a query.

"Ten, more than anyone, ever," Paulsen said. "If he hadn't done for himself by fifty-one, would've been more."

"Plenty more," Robert said. "If he'd stuck around, I'd never have won. He'd have my six, plus his ten, and... who knows?"

Michael Standish sipped. "The man was eternal. Even that word doesn't cut it."

"Not one of us is poet enough to name the loss of Karlring. To even try seems phony." Robert leaned down and touched the glass front of the fireplace. "Phony, like this damn fireplace. A fire isn't gas flames, it's wood burning. Smoke, and unpredictability." He was still thinking about another fire.

Milla moved toward the kitchen, gesturing at platters on the counter. "Karlring wouldn't stand for wasting food. Remember your early years, all coming up together, poor and starving?"

Dinner was a buffet of local seafood: Yaquina Bay oyster shooters with lemon and sea salt; blackened razor clams from Agate Beach; Dungeness crab cocktail in martini glasses with sweet habanero cocktail sauce; smoked Pacific salmon with aged gouda and caper chutney. Each filled their plate and returned to eat near the fireplace.

By the final bite, the Lagavulin too had been depleted, dispersing a cloud that had loomed since the mention of Karlring's name.

Paulsen fell into teasing Jack Irons for being too young, fit and trim for a writer.

"Is it true you're planning a triathlon? What, last time you ran a marathon you thought, that's not hard enough, maybe next I'll add a bike ride and swim?"

"It's just a Half-Ironman," Jack Irons said.

"And let's discuss that nonsense you spouted in that *Rue Morgue* interview. Dictating your book with a voice recorder on all-day mountain hikes?"

Jack Irons shook his head and laughed. "This weekend with you guys, it's like *The Big Chill* for alcoholic grey-beards with bellies swollen and backs ruined from too much sitting."

All laughed, not least the gray-bearded alcoholics.

"All right, pup!" Paulsen roared, striking a pose. "Which of us is Meg Tilly in a leotard, doing splits?"

"What next?" Michael asked. "More Scotch?"

Robert went to the cabinet, and came back uncapping a bottle of Glenlivet.

"I prefer Irish whiskey," Agni said.

"Fuck Irish whiskey," Robert said. "And I say that as half an Irishman. Tonight we'll be drinking this here single-malt."

"Scotch aficionados are such tiresome snobs." Agni briefly withheld her glass, then held it out.

"You're married to this woman, Michael?" Robert poured around.

"What should we toast to?" Michael Standish asked.

"Publishing," Paulsen said. "The only thing I hate more than ex-wives."

"To Karlring, and publishing, and Paulsen's ex-wives," Michael Standish said.

They drank.

Paulsen blinked, red-faced. "Please, no more Karlring talk tonight. As an alternative, I suggest we start a rumor as follows. The only reason our Doret won his latest HPL—"

"My sixth."

"—is because World Horror was in Portland this year. That's home field advantage. Not to put too fine a point on it, the fix was in."

"Scoreboard, chum." Robert clinked Paulsen's glass. "Six is more than two. Nearly twice as many."

"Cheers." Both Standishes toasted in tandem.

Paulsen slapped Robert's back. "Congrats, my brother."

"My sixth HPL." Robert sighed. "I should be on top of the world. I am really."

"I feel a cloud hanging," Michael Standish said.

"Things feel heavy, like some persistent lament," Robert said. "Is it Karlring, the Lagavulin? Maybe I shouldn't have. But we've been avoiding it so long."

"That's just life," Paulsen said. "The ultimate fade to black."

Agni took Michael's hand.

"Is that all it is, just recognition of mortality?" Robert asked. "Not just Karlring's. Ours."

"Our careers have progressed, especially yours, Robert." Michael Standish chewed his lip. "Yet I barely recall the enthusiasm that got me here."

"You hit the level of multi-book deals, then keep your head down. One house, one relationship." Paulsen hunched, stroking his beard.

Jack Irons made a rude noise. "One relationship. Do you even hear yourself?"

Paulsen's face remained serious. "You stop walking the edge, and that's good, the edge is dangerous. But really, you stop living life. When's the last time I got arrested? Woke up beside a stripper?"

"That's the experience you're missing?" Michael Standish laughed.

"Nah, you know. It's fuel for the work, certain experiences. Earlier we took risks, stared demons in the eye. Suddenly thirty years gone, spent typing, vision wrecked from computer screens. The edge, gone dull."

The Standishes and Jack Irons appeared occupied by thought.

Paulsen continued. "When's the last time you felt afraid?"

"That's it," Robert said.

"What?" Jack Irons asked.

"What we need, Paulsen's right." Robert hurried to the kitchen.

The others waited expectantly, wondering, looking to Milla. She shrugged.

Robert returned with a small branch of driftwood, a salt-bleached ornament from the window sill. He knelt at the fireplace, opened the glass and placed natural wood atop the artificial logs. It surged to life, flared. Blue flames turned orange.

"Tomorrow, we'll show you something." He looked meaningfully at Milla.

"You mean take them to Smoke Lodge," she said.

"Oooh!" Lisa jumped up. "I've never been to the lodge, only heard about it. Yeah! Big fire."

"Can't be an equal third in the Doret *menage*," Paulsen began, "sorry, I meant marriage, without that. Not that I know what this Smoke Lodge is."

"If they let me, I'm going to take the Doret name." Lisa glanced at Milla, suddenly embarrassed, covered her face with one hand. "We haven't talked about it, but I just…"

"Three Dorets are better than two." Milla reached around Lisa's waist and squeezed possessively. "We're all libertines here, aren't we?"

"Maybe not all," Paulsen said.

"Think of Scott and Zelda, all their friends," Milla teased. "They really knew how to live."

"Worked out great for them," Michael Standish said.

"Listen, everybody wants this?" Robert asked. "I'm serious."

General laughter and lighthearted dismissal trailed off before Robert's continued sombre look. Finally, all assented.

"Tomorrow," Robert said. "Smoke Lodge."

After an oceanside lunch of chilled half-shell oysters and excellent bread and butter, with spicy salted Bloody Marys all around, they continued down Pacific Coast Highway, then turned off at Siletz River.

Paulsen, riding shotgun, turned. "Milla, what's this secret lodge your

Robert's taking us to? When Uncle Paulsen asks, you must tell."

Milla, seated in the second row between Lisa and Agni, ignored him.

Lisa laughed. "I'm just excited."

Paulsen hailed Jack Irons and Michael Standish in back. "Either of you know anything?"

"Be patient." Robert gripped the wheel one-handed. "Enjoy the scenery."

Dead piers spiked the inlet where bay transitioned to river. Mist drifted marshlands beneath hills of birch gone yellow and orange. The gap between river and road widened enough to allow homesites and sodden grazing land.

Robert pointed across the river. "There's the *Sometimes a Great Notion* house."

"These little seats aren't fit for grown men," Jack Irons groused.

Paulsen laughed. "Luckily that doesn't apply to you, waif."

"Speaking of lucky," Michael said, "if Karlring were here, he'd displace three of us."

"I've seen pictures," Jack Irons said. "Karlring was a bear."

"A giant man," Michael agreed. "A lion's mane. A mighty beard."

"Heart the size of a yoga ball," Agni added.

"His girth exceeded most doorways," Paulsen said. "They had to be broken out to make way, and rebuilt after. And when he was in his drink, he grew six inches in height. Could raise two ordinary men overhead, one in each hand, as I might lift kittens."

Unlike last night, when mention of Karlring had left the mood heavy, this outpouring seemed to please everyone. The mood brightened, and talk of scenery and destination resumed.

Paulsen read a roadside sign. "*Ichwhit* Park. What's Ichwhit?"

"Allegedly it's *bear* in some Native American dialect," Robert said. "Siletz Indians… I don't know, does every tribe have their own language? Standish, don't you speak all languages?"

"All but three," Michael shouted, "and Agni speaks those."

"There are bears here?" Lisa asked. "There aren't. You're making jokes about old bear Karlring."

"No bears," Robert said. "Not around here."

"Good," Jack Irons said.

"Bears fucking scare me." Lisa shuddered.

"Plenty of *ichwhit*, though," Robert said.

In fields softened by encroaching water, a half-sunk Caterpillar tractor sat abandoned and rusting beside a fallen tree from which cut sections had been dragged to the house and split for firewood, the remainder sodden in the emerald marsh. This seemed to be the last house beside the river. Trees took over. Spruces leaned over the road from both sides, almost meeting above the center, and in the occasional lesser valleys which shot sidelong uphill, trees leaned more steeply and managed to intermingle dying leaves above the very streams which cut downslope.

"Almost to the turnoff," Robert announced.

"Beautiful land," Michael Standish said. "You're doing well, you Dorets. The Portland place, a beach house, plus this lodge."

"The beach place, my grandmother left. The lodge, you'll see, it's pretty rustic. No electricity. We built on land owned by our friend Jarrett. He owns most of this forest."

Milla laughed. "Jarrett's crazy, shut away in his plantation-style mansion. All these weird collections."

"Permanent coast-dwellers," Robert added, "they're pretty much all misfits and loony tunes."

"What kind of collections?" Paulsen asked.

Robert looked sideways. "All kinds, almost a museum. Wood sculptures, maritime paintings, old records. Mostly books, some that might impress you. Here's Lost Lake Road."

A yellow car ahead turned left into a gap between trees. Robert slowed the Expedition and took the same turn. Up the narrow gravel road a metal gate blocked the way.

"Where's that other car?" Paulsen asked. "It turned ahead of us."

Robert removed his seatbelt. "What car?" He jumped out, unlocked the gate and swung it open.

Through wavering leaves, intermittent sunlight filtered gold. The road wound through trees falling barren, summer's overgrowth lost. In another mile, the incline diminished. To both sides, fields of wild grass were weighted by damp orange and brown leaves. To the right, beyond tumbled rocks and vines, an irregular lake reflected slate sky.

"Your own lake," Paulsen observed.

The road curved past a scrim of alders to dead-end at a log structure.

"Smoke Lodge," Robert announced.

Out front, a bonfire burned in a stone firepit. In the field, overgrown corn stalks sagged in rows. Overripe pumpkins slumped on their vines.

"Who built the fire?" Lisa asked.

Robert set the brake. "Probably our friend thought we might come today, wanted to welcome us."

"Why not inside?" Paulsen asked. "There's a chimney."

"You need the outdoor experience first. Later, we'll go in."

Rain fell, visible but soundless. Perimeter trees swayed independently in surging wind.

"What's that rotten smell?" Agni asked.

"Pumpkins," Milla said.

Around the fire, upended crosscut log sections made eight stools. The seven sat.

Robert hoped nobody would say anything about the empty stool. "It's always damp here. The ocean uses the rain and mist to reach inland, and the ground's a sponge, but if you build big enough fires and leave them burning, eventually things dry out." He went to the lodge's outer wall where an ancient rake leaned, and with this, began gathering leaves into piles, some like yellow parchment, others red or brown and hole-shot with decay.

He took up one mound and tossed them in the fire. The leaves sputtered and hissed. "No matter how wet," Robert said, "they always burn."

A column of smoke rose to vanish against clouds. Darker ground-level smoke sound tendrils among the visitors.

Jack Irons coughed. "Is this why it's Smoke Lodge?"

"Nope," Robert said.

From a paper bag Milla produced a magnum of Shiraz, pulled the cork, and filled clear plastic cups.

"No wine for me," Paulsen said. "Anything else?"

"Inside." Robert stood. "I'll go. Enjoy the fire."

Michael Standish and the women sipped the wine, while Jack Irons and Paulsen waited with empty cups.

Robert returned, carrying a brown glass jug full of obscure liquid.

"What's this?" Jack Irons asked.

"Jarrett often drops off a gallon or two from a new batch." Robert poured. "He claims it's mead, but I think it's something else."

"Fireside mead," Paulsen observed. "In the forest, by Lost Lake."

Michael Standish angled his cell phone at arm's length. "Untethered from the world."

"Try this," Robert promised.

Paulsen tasted. "Extraordinary. Spice on the tongue, sweet. Burnt grain."

Lisa quickly finished her wine and tried the mead. "It's like pumpernickel."

They sat a long time around the fire, fetching their own refills, mostly not speaking.

Finally Jack Irons stood. "Damn, I'm sweating."

"Feel free to wander," Robert said. "I'll start dinner soon."

"It's early, yet," Paulsen said. "Not that I couldn't eat."

Milla stood. "When people lived outside, they ate early and slept at sundown."

Agni looked around. "We aren't sleeping out here."

"We won't stay overnight," Robert said. "Explore the field or the lake. Just don't go far."

"Let's explore," Lisa said.

Milla led Agni, Lisa and Jack Irons through the pumpkins and cornstalks to the lake. Robert watched, despite knowing Milla would keep track. He gathered more fallen limbs and leaves.

The fire enlarged, intensified.

"How do you transition from two married people, to this?" Paulsen asked.

Robert shrugged. "It wasn't how you'd think. We just took her in, like roommates at first. She needed friends. A stable place."

Paulsen looked dubious. "But now you three…"

"Now, yeah," Robert said. "But that took a while. Actually, the women worked it out."

Pointedly ignoring the subject, Michael Standish indicated the lodge exterior, where hung constructs of branches, dried plants and animal bones. "Pagan influenced, I think, also Native American."

"Maybe."

Robert reentered the lodge, shut the door, and emerged minutes later carrying a heavy cloth-covered basket and four yard-long metal skewers. He placed these on the table and ran each spear through chunks of seasoned game meat, whole potatoes, red onions and yellow squash, then poised these over the fire.

After a while meat sizzled and spit, vegetables steamed and blackened.

"Food enough for twenty," Michael observed.

"Where'd you get fresh meat?" Paulsen asked. "We didn't carry that in."

"Inside. Jarrett leaves provisions, if he guesses we're coming."

Robert refilled his cup, then Paulsen's.

"I'll try that." Standish shook out his cup, but drops of Shiraz remained in the bottom. "I'm sorry, could I get a clean cup?"

Robert poured and they all drank, contemplating the transformation of raw food over fire.

Paulsen sniffed. "Real caveman time."

Robert shouted toward the lake for the four to return.

Through the trees, shapes emerged into the field.

Agni ran ahead of the others. She kissed Michael's hand, and froze upon noticing his switch from wine. "What's this? Speaking of wild transformation."

"Wild food, drink, and fire." Jack Irons walked up. "Have you heard of Paleo Diet?"

Robert crouched to remove the first giant kebab from the fire. He placed the cool end into one of several angled holes drilled into the table.

"Wondered what those were," Paulsen muttered.

"Can I help?" Lisa asked.

Robert shook his head. "No silverware. No plates."

"Bare handed like animals." Milla selected a blackened oblong of elk. "Careful, it's hot."

"Our hands is tender!" Paulsen slid a blackened potato off the spear.

"Oww."

They ate carefully, fingers juice-slick, lips black with smoke char. Some complained at first of burned fingers or mouths, then gradually, as if remembering, each ate with solemn purpose.

After, following Robert and Milla's lead, all cleaned their hands with damp leaves. There was no water to drink. Agni finished the Shiraz.

"Regrettable the mead's gone," Paulsen observed. "That brew opened my skull rather nicely."

"I have a surprise." Robert started inside.

"Are we going in now?" Jack Irons asked.

"Not until true dark. But I've stashed more mead."

Robert shut the door behind, and reemerged carrying two more gallon jugs, along with something else under one arm. He handed Jack Irons the brew, and showed the others a book. Worn black leather, thick as an old bible. No words on the cover, just a silver hexagon bounding an asymmetrical asterisk. In six corners within were arrayed indecipherable letterforms.

Paulsen's eyes widened. "I've seen that before, Karlring's shelf. He wouldn't let me see."

"I know it bothered you, Karlring making me his literary executor." Robert handed Paulsen the book. "You'd known him longer."

"I wouldn't say…" Paulsen opened the cover. Pages crackled like dry leaves.

"He never let me read it either, until he was gone," Robert said. "I figure it's why he picked me. Not to caretake his own work. This."

"Who wrote it?" Paulsen turned pages.

"It contains many hands, and languages," Robert said. "Diagrams, poems. Tables of figures."

"There's no title."

"*Wyentenja Isvosk Nia Tenjmako*. My best translation is *Through Smoke Into Fire*." Robert indicated the symbols on the cover. "Every line I've translated, I've found referenced within Karlring's later stories. This book is the foundation of all Karlring's most acclaimed works." He paused, gave them time to absorb. "And all my own, since the book became mine."

None of the others spoke. None moved.

Robert took back the book, flipped pages. "Here's a taste, untranslated."

He recited, glancing up periodically to make eye contact. The lines were metric, strangely incantatory, almost songlike.

Michael Standish leaned in, head angled as if still listening, even after Robert stopped. "Some words are Latinate, but I can't... It's none of the major Romance languages. I'd recognize Galician, Corsican, Catalan."

Robert offered Standish the book. "The languages are mostly obscure, not taught in universities. Those lines hybridized Quechuan and Andean Spanish, rare even in Chile, where Karlring found this."

"Karlring spoke only English," Paulsen insisted.

"No," Robert said. "He'd been using it."

"I can't..." Michael shook his head.

"It ends as follows, in Karlring's hand." Robert flipped to a later page. "Many before tied their lines, end to end. Fix yours at the last; others will join. The thread lengthens forever."

Paulsen whistled. "Did you know about this?" he asked Milla.

"She knows everything." Robert looked up at the darkening sky. "See that?"

Paulsen followed his gaze. "What?"

Michael pointed. "Is it the moon, breaking through?"

"No moon yet." Robert picked up the mead. "But something's coming."

He poured while Jack Irons distributed filled cups.

"And when there remains no water or wine," Paulsen intoned, "all the world's people must content themselves with what brew the devil provides."

Everyone encircled the dwindling fire except Robert, who set the partial jug between the full and empty ones, then ventured into the mist to gather more wood. He returned, threw limbs onto the fire, and went back for more.

"That's enough, Robert," Lisa said. "Join us."

"He knows what needs doing out here." Milla smiled, gently disarming.

"Getting cold." Jack Irons squatted before the fire.

Robert fed another armload to the blaze, then more damp leaves, which hissed out eye-burning smoke. The fire broadened, seething with the yellow ferocity of a captive sun.

"Lean close," Robert said. "Breathe it in. If smoke burns your eyes, you're not drinking enough. Let it darken your skin. Preserve you, like smoked meat."

Michael Standish refilled his cup and went to Robert's side. He breathed deep, blinked his eyes, and laughed strangely through coughing.

Agni approached, touched her husband's shoulder. "Michael, you should—"

Michael roared like an animal at the fire. His cry ended ragged and hoarse.

"You're making me afraid," Agni said. "This is—"

"You should drink." Bug-eyed, hair upstanding like Eraserhead, Michael offered his cup.

"Try some, it's good!" Lisa leaned against both Standishes, then unzipped her tall boots. She stepped out of them, looking about wild-eyed.

Despite seeming afraid, Agni drank.

"Who wants to run?" Lisa sprinted off, soon vanished into mist. Only her laughter and the rustling of disturbed leaves hinted her trajectory.

Jack Irons pranced, kicked off shoes, and started after Lisa. He fell, laughing.

Agni Standish finished the drink. Michael forcefully clutched her to himself and kissed her with uncharacteristic animal passion.

"Is this for real?" Paulsen regarded his cup. "Is it? What's in this stuff?"

Milla leaned in close, as if confiding a secret. "It's not ordinary mead."

"Not ordinary." Paulsen laughed and roared, like Michael before, then pounded his chest like Tarzan and cackled as if surprised at himself.

"Good?" Robert asked.

Paulsen's red face beamed. "I'll take more, if you're pouring."

"Do you have enough smoke?"

"No, more please. More smoke."

"Is this what you wanted?"

"I did say... We talked about Karlring and—"

"Why did we come?" Robert insisted. "Remember what you wanted?"

Michael and Agni approached, huddled in.

"To remember," Paulsen said.

"Look up." Robert pulled back.

The sky above cleared to transparency, while ground-level remained shrouded. The moon loomed red, impossibly large, filling a quarter of the sky. The massive disc, no real moon but a looming world, occluded or outshone all stars.

"Now it's time." Robert held a branch into the fire, raised it burning. "We go in."

The interior log walls were honey-gold. A massive river rock fireplace, black mortar speckled with metallic glass, dominated the near end of the open rectangle. Within the hearth, already loaded with kindling and splits, Robert struck a fire.

The prospect of finally seeing inside seemed to calm the group. At least briefly, they reverted to themselves.

The fire surged, blasting heat and light. Robert held the book and watched his friends exploring. At the far end, a trio of double bunks, each with shelves of rough-sawn lumber, were separated by delicate scrims which first appeared to be Asian paper screens, but were actually stretched hide painted with the black symbols from the book's cover.

Milla helped Paulsen open the last jug of mead.

Cup extended, Lisa bounced on tiptoes. "Me, me."

"Gotta love ladies who tipple," Milla said.

"These ornaments," Michael Standish mused, facing the side wall.

Jack Irons shrugged. "Sculptures of sticks, colored leaves."

The arrangements combined natural browns and reds with other colors less organic, which lent these dead things, despite brittle desiccation, the vibrancy of persistent life. At their center hung a wide, unframed painting, frayed edges dangling canvas threads, depicting an orange seething globe whose surface spit tongues of fire. Visible outlines of continents indicated this was Earth, not Sun. Beside it, a bear straddled the white moon, arms outstretched with elongated needle-sharp fingers, striving toward home.

"Getting smoky, Robert. Your chimney's got the flue. Get it?" Jack Irons cackled.

"Ha," Milla said.

Agni approached stiff-legged, staring into mead dregs. "It feels like clockwork elves are controlling my body."

Michael alternately squinted and opened eyes wide. "I have post-anesthesia fog."

Robert drained another cup. "The mead contains its own secrets."

"Where do you want us?" Paulsen's eyes bulged, his face red.

"On the floor, by the fire," Robert said.

"It's hard to look at it." Lisa rubbed her eyes. "Like staring into a foundry."

Milla sat beside her. "Nothing can cut this smoke."

Even as the fire burned hotter, the interior seemed to darken.

"Everyone here?" Robert faced them. "Anything missing?"

Paulsen coughed, waving a hand. "Some air would be nice."

Robert held up the book. "This didn't begin with Karlring. But he left it to me, and it continues."

Michael Standish reached. "Can I see it again?"

Robert ignored him. "Karlring studied languages, delved into arcana, trying to understand."

Milla rose and crossed the room to the shelves near the left corner bunkbeds. Robert's eyes followed her, and the others twisted to watch as Milla started dragging what looked like an unrolled sleeping bag, lightweight, as if stuffed with dry leaves.

"Starting where Karlring left off," Robert said, "I learned more."

Milla passed behind her husband toward the fire.

"What's in that?" Paulsen asked.

Milla easily lifted the bundle and tossed it onto the fire. The flames caught, made it part of their burning.

"It's Karlring." Robert held the book so they could see only the cover, and resumed speaking in the same bizarre tongue he'd intoned outside.

The others stopped questioning, merely watched.

Robert halted, turned and threw the book onto the fire, where the bundle still burned.

"Robert, stop!" Paulsen fell sideways and scrambled forward, as if he might snatch the book from the flames.

Michael Standish stood easily, straight up, eyes bulging in surprise. Blinking at the smoke, he stepped around Robert, who made no move to stop him.

Words emerged from the fire in a deep male voice. Not Robert speaking, but the same language as before. A pause, then new words in another language, stranger still. Robert stood away, Paulsen and Michael fell back to their places. Dark smoke swirled thick. Within the core of yellow-orange flame, a human shape clarified, sat up and slowly stood. No longer a formless bundle. A broad man-shape unfurled, details lost in the smoke. It was this shape, speaking.

"What are these words?" Michael flinched, as if the sound caused pain.

"Ask him." Robert pointed. "Ask Karlring."

Giant's stature, wild mane, formidable beard. Karlring's voice.

It murmured, standing at the limit of the fire, yet not detached from it. Robert had seen this before, had never been sure whether the form was a solid thing, or merely some uncanny formation of fire. The bearlike physique, overlarge head crowned with bushy hair. Copious tears streamed from its eyes, glistening, flowing ever faster, pattering heavy on the fireplace verge. The ground remained dry. Not transparent tears but something darker, like dark tea or whiskey, which sizzled and steamed away.

"Heard you say." The voice creaked like a broken chair.

"I brought everyone," Robert said.

It resumed speaking, now English in short bursts, not Karlring's characteristically fluid complex sentences. Each fragment triggered sequential images, memories spun rapid and disordered.

A woman falls stricken, dying on cold concrete. Paulsen's second wife, Ellen.

Hooded figures hunch over scrawled vellums, edges curled. Corner insignia black, wax seal red.

Hotel bar, Karlring, his agent, and Len Totts of Euclid Press. Three hands toast whiskey.

Third wife, Anne, first encounter. Hotel suite champagne, she strips off green satin.

Anne remarries, Len Totts, Karlring five weeks buried.

Providence with Robert and Milla, New York with Agni and Michael, later all in Boston. Thai dinner meeting Jack Irons.

Tar smeared on stone by many hands. Firelight outlines robed shapes against cavern wall.

Faster, others flash, indecipherable.

The voice stopped. Robert heard his own breathing, saw other faces twisted in fear and distress. The images, if all had seen the same, as he assumed, what would the others make of them? When Milla first accompanied him here, their experiences had matched.

It had to be Karlring. Events they'd shared, also things after his death. What explanation?

The voice resumed. "A dream remembered is not the dream itself."

"You can't be Karlring." Paulsen's voice broke.

The shape faded, edges softening into fire, then resolved again. "Many different kinds of dying," the voice croaked.

"If it's you, Edward, what do you want to tell?" Agni asked. "What can you give us?"

"Nothing," he said, then repeated the word, the last almost a whisper, like candle flame sputtering in the wind.

The shape finally vanished. Nothing remained in the fireplace but flames and smoke. Already the fire shrunk as if starved. The embers diminished, yellow to orange to red, dying until finally the black remains gave no light at all.

Robert couldn't pinpoint why he believed. So much felt subjective, experiences that couldn't be shared even by those in the same room. But looking at his friends, their expressions made him believe all had undergone something similar. This relieved him, comforted him. Always he felt such desperation, urgency in the face of fleeting time, the need to forestall death's encroachment. Eventually, tempted to face this again, to delve into the book, trying to learn more. What would it grant him? Would it season him, toughen his resolve, allow him to squeeze more life out of what time remained? He didn't know by what increment he should measure. New mornings, breaths drawn, seized recognitions?

He couldn't stop time spinning, accelerating, could only grasp what lay within reach. Life wasn't done, not yet, not today. More books ahead, more travel, new discoveries and friends. And what he possessed already. Things with Milla, stronger than ever. Lisa, good and true. They needed each other.

Was that enough? Still the Earth raced its flaming circuit, each year dwindling under the widening shadow of the past.

Nobody spoke. Just breathing, all around.

Robert went to the fireplace, delved barehanded into ashes. He retrieved the intact book, unburned and steaming.

Dr. Agni Standish rubbed her eyes. "Did we all just…"

"We did." Lisa looked from Robert to Milla, visibly stunned by the secrets revealed, seeming to guess what other concealments might remain.

"He only remains long enough that we're sure it's him," Robert said. "No more. And every time, sometimes days later, sometimes within minutes, we find ourselves questioning whether he was ever really here."

"Did we bring him," Paulsen asked. "With all our remembering, our nostalgia?"

"Nostalgia, it's nothing but pain," Robert said. "It's memory poisoned by the anguish of loss."

He went to the doorway, opened it. The smoke drew out, sucked by cold wind, and dispersed. Robert inhaled fresh outdoor air.

"It's all new." Paulsen came outside, shaking his head. "Everything."

The mist had cleared and the moon stood overhead in brittle clarity, no larger than usual, no sign of the strange earlier redness and exaggerated size.

Michael led Agni out, heads swiveling as if observing an unknown world. Leaves crunched underfoot, dry and brittle.

"Like I promised," Robert said. "Let the fire burn long enough, it dries everything."

"I never thought Karlring would terrify me," Paulsen said.

"Fear is something we used to love," Robert said. "Now we write stories meant to be scary, without ever feeling afraid."

Milla came to his right side, Lisa his left. Two decades had passed since Robert and Milla had decided against having kids. Lisa, though newly arrived, felt the same. They had no regrets, never felt any lack, but now Robert wondered who would summon him from smoke, after he was gone. None of these friends had offspring.

"I know what I'll write next," Robert said.

Both fires had died, inside and out. Already, Robert was thinking about the next time these fires would come. Out of the chill night, a coil of wind swirled brittle leaves, and spun them so they screamed, one against another.

EVERYONE GATHERS AT
HAYSTACK ROCK

A t eleven o'clock on the final morning of the event, Daniel awoke after only a few hours sleep. He fought through fatigue and a skull-piercing hangover, hurriedly showered and dressed for a day on the beach. As he approached the hotel's continental breakfast bar, the food was being carted away. He managed to grab a Greek yogurt and fresh blueberries. At least coffee remained plentiful.

The few bright-eyed tourist families in the dining room seemed bewildered, outnumbered as they were by clusters of event attendees, all wild-haired, black-clad and tattooed. Though Daniel was himself one of them, he'd always ignored those affectations of style, which he disliked for seeming compulsory. Outwardly at least, he resembled the vacationing suburbanites who must have been wondering what the hell was happening in Cannon Beach that weekend.

None of his eleven sisters of the Medusae remained in the dining area. On the way down past their rooms, he'd observed door hangers requesting maid service. So they'd left him behind, presumably gone to the beach, desiring like all the rest to spend every moment of the long weekend taking in the gravitas of Haystack Rock while they waited for this final day's climax.

As he ate alone, Daniel looked out the broad window, past an expanse of sand and beach grass, to the natural monolith which loomed over the beach. He'd heard stories, understood the importance of this place and time. Though prior attendees of the last event seven years earlier seemed terribly excited, all remained vague as to exactly what should be expected.

He was sure he could find Medusae's parcel of sand, but remained concerned the others might be avoiding him. What if they knew where he'd gone last evening? Somebody might've seen him talking with Lin, who was a notorious, recognizable figure in the narrow worlds of esoterica and cultic worship. Divisions between houses seemed important to many, though actual distinctions between them were so subtle, most seemed homogenous even to insiders. To the public, the various houses were known only by cover identities: art schools, gentlemen's clubs, or the New Age feminist collective Medusae pretended to be.

All seven years were focused toward this long weekend event, which was never given any real name. Some called it "Cannon Beach Weekend," or "The Seven Year" or most commonly, "Gathering at Haystack Rock." This had always been the way.

Some insisted every seventh event, the forty-nine-year interval, carried still greater significance. This weekend was such an occasion.

Upon arrival Thursday night or Friday morning, houses and factions had begun claiming parcels of sand from which to observe Haystack Rock over the course of the weekend. They'd settled into rooms, sipped Oregon microbrews, and devoured seafood caught within miles of here. Oysters were especially popular, and rock scallops were making a comeback. Superficial mingling between groups occurred, but most considered insularity a virtue.

Everything aimed toward Sunday. Then it would happen. This everyone agreed.

The outsiders in the room, Daniel realized, families and retirees and suburban-looking couples, regarded with open bewilderment those present for the event. None seemed to notice Daniel, and he guessed some of his fellow seekers might likewise misidentify him as a "normal." Daniel had always considered himself an outsider among outsiders.

Behind him, a young woman whispered. "Why do we even do this? It's so old-fashioned."

Daniel snuck a look at the almost identical pair. Early twenties, black lace gloves and nail polish, exaggerated Gothic eyeliner.

"You do know what's happening." The second wore long bangs in red spiral curls.

"No, I don't." The first frowned, accentuating her overbite. "Everybody either says nothing at all, or they say seven years ago fizzled."

Daniel was tempted to dismiss them for their seeming immaturity, yet he hoped they might reveal some hint of what might be to come.

"It didn't fizzle," the second said. "Just, it was only revealed to a few."

"You know what that Eugene hippy dreadlocks guy said?" She transformed her voice into a throat-rasping croak. "If you missed it, that's on you, man. Don't mean nothing happened."

"Roseburg, not Eugene. That Lookingglass Forest stoner collective. Kickass weed."

"Hells yeah. Anyway, who knows? We'll see for ourselves."

Daniel tried not to stare as the young women stood, gathered bowls, empty chocolate milk cartons, tiny boxes of Cap'n Crunch and Fruity Pebbles. The second noticed Daniel watching, looked away, then stole another look at him. As both took up their trays, she whispered, "Oculum" to her friend, who glanced at Daniel and nodded agreement.

Oculum Press was Daniel's publishing house. The recognition surprised him, though the other Medusae had often teased Daniel, said he was becoming a rock star within their little scene. Mostly he kept to himself, focused on the work. Of course he realized people must be purchasing the books, and the audience for such materials was overwhelmingly likely to be here this weekend, but he'd never actually met any collectors.

He felt momentarily giddy, then like a phony or egomaniac. Initially, he'd felt dismissive toward the attitude of the young women, as if they expected this event ought to be some gaudy spectacle, a fireworks show, rather than a matter of profound wonder. Then, the very instant they recognized him, suddenly they seemed more interesting, their notice flattering. He knew it was a superficial reaction. Pure vanity.

One of the primary concepts that had first drawn him to this philosophy, which he now counted as a religion, was the value of aspiring to transcend ego and materialism. He'd always believed the universe to be grander than what was revealed by the senses, deeper than solid matter. Time existed without beginning or end. Distance was meaningless. His pursuit of these truths had brought Daniel to Medusae in the first place. Outsiders guessed he'd sought this group of hyper-sexualized women for the obvious reasons, but what had actually inspired his pilgrimage to the Ghost Mountain retreat had been Maya Dancer's book. *Deep Time: Diving to Infinity* was an expression of belief in the mind's ability to comprehend, even to own the limitless. So inspired, Daniel had travelled to California, found the compound in the mountains between Sacramento and Lake Tahoe without any knowledge of Medusae, the cultic sect Maya Dancer had covertly founded in 1950. He'd stumbled into their midst, not yet twenty-five, and soon become the first male Medusae since the death of Maya's last male consort thirty years earlier. The Medusae had accepted Daniel like a brother. Between Maya's mentorship and Daniel's own efforts, Oculum Press had rapidly ascended to the pinnacle of esoteric publishing worldwide. Then Maya had died, reputedly aged ninety-eight, though she'd appeared closer to half that. The IRS had seized all her financial assets, but not the Medusae compound. Since then, Oculum had provided Medusae with most of its income, not to mention prestige among rival factions.

Strange as some might consider his presence there, Daniel insisted he'd found the right fit. A quiet, supportive background for his studies, and home base for his explorations. Never mind that he was so often alone.

The other Medusae had arrived at this weekend's event proud and expectant, having proclaimed themselves all the past seven years as sole recipients of the previous event's vital revelation. In those years, some Medusae had often made aggressive claims as to the significance of their little group, while outsiders had openly cast doubt upon the Medusae account of the revelation. It pained Daniel to hear such aspersions, to witness controversy overtaking Maya's reputation. He'd even come to worry this might harm Oculum, which many assumed to be run collectively by Medusae, not solely by Daniel.

A particular matter of contention had been Medusae's refusal to specify what Maya and her two consorts had actually witnessed. Still, this wasn't unusual. Though revelations were most often shared by all present, in instances where only a few had received rare truth, they'd often guarded it jealously. Neither of the two surviving witnesses to the vision had ever told Daniel anything specific. Only vague hints.

Beyond the dining room window, clouds shifted to reveal radiant blue. Daniel knew he couldn't escape this morning's reality. He should track down his friends, but part of him wished he could escape. Last night he may have crossed a line. He couldn't stop thinking what might come of it, good and bad. Connections, opportunities. Not least, the personal, intimate aspect. Getting close to Lin was exciting, but he tried not to think about it. He might not even be able to acknowledge it to the others.

Daniel stood, crossed the dining room and started down the stairs. He didn't hurry. The parking lot curved away to an asphalt ramp, transitioning to sand. There Daniel halted, surveyed the beach. His friends must be waiting.

He turned away, surveyed the row of oceanfront homes beyond the hotel.

"Daniel."

He spun, startled.

Barefoot in a red bikini, Apia squinted in the glaring sun. At thirty-nine, she was the second youngest Medusae, a decade older than himself. Wind gusted. Apia crossed her arms protectively.

"Aren't you freezing?" Daniel asked.

She nodded. "Just running inside for my wrap. Where the hell did you go last night?"

"Ah… I assume everyone's still in the same spot? I'll be down soon. Going to walk a bit."

Apia shrugged and continued up the ramp.

Daniel felt tired, mentally foggy. He hated lying, even by omission. His intimate activities could be kept private, but he knew the others would be interested in his liaison with the leader of a prominent rival faction. The Esoteric Order was a grand house, possibly the oldest. People whispered of vast EO fortunes, outposts hidden around the globe. Even an enormous yacht where Lin supposedly resided much of the year, stopping at various ports, visiting EO satellite facilities. Daniel had wanted to ask, but hadn't wanted to seem starry-eyed.

Of course the others would want to know.

But Daniel wasn't prepared to reveal he'd spent the night with Lin. Not yet. Nobody had ever clearly explained the rules regarding cross-group consorting. He really had no idea whether he'd transgressed unforgivably. Maybe it was no big deal. Just another example of his outsider status within Medusae, always literally odd man out. The only male in a feminist collective for whom lesbian sex magick formed the core of ritual practice. The others had often joked that one day, they'd find a way to truly initiate him, break him in. He'd always wondered if they realized how he really felt about that prospect.

Medusae could wait a little longer. Daniel diverted south through mounds of dry sand spiked with beach grass. The seventh house was older, grander than the rest, surrounded by a dark concrete wall surmounted by rusty ornamental spears. He could discern no way through the prison-like barrier. He couldn't remember how Lin had gotten them inside last night.

Above the wall, a second floor patio overlooked the beach. Beyond wrought-iron railing stood a Chinese man wearing only khaki shorts, torso heavily tattooed. Last night, everything had been dark. Daniel hadn't been able to ascertain how much older Lin might be. Possibly fifty? Maybe a very trim fifty-five.

Daniel realized he was staring. Lin might see him. Should he call out? If he did, whether or not Lin recognized him, the Medusae on the beach might hear. What if they saw him here, beckoning to Lin outside the EO house? Everyone at the event knew this house, all the stories and legends. His friends might guess where he'd spent last night.

The gravity of Haystack Rock turned him around. Maybe he should look for his friends. The Medusae pavilion, midway between the hotel and the rock, where dry sand began to firm in proximity to the water. His own people. Daniel felt torn. One direction, another. The life he'd been living, all secrets and repression. Or new possibilities.

"Daniel?" A voice from behind, from the house. Familiar. "Is that you?"

He turned.

Lin was peering down, beckoning.

Daniel saw no doors or gates. No way in.

"This way." Lin indicated the north wall, hidden by tall greenery, then started down stairs.

Daniel slipped into a narrow gap of darkness behind a groomed hedge, continued until he reached a metal door flush with the concrete. A latch clicked. The door creaked open.

"Here you are." Lin's hand gripped Daniel's forearm, pulled him in. Physical, possessive, just where they'd left off last night. As if he'd never quietly fled the room while Lin slept. Beyond the wall, under the sun, Lin's tattoos were vivid red and black. Tentacles curved around from his back and up. Suction-cupped tendrils grasped across the front of his torso.

Thrilling. Frightening. Something trembled within his chest.

"Nice seeing you in daylight," Daniel said. He imagined Apia returning from the hotel to tell the others she'd seen him. What if someone had seen him call out, Lin beckoning, Daniel slipping inside?

One side of Lin's mouth lifted. "You might've stayed."

Daniel grinned, abashed. "My group. They don't really know."

When Lin laughed, crinkles formed around his eyes. "Seekers of truth, supposedly. Yet they expect followers to falsify themselves?"

Daniel couldn't answer. He knew the weekend was supposed to be about addressing cosmic truths, not individual concerns. Yet what felt most vital, most immediately desirable, was this human connection. He'd long been frustrated at needing to conceal himself. Now here was a man who was kind to him, generous with his attention, with his body. All Daniel could think about was last night's experience. That feeling of intimacy had managed to transcend even the grandest rhetorical language invoked in worship or found in the reading of sacred texts. Since that frozen moment in Lin's room, everything felt expansive, tinged with far-reaching significance. Two people alone. Intimate warmth, texture of skin. Promise of release. Afterward, talking ideas, books, philosophy. Already Lin knew him better than any Medusae ever did.

"Sorry," Lin said. "I don't mean to denigrate your sect's approach. Medusae is small, but you've achieved important things. Not least, your Oculum editions."

Daniel said nothing.

"Have you eaten brunch?" Lin gestured at the EO house. "Cannon Beach has very good food for a little town, but I think you'll find inside, we can do better."

"But I'm not a member." Daniel felt foolish, telling Lin something of course he knew.

"You're my guest." Lin withdrew from his shorts pocket a metal wallet-like case, oil-rubbed pewter. He flipped it open, revealed an insignia. Ornate black tendrils enwrapped a brilliant green gemstone.

"I've never seen one in person," Daniel said. "It's beautiful."

Lin turned, opened a door in the house's side, held it open.

Daniel entered. When the heavy metal door swung shut behind them, it made no sound.

"Some little beach house," Daniel said inside. "It's all Downton Abbey in here."

"Downton…" Lin trailed off. "Sorry, I don't know what that is."

The interior was chateau or mansion style, far from the usual driftwood and seashell beach decor. The entry hall and wide, curving stair were adorned with surprisingly straightforward classical paintings and sculptures, rather than the oddities Daniel had expected. But upstairs, the long upper hall into a wide open upstairs room displayed symbolist works, various cultic memorabilia and artifacts of the arcane, some of which seemed genuinely ancient.

"Must be some deep stories in a place like this." Daniel searched the vast dining room, unoccupied but for a pair of attendants. "I did expect more of a crowd."

"It's true, membership's declining. Inevitable outcome of exclusivity, I'm afraid."

A white on black Cephalopod-themed Expressionist painting dominated the room. Tentacles coiled, intertwining. Repeating patterns of suction cups, reminiscent of Lin's tattoo.

"Size isn't everything." Daniel kept a straight face. "A small group might achieve something a massive crowd missed."

"For example, your Medusae's discovery at the seven-year-ago?"

"Some dispute it, I realize." Daniel tried not to be obvious about checking out the bottles above the bar as they passed.

"I believe it's true. Maya was an honest woman."

Daniel stopped, spun. "You knew Maya?"

Lin waved off the question. "Not intimately. But attend enough of these, you never know who you'll end up sharing meals with. Or a bed."

"Attend how many?"

"You mean, how many events have I witnessed?" Lin's mouth narrowed. "Clever attempt at age-guessing, though a bit obvious. The answer is, you'd be very surprised how many."

"Of course it's your first forty-nine-year event."

"That would be telling." Lin gestured to an attendant, and chose a table midway between window and bar. "And yes, this lodge bears the burden of a most interesting history. Perhaps a book, some day? An exclusive for members of our Order. You might consider it while we eat. We have wonderful lox, capers and bagels from New York. Crab cakes Benedict, very fresh. Applewood smoked bacon, potatoes fried with garlic and rosemary. Mimosa, though I always think it a shame, muddling fine champagne with orange juice."

"I ate at the hotel. Free continental breakfast."

"Ah, the Shoreline." Lin made a face, apparently fighting against seeming dismissive. "You seemed bashful, your approach this morning. It's cute, charming. But why?"

"I assumed we..." Daniel leaned across the table, whispered discreetly. "Shared a secret."

Lin allowed a grin. "You're closeted among your sisterhood?"

"Are you saying you're allowed to be out, here?"

"Me?" Lin laughed with such sudden force his chair slid back from the table. "You're serious! Bless your innocent heart."

"How should I know?" Daniel looked at his silverware, rearranged it. "I'm used to sneaking around."

Lin fixed Daniel with a direct look. "I've been sucking strange cocks at these gatherings since before your birth. Many mouths, many cocks. Most of those strange boys have by now grown much older. Bodies withered, mouths not nearly so pretty. And their cocks?" He shuddered theatrically. "I hesitate to imagine."

Daniel's cheeks burned, both in surprise at Lin's bluntness and embarrassment at his own presumption. To think he might have been Lin's first Cannon Beach encounter. So naive. "I guess I'm relieved. I admit I assumed this might be compromising. Still is, for me at least."

"You're concerned over the gay issue, or fraternization across boundaries?"

"Both."

"There was a time, men like us were vulnerable. Susceptible to liaisons being used against us. Leverage. Blackmail. But really, I assume your Medusae know more than you realize. The cat's always out of the bag long before the closeted boy supposes."

Daniel blinked.

Lin's hand motioned up and down, indicating all of Daniel. "I mean darling, look at this. At you. White skinny jeans, rayon shirt half-unbuttoned. Yellow espadrilles, and bleached hair falling fetchingly over your right eye, like a young rave dancer or rent boy. Aren't there still raves? We could call you DJ Oculum, couldn't we? You could spin records."

An attendant approached in a cream suit, gold piping on the sleeves.

Daniel straightened in his chair. "I don't mind if you eat breakfast. I might have a mimosa."

"Two mimosas," Lin ordered. "One without orange juice, please." The attendant departed, and Lin unfolded his napkin. "If you have questions, Daniel Ayhdehan, you should ask. I follow your eyes, your wondering gaze. I smell questions a-burning in that singular brain."

"Such as?"

"Your eyes widened at my Order insignia." Lin took out his ID again. "The sigil derives from a book discovered on a ghost ship washed ashore on Argentina's southernmost tip, at the port of *El Fin del Mundo*."

"End of the world."

"Yes. Sounds grim I realize, but there are as many ends as there are worlds. A matter of perspective. Picture Tierra del Fuego, Cape Horn, nineteen and nine. A ship without logs or maps. Cabins outfitted for sixty-three. What scraps of understanding we derive from this book have formed our second foundation. A new testament, if you like. By this time, our Order had grown decadent. Distracted, enfeebled by three millennia of dissecting the original Atlantean texts. This newer text we call *The Line of Stones Beneath Sand*. Arguably, it describes a layer of text, quanta of words hidden beneath granular ice, like sand. The language is very like code."

The attendant delivered mimosa and champagne.

Daniel sipped. "Why are you telling me this?"

Lin leaned forward. "Don't you want to hear?"

"These are your secrets. Closely guarded by your order."

Lin waited.

"Yes!" Daniel blurted. "Of course I want to know. Of course."

"In exchange, maybe you'll discuss your interests. Book arts, esoterica. Ancient texts."

Exchange? Daniel's mind spun. Trade not just ideas, but secrets? He doubted he had anything to offer. Lin's revelations were exciting. He decided to shut up, let Lin divulge all he wished.

Lin continued. "Our seal's stone, everyone supposes it's emerald, but it's green garnet. Less precious, less valuable, but—"

"More powerful."

"Yes. *The Line of Stones Beneath Sand* clarifies the relative powers of minerals. The floor of this room, did you notice?"

"I did. It's not jade. More transparent."

"There are two different stones, alternating hues. Brazilianite and green calcite."

"Membership may be on the wane, but you don't lack for luxuries."

"We consider architecture and design among the highest attainments, along with the written word." Lin finished his champagne, tapped the empty flute with his fingernail. "This room overlooks Haystack Rock. Most often I've taken in these events from up here."

Daniel felt disappointment. He wanted to remain with Lin, enjoy everything on offer. But all he understood of the seven-year events, he'd learned from hints given him by Medusae. Everything indicated the experience should occur on the sand at the foot of Haystack Rock. What would the others think if he never showed?

"There was a time I ventured to the beach," Lin said. "I do miss that engagement with other aspirants. Seekers, barefoot in wet sand, lapped by waves. The briny tide-pool smell. Contemplating what might arise. It's been too long."

Daniel tried not to show his reawakened curiosity.

"I'm older than you suppose." Lin seemed burdened, whether by this revelation or by memory. He signaled to the bar. "I'll have lunch. Maybe something else for your hangover?"

The attendant returned.

"I'll try a brandy," Daniel said.

"You mean cognac," Lin said. "Try the Marie Antoinette, aged twenty-five years. Sublime."

Daniel nodded. "Sure."

"I've granted you information, partly because of what we shared. Partly because you offer something in return."

Daniel wondered what this meant.

"You're more respected than you realize. Your books. Can you think of anyone, among the many splinter groups and sub-cults, denominations, sects, brotherhoods and sisterhoods... anyone with your ability to cross lines? To get everyone talking again?"

"I just make books out of words written by others."

"Please. You're an opinion leader. You manifest works of art, worthy not only of study. Worthy of devotion."

Daniel wanted to object, accuse Lin of overstatement. All he did was select texts, assemble and edit, find appropriate artwork. "It's what I love." Somehow, he'd been fortunate enough to do exactly what he desired, almost since he graduated university. To present esoteric texts, many otherwise lost, in ways that respected the source while alleviating flaws of deterioration or damage. Grimoires and secret histories, texts more meaningful than any of the modern age. "You say you're older than I suppose. Do you know I'm only thirty? Just now, today. It's my birthday."

"Yes, you said last night. Remember, when midnight chimed? The two of us, coiled together in my room."

Daniel looked down, embarrassed, shook his head.

"Our bodies a circle, a double ouroboros. Two men. Two mouths. Beginning and end."

The attendant returned, offered Lin two plates, berries, and lox with lemon. Daniel accepted brandy in an oversized snifter, the glass delicate as a light bulb. He raised it, inhaled. The vapor overwhelmed him, a smell of years, of decadence and luxury. Daniel was hesitant to taste. He studied the room, took in details. Elements noticed in passing before, like the tiles, he now understood. How many other treasures surrounded him, as yet unidentified? A depth of riches, wealth accumulated over centuries, not only in this very lodge. EO possessed so many hideaways.

Anyone would be tempted by what Lin seemed to be offering. For Daniel, the enticement seemed a perfect match, impossible to resist.

Someone approached his shoulder, a peripheral shape more felt than seen. Daniel turned, found not an attendant, but an older man in a silver double-breasted suit, eyebrows wild, silver hair dramatically upright. Pinned to his lapel, a scarlet "S."

Daniel awaited Lin's introduction. Nobody spoke.

The arrival touched the arm of Daniel's chair, leaned in close to his ear.

"You're not welcome," Lin said.

The silver man ignored this, and spoke slowly, just above a whisper. "This Order conveys no truth. The Salamander Lodge priesthood is established, our membership grows. We enjoy the cooperation of Jarrett Haas, of Six Sided Circle, of the South American cultus. Only one group has achieved detente with Obsidian Group. The Salamander."

Lin stood. "Unless you have an access pass, you'll have to leave."

The attendant behind the bar spoke into the cuff of his own jacket sleeve, looking over his shoulder at the doorway. From there, a younger man in sunglasses and a dark suit, which stretched tight across his bulk, rushed in.

The silver man produced a metal identity case, apparently identical to Lin's. He flipped it open. Familiar black tentacles, like vines enwrapping a green gem.

Lin leaned in to read the engraving. "Your pass bears the name of a dead man."

Appearing unperturbed, the silver man delved into the same pocket, came out with two more passes. "How about these?"

The bulky security man strode up and knocked the passes clattering to the tiles.

The silver man whispered again to Daniel. "Remember this. Code word, volcanism." He straightened as the security man took his arm. "I'll go."

The attendant grasped the other arm and the two began hustling the silver man away. The intruder squirmed, pulled loose the arm held by the attendant, and tried to run. The security man yanked the intruder back, flung him to the ground. He removed his glasses, produced from within his jacket a telescoping tactical baton, black like a thick wand. A wrist-flick extended this to arm's length. The first swing broke the silver man's upper arm with a meaty crack. The second fractured his skull.

The attendant regained hold and the two resumed dragging the silver man out. The second attendant followed with a bar towel, wiping up a trail of blood as they left the dining room for the hallway.

"Costly way to deliver a message." Lin looked at the unmanned bar.

This was the first time they'd been alone since last night.

"This extreme factionalism bothers me," Daniel said.

Lin sighed. "It bothers me, too. But it seems an inevitable outgrowth of this world."

The first attendant returned, hair disarranged. "Sorry, sirs. More drinks? I'll just…"

"You already brought them." Daniel gulped, swallowed, then realized it was something rare, meant to be savored.

"What did he say at the end?" Lin asked. "It seemed inflected in a way I couldn't understand. Like he hissed into your ear."

Daniel considered, tried to remember. Some strange word. Volcanism? "I'm not really sure," Daniel said. He might tell Lin later. Probably he would.

Lin sighed. "The Salamanders have been trouble for us."

"Did he really come here looking for me?"

"I said before, you don't realize how Oculum is regarded. You could ask almost any price, for switching allegiance. Name a—"

"I'm not a deal-maker," Daniel interrupted.

"Jarrett, then." A pause. "Would you like to meet him?"

"Jarrett Haas is here?"

"He's a friend of the Order. The two of you share many interests. I could bring him."

Just hearing the name excited Daniel. Jarrett Haas was a recluse who resided in an obscure estate in the coastal mountains somewhere south of here, but still within Oregon. Daniel's mouth watered at the prospect of meeting Jarrett, discussing his priceless library of manuscripts, scrolls and incunabula. The prime mover for Oculum had always been the unearthing of secrets in unpublished manuscripts, underground collections, obscure archives. Forgotten and neglected, these had disappeared from the world. Daniel wanted to reveal these buried gems, make them available to seekers and acolytes.

He had to meet Jarrett. He would.

Another sound of intrusion from the doorway. Daniel jumped.

"Someone was yelling." A very thin teenage girl staggered in, wearing vertical striped pajama bottoms and a lavender Cocteau Twins T-shirt. Clearly she'd just awakened. Her short platinum hair was wildly messy, her eyes red.

Lin didn't look at her. "Don't worry."

The girl seemed dreamy, unfocused. "Why did nobody wake me?"

"Nothing to worry about," Lin said. "Save yourself. Go to sleep."

"Save myself?" The girl nodded, seeming to recall something. She turned and started out the way she'd come, wobbling on colt legs, loose white socks slipping down around her ankles.

An attendant swerved to give her a wide berth, and nearly spilled his tray. "Glad we got that Salamander out," he said to Lin, plainly nervous, "before she came down."

"Much safer letting her sleep." Lin turned to Daniel. "She'll sleep for weeks, lacking any threat to arouse her."

The attendant placed two snifters, fresh cognac for both Daniel and Lin.

Lin brightened. "I envied your Marie Antoinette. So. Tell me what you're working on."

Daniel hesitated, not only from reflexive secrecy. "You might consider it heretical. At least, misguided."

"Your new direction interests me. What was the title, the *Niger Praetium Sol Patris Coronam* introduction? *Post-Belief Skepticism Reconciled...*" Lin trailed off.

Daniel finished. "*...Reconciled to the Need to Desire.*"

"Yes. I'm intrigued, though I hope we retain, if not belief, then the capacity for wonder."

"Pure faith is beautiful," Daniel said. "But I wonder if that era is dead. The search for the numinous, abandoned for rational materialism."

"Oh." Lin appeared momentarily unable to swallow his cognac. "How mundane."

"I'm not trying to eradicate belief. Just trying out new eyes. Looking in texts, seeking wisdom. The bloody poetry, rather than the rules and models for behavior."

"Post-belief," Lin pronounced, as if tasting foreign words.

"My current project is actually a clarified reproduction of a transcendentalist manuscript, *The Motionless Pool*."

"I haven't heard of this."

"Nobody has. It's perfectly obscure, really. An incunabulum, interleaved with woodcut prints. Five hundred years old. Two copies were found, one in Chile, one in Peru, speaking of South America. Both damaged, incomplete. Between them, one complete original."

Lin nodded. "What language?"

"A weird mix. Andean Spanish, Chilean native dialects. I can't translate it, but found someone. Other than that, the book arts aspects you'd probably find boring."

"Not at all."

"Letterpress chapter header inserts and limitation page. Calfskin cover, cerulean blue, hand tooled, silver inked. Typeface crafted by a type foundry here in Oregon."

"See? Everything fits, connects."

Daniel considered. "I do see."

Lin stood. "Why don't we go down to the sand?"

"Now? Together?" Not only terrified at the prospect, Daniel also felt guilty for withholding the Salamander code word. Why hadn't he told Lin? "I was thinking of the word that Salamander whispered. Volcanism. Does that mean anything?"

"It might," Lin said. "Keep it secret. A day might come, trading that code is all that stands between you and an invitation to Six Sided Circle. Or maybe it gets you out of Obsidian lockup."

Already, so much had changed. They stood.

Outside, Haystack Rock loomed, a rough mountain in miniature, the north side near-vertical, the south more gradually sloped. Above, scalloped clouds stretched into the Pacific. Seabirds wheeled in clusters, occasionally settling near the summit. In the ocean nearby, several lesser rocks jutted, lacking both the imposing majesty and occult power of their parent.

Barefoot and still shirtless, Lin led the way through mounds of dry sand built by wind. To Daniel each step was a struggle, though most of his burden was reluctance. He did want to see the beach, to stand in the shadow of the rock on his first seven-year event.

"I can feel you worrying," Lin said, with kindness rather than chastisement. "Excess of caution seems a trait of yours."

"I have to tell them." Daniel felt more terrified than ever about his place in Medusae. So much of the day had passed, his absence unexplained. "Either the others will accept this, or not."

"That's right. In any event, you'll persevere." Lin glanced back, a glint in his eye. "But I'll keep teasing you about remaining too cautious. You remember the first time?"

"What, last night? When I asked about condoms?"

Lin laughed, delighted. "Most of the time, better safe than sorry. But not with us."

"What's different about us?" Daniel asked.

"I've always been careful," Lin said. "And you're a near-perfect celibate."

"No, I've…" Daniel began, but trailed off.

"It was worth the risk. To feel skin on skin."

Daniel was startled to see the Medusae where he expected them, halfway between the Shoreline Hotel and the rock. He veered subtly away, to the south.

Lin followed his lead. "Shall we face your people, get it over with? Or would you rather walk a while first?"

Daniel rolled up his jeans, took off his shoes and carried them in hand. "Let's walk."

It was easier, letting his feet sink in, not having to worry about getting sand in his shoes. He knew he needed to relax, stop fretting. But he'd invested so much of himself into Medusae. The group now felt intertwined with Oculum. He'd put everything at risk, being reckless with Lin. He guessed Medusae might be tolerant of the gay question, given they were all lesbians. But had he compromised group security, being intimate with an EO leader? Even if he really hadn't said anything he shouldn't, the others might not believe that.

Lin looked around, as if the event were entirely unfamiliar to him, but with an air of self-containment that only worsened Daniel's anxiety. Lin's earlier question echoed. Was he really more worried about being seen coupled with another man, or with a prominent member of EO?

"Do you think Obsidian Group is watching?" Daniel wondered aloud.

"What would Obsidian want here?"

Daniel shrugged. "Information gathering."

Lin looked confused. "Obsidian knows everyone. The day you arrived at Medusae, before you signed up, Obsidian knew your name, your history. If Obsidian's never co-opted you, vanished you into some basement cell, it's not because they can't find you. It's because they don't care, or it serves their purpose that you remain at large. They have bigger, badder things to worry about than us."

Pondering this, Daniel felt a new tangent of worry, which actually alleviated his Medusae concerns. What else was out there?

"See here?" Lin indicated a group of women, all dressed in brown and green, with silver V-shaped medallions. They moved around a roaring bonfire, not exactly dancing, but moving in rhythm together, as if executing some preparatory routine. "At first I found it strange, this crossover with Wiccans and Pagans. They don't believe as we do, yet still they feel connected."

"As if they might gain something by proximity to this."

"What was your trigger?" Lin asked. "What brought you to this? For me, it started from two vectors of exploration. Ritual sex magick, and silent nature retreats. Realize, this was long ago. I tried various groups, discarded one after another. From each, I retained tiny kernels of useful truth, then sought toward the next thing. Until I met Jarrett."

"Jarrett." The very name excited Daniel all over again. "Is it true Jarrett's now in Six Sided Circle? You're not one too, are you?" He had to restrain himself from hyperventilating, let alone asking too many questions.

Lin laughed, both coyly, as if protecting secrets, and from pure amusement. "Of course I'm not. Jarrett's not either. He's isolated on his Siletz River estate, not two hours from here. If anyone deserves a look at Jarrett's library, it's you. I'll arrange it, if..." Lin paused, exhaled.

"What?"

"If we're still... in touch. After your Medusae have their say."

Daniel wanted to assure him, of course they'd remain in touch. "It's always interesting, hearing people describe their beginnings. Most of us stumble across books."

"That's their power."

"Someone starts out seeking magic. Demonology, grimoires, spells. Then, stumbles onto this. For me, no surprise, that's how it started. Reading in occult libraries in Ukraine, in Norway and Wales. Seeking singular books. I started out copying interesting designs, creating tables, lists. I began wondering about exotic editions. Lambskin, papyrus, vellum. The more I studied, the more the words took hold."

The sound of the gathering fell away behind. The beach curved right, became narrower, more rocky. They walked until the beach disappeared into jagged rocks struck repeatedly by waves. There Daniel stopped. He wasn't sure how Lin felt about all this, couldn't understand why he was being so patient. Then it occurred to him, while they were out walking, trying to avoid the crowd, they might miss the very event for which all had gathered.

Daniel turned, started back. "Have these seven-year weekends always been nameless?"

"So long as I've known. No name is needed."

"And the forty-nine-year. Is this really different?"

Lin considered. "Nobody knows. It's not written anywhere. Just speculation. That's the nature of belief, of faith. Worship of the unknown. Hope without certainty."

Nothing had changed in the core of Daniel's own philosophy, since his idealistic post-college years. But getting to know other practitioners, he'd often found himself disappointed in the way limits accreted upon them. Rules and expectations, self-imposed boundaries, limits no different than those affecting any rat-race drone. Timidity of thought and narrowness of conception stood perfectly opposed to the very belief system of expansive Cosmicism to which they claimed to adhere. Worship of infinity ought to remain pure, yet inevitably became just another routine, or a commodified object of exchange. An enlightened few carried on worshipping elder gods, insisting they would return. Some believed only in the symbolism, that Great Ones might share knowledge without actually appearing.

Others expected unequivocal material manifestation. The Great will rise up, and speak. Proof incontrovertible.

"I agree, no name is needed. I have so many questions." Daniel didn't want Lin thinking him frivolous, distracted from this serious event by personal circumstances. "This is my first."

"You're thirty years old." Lin veered as they approached a large group clustered around a low fire. "You'll see many more."

As they circumvented the group, they met the stream of pure rainwater runoff that cut the sand between the hotel and the ocean. Opposite, north of most of the gathering, stood a cluster of eleven women.

"There they are," Lin observed.

The Medusae. They appeared bored.

"Are you ready to face your friends?"

Daniel tried to bear in mind what Lin had suggested, that he was respected among the broader community. Even the Salamander had approached Daniel with respect. "It's time they actually see me. Whether they like it or not."

He felt greater fear, facing these women, than any he remembered. The absence of Maya Dancer ached like a wound in his gut. If only she were here.

Now something would be revealed, if not by overt declarations, then hints and glances.

Daniel was ready to call out, announce himself, but Apia saw him coming.

"We were worried about you, man."

All eyes moving. On Daniel, on Lin, glancing among themselves. A moment of appraisal, connection, then expressions of welcome. The circle opened for Daniel, even Lin beside him.

His fear had been pointless.

Like a big sister, Apia nudged Daniel.

The new Matriarch Fossa greeted Lin. Several others shook his hand. A few seemed impressed, almost starstruck at his presence.

"Figured at some point you'd need to branch out a bit," Apia told Daniel.

He felt himself in unfamiliar territory, elevated, airless. Already he felt sorry for the version of himself who had existed until this weekend. Now he was someone else.

Everyone watched, waited. The last daylight traces slipped away, like the last guest at a party, vanished without a goodbye. Sky no longer a source of illumination.

"It's time," Daniel said. "The seven-year night."

"This is forty-nine," Lin said. "Something will happen."

"There's some controversy. I heard someone say this event always ends in broken promises. Always, *Maybe next time*, and that's why participation is dwindling. If everyone drifts away, will this even still happen?"

"Earlier," Lin said, "you told me a few can accomplish as much as a crowd."

"But everybody I ask what they've seen, they shrug, say nothing." Daniel felt exhausted by the burdens of tradition, of expectation. "Do you still believe? Or just attend out of habit?"

Lin paused, perhaps thinking, or considering whether to condemn Daniel's faithlessness. "I believe something always happens. I also believe it's possible to be here, eyes and ears open, and still miss it."

He squeezed Daniel's hand. Such a simple gesture, conveying so much. Daniel felt as good as anyone out on the beach, in the EO house, or anywhere else. Good enough to believe whatever seemed true, say whatever he wanted. Comfortable standing beside a man like Lin, perhaps older, of a different denomination. They weren't so dissimilar. He even felt kinship with the others assembled, most watching the sky, others attending the rock itself or water behind it.

After a time within the circle, Daniel felt the Medusae loosen. All scrutiny lifted like mist. He felt no awkwardness, no uncertainty at all, when Lin suggested the two of them walk alone to the water. Outgoing tide had receded almost entirely beyond Haystack Rock.

"You can see all kinds of life in the water," Lin promised as they went.

Daniel sighed, overwhelmed. So many new possibilities. Infinite openness above, all around. Life might easily take him in any of these directions. "So much offered to me."

"Your life," Lin clarified. "It's like all the rest. Only more so."

"Funny."

"What would you do next, if you could do anything? Which you can."

"I'd love to meet Jarrett. See his collection, discuss it. Maybe someday, but now…. I'm overwhelmed. This is the first time I've been able to do this." He reached an arm around Lin's waist as they walked across wet sand.

"And yet," Lin said, "you didn't seem entirely inexperienced."

"I had plenty of experience. Just, it was all secret."

"Such is our life, as chosen," Lin said. "Always secret, possessed of hidden knowledge."

He led Daniel into tide-pools. Black rocks half-submerged, thick with barnacles, mussels, anemones. Within pools, starfish green, orange, even violet. Water cascaded in, splashed across Daniel's front. He tasted cold salt. "It's too dark to walk out here."

"Just follow," Lin said. "Walk where I walk."

Daniel stepped only where Lin stepped. He imagined tiny fish in the water, invisible in the swirling black.

Finally Lin stopped, squatted over an oblong pool. "Come closer."

Daniel tried to kneel, almost fell, laughing as he caught himself.

"What?" Lin asked.

"You've already shown me more in a single day—"

"And a single night." Lin flashed a lascivious grin, then bent and stirred his hand in the pool, agitating the frigid water.

Daniel tried to pull Lin upright. "Come on, let's go back. We'll miss it."

"What do you believe is meant by Cosmic? That word. Think Cosmos, Cosmology. Like universes, very large. Earth resides within a universe. Cosmos must be larger than Earth. This rock, it grows out of Earth. Must be smaller than Cosmos too. Such hierarchy only follows."

Daniel hesitated, wary of a catch. "Most would agree."

"What about you? Reader of books. Publisher of great renown. What do you believe?"

Daniel's mind spun, trying to address the question. "It's a concept too large to readily debate."

"The sky darkens." Lin looked down. "That darkens the water."

Daniel awaited the punchline, but none came. He looked down, at where Lin himself stared. A pool at his feet, contents invisible.

Was Lin's point that the cosmic needn't be large, on a human scale? Infinity might not blot out the sun, or rise from the sea, a timeless leviathan. Cosmic could mean very slow, or deep, or old. Infinitesimal, yet conveying the light of suns long dead. Such an infinity might occur in a flash. Might pass unnoticed, even by eager crowds standing, eyes open.

Daniel focused beneath the water's motile surface. Pinpoint lights moved, almost imperceptible. He leaned near, bent so his eyes almost touched the surface. So close, the points became everything. The water itself, a lens.

Remembering Lin, he looked up. "Do you see—"

"Of course."

Together they absorbed immeasurable visions, projections from another time, vastly distant. The phenomenon lasted only moments, noticed only by two. So it had always been. Waves crashed endless upon ancient rocks, eroded them to sand. All the time new things were birthed and lived eternities, ever hidden from sight.

THE SLIPPING OF STONES

My long-established practice of mornings and evenings was to walk until the beach ended in a high cliff wall, then return home. Even in winter, chilled by an hour's exposure to wind and spray, I preferred walking the beach. Out on the sand I remained solitary, anonymous. Locals never ventured north of Road's End park. Tourists, of which in December few existed, wouldn't impose themselves upon a local who pointedly ignored their greetings.

It was on such a walk, before vacant oceanfront getaways for Portland and Seattle millionaires, that I heard the child screaming.

I paused, strained to hear through the wind. I scanned the slope of sand and beachgrass, beyond which stretched dark houses.

Another repetition of the sound tightened my nerves like an overwound violin string. What was that high wailing? Could it be laughter? I wanted to believe it could be anything else, anything but the terror of a child.

Along the shore, nothing moved. I turned toward the water. The sun lowered on the horizon, a fire dying into red futility behind the ocean's boundless, indifferent slate. The shriek came again, clearer and so piercing that this time I discerned the direction. It came not from the row of oceanfront homes, but out in the water. A long, narrow island ran parallel to shore, not far out. I'd never seen the island accessible from land, even at lowest tide. Always before, a roiling barrier of white foam had separated the beach from the strip of black rock and pale sand. Upon that edifice towered a massive house built of granite blocks, like an old world museum somehow landed upon the shores of Oregon. As I'd passed this stretch of beach thousands of times before, it seemed strange the house only now penetrated my awareness for the first time. If indeed I'd noticed it before, I must've assumed the place to be abandoned. The island had long ago receded into a sort of backdrop, no more than a picturesque rock formation offshore, rather than site to a noteworthy and potentially curious building. I'd never imagined someone might reside there.

The tide was already shockingly low, and continuing to go out. As I stood wondering, waves rushed out from shore, as if a drain plug had been pulled. The way cleared between where I stood and the island's southernmost tip. A path seemed to rise out of the water, a ridge of sand sufficient to cross the gap, then climb toward the house's crumbling foundation.

No reasonable justification existed for me to trespass. I knew I should walk away, yet the child's screams had startled me to alertness, imposed clarity upon the mental fog that had pervaded all my years in this place. My heart thudded. Should I go forward, or turn back? I strained to discern movement, or hear the cry again. Any confirmation this was not foolishness. What if I'd heard nothing but a seagull's cry, or wind whistling over sand?

High in the structure, the inland-facing windows were dark, all except the endmost. That broad rectangle, the sort of picture window that might dominate a living room, flickered orange like firelight.

I stepped out onto damp sand, wrinkled like a fingerprint. Having crossed a line now, I ran.

Once I was on the island, nearness exaggerated the angle at which the imposing structure loomed. It seemed to sag under the weight of ominous sky. The upper structure was intact, walls straight and windows unbroken, yet the foundation cracked and sundered. Seams opened between massive blocks, which drifted and slow-tumbled down to where waves encroached upon sand. Still the higher portion remained perfectly square, certainly more impressive than any of the newer beachfront homes opposite. Enormous stones might slip, the foundation might break and shift, yet somehow despite such lower disarray, the body of the house stubbornly refused to give way, and remained upright in defiance of the sea's patient efforts at reclamation.

Another cry. Still I saw nothing, no one. My hands trembled in my pockets.

Many blocks had shifted sufficiently to create dark gaps wide enough that a child might crouch within, hidden from the wind.

I scrambled up the slope, driven by urgency. The sound of a child in trouble would affect anyone. Considering my own history, what I'd lost, how could I possibly turn back?

I slipped into a black opening.

Blindness prevented any guess at the measure of space into which I intruded. I pressed through a cleft, angling my chest to squeeze between slabs. Massive weights seemed imminently about to fall, a perilously heavy world ready to crush me under. I threaded a cracked maze, where elevations shifted on sands too unstable to bear their burden. Gravity, wind and sea collaborated to undermine by subsidence.

Beyond a corner, I felt walls part, and beneath me, a floor of flat stone. Perhaps basement or cellar. I couldn't see if proportions were regular enough to call this a room. At least here were breadth and height enough to stand upright. Already after only a minute in the dark, I doubted my own internal compass. I crept in what I hoped was the direction of the house's center.

In the next narrow passage, I stuck fast, almost turned back, but thought of the child. Fear compelled me onward. In boyhood, I'd squeezed through missing slats in a neighbor's fence. So much time and experience, a million pleasures and tragedies, separated me from that boy, but I remembered. More, I remembered another boy. The thought of my son spurred me. I exhaled, trying to compress my body, become a smaller version of myself. Somehow I slipped, stumbled forward, arms flailing, into space.

The ocean's churning sound silenced. Now I was within. The outside world seemed distant.

The floor inclined, first smooth, then regularly notched, like grooved steps in a medieval church, which slowly resolved to the perfected right angles of proper stairs. My hand found a varnished rail. The air changed, dry warmth on my face. This was someone's home. I was intruding. I kept hesitating, wanting to turn back. It wasn't too late.

As if in answer to these doubts, another shriek pierced the air. This propelled me forward, racing toward illumination at the top of the stairs, forgetting any concern for the noise of my breathing and footfalls. The glow took on the same golden firelight warmth I'd seen from outside, through the picture window. I came to a verge, where stairway became room. This was no place of menace, but polite, civilized. I heard lively fire crackling, peered around to glimpse ocean through a far window.

My worry at trespassing increasing, finding no hint of the imagined dark threat which had drawn me, I listened for any confirmation to justify my presence. No cries or whimpers, no sounds at all of children. Just snapping fire, and the distant, foamy hiss of waves.

From within, a small movement. Firewood popped. A presence shifted.

"Who's here?" a voice rasped, a sharp threat.

I froze, concealed behind a corner. There was still time to turn, retrace steps at a run.

The certain recollection of what I'd heard fortified my resolve. Somewhere, a child must be in trouble.

I stepped forward, past the corner of a tall shelf of brown wood. The room was dominated by a fireplace broad and tall enough that a man could stand within, if not for the blazing mound of stout logs. Reclined beside the fire was a childlike figure entirely swaddled in white blankets. One pale hand emerged to rest upon a work table next to the lounge. The small shape was otherwise covered, even the face hooded.

"Who is it, here?" The voice was different now, hostile, but childlike.

Uncertain, I stepped back, just enough to hide behind the cabinet. I averted my face, as if to avoid being seen might buy some time.

In the corroded silver of a mirrored door, I glimpsed a reflection, eyes which terrified me briefly, until I recognized myself looking back, disturbingly gaunt and harrowed. After a jolt, my heartbeat subsided. The staring face resolved into an arrangement I saw mornings when I shaved, and otherwise sought to avoid.

When the figure by the fire spoke again, the voice sounded clearly like a young boy, but with none of the submissive tentativeness of children I'd known. Had the startling change in voice been a matter of misperception, just as I'd failed to identify my own reflection?

"You look like the man I saw out on the beach." Less hostile now, he seemed almost welcoming. "Was that you?"

The time for retreat had slipped past, like so many life events, recognized only too late.

The boy's gesture reclaimed my attention.

"Yes, I heard a child," I began. "Heard a child screaming."

"Screaming?" He pushed back the hood-like part of the blanket to reveal wild blond hair, and eyes which pierced as he appraised me. "There are no children. Maybe you're thinking of someone, so you imagine hearing them?" Certainly he was older than the voice had first seemed, perhaps approaching teenage.

I wanted to protest his presumption, but held back. "You're alone here, then?"

He gestured at the table, papers and very old manuscripts. "Yes, working." A fountain pen rested beside a bottle of ink. The fingers of his right hand were smudged black. "I copy histories. New papers and ink, new languages. Nobody likes the old stories, so I have to update them. Otherwise there's no chance of people wanting to read them."

As a repairer of books at Lincoln City Library, I understood something of what he meant. The volume he currently transcribed was vellum darkened by centuries. It disintegrated like the Nag Hammadi codices, which of course I'd only seen in photos. My own work involved nothing so esoteric, merely rebinding, tape and glue repairs. "I wondered if the house was abandoned."

"Abandoned, a place like this?" He shrugged. "Pieces may be slipping away, but new ones always come along." A lively giggle escaped him.

Not understanding the joke, I took a step nearer the window, wondering about the incoming tide. Before I could see, something stopped me. I felt the strangest, almost ominous certainty that if I looked outside, some spell would break. The ocean would surely have rushed in, cut the island off from land. It would be too late. All this would fall apart.

More rationally, I felt presumptuous, ranging about this room, where I remained a stranger. What business did I have?

I turned back, found the boy wriggling within blankets, trying to shrug them off. I should have excused myself, but couldn't shake the idea of someone in trouble. If not this boy, then another. The possibility of rescuing a frightened or menaced child trumped all considerations. To achieve that, I might have sacrificed anything.

"There must be… some adult." I surveyed the room.

"Now listen, don't go all parental." A confident smile played at his lips. "I welcomed you, but you still haven't introduced yourself."

"My name's Diment." First name or last, I didn't say.

"Mine is Aon. People's names never change, you know, even if we keep trying to become someone different." His eyes narrowed. "You know what I mean, Mr. Diment. Trying to shift yourself. Never quite managing."

This assertion sparked indignation, as well as an embarrassed wish to over-explain in compensation. It was none of his business. I wanted to assert dominance over this child.

I stopped short. This was his place. I was the intruder.

Aon swiveled toward the large red painting above the fireplace. My own attention followed.

"*Per Voluntatum, Ad Astra*," he pronounced. "By Will, to the Stars."

The scene depicted a woman in a drifting white dress so ethereal and undefined as to combine aspects of garment, of cloud, and extended wings. To her left hip she clutched a young child, his body lost in the blur of movement, facial features obscured in burnt umber and crimson brushwork signifying shadow. The woman's own face appeared pained, eyebrows peaked, eyes angled down and away in despair or terror, as if enigmatic monsters lurked just out of view. As if she resigned herself to death, along with the child to which she clung despite—

"My son was killed…" I stopped myself. Part of me wanted to resume, to keep telling. A war waged in a flash of contrary impulses, between the urge to halt my divulgence, and the desire to say what needed revealing.

The wish for sympathy, and hope for the opportunity to explain my intrusion, overrode the pain of remembering. "I was a father." I halted and bit my lip. "I wish someone had tried to help my son."

"You said, *was a father*," Aon said. "You are a father. Ever were, always are."

Again I felt drawn toward the window. The tide, the world's inexorable turning. The influence of bodies external to myself. Too late to turn back. Another step.

Aon shrugged the wrap fully off his shoulders. Both hands free, he made a tiny gesture, a grasping. I froze, looked down at my own open hand. If the boy were nearer, the way his hand extended, his gesture would allow him to grasp mine, to hold me back. From a distance, he reached to me. I felt prevented from the window. The boy never moved from his seat.

"After my son died, my wife couldn't..." I still couldn't remember, couldn't face it. Our son's death had been an accident, impossible to prevent. Voia's dying had come later, after months of retreating within herself, ever deeper, multiplying the agony we both felt. Finally, she'd gone after him, despite no chance of catching up.

"You imagine your wife gone, but your son still near." Aon spoke with a certainty, an almost monk-like wisdom. So unlike a child.

"Near?" I tried again. "Yes. That's why I came. I told you, I heard screaming."

"You believe you heard screaming. You needed an impetus." Aon gestured to the second chair. "Why not tell me about Walker Diment?"

Were others here? My son's ghost lingered, though I no longer expected to find him, or any other child. Finally, I felt myself near, suddenly aware what I'd missed. Aon reminded me of the lack.

"How often does the tide retreat far enough that someone can walk out?" I asked.

"Never."

The fire warmed me. I answered Aon's questions, discussed the mundanities of my life in Lincoln City. Then, perhaps worried Aon might ask after the trouble which brought me here, I digressed into maudlin self-examination. My life had become lonely. I realized this truth at the moment I spoke the words. Aloneness, a stale habit. How long since I'd truly desired it? Where solitude was by design, there was no loneliness. That preference had slipped.

At a pause for breath, I jolted to awareness of time. Was I too late to depart? The sky beyond the windows was growing darker. Rain fell through chill mist. I imagined waves rushing in, like milk spilled from a crashed-over cup.

"You're ready for more." Aon shrugged off his wrap and stood. Within the nest of white blankets where he'd been sitting, there remained a large, damp red stain.

My awareness spun in reaction, mindful of some memory dangling overhead, seeming imminently ready to return, only I lacked the acuity of perception to locate the thing and pluck it from the air.

Aon wobbled past the fireplace. His khaki trousers and olive sweater were unmarked by blood. His body showed no sign of injury, just that crooked, almost elderly gate. He moved toward one of many artifact-laden cabinets, and strained to reach a high shelf. Despite his sharply bent spine, he stretched tall.

"It's not necessary." I too rose. "I should go." I started not for the stairs, but the window.

Aon shuffled quickly past, into my path. "What do you have…" He pointed.

I saw what he indicated, my hands clutching an object, obviously something I'd taken from a shelf without realizing. It was a sculpture, five vertebrae in white marble, paler than real bone. Despite a crosswise crack, the sculpture remained a cohesive piece, not loose or fragmented. The crack was not damage, but a feature of design.

Seeing the other cabinets, I could not deny the attraction exerted by such diverse oddments, a whole spectrum of casts and specimens. Figures on the nearest display mostly resembled parts of the human body, both internal and external, in colored stone.

The boy limped ahead, identifying floor-standing artifacts in passing.

"The interlocking panels of this bronze table slide," he said. "Useful for calculating changes in orbits."

On its surface, tarnished circular arcs spun varying radii.

"The spectrum." He pointed eagerly.

A semi-circular meter, black speckled buttons arrayed below a window, and a gauge needle wavering beneath possible readings: *illuminato*; *hic sunt futurum*; *tenebrosus*; *materia…*

Aon darted, excitedly pointing out relics faster than I could follow.

"*The Suicide of Queen Dido*." He indicated a white sculpture.

"It's by Cayot," I said. "I saw the original in the Louvre. A scene from Virgil."

"This is the original," Aon stated flatly, then continued. "And this globe."

An ivory sphere, etched with silver lines delineating land masses, oceans, national boundaries. Several maps overlapped, continents of unknown worlds superimposed in three-dimensional collage with the familiar lands of Earth. Aon's hand traced the surface, momentarily gripped and spun it in its wooden nest. A darker hemisphere came into view, a side of graphite stone. A small ebony door was inset, and beside that, a green window to the globe's interior the shape of a human eye, including lashes in gold leaf.

I thought of looking into that window, even started to reach for the tiny door, but stopped short.

"I knew," Aon said. "I knew this was in you."

My hand jerked back. "What do you mean?"

Aon was not innocent, no child at all, but some bent philosopher. Always guessing.

"You were a man of art," he said. "You painted new lives into being."

"I'm a librarian." *Painted new lives.* What had he meant?

"Is that all, a repairman of other people's stories?" He regarded me critically. "No. You're someone else."

"Who?" I was sure I didn't know.

"You said your name," he insisted. "Walker Diment, the celebrated painter of figures, who moved from New York to this little town. Walker Diment quit painting, not when his son died, but soon after, when his wife followed. Only then."

I blinked. "My name is Walker Diment."

"And you know about art."

Fingers sticky with oil pigments, the smell of linseed. These seemed aspects of someone else's life, vaguely appealing. A place I'd enjoy visiting someday, at least to look at paintings again. Discuss the work. "Yes, that much is true."

"You stumbled in, through some crack newly made." Aon straightened. "Uninvited, but now you're here."

I was not that man.

An object on a shelf, a voluptuous female nude, in copper wire. I reached—

"Your wife. What did you say her name was?"

"My wife?" Memory swerved, tried not to return. "Voia."

Aon left me there, ventured away to a far corner. He returned with an antique phone receiver, holding it to his ear, listening.

"Is this her?" He offered it to me.

A voice crackled, indistinct. A woman spoke my name. Pain of loneliness flooded, delayed realization of suffering felt suddenly, a pent-up wave crashing after long repression. How I'd craved contact. Even brief conversation.

"Wait." I shook my head. "There's no cord."

Aon set the phone on the floor.

"I ought to go," I said.

"Stay. We lose track of fundamental needs. So rarely we form real connections, then relinquish them, stupidly, in the name of phantoms."

These words seemed true, even compelling. When was the last time I'd shared a meal, wine with a friend? The last time I'd touched—

Aon raised a finger. "I have something to give you, then another thing to show you downstairs, so you'll forget leaving." He went to yet another shelf and brought back an ornamented wooden box, green and gold, the size of a child's shoebox.

I started to open the lid.

"Not yet." Aon's hand darted with startling urgency. "Come." He walked toward another dark corner, one hand trailing as if to pull me after.

One moment at my side, the next, gone.

"Wait," I called. "What do you want me to see?"

Clutching the box, I followed.

At the top of the stairs down, we passed an ornamented mirror. I was startled at the difference between the image of Aon's reflection and the face I remembered seeing. His years were impossible to judge. I wondered, what age would my son be now? I imagined him forever a toddler, grinning, oblivious to the world's threats. Today, he'd have been thirteen.

I hurried to keep up, careful not to drop the box Aon had given. It was light enough to be empty.

The stairs reversed endlessly down and down. We delved seven stories deep, eleven, penetrated rock beneath seabed sand. Far below the waves, so deep, all became dry, silent. Tides exerted no pull.

After so many featureless landings, on the thirteenth we found a closed door. I stopped, captivated by the hidden potential. What lay beyond such a thing? I imagined sidelong digressions.

Aon continued past, still descending.

Finally I broke away, hurried after. Down uncounted levels, until we found a limit. The last stair brought a sense of finality, yet another doorway suggested, like the last, the possibility of something more beyond.

This door was unvarnished black walnut, carved with a sigil. Eight ornamental forks radiated from center, tines outward.

Grasping the knob, Aon cleared his throat. "May we enter?"

I stepped back.

In reply came a woman's voice. "Please come in, son."

"She calls me that," Aon muttered confidentially.

The door popped open, swung to reveal a closet-sized room. At its center, a woman turned slowly toward us. The many surrounding shelves contained objects and statuettes of the kind found in the upstairs cabinets, illuminated by tiny copper lamps with murky red glass.

Aon gestured. "This is Jova."

A young woman, warm with life, naked skin fully revealed.

No.

A mannequin, made of gems and copper wire.

She seemed to be both at once, her lovely face brilliant with color. Lips of ruby, fingertips oblong sapphires, eyes emerald and opal. Not a construct or statue, but a being organically alive, watching me. I craved to explore her every detail. More than attraction, I felt familiarity, as with someone whose mind and body were already intimately known. Recognition. Was she a woman, or something I'd made? Memories spilled like waves. A bundle of epigrammatic words, perhaps titles. Canvas wet, glistening with aromatic hues. A rush of ideas, subjects I'd always intended to paint, but never manifested beyond vague intention.

Was she some last creation, before life unraveled?

I felt myself compelled nearer, drawn by another chance. A new beginning.

Jova's ruby lips parted to reveal bright teeth. A wild strand of hair fell, a black curlicue between white breasts. The ratio of hips to waist, as if I'd designed her. My gaze fell unavoidably to her naked sex, which resembled a florid bloom. Her hip shifted sideways, one knee slightly forward. She swayed into me, nearer not just in physical movement, but focus. Her warm, living smell, a sensation somehow forgotten. Not an echo from lost paintings or dreams, but a matter newly discovered, fresh with surprise.

My fingers twitched in motions of phantom brushstrokes.

Her nearness.

"The name Jova," Aon said, "it's a word that means future."

My eyes found the absurd sculptures.

A black crystal skull shot through with silver stars.

A pink marble couple in copulation, the woman double the man's size.

A bird's nest of pewter needles cradling a limestone fetus.

A terra cotta woman's head, vulva in place of a mouth.

"You're welcome here." The movement of Jova's lips forming these words hinted at voluptuous desire. The plushness of her mouth evoked such overwhelming lust. Real flesh wild with electricity. Her hands touched her belly, moved lower. Between her fingers glowed radiant skin, hot as embers.

She curved nearer. I believed this aching to be hers, then realized the feeling was my own.

Stop fighting. Give in. The need, impossible to ignore.

My gut clenched. "No."

Terrified I turned, opened the door, stepped out of the surreal gallery. I felt a shock within my chest, a jolt powerful enough to stun. I leaned down, caught my breath. The ground itself rumbled, a physical heaving profound as an earthquake. The wall I touched to steady myself shuddered.

"Stones are slipping," Aon said, still within the room. "Come back in."

When I hesitated, he swung the door nearly closed.

My ears popped. The world churned in new configurations. Past synchronized with future. Where mind resisted, strained to project unchanged reality, everything outside me went on reconfiguring until the shift could no longer be denied.

I desired escape, but knew no deeper place to go.

I fled. No focus but *Upward. Keep climbing.*

My legs burned. Hyperventilating, I staggered until I caught my breath, then resumed my feverish upstairs run. Muscles failed again. Dripping sweat, I slow-climbed, hands on wobbling knees.

I came to the pale, unmarked door, and stopped, dizzy and swaying in exhaustion.

Thirteenth level. Halfway down. Halfway up.

Doubt began to intrude. Why was I running? I felt deserted by certainty, perceptions unreliable. No such thing as escape.

Footfalls on the steps below me. Someone climbing.

Aon rounded the landing and came to my side. He looked at me. "You see your desires as enemies out to conquer you."

I knocked. "What's behind this?"

This door was uniform pale birch, offering no hint, unlike the one below, encoded with symbols, carrying the kind of meaning that might enable one to guess. Might enter, without help.

"Behind?" Aon asked. "What's behind every locked door?"

I took the knob, tried to turn. Locked, of course.

"You knew, but tried anyway." Aon seemed impressed, or at least surprised.

"Doesn't it bother you, every time you pass? Wondering?"

"Most doors are like this," Aon said. "Learn to ignore them. Instead, find the one door. Open it over and over."

I wanted to believe he was trying to help, that he understood my suffering. "Tell me something. I need a push." I looked at him, pleading.

Lip curled, he leaned close, almost tall as me. "Eleven years ago I took your wife. So you would be here now."

I considered his words, tried to dismiss them as nonsense. My mind resisted, sought to deny.

"I took your son first, so your wife would follow. I knew what would bring you. That you would cross the country, walk this beach, until after eleven winters, with the whistling made by the very wind that always blows, you'd believe you heard the screams of your son dying. Heard them in time."

I remembered. The scene flooded back, shattered inside me. I twisted, clenched. Sharp edges dug in. I wept. "Why?"

"All your works, meant for these walls." Aon gestured overhead, toward the house far above. "Walker Diment, noted artist of erotic and surrealist figures, painted in this house until he died. Those paintings, all the objects in this house, none existed until you made them. They're stories you will create."

This implication stunned me, despite its impossibility. "I haven't said I was that Walker Diment." This was futile, but I could think of nothing else. I couldn't look at him.

Slowly, I moved to descend.

Aon followed me down.

"Why?" I tried to repeat. I choked on the question.

His only answer, footsteps.

We attained the bottom so quickly. I reached for the knob.

Before, Aon had asked to enter.

I gripped, didn't turn. "None of this brings back…" Let go.

"Voia gave up," Aon said. "She withered. Jova will always thrive with constantly renewed potential. Charged forever with moist electricity."

The door sprung open.

I saw her gloriously revealed, surrounded by representations of bodies partial and entire, depictions in varied sizes of all the aspects by which woman differs from man. Transfixed, I stared. Figures copulating. Anatomy lessons in disembodied parts. How much could I—

Jova made a small movement, startled me to awareness. I was here, her room. My body, hers. This was an instant, a fleeting present, not stuck memory. Some difference existed in each new time before it was lost to the next.

She was tangible, not some ghost.

Aon spoke. "Your boy, beside a road. Your wife, shut in beside a fireplace. Your refuge, a closet at the bottom of a stair."

Past and present slipped, held me pinched between.

"What will I do?" My question sounded foolish the moment I spoke it. I believed Aon would know.

"Your future?" His eye twitched. "It's already done. It's here, above and below."

Automatically, my finger cleared dust from the corner of my eye. My hand trembled. "Can I at least look out a window?"

Aon stepped outside the tiny room. "Not yet. Not until you no longer care what's out there." He swung the door shut.

I was alone.

Jova leaned nearer, breathing warm. Into my ear she whispered seventeen syllables, words meant only for me, surprising in their intimate knowledge. Past, present, were they still near? From frustrated desire to limitless potential. Keys for secrets locked away.

A reflex said, *Step back, change the subject. There will be time, later.*

I ignored the voice, made myself face her. It was foolish, always trying to leave, always thinking of another time. I might remain here, with the fast-shifting child, pressed into proximity with a woman whose flesh might tick forever. What was life outside? At home, nobody waited. I remembered little of the place. Doors swung unlatched, windows open to the world. Everything was permeated by wind. Some vague fear, loss possessions I couldn't name. All I'd ever done was walk on the sand, every day. All I remembered.

Out along the sand beyond Road's End, to where waves died and wind stilled. Only when there was no more North to chase, turn around, walk South. Finally, I'd heard the cries, had wandered, drawn by what I guessed was fear. But what really carried me?

The imprint of a child's blood flowing out. Guesses at quanta of suffering.

Jova spoke again, reiterated suggestions. The physical details first shocked me. Part of me wanted, was ready. The words terrified, even as my interest was sparked. To feel myself pulled into her this way elicited a panic reaction. I had to resist it. She leaned toward me. Now I shifted, wondered.

Couldn't help it.

"How is your life here?" I asked.

The smile flashed rubies. "How was your life, in your place?" Her fingers stroked my arm, my hand, with care. "You wear your grief, a glove so close-fit you forget it's not skin." Her words carried no mockery. The look in her eyes seemed gentle.

Still part of me resisted. I should want to go home, to a place that contained things I'd purchased over years. None special, but their selection and arrangement was my own. I should care about maintaining them. The science of how specific things were kept intact, safe from wind.

"Will you show me the rest?" I asked.

"Aon will show you," she said.

I heard no sound beyond the door. Aon had gone.

"You can't come out?" I had seen her moving, hands and eyes, had felt her breath.

"Many rocks fall away, without undermining the house," she said. "To-day, so many slips. It's rare, this way you entered."

"But—"

"But I'm rooted here." She displayed no sadness. "My room contains everything. Aon helps, and you will. You can always come back. Or just stay. If you like."

The invitation felt genuine, seemed possible. *I might stay.* "But my own house. I left windows open. Doors."

"But it's empty," she said. "What harm could the wind make?"

I thought of lack, of longing. My desires asked nothing of others.

Her gesture indicated my hands.

Looking down, I rediscovered the box Aon had given. I'd been carrying it, up and down. "I forgot."

"You can open the box," Jova said with obvious interest. "You can look."

The burden had so quickly become part of my body. Small shifts compensated for the new weight.

"Why not open it?" Her lip trembled in eagerness.

I held the box by its bottom, avoided touching the lid. Shifted it in my hands. Listened.

I knew what this contained, could see without looking. I staggered at the shock.

"What do you think it is?" Jova asked.

My eyes opened. The lid remained closed. Would stay that way, always.

"Bones, shattered." My voice trembled. Sweat dampened my back, trickled down my neck. "A child's bones."

Jova's eyes. A gesture of tenderness.

I bore up, straightened. "What do you think it is?"

This room, so hot.

"If I tell, will you believe me without looking?" Jova's hand descended slowly. Past her breast, her belly. "If you do, it will be true."

Her eyes held me, saying, *Wait...* The hand slipped lower, as if outside her control. Her eyes, upon the box. "A key. A copper key."

Many fires burned within the house. Not just the fireplace above. The whole place was fire. Surrounded by ocean, there's no way the flames might ever spread.

If I stayed, I might—

The floor rumbled, a shifting of stones. Wind rose, a wail so high and piercing it could be heard even here, far below. The screaming was only wind. The wind would never stop.

THE TIDAL PULL
OF SALT AND SAND

Waking comes on slowly. I sprawl, wet beach, morning. Waves crash, subside. Sea foam dies away, sizzling into sand. Cold numbs me. Tingling skin, brittle in the wind.

Memories of last night tumble. Back and forth, from there to here. Between vague recollection, and wishful dreams, like pleasurable hallucinations. I'm stuck.

Go back. Want to—

Awareness floods in, another rush. A wave. Naked, freezing. How the hell did I get here? No idea. Somehow, yesterday turned into this.

"Atra?" My voice, an unfamiliar croak.

No answer, no sign of her. No footprints around. Just waves rushing in, smoothing the sand. A perfect expanse, traceless.

Where am I? Try to sit up. Some rocky dead-end. A beach, never seen before.

Sound of an approaching motor. A police Jeep stops a short distance off. Blond cop in a yellow rain poncho, approaching. Behind him, a half-dozen beachcombers, loosely gathered. How long have they been standing back there, watching me? The cop approaches, maybe a little cautious. Mostly amused.

I want to defuse this, invent some harmless, funny explanation. Sorry, officer, must've gotten a little carried away last night with the new girl-friend. Not sure where she's off to. Sure didn't mean to scare the locals, combing for agates or shells or whatever washes up around here, other than naked guys from out of town. Want to laugh it off, let him know there's really no problem. Just need a little help, a cop on my side. Maybe borrow something to cover up with, until I can… what next?

Find Atra. Go home.

I say none of these things. My thoughts drift back, that intimate place. Secrets revealed by Atra. So many sensations, a sense of the alien. The new.

Can't let myself imagine yet, not now. No time for that here.

"Had reports of a naked fella down here. Figure that might be you." The cop pulls off the poncho he wears over his Lincoln City Police jacket.

I slide the poncho on, look around. She must be somewhere. "Atra, where would she…" My lips numb, slurring. Throat rough. A different man's voice.

The cop looks skeptical, but pulls out a notepad, flips back the cover. "Atra, who?"

I give our full names. She's Atra Persons, I'm Nick Ravenna. I spell it. Both from Portland. I live in the Goose Hollow neighborhood.

"I'm guessing you don't have any I.D. hidden somewhere."

I give him my address, my driver's license number.

"Atra Persons. Her address?"

I hesitate. "I don't know it."

"This woman, you knew her?" Skepticism back on his face. "Not just someone you… just met?"

I can see his mind working, wondering if I've been rolled by a prostitute.

"Nothing like that," I say. "She's my girlfriend. But things are new, just a few weeks. I haven't been to her place." That's all I can tell, all I know. My hands tremble, seeking for something to grasp, any solid object nearby. I plunge my hands into the pockets of the poncho.

The cop offers me his cell phone. "Maybe try calling her."

I want to dial Atra's number, hear her voice. Fix all this. "I can't. I haven't memorized her number. It was saved on my phone, but… I don't know where that is. I guess with my clothes."

The cop cocks his head toward the Jeep. "I'll radio in. Maybe somebody's seen her." He heads off.

The beach terminates in a cliff wall. Black stone looms over tide pools and barnacle-stubbled rocks. Waves roar and disintegrate into cream-white foam. Further out in the water, a rock pillar rises tall, monumental. In a hollow near its tip, a single seagull perches. Watching.

Memory threatens to return. Fantasy, whatever it is.

"No sign of this Atra Persons." A voice behind.

I turn.

"Checked Portland too." The cop looks a little more skeptical now. "No Atra Persons listed. You sure of that name?"

I shrug, shoulders trembling, trying to fight this rising panic. "Maybe she's unlisted."

"You just met this girl? Hook up online, I'm guessing. Things don't go as planned, maybe she doses you? Runs off with your stuff?"

"No. We're in a relationship. We've been together, every night for two weeks. If she wanted to steal, she could've—"

He nods. "Yeah, okay."

"We hiked all afternoon, ended up in this hidden cove where… It all happened." No way to explain. Can't even give the first hint what it was like. Not without sounding crazy. "Not sure where, it was dark. But it has to be close by. Any coves near? Inlets?"

The cop gestures at the jutting black stone rise. "This is where the beach ends. Past here, it's just rocks and waves, no beach access until up around Neskowin. Proposal Rock, that's seven, eight miles." He holds onto his notepad and pen, keeps asking me a lot of things I don't know, including things he's already asked. What part of town she lives in. Names of friends, next of kin. Workplace. All I can tell is where I met her, on Portland's South Waterfront. We were both walking, and somehow ended up talking. From there, to a beer afterward, then dinner. A swirl of intimacy, two weeks blurred into this.

It's a test of sanity, a waking nightmare. My guts burn, reacting to this fear and uncertainty. I try to calm myself, but can't. Even though I'm sickened at this morning's turn, last night's pleasures keep returning to mind.

Those memories don't calm me, only add to the trembling, the sense of impending overload. Remembering that weird disembodiment. A whole-body tingle, like electric shock.

I'm sure back at home, Atra will explain. There must be some reason.

My brother drives down to get me, two hours from Portland. In the car, at first he jokes, shaking his head, teasing. Just another of my stupid misadventures. His questions sharpen, half-kidding. I can tell he wants an explanation. Then he says he doesn't care. It's all stupid, pointless. He hopes this is my idea of a swell weekend.

But I know him. It's his way of trying to get me to offer up what he wants. What happened?

My indifference to his questions starts irritating him. "How the hell do you wake up naked on the beach?" he demands. "All by yourself, with your car back in Portland? How did you even get there?"

"I don't remember." That's mostly true.

"Was it some woman?" he asks. "Sure it was."

Of course, I don't tell him about Atra. He's never heard of her, never met her. My brother's inclined to treat all the women I meet as identical. Dysfunctional types, in need of saving.

"Nick's Lost Kitten Rescue Service," he says. "Drop off your broken, helpless crazies. Long as they've got… Something to offer." He smirks, a mocking laugh.

It's always like this with him, as if they're all the same. But he's been married since high school to the same dull, brown mouse. How would he know what it's like, to come together with a person, get to know them in the dark. Learn their secrets, and try to understand all the suffering that made them who they are? To someone like him, the idea of feeling love for a person after such a short time is a joke. Just an invitation to ridicule.

Atra is different, worlds apart from the rest. It's hard to explain, but there's something about her. Like another species. It's depth of experience, I think. She's a woman, not just a stunted girl in a full-grown body.

Home again. My car, still parked outside. Nothing's changed.

My brother hands me his spare key. I offer to go inside, change my clothes and give him back the jeans and sweatshirt and socks he brought down for me. He shakes his head, says he'll get them later, drives off.

Such a relief, just being back at my home. It's an unusual place to live, I realize, the outcome of a design and construction project made by architecture students at Portland State. If I didn't rent it from the college, I'm not sure who else would want to live in a windowless cinderblock cube. It's perfect for me. Two stories, concrete-gray, as tall as it is wide. A form of perfect, symmetrical balance. Distinctive geometry and design is a must for me. People fret over the aesthetics of their car, their clothes, their hair, yet they live in nondescript, boring houses. Cookie-cutter places without form or shape.

Some would consider my place cold. The floors are concrete, the fixtures stainless steel. Fluorescent lights hide behind angled blinds, so illumination is always subtle, indirect. Here I feel safe, warm and comforted. I'm at least as settled as possible, without answers.

I begin to rebuild, knowing I won't be right until I see Atra. At least talk to her. I get myself new ID, another wallet. Replace the lost phone and camera. There's nothing to fill the vacancy I feel. A loss, a wanting, much more profound than hunger.

I keep waiting, because I have no choice. Atra never calls.

I don't know where she lived, can't find any trace. I return to the waterfront, walk the park, the brewpub where we first ate and drank together. No sign. Maybe I could accept never seeing her again, this woman I barely knew. I might do without Atra herself, if I had the answers only she can give.

My memory's wrecked. A broken mirror, many crucial shards lacking.

I pass evenings at home, without books or videos, eyes closed. I recline on my bed, perfectly centered in the upstairs room. It's a matter of geometric ratios, placing myself equidistant between four walls, each wall decorated with a painting forty-eight inches square, each painting based on a single color of the CMYK color-space, offset against a monochrome counterpart.

I made the paintings while still a student myself, obsessed with graphic design and four-color process printing. Cyan and silver. Magenta and gray. Yellow and graphite. Black and white. These exercises in understanding, in breaking complexity down into simple component parts, surround me as I try to remember.

Sorting memories through a four-color filter. Sift the detritus of recollection, someone else's junk drawer.

If I still had my camera, whatever pictures I took that day, what would I see? Blue sky, steep vistas, dense forest, sprawling ocean. Atra's face? I can only guess. So few details remain available to me. Our night together, before that disoriented morning. Some aspects clear, most obscure.

What do I remember? I have to establish that much, before I lose it.

We covered miles amid giant trees, climbed toward gaps of blue-white sky. Atra playfully affectionate, mostly. Sometimes distant, as if preoccupied.

We walked much farther than I expected, sweat trickling down my back, blisters on my feet. Hunger, dehydration. These sensations I recall with vivid clarity, but not where the hike started. Not the drive to the coast. An all-day walk landed us in that cove, somehow. By what path? A patch of warm, dry sand at the cove's apex. Mist drifting off waves crashing nearby.

Tingling, sensitive skin. Atra's breath, her lips. An intimate touch inflamed to... What?

Here, memory becomes painful. The nearer to her, the more fraught. Exaggerated, intimate intensity, like staring at the sun. I blink the vision away.

Together, then alone. What happened? Why the shift?

If I could zoom deeper, study the photographic negative of memory under a magnifying loupe, what would I find? Some trace of a secret in her smile? I remember hair blown across her face, a fringed outline. Smiling shyly, lips covering a slightly crooked front tooth.

Atra took me there. It was her idea, something urgent and specific. Why?

The night before we left, she tried to tell me she was done seeing me. That she had to go away, things had to change. Wouldn't say why.

When I demanded answers, some explanation, at least a single reason, she wouldn't look at me. She'd start to offer some reason, then back off, realizing there was no truth in it. Try another angle, abandon it. Wanted to call off the morning hike, walk away, stop seeing each other.

I held to her, wouldn't let her go, no matter how much she protested and cried.

Finally she relented. I was right, she had no reasons. Everything could go back to the way we planned. The early drive, the hike. Whatever it was she wanted to show me.

There was tenderness, sadness in the way she looked at me. I could still see it, something remained wrong. I wouldn't let her end things, not without a reason. Not without talking to me, at least. I was sure she'd see I was right.

I remember that day in the high trees, somehow arrived near the ocean, overlooking the curved horizon of water. She undressed, pulled us together, wild with desire. Both of us hot, already sweating from the hike. She made love to me, unbridled, half-crazed. Like never before. Full of anger, and regret.

"Just for me," she said, from the delirium of her orgasm. "For me only."

From there, nothing of the rest of her hike, how we made it down from high cliff overlooks, to the sand below.

What about the cove itself?

We weren't alone there. I recall strange women, in anachronistic dress, like Amish, toiling along the cove's edge. They fumbled in the water at the foot of the cliff wall, still ponds where something was being cultivated. Blank faces, impossible to read. Was this part real, or my imagination filling gaps? Other women, working. Why would Atra take me to a place like this? It carried some meaning for her. Something she wanted to show.

The mind strains, recollecting details. I sometimes think the subconscious offers bits invented to fill gaps, to relieve the stress. My only persistent memories of the time are more like erotic dreams than waking experiences. The way her body felt, my own sensations exaggerated, hyper-intense. Before me on the sand, Atra reclines, never fully unclothed. I taste salty skin, gritty with wind-blown sand. Her legs part. She encompasses and surrounds me, seeming to split open, to divide. She writhes, flailing, and

I swim within her, touched by a multitude of hands. I taste sensitive flesh, secret and exotic as the ocean deep. I float, held aloft in a pool of buoyant lust. Like madness shared between us. A sudden exit from the familiar.

The ache of desire, so intense. A tangible thing. The need for release, a burning pressure.

Ocean roils all around, full of anger, black and primal. Wild, manic. Atra's body changes, shifts. She climbs over me and we tangle. Hallucinatory.

None of that seems part of the reality I inhabit, sitting alone in my room. Yet it's as real, as sharp as a blade in the gut. This sense of being devoured, dissolving into a crowd. Giving into desire. Relinquished selfhood, ego dispersed irrevocably. All that's still with me.

I want to go back. More than obsession, it's love, passion. So powerful it hurts.

Sit by the phone long enough, waiting for that ring, and eventually something fades. It's impossible to sustain the same intensity of hope forever.

I spend less time obsessing on memory, hoping for a return, and gradually return to an awareness of the necessities of living.

I do graphic design and layout for a famous Portland ad agency. Working from home allows me freedom to set my own schedule, work at my own pace, and avoid the grating din of the agency's open-plan office.

Days stumble past, blandly routine. Every day, nine hours work, two meals, one hour meditation, two hours reading. Music, from the time I wake until I sleep. Try to sleep.

Weeks, no glimpse of hope. How to escape from the oppressive weight of life itself?

Lately I try to remember what I wanted before I knew Atra. She left me, never said why. I've lost other relationships before. I've always moved on.

Is this torment over losing her, or is it the place she took me? I'm afraid without her, I'll never get back. Hopelessness grows.

I think what I always wanted, what I was always seeking, was the idea that there might be something more. This life seems too mundane, too colorless. Something more must exist, somewhere out there. I've always suspected I might find it someday. Maybe in books, or in nature. Art, music. All these things hint at the sublime, at wide open spaces, deep time, grand scale.

That's what I wanted before Atra, what I still want. It's what I believe she might have shown me. Just a glimpse, and only for one night.

What was it? The place itself, or something felt or heard or smelled within that secret cove?

Salt water and sand. Cyclical waves. The cove, powerful in my recollection.

What's happening in my mind really makes no sense.

I start believing I'll never see Atra again. That doesn't mean I've given up on finding the cove.

Think back, try to remember. Every conversation, even things that seemed unimportant at the time. Maybe she dropped hints, mentioned places she'd visited. Maybe where she came from?

One thing I remember, the tiny notebook she always carried. The microfine Japanese marker she used to scrawl notes. Maybe jotted a few words, or sometimes longer things while I was busy working, or cooking. I might see her doodling shapes, but she never showed me what was inside the book.

What obsessions worked on Atra's mind?

I saw her experience joy, dejection, pleasure, boredom.

"I was dreaming of sand."

Is that something she said, in the blurred black of night?

Waves on the shore, the place where ocean infringes upon land. Striving always to encroach, always tiring, falling back.

Riptides lurk. Dangerous, always ready to pull us under.

What could take a person from safety, wading within reach of dry land, and yank them away from their life? Pull them out, away from shore, and down. Currents beneath the surface. Invisible, but powerful.

Whirling ways, down deep.

The ocean floor is sand, but it's more like firmament above. Black as space. Some ultimate, profound unknown.

Strive downward.

Finally, clarity. I realize I'm dreaming. It helps me see.

I tumble out of the dullness of my room, from tangible, well-lighted concerns, into vivid realms of opioid fantasy.

The secret cove. Atra greets me, not alone. We're surrounded, swarmed. Many of the throng share her face. We fall together, the intimacy I crave. I dissolve in engorged, voluptuous wetness.

That ache in my gut. Desire poisons as it compels.

A perverse cycle, need and loathing, lust and destruction. Fuck the world. Submit to the world and let it fuck you.

I wake knowing I'll try again.

I gather hiking guides and maps, conduct online research. Spend weekends in the car, driving up and down Highway 101. I seek any recognition, feeling certain all it will take is some detail remembered. Landmarks, trailheads, signs. Anything we passed that day. If I can't find where we parked, at least maybe I might recognize where we turned off the highway.

This new obsession occupies all my free time, and sometimes afternoons when I should be working. I wander in my car, and find nothing. Rather than killing my enthusiasm, this futility causes my existent preoccupation to ferment into a drug-like madness.

I will see it again. The cove's surreal yellow light. Ground mist rolling in, despite cloudless skies.

These images bear no resemblance to the world in which I was born and now live. The cove is hidden, reachable only by trails, steep and remote. An invisible path I need to find, somehow. Maybe impossible. No choice but to try.

I focus on the forty miles between Depoe Bay and Pacific City, with Lincoln City at the heart. I don't know for sure that the cove is near where I was found, but it must be a distance I could've walked during that obliterated night, before the next morning.

All along Pacific Coast Highway, I stop in at restaurants, hotels, gift shops. I want to ask for help, want to explain. Mostly I show my picture of Atra, the only one I have. Ask if they've seen her. The sympathetic ask for details, but I have none to offer.

It's a picture of my girlfriend, I say. Her name is Atra. She's gone, I don't know where. If I told them Atra lives in Portland, they'd want to know why I'm searching here. That's something I can't explain.

My search is blind.

There are dozens of hikes on Oregon's central coast. Over the months, I try them all, at least all the trails listed in books.

I find no triggers for memory, nothing familiar in any way. Only mile after mile of beautiful forests, fields, hills and beaches. Rocky coves without sand. Inlets the wrong shape, or ruled out by obvious landmarks, or too-near street access. Rock faces, dead ends. So many places, all clearly wrong. Nothing close.

Not one contains my secret. That flavor of mystery.

Atra fades, like someone known only in a fond dream, but my vision of the cove grows more tangible. How can that be? Tireless waves, rocks immune to erosion. And something more. I'm not sure what.

My outings blend together, take on a sameness, like a mantra repeated. Passing through trees, the repetition blurs.

Somehow I come to a high place, not sure how I even arrived. But I see the water, an arrangement of rocks that seems familiar, even from so high above.

I'm nearly there. But how did I come?

I can't help my excitement, become frantic, thinking I've found it. It's there below me, but I can't find a way down. Never mind how I got here, I can trace my way back later. Find my car, somehow. All I need to do now is find a way down.

I scramble off the trail, heart pounding, trying to find my way nearer the edge. Peer down sheer cliffs. No way down. Backtrack, running through tall grass. I realize, only now, I'm not really sure about the water. The rocks out there. Hint of a cove, or inlet. The light is dim, worsened by dark clouds moving through. The sun, already low on the horizon, and I have to make it back to my car. At least two hours out, nearly that long to return. I'm afraid of being unable to find my way. Still my eyes fix on the water far below. I see it come together, the formation of something beneath the surface. Light reflects from low on the horizon, glittering silver. What am I seeing? An entire open field of water is churning. Do I see limbs, arms, other body parts popping up from underneath? The water's too dark, with these clouds. Not a cluster of people swimming, but some formless mass, dark gray. Barely more solid than water, trying to rise only to become formless, unsolid, and sink back into the churn.

I want to get down there, more than anything. The obsession rises in me, with all the power of passion, lust, jealousy. It's almost worth leaving everything behind, ignoring the trail, my car. My home, all my life back in town. But if I don't go back to Portland, return to work in the morning, what then? Without income, I can't afford to continue searching. I'm not even sure how I came here. How would I find this again?

By the time I think of taking a photograph of the movement in the water, I see everything has gone still. The gray clouds are past, but the sky is still darkening.

I'll come back. I'm closer than ever. Just need to keep looking. I'll find a way.

Home again, preoccupied with new memories. Trying to sort out what I found. How does all that fit with what I already knew? I try to settle back into my quiet life, get my mind back under control.

Lie on my bed, at the exact center of the room. I need clear, geometric music to clarify my thoughts. Try to meditate, starting with early Philip Glass suites. When that's not enough, move on to Phrygian Gates and China Gates, by John Adams. These constructs of human artistic intention offer up their intrinsic form, impose it upon me. There's a rhythm, a spacing. Gaps exist, slots into which I should align myself. Grid-like structures, clear and profound.

I'm afraid the increments are all wrong. The four-color paintings are no help, either. It's a lie, trying to reduce everything to simple categories. The possibilities are too numerous. The world's so much more complicated. Especially people.

I stand, descend the stairs to my work alcove on lower landing. The dark computer stares back. Not sure what I'm looking for, just that it's here.

Switch on the desk lamp, open the drawer.

A letter, folded in quarters, inside a square envelope. Metallic silver paper. Green ink. My name.

Atra's writing.

Why now? Haven't seen this before, yet it's here, in plain sight. I must have opened this drawer twenty times in the span since Atra left.

How long?

The exquisite stationery. The expressive writing, brilliant green. Before I read the letter, this reminds me of Atra. Her love for fine paper, her obsessive collection of fountain pens. Even in our short time, she told me all about her dozens of pens, in wood cases or on special stands. I never saw most of these, other than the few she carried at various times. But she talked about her pens and inks with such joy and such love, they seem as real as anything I know.

Now Atra speaks to me, by her own emerald hand.

"My Dear Nick—

You don't hear my warnings,

too hungry for what you want.

Always pressing forward,

rushing headlong at the unknown.

Desire will eat you alive,

until there's nothing left for me.

Love,

Atra"

A scent in the paper evokes memories of her, and other images. Rows of pens on display. Shelves of unusual inks, vivid colors in exotic glass bottles, all shapes and sizes. Something I see so vividly, can envision in every detail, as if I've actually seen it. But I never have. Never even saw where Atra lived.

Just like the cove, and Atra herself. Maybe it's all false memory. Nothing more than wishes.

No progress, can't even find my way back to where I've been. Feeling morose about my search. Self-defeating. Stuck in my own head.

I stop for dinner at a waterfront inn and restaurant on Nestucca Bay. At the bar, I sit alone. Almost the whole place is empty. An older man in a fisherman's slicker and ear-flap hat sits by the fireplace, sipping liquor from a leather flask.

The bartender takes my order, a cannonball of clam chowder in a sourdough bowl, and seems not to notice or to mind the old fisherman drinking on his own, rather than ordering from the bar.

My food arrives and I can't help watching the old man, still sipping, mostly looking into the fire. He seems not to notice me, but I wonder about him. The way he seems so self-contained, despite being alone. Unworried, even carrying his own drink. What does he need with this place? Maybe just the fire.

After I pay my bill, I approach the fireplace.

The old fisherman doesn't look up, but clearly notices my presence.

I sit in the chair, next to the sofa on which he slumps diagonally. The brown leather squeaks as my weight settles in.

The fisherman holds out his flask toward me, without meeting my eyes.

"Hello," I say. "I'm Nick."

"Care for a sip?" the fisherman says. "I'm offering. You're bothered, plain to see."

I hesitate. Normally I'd walk away, but I feel stuck, dead-ended. Why not try something different? Maybe it's time to step outside myself.

I take the flask, and sip. The liquor burns my throat, all spice and smoke. I take a second drink, hand it back.

Then I tell the old fisherman my story, at least part of it. How I met a girl in Portland, in an improbable way, and very quickly felt close to her. We seemed obsessed with each other, not just me with her. Then that day when things seemed to swerve between worst and best. In the morning, her distance, and trying to end things. Then later, the beautiful hike, the impromptu sex out there, overlooking the ocean from a cliff. Last, the discovery of this hidden, almost magical location. Worst, awakening to find her gone.

"No trace," I say. "Even now. As if I never really knew her at all."

The old fisherman offers the flask again. "You have to start looking."

I sip, welcoming the burn. "I am, have been. Won't stop."

"No, that's not good enough," he says. "My advice? Don't keep doing the same. Why continue what never worked? Assume all of that is wasted effort, searching in the wrong direction. Like with the white sturgeon fishery. Most kinds of sturgeon's endangered, so while we're still allowed to take some, they're harder to find. There have been sturgeons on the earth much longer than people, do you know that? Unchanged. Sturgeon's an ancient thing. Some think it's beautiful, some horrible. I'm not sure myself. I just know how to find the sturgeon. Always manage to find it. I look in one place for sturgeon and don't find it there, I try different places. Not just different places, though. Different ways of looking."

"You fish for sturgeon?" I'm not sure whether he's being literal.

His eyes narrow, without seeming unkind. "You hear what I said, my advice?"

I stand, slow and stiff. "Maybe you're right." I'm unsure about the advice, though, unconvinced that seeking a lost girlfriend or her secret place somehow pertains to hunting white sturgeon down rivers and into the ocean. "I appreciate it. The drink."

The old fisherman nods, already looking back into the fire.

I start to head out to the parking lot, but feel woozy, too tired to drive. What was in that flask? I veer back toward the inn's front desk, and inquire about a room. It's expensive, more than I can afford to spend if I want to keep searching like this every weekend, but I'm so tired. Can barely keep my eyes open.

I pay, and take my key upstairs.

The room is clean, well-maintained, but the bedspread is hideous, the art on the walls is ugly. There's no symmetry. The colors are a swirling nightmare, everything all scrambled, disproportionate, out of balance.

I don't have any of my own music with me.

Collapse on the bed, struggle out of my jacket, fall back. Eyes closed, it's better. Don't have to see the visual assault of the decor. Seascapes, beach theme, that I could understand. This is worse, all peach and yellow blossoms, pastel stripes. Heartbreakingly awful.

I'll fall asleep soon. Have to escape this place. Just sit up long enough to take off my shoes, and lie back. Eyes shut.

I realize my struggle is mostly internal. There's no enemy out there in the world, trying to stop me from finding what I seek. No physical barriers impede me. My problem is lack of information, a shortcoming of knowledge. This leads to frustration, a demoralizing sense of futility. Can I seek forever, without ever making progress? I'm terrified I'll continue this way for a thousand years. What if I forget what I'm after?

Another coffee stand in Pacific City, a drive-up on Highway 101. I think I've stopped here before, but the counter girl is unfamiliar. Her crop top reveals a jeweled belly ring over shredded low-rise jeans. Bleached hair, defeated by coastal humidity, hangs limp into her eyes.

I order coffee, then spill my disorganized questions.

This girl I knew. Maybe you've seen her, or somebody knows her. The forest, leading to the cove. Even as I'm speaking, I realize how unformed and vague all this sounds.

Mention nothing about secrets.

I bring out Atra's picture.

The girl flinches, rubs her face as if I've slapped her. "Why don't you call the police, instead of going around yourself, asking after her?"

I can't tell the truth. I don't know enough of Atra's details to get help from the police. Her address, where she worked. I only know her voice, her body. Her love of ink and antique pens and vellum paper.

"Maybe you're a stalker?" the girl continues. "Got yourself dumped. Can't take a hint?"

I take back the picture. "We were together. She disappeared."

"She shouldn't-a taken you where she did." Behind the glass, her face pales. It's the first recognition I've encountered, the first hint I might not be crazy.

She slides the window shut, steps back from the glass, out of the light.

"Wait!" I rap hard on the window, heart thudding with excitement. "You recognize her."

The coffee girl steps closer, arms wrapped around herself, then she turns away again, shaking her head emphatically.

"What is it, then?" I shout. "You know something."

She comes back, opens the window a crack. "You promise to go away?"

"Yes, of course."

She looks down at the counter, not at me, as she speaks. "Sometimes they seek outside Neskowin, that old forest on the ocean side. You know Agate Beach?"

I nod.

"Some get lost there, in the trees. Bad stuff. Cults or... Who knows. Dark things, there to Cascade Head. Locals know. Enough disappear, you don't go looking. Don't go near."

My mind spins, wondering if I'm getting everything she's saying. Does it even make sense? "Disappear? Who takes them?"

In that instant, her eyes look much older, full of regret and the burden of memory. "I've got to close up now. You should take a hint." She shuts the window, latches it, hangs a CLOSED sign, then stalks away into the dark interior.

I sit still, trying to catch my breath. After a while, I pull out onto the highway, headed south.

Saturday evening, almost dusk. Too late to start exploring.

I drive a few miles, most of the way toward Neskowin, and stop at the first little hotel. The place is faced-up right against the highway. The whoosh of traffic kills any chance of sleep. It's too random, the gaps between cars unpredictable. Probably sleep would remain beyond reach, even in my own bed at home, where I play CDs of ambient background noise to help block out distractions.

For the first time, I have something to go on.

Lying there, I wonder if I remember something Atra said to me that last night before the hike, or maybe it's just an echo of the coffee girl's last words.

"You need to take a hint."

Friendly advice, or warning? Any sense of tone or context is obscured by the fog of memory.

I toss in anticipation, tense and sweat-drenched, like someone adrift at sea. There's no clearing my mind, no relaxing. I'm not awake, not asleep. Stuck between.

Four A.M., sky still black. Dawn, hours distant. Somehow the darkness clarifies. I drop the hotel room key into the return slot, and head out.

South of Neskowin I veer off 101. The old forest which hugs the entire coast, north and south, exerts a powerful gravity. These ancient trees, huddled in their millions. Far south looms the black hump of Cascade Head, against the deep gray sky.

Yes, darkness clarifies. I see what I've always needed, in the interstices between two worlds, daytime and night. I've searched the right places. Just the wrong times.

The road is a dream pathway, familiar by feel, rather than sight. Acres of midnight green swarm with the menace of hidden life, alert and watchful. A wide spot at the edge of the road. An unmarked trail opens into tall overgrowth. Even overrun, tendrils grown long and streaming to the ground, I recognize this. The entrance.

I venture into the chilly realm of darkness beneath the trees, follow ways that may not be visible trails by day. Climb across streams, clamber over broken rock fields overgrown by moss. Sometimes, underground. I'm convinced the way is impossible, a network of paths without signposts leading me out of lonely darkness. After seven or eight miles, I move out of forest depths, into a place where gaps between trees begin to allow for hints of light. Finally I break into the green-filtered aurora of morning. I only hope my path, undertaken by night, remains true in a world remade by daylight. How did this happen, with Atra? I remember the dark, being together early. In fact now, I remember an uneven night, after we argued. Her tears, our sleeplessness. Rising early, to drive in the dark.

The path broadens to the width of a road, and climbs high into the coastal hills. Trees part, exposing me to the first full sun of morning, until sweat soaks through my shirt, drips into my eyes and down my neck. I push on through fatigue, still unsure what I'll find. This seems right. At least I've found the way. Maybe it leads to some clue what happened to me. Maybe just to Atra's body, reduced to bones. No way I can stop, not until the cove.

I halt, stand silent, and strain to confirm what I think I've heard. The ocean. Realizing I'm so near, I take off up a bank, then zigzag down a steep slope. I pass wind-blasted trees, weathered gray and bent steeply, like crones seeking shelter, their wild hair flailing in the relentless blast of salt mist headed inland. Here ahead, an overlook. Unobstructed view of an inlet below, the same stretch of coastline the Lincoln City cop told me was nothing but miles of rocks. It's sand, encroached upon by thin waves, in a half-circular protected cove. Further out, the many rock mounds I remember, twenty or thirty feet tall.

The tide is higher than I remember, but this is it. The place is real. Not hallucination, not dream.

Still, no way down. I'm swaying, weak-kneed from exhaustion. How long have I been hiking? Past noon. I must've gone fifteen miles, maybe more. I turn from the edge, wishing I could dive off, take the most direct path to what I seek. Another part of me would like to turn back, not just try another day, but forget all this.

I can't turn back.

Hope compels me. More than desire, I crave knowing. To recover what I've forgotten. Another reality, a new way of feeling, of living. I'm possessed, overheated with urgency. I range southward, always keeping a sense of where I am in relation to the cove. Outgoing tide exposes more sand. I keep hiking, keep peeking down, over the edge. Trying to find a way down the cliffs, more than a hundred feet over wave-pummeled rocks, I edge along, hoping for a lower point. So familiar. I lean out, straining to see.

Just then, the sandstone lip breaks away. I fall, skidding and pinwheeling down the slope. Not a sheer drop, but I skid out of control, pelted by loose rocks and chased by a rush of sand until I hit bottom.

Dazed, bleeding, I come back to awareness. Nearby, crashing waves. A landmark I recognize, a rock spire just offshore. A seagull perches in an alcove-like hollow, near the tip. The same rock I saw that morning, months ago, shivering naked on the sand. I'm here, the beach at Road's End. The very spot where the Lincoln City cop came out to meet me in his Jeep.

The cove is here, just around these rocks.

I try to stand, scraped and still dazed, but not badly injured. My wounds are nothing, next to my excitement. In the pools at the foot of the rocks, starfish sprawl, exposed and vulnerable. Green and pink anemones, like gasping human orifices, struggle in the sun. A narrow rock bridge leads up, past the outcropping, first higher then back down again, around the corner. All this is usually underwater, not just on the morning I awoke here, but all the times I returned. The tide's much lower now than ever before. I don't know how often the water drops low enough to pass, but I won't miss this opportunity. I climb the bridge, balancing over a twenty-foot drop to roiling ocean on my left, and to my right, a narrow gutter filled with jagged rockfall. After I make the corner, and start back down toward sand level, my head begins to spin from the impact of the fall, the danger, and the onslaught of memories and dehydration. So much emotion here. I want to drink, to dive into the ocean and fill my gut. The sun, so bright already. The very air, yellowish and hazy. Just minutes ago, where I came from, the sky was blue, dotted with white clouds.

Here, everything is different.

I need to rest a little, get my bearings. Want to relax, catch my breath. I make my way up to the most inland extreme, where sand remains dry at the cove's highest point. I sit, then lie back, feeling dizzy. I'm afraid if I close my eyes, I'll wake up back at home.

Hundreds of dreams. Thousands of waking fantasies. Finally here.

I sit up, startled, suddenly remembering where I am.

The tide, so much higher now. I must've slept.

And I'm no longer alone. Along the northern rock wall, near the water, a cluster of women in old-fashioned garb hunch over tide pools. They wear white hoods, hiding their faces from the sun. Their movements are slow, deliberate, as if they're uncomfortable moving this way. Awkward but persistent, they work.

Not what I expected to find.

The nearest of the women glances up.

I recognize her. Atra.

I raise a beckoning hand, start to run toward her.

I stop. Not Atra. Her face similar in shape, and the eyes. But it's not her. Strange, how I seemed to know her. This woman's eyes are pure black, her complexion inhumanly pallid. One hand rests on her swollen belly.

Pregnant.

A second woman looks up, recognition on her face. She too seems to know me. Like the first, she reaches instinctively to protect the bulge, the child she carries. Another face, so familiar. One more variation on the woman that haunts my dreams.

I'm not afraid. Start to go closer.

"Not her," I whisper.

Still the weird, impossible certainty remains. It's Atra. Cold-eyed. Beautiful.

A third stares at me, eyes steady as I approach. Behind her, the rest look up. They follow, six or seven of them, drawing nearer. I can't read all the faces, yet all seem to know me. That same haunting resemblance, one after another. None truly the woman I knew, yet all so similar, I know I've found what I sought. They move slowly, curious, coming toward me as I approach them. Every one of them pregnant, and always mindful of what they carry. Closer, I see their eyes. All shiny black.

Nearer the rocks, I try to look into the tide pools, curious what labor occupies them. Every shallow, individuated pool, each with its own walls, contains a pale yellow-green egg, like an elongated melon. A few of the women remain at work, keeping the eggs covered with seaweed, until the tide returns.

As I step closer still, the woman nearest me seems about to speak. Her mouth opens, and she hisses at me, a throaty sound of warning. Her gums are black, teeth silvery and patterned like coral. I back up, away from the egg beds, and she calms.

Something moves, out in the waves. Another woman, like these yet uncovered, walking in out of the rushing water, naked skin pearl white. Unlike the rest, those tending the eggs, she is not pregnant. She carries strands of seaweed in her hands, but when she sees me, drops these and approaches quickly. She comes toward me rather than the others, and with none of their lassitude or caution, seeming eager, excited. When she smiles at me, her mouth is pink, not black. Teeth white, rather than patterned. And her eyes, the eyes of a human woman, green surrounded by white. Only the pupils black.

Atra. This time, it's her.

That look, so loaded with implication. She takes my hand, and I'm certain. The others bear a sister's resemblance. This one, newly risen from the dark water, smelling of the ocean's fresh and living depths, looks me in the eye. She takes me by the hand, leads me away from the tide pool beds, up toward the sand still dry and warmed by the sun.

Her belly is flat, her shape exactly as I remember, yet like the others, her hand goes instinctively to that place. Expectant, as if feeling for a bump. Waiting.

When we reach the apex of driest sand at the edge of the cove, where before I slept, I stop.

Below, more women rise out of the waves, identically lean, pearlescent. Seeing so many of them, so much alike, my certainty wavers. Heavy surf crashes without effect against their bodies, moving them no more than a gust of wind. All carry strands of seaweed, green ribbons trailing from both hands. Ashore they drape the fronds over the eggs, then redirect toward us.

Atra kneels beside me. Her lips part. I try so hard to remember. Her eyes convey recognition, pleasure. Something more, some deeper wanting. She unfastens my shorts and tugs me down beside her. She gestures to another, approaching from behind. All the rest, those thin like her, approach and surround us.

What the others already carry in their bellies, these desire.

Here there are no other men. Others must have come, both before me and since. The swollen bellies, the eggs in the pools, are too many to be explained by my one night. Or have I been before, more than I realize? I only remember once. Where will I wake tomorrow?

I'm just trying to cope with compulsions, drawn by fierce and restless need. Anything to tame these wild dreams, quench my desires. At least for a night. Maybe I'm stuck in a doomed cycle, find and forget, always return, thinking it's for the first time. Every new search, undertaken from the ignorance of a blank mind.

Can I ever learn to remember? I want to remain.

They pull away my clothes, support me with fluttering hands. I'm weightless, carried on the fingertips of all those without child.

Atra. Almost-Atra.

The burning, tugging force of their wanting calms and subdues me. The ring draws nearer, encloses. Communal skin, feverish and damp. Nobody speaks.

I recognize this. I remember.

I've known women, felt pleasures, but none like this. The sensations exchanged transcend body, overload the mind's capacity to process, to remember. Fulfillment of primal imperative, a metaphysical pull. I'm drawn toward Atra. To give to all. Not to possess.

The primary encircles me, draws me in. Others press closer, almost identical. Beautiful, full of grim potential, fragrant of the sea. They press in, ready to receive. Bodies aching to transform. They merge with me. Part of her, part of them.

The most powerful change, the sensation that proves the reality of all I dreamed, is my own transformation. I grow into them. Become one.

Not male, not female. Not a single one alone. All of them Atra.

All of us.

DELIRIUM SINGS AT THE MAELSTROM WINDOW

woman calls, says she's FBI. My daughter's been found. So many years I expected this call. Eventually, I stopped waiting. First I think it's a joke. She goes on about transfer protocols, cooperation with Interpol, that kind of thing. My daughter's no longer a minor, but my presence is requested. One thing that zaps me right in the heart, she says the girl asked for me.

Thoughts and feelings, all kinds, unsorted. Eagerness. Fear.

I rush downtown, envisioning a reunion with the eleven-year-old I last saw. Maybe slightly grown, but I'll recognize her. Sure, I know the math. She'll be nineteen now. Somehow that part doesn't register.

I check in, someone guides me to Interview Room B. Observation mirrors, microphones, video cameras. There's this woman sitting there waiting, platinum blond, exotic, maybe twenty-five. She stares, expectant, trying to puzzle me out. At first I take her for the agent who called, but she's wearing an outfit more suited to a fashion runway. In her smile, I recognize something of my wife when she was young. It's her, my little girl, a glammed-up version of her mother.

No time for any big reunion. The female agent arrives, black suit, straight brown hair, dangling plastic badge. My daughter's not suspected of any crimes. The agency's interested in what her mother did, anything she remembers. Questions fly.

Can't believe I'm sitting here beside her. I try to pinpoint her accent. French, maybe Belgian or Swiss? There's this superior, unimpressed manner. Insists on being called Bettine, not her birth name, Elizabeth. We called her Betty when she was little. At least the name's in the ballpark of what I know. The girl herself, totally unfamiliar.

Black suit's interested in that other Elizabeth, my wife. The questions are old news to me. Scars heal tougher than the skin they replace.

"Did you observe your mother assaulting your father?"

Sliding across the table, photos I've never seen. I wonder why she's making us look at some corpse, poor guy chalk-white, twenty stab wounds over his chest and shoulders. Then I see the right hand dangling, half-severed.

It's me.

"What reasons did your mother offer, after the attack, for what she'd done?"

"Where did your mother take you, after she fled the country?"

Lots more questions. Few answers. Don't know. Can't remember. Her accent fades out, returns. They landed in France, crossed into Belgium. Moved a lot, especially at first. Always old towns, out of the way. Five years ago, her mother took off. Some unspecified drug problem. This left the girl alone with an older man they'd been living with.

There's a revelation.

"The last five years," she says, "his home was mine." Claims she never knew his name, doesn't know how to find him. Can't name the town.

I can see the secrets, withheld behind her eyes. Just not sure what she's saving them for. Her self-possession seems alien, especially in someone so young. She's the same age as Elizabeth and I, when we met. Now I'm forty-four, a quarter century older than my daughter, and still less in control. I've grown adept at redirection, the way a magician hides whatever he doesn't want you to see. After Elizabeth tried to kill me and took our daughter, I entered a bad spiral of self-pity and solitude. Self-prescription: a river of Black Velvet. Pills for pain, prescription at first, then the real trips. Any pleasure I could taste without breaking seclusion.

Even after my anger faded, everything felt so broken.

Rehab saved my life. I'm clean, and plan to hold onto that. The hard part's knowing I'll never feel pleasure again. Not without the drink, and the white powder. Too many scars to cover. Not just stab wounds, and the useless, dead hand.

Black suit decides we can go. My daughter throws me this purposeful look. My inference is she's promising to let me in on whatever this is. She's my girl, I realize, but it feels more like my wife is finally ready to explain.

On the way to the car I notice she's tall, probably taller than me even without the heels. Just like her mother. Makes me wonder about her upbringing. How down and out could things have been, if she grew up looking like this?

A question coalesces. *Is it really you?* I almost say this aloud.

Maybe a scam artist? Someone sent by my wife, working some angle.

All I really know is I'm supposed to call her Bettine.

This narrow, angular creature follows me into the house, carrying her glossy black leather bag. Charcoal couture dress, oversized sunglasses, that regal platinum mane. Like a poised starlet, strutting out of a Fellini picture.

She greets her old room like a houseguest seeing it for the first time. A half smile at the little girl decoration. Shit, embarrassing. I kept washing the sheets, changing the bed, just in case. Drifted way out of touch. So many years.

She sits, knees together on the little bed, seems to shrink, drawing herself in, as if imagining how she might cram herself into this tiny space she once occupied. Her eyes flit to the space beside her on the bed. Wondering if I'll sit down? Hoping I won't, or that I will?

"No FBI here now." I try for casual, feeling awkward, nervous. "You must remember something." I expect her shell to crack. Show some vulnerability, at least let me in on the secret.

She shrugs. "I thought I was born there, speaking French. Mother and I, first we lived alone, always moving. Then we settled, this very old town, living in the gentleman's house. Mother said she belonged to him." She pauses, looking around. "This house, it's not familiar. If you say I was here before, I believe you. I remember this *couvre-lit*, this bedspread. Speaking

English, that must come from somewhere. I took no lessons."

"Where were you trying to go, when they stopped you at the airport?"

She sighs as if tired. "I told them my passport was false, so they would deliver me to you."

This doesn't make sense. So many questions. It's torture, holding back. "You said you don't know where your mother is," I venture. "We might try looking for her. With or without cops—"

"Elise?" She makes a face, as if remembering something unpleasant. "You and FBI, you call her Elizabeth. Mother never called herself that."

From the interview, I knew their aliases. The only surprise is how little she remembers.

"Elizabeth Dahut Nix was your mother's maiden name. You're Elizabeth Melusine Sky. We called you Betty until you were ten. You asked us to start calling you Elizabeth."

Bettine leans back, propped by thin arms.

"It's OK," I say. "I'll get used to calling you Bettine."

She sits forward, darts one hand into her bag, produces a silver case and a lighter. Withdraws a black cigarette, lights it. I'm shocked, about to protest, but stop myself. What right do I have?

"There's no need, looking for Mother." She exhales. Clove smoke drifts, unexpectedly pleasant. Burning sugar overpowers the tobacco aspect.

"What?" Distracted, I missed her point. The sweet, spicy smell. Wondering how it tastes.

"Her problems I mentioned. She was lost to addiction, victim of unrestrained craving. I should have told you. Many in our circle succumb the same way."

What's she saying? My head spins, dizziness, panic. "Did I understand… You're saying your mother's dead?"

She nods, resting her hand on the glossy black leather case.

Everything seems far away, clouded. My head buzzes, tingles. Must be the clove smoke. I can taste the sweet burning paper on my lips. It reminds me of something else I smoked, some high barely recalled. Nothing else explains this feeling. I crave numbness, escape. Want to run.

"I'll let you sleep." I back out, shut Bettine's bedroom door.

From the dark hallway, I hear leather rustling, and the click of steel fasteners.

Two thousand black midnights alone. Now this. How long have I wavered, not existing, merely remembering? I sprawl atop the bed, still dressed, in frustrated wakefulness.

Music intrudes at the lowest reaches of my awareness.

I rise, open my door. A song from another room, something I don't recognize. I work in the listening room at the university music department. I've heard everything. Not this. The scratch of an old record, classical strings. Voice distinct from the music. She sings along, tentative, slightly out of sync. In that hesitation, something familiar. A hint of the girl I recognize.

I cross the hall, touch the door, trace fingertips along the wood. I want to knock, but still feel a stranger in my own house. It's Elizabeth's ancestral place. Probably I'll always feel unsettled, like a visitor imposing on hospitality.

Eight years.

She took everything. Lots of men say that, meaning the house, the 401k. Mine took our daughter, left me bleeding to death, riddled with stab wounds, hand almost severed. Punctures became scars. Healing floated away the pain, left behind a brittle shell. Not a man, just a bloodstream pumping a prescription cocktail so powerful it prevented me from caring about the one miserable truth I was sure of: I was done living, at least in the real meaning of the word.

The university held my job longer than I'd expected. After ninety days, someone in HR finally said, now or never.

I decided on never.

To the rest of the world, I was lucky to be alive. Is everyone really unaware there are worse things? Do they only pretend? Despair so bottomless. Each breath, agony. Every morning, the most sickening hangover. Of course, whiskey played a part.

This house is the only thing Elizabeth left me. Now that I'm sober, I don't want it. If I can stay clean, hold onto this job, maybe I'll climb out.

Something like Bettine coming along, that's a potential trigger for re- lapse. Recovery 101.

My knuckles strike the door.

Singing stops. The door swings open.

"Oh, I woke you."

She's wearing a white sleepshirt so diaphanous, I have to look away. Smell of burning candles. Warmth. On the bed, scattered ancient records in brown paper sleeves. Without makeup, she looks like the Elizabeth I first met.

"Those look like 78s," I say. The library collection has rooms full of these.

"That's all I kept, from over there," she murmurs.

"Where'd you find the old Victrola? I've never seen it around."

"There's so much here." She points beyond the east wall, toward the stor- age rooms. "I think you never explored."

"This house must seem… humble. You're accustomed to being kept with money."

"You don't mean Mother. You mean—"

"Yes, this man. She… left you to him." Trying to remain neutral. Can't seem judgmental.

"I never knew his name." She looks down. "He asked me to call him Daddy."

I manage not to flinch. No response at all.

She shrugs. Her gaze flits to the ceiling. "He owned the tallest house on *Rue d'Auseil*, the oldest block of the district. A gigantic house, like a loom- ing range of mountains, seeming to lean out over the road."

"You describe it like a fairy tale." Can't help frowning. "You were too young."

Her persistent half-smile flares into stubbornness, something like aware- ness of advantage. "It was not what you imagine. Not at all. More like being mistress and paid research assistant to a brilliant scholar of the arcane."

The word *mistress* sticks. I try to move past. Instead: "Scholar… arcane?"

"An eminent occult experimentalist, founder of *Maîtres de l'autel de verre*, that is, Knights of the Glass Altar." She nods. "One of Europe's wealthiest men, yet anonymous, exerting power in stealth, within his secret society. I learned much. Took these records, and many secrets."

I move closer, seeking angles against her inscrutability. "Tell me about your mother. What you said about her addiction."

She holds my gaze, then looks away. "Yes, the white smoke. Within our circle, the Glass Altar, of course we all experience it."

"White smoke? What is that? A plant, or—"

"It's not a drug, not something you buy. Like so many pleasures, the aim is to approach as near as possible, while avoiding the harm of too great proximity."

My heart, a blunt hammering in my chest. Seeing her smile this way, talking so casually about this strange high. She has no idea all I've been through. The horrible depths, recovery, relapse. I don't want to tell her, but she has to understand how dangerous this is.

"The high used to be all I had," I begin. "I can't do that anymore."

"This smoke is different." Her gaze intensifies. "Better than anything you've known."

I shake my head. "I'm in recovery. It's fragile. You need to respect that certain things are dangerous for me."

Her lip curls into a teasing smile. "I do understand."

Though I'd like to remain, try to draw more out of her, I feel uneasy. Smiling vacantly, I wish her good night, and back out of the room.

Sleep, that's my intention. I lie atop the still-made bed, mind rushing, hyper-sensitized.

There's no mistaking the sound of the needle drop. So attuned to solitude and quiet, the slightest noise pierces my attention. Bettine's singing elevates, flits delicately, a white butterfly in the aggrieved blackness. The vocal line entangles with high jagged-edged strings, I think solo viola. My daughter's voice, accompanying a song recorded before she was born. Before I was.

Eyes close. Jagged lysergic colors swirl, worse than ever. In our twenties, Elizabeth and I pursued such kaleidoscopic stimuli, found pleasure in them. Finally I was the one who insisted we had to stop. It was her leaving that plunged me back in. Now my gut churns, and I'm filled with fear of the depthless vacancy I feel, tugging.

The song ends. Scratchy background noise repeats, the needle stuck in a run-out loop.

The record restarts from the beginning. This seems familiar, the scenario if not the voice. Perhaps her mother. Did Elizabeth sing along with records while I tried to sleep?

I'm out of bed again. Outside her bedroom, ear pressed to the door.

The voice pursues a more ethereal, almost angelic line than the main thrust of the recorded song, which is more aggressive, raw-edged and strident.

I drop to one knee, fit my eye to the keyhole.

In the center of her room, she stands looking up, arms raised in the same delicate nightshirt. Her orderly hair and intact makeup tell me she hasn't yet been to bed. I can't see what's overhead, attracting her attention. Our bedrooms match, mirror images. Must be the skylight. In my own room, the glass is a black rectangle framing a few scattered stars. A million hours I stared up through that portal while the world slept.

Straining upward, she sings as if rhapsodizing some beauty unseen to me. The melody she weaves is strange, angular and swerving, yet beautiful. Beneath the startling bluish moonlight penetrating from above, her skin is radiant, her garment transparent.

Look away. I'm curious, fascinated, yet overcome with the exhaustion of many sleepless nights. Better to return to my room before she catches me watching. Close my eyes, try to dream.

By the time I'm ready to leave for work in the morning, there's no sign of Bettine waking. I leave a note on the kitchen counter.

My boss knows my history, my scars, and the right hand I drag around like cold meat attached to my wrist. When she hears about Bettine, she suggests I head home early, catch up tomorrow. I think she feels sorry for me. A lifetime ago, I was a teaching assistant in the music school, hoped to become a professor. I lost all that, lost everything. Can't be bitter, though. They didn't have to let me back in the department at all.

Anyway, I don't mind playing sympathy for a few extra hours at home. Maybe Bettine and I will reconnect. Whether I need it more, or she does, I'm not sure.

At home, everything downstairs is exactly as I left it. The only sound, hardwoods creaking under my feet. My note sits untouched on the counter.

Then I hear the record playing.

As I climb the stairs, music clarifies. From the upper landing, I see her door standing open. I don't want to burst in, frighten her. Having an adult daughter, I don't know where to begin. No point of reference. Technically she's still a teen, but I'm out of my depth, have no idea how to approach. Should I leave her alone? Who knows what she might be doing. I want to help, but I'm afraid she might be dangerous. All her talk of ecstasy, and white smoke.

Outside the open door I stop. I should announce myself.

Bettine's standing next to the bed, just where I saw her last night, through the keyhole. This time, she's surrounded by a white, whirling cloud. I expect a druggy smell, pungent like weed, or the plastic tang of a sizzling boulder, but what I get is airy, light and sweet, like a puff of powdered sugar inhaled off a donut.

"Is that…" I step into the room. Of course it is. "You can't, Bettine! Not here." I think to hold my breath, back away. Already the taste on my tongue is incredibly sweet. I should spit it out, but can't. The intense, unexpected sensation brings me up short. I feel an urge to open my mouth, to take it in. I want more.

Only a man's unbuttoned dress shirt and panties cover a model-thin body, legs impossibly long, the crest of hipbones visible through her flesh. Arms aloft, head tilted back, as if she hasn't heard me, still thinks she's alone. No paraphernalia visible. Just the music, and a girl gathering clouds to herself. Reveling in it.

I want to forbid this, drive it away, but there's nothing tangible here. Nothing to prevent.

She notices me, turns. Upraised hands flutter, as if playing with something invisible, trying to catch butterflies I can't see. Lowering her arms, she smiles like she knows I'm wondering what to make of this. As the cloud dissipates, she moves the needle back to the beginning of the 78. She drops playfully onto the bed, then reaches for something behind her on the mattress. Her hand goes between the old records, produces a black leather book.

Not the black polish of her luggage, but aged and worn.

She pulls me down next to her, and scoots up close. It's strange, touching her for the first time, feeling her warmth. I want to put my arms around her, squeeze her to me. I'm afraid of how that would feel.

"Within these pages," she says slowly, dreamily, "all the secrets."

"What…"

She flashes the book's cover, illegibly titled. "Mother found the book here. In this house."

"You said you didn't remember, before."

"She told me, as we departed *Liège*. Said she found it in her ancestral home, in Oregon, in America. Here. This book ignited her search, our trek to Europe. It fired her great hunger."

Bettine doesn't open the book, but allows a closer view of the florid script, waxy metallic ink the color of molten lead on the cover. *Chansons de l'extase lumineuse.* A scent, pleasantly earthy, almost pungent. As I reach, she withdraws the book to its hiding place, between records in brittle sleeves.

"I'll be careful," I venture. "It's part of my job, repairing old books and records."

"You said before. At a library." She shifts slightly, hiding the book behind her.

I try another approach. "How did your mother really die?"

"Why should you want to hear about her?"

I don't answer.

"You should hate her." She looks up. "This book was all she cared about. Until the smoke."

"I've never seen it before." I regain eye contact. She's holding something back.

She hesitates. "She suffered. Those of us most susceptible to pleasure, we suffer most."

That was me, before. Don't want to remember. "You mentioned this man." Despite all she's experienced, I feel I should protect her. My stronger impulse, though, is the desire to know. I have to look away. "You called him Daddy."

I glance back, catch her looking with pity at her poor father, scarred and broken. Carmine lips a recurve bow, her mother's mocking smile. Maybe she wishes she found this place empty, enjoyed a solitary homecoming, free to pursue whatever inspired her return.

"It's not answers you need." Her accent thickens. "You have so much pain."

"I'm glad you're here. But you seem fully formed by your life over there."

"It did offer many rewards." Her eyes focus far away.

"So, why return?"

She exhales slowly. "Daddy decided Mother was right. He gave himself over to bliss."

"What do you mean? He overdosed, thinking he'd be with your mother?"

"Something like that. Perhaps an accident. Some believe everyone who gives themselves to the smoke does so willingly. I had to leave while the *Gendarmerie* sorted things out. I thought I could return, that his house would become mine. I retained a lawyer to fight for me, but Daddy's secrecy had been absolute. He had no public identity, no will. I could never return to the house on the *Rue d'Auseil*. I was homeless, and possessed only the essentials I carried with me that day, expecting within weeks I would return."

"How lucky you took the records with you. And this book, something about songs."

"As I said, some believe every seeming accident disguises secret intent." She chews her bottom lip, eyes darting up, to the corner of the ceiling. "Perhaps I knew this was my journey's next stage."

"Your mother's ancestral home." I stand, shrugging off suspicions, feeling more settled than I can remember. Do I have a part to play? "Are you hungry? I'll make dinner."

She looks surprised. "I don't need food."

In the doorway, I stop. "I'll make enough for two."

After it's clear she's not coming down, I eat alone. What's left, I put in the refrigerator.

In solitude my mind settles. The house is dark enough, quiet enough. I might sleep.

Distant music shoves me sideways, from cramped sleep into sweat-drenched wakefulness. Such a song echoes in and out of uncomfortable dreams, carrying into black delirium the dizzy significance of half-forgotten mad hallucination.

I'm out of bed before I know it, standing in the hall, searching for recognition within the tune drifting from Bettine's open door. A restless song, sharp thrusts and tension-fraught lunges.

Though the room seems empty, I'm hesitant to enter. Recently I'm always up late, listening at her door to the sounds within. I creep as far as the doorway. Bettine hasn't left the bedroom since she arrived. Where could she have gone?

The Victrola spins unwatched under the pewter lamp's glow. The old leather book amid lacquer records spilled across the bed evoke an age when Elizabeth's forebears built this place.

Shadows shift on mahogany floorboards, the quality of light altered as if the lamp has moved. Stepping inside, I see at once what's changed. It's the skylight, not transparent to the dark sky, but full of milky liquid. What I'm seeing makes no sense, this glass portal filled like a shallow pool, contents held up by inverse gravity. A shimmering, seething maelstrom. Out of the surface—liquid, yet weightless as air—a white tendril reaches down, wavering like ivy growing at time-lapse speed.

My hand extends, against my will. The right hand, the dead one. This pale, wavering finger strains toward me from overhead. I want to touch it, despite knowing my dead nerves will feel nothing. I raise my left as well, strain on tiptoes toward the ceiling.

Pleasure tingles all my fingertips, hyper-stimulation that makes me suck in breath. Both hands are alive with sizzling, electric sensitivity. It's too much. It's wonderful. Dead nerves, thrillingly alive.

"I didn't bring that in." A woman's voice, behind me. "This time, it was you."

I spin.

My wife in a towel, wet skin flushed from a hot bath. Years spin past in reverse, before my eyes. Elizabeth, as I first knew her.

No. Memory is a filter, overlaying what I see.

It's Bettine.

She approaches. "Now you've felt it. You understand."

My heart pounds, fingers tremble. "You can't have this in the house."

"It's always been here, and it's sublime." She stands beside me, rises on tiptoes, one hand grasping my shoulder as the other reaches. Her towel slips from her breasts. She reaches to catch it, but not before I smell her skin's hot dampness, fragrant of gardenia. "What must change is your perception."

She strains upward and the wet surface above her breaks. A misty hint of white reaches toward her, solidifying.

"What is this stuff? How'd you bring it with you?" I remember that sensation, desire to feel it again. I'm more afraid than ever, yet the temptation has also grown. I'm hungry to know that feeling again. "We have to stop. Otherwise... I'll go."

I turn away.

"Wait." Her voice, softer. She reaches down, adjusts the Victrola. The strange music clarifies. "Every pain can be soothed. Nothing need trouble us, ever again."

I try to flex my right hand, already deadening again. I crave that dazzling tingle, remember it clearly. "I'm an addict. Pills, powders, everything. I have to be afraid."

"We've learned to approach the danger." Bettine sits on the edge of the bed, daring me. Her eyes go to the skylight, where the gelatinous substance is now settled, motionless. "Reach, once again. I want you to breathe it in."

My hands tremble. I mean to refuse, but no words will come. The strange wet surface shimmers into gaseous drift, subtly glowing.

"Inhale." Her towel slips again. She starts to reach for it, then with a half-smile, allows it to fall. "Let it penetrate your lungs, gentle as a whisper. Let another reality shift into place, superimposed onto this one, like a slow film crossfade."

"It's dangerous," I whisper. "You said it killed your mother."

"It's not the smoke that kills, but the ancient beings behind it. They use the smoke, a conduit to rapture, to tempt you nearer. It's accessible only at certain windows, in a few houses in all the world. This is such a window. You only have to open yourself. Take from them their pleasures. Use the music as your shield."

I force myself to look down, away.

She takes up the black book, broad and thin like an artist's folio, perhaps fifty pages.

"*Chansons de l'extase lumineuse.*" Fingertips trace words standing out in thick relief. "The name, it means Songs of Luminous Ecstasy. It's our instruction."

I lean in, tentatively reach for the book, expecting her to snatch it away. She moves it just beyond my reach, and opens the cover to reveal pages lined like musical score. Some sheets are scrawled with dots and loops like alien musical notation. Others are handwritten in a mix of styles and colors, or annotated with diagrams.

"The only copy," she says. "The work of many hands."

"You helped write this?" I ask.

She laughs, surprised. "No. It's very old."

The words seem plain enough when I glance at an entire page. When I focus on individual lines, try to follow the thread, they shimmer out of focus. A smell of rotting flowers and incense, perhaps memory again. I rub my eyes, shake my head. "What does this say?"

Her finger traces a line, the hand's proximity focusing my attention. Vague letterforms clarify, resolve into words, punctuation. Violet English cursive, needle thin, precise. Sky blue French, looping and textural. Inky black German, fraught with blotches and smears.

"Entice them," Bettine reads, "take their sweet fruit, but beware, they would devour."

The words on the page come clear.

"Desire of mind to bring them. Music of Reich to sooth them. *Songs of Zann to drive them away.*" She turns the page, hands the book to me.

I read where she left off. "We feed of their fruit, they feed of our worship. Such is the ecstasy of the Glass Altar."

"For years uncounted, this music, has kept at bay the harm approaching the callers of the white smoke." She kneels naked at the phonograph. Though the song isn't finished, she lifts the needle back to the beginning. "Some, like Mother, believe it possible to ascend. To become a higher being, dwelling forever within bliss."

"I'm not going that far," I whisper. "I just want to feel good. Just for one minute."

"I know what you need," she sings, voice light as the mist. "I'll protect you."

I crave something I barely understand. I'm tired, weak from lack of sleep. Too much worry. Not enough happiness. I stand, raise my face to the glass. Let it come to me.

Beside me, Bettine looks up at the skylight, filled with liquid clouds. A pale, barely tangible finger extends. She sings a brief, urgent melody, and the snaking tendril withdraws, leaving behind an airy puff of floating powder. She flicks out her tongue. I taste what she tastes, sweetness like powdered sugar inhaled. The flavor of her mouth, like a kiss. I can't help swallowing. A rush of pleasure floods my body, the swirling embrace like a warm opiate cloud, but more energetic. The perfect balance of peace and stimulation.

Against this, I have no defense. I desire nothing more.

What paradise would I choose? A shimmering ecstasy of safety, comfort, belonging. Blackness of night transformed to a limitless, accepting universe.

Swallow deep. Again. Who could ever want anything else?

I wander hallways, explore an infinitude that has always existed, all around. Every time I think I'm dead-ended, new doors swing open. Unfamiliar rooms, passageways to my past, my future. I thrill at possibilities, certain this wondrous potential will remain, available to me after my head clears. My bitterness no longer matters. Without it, I'm weightless. All the pain, memories of blood, acid rage. All set aside. A lifetime of unmet desires and cumulative defeats. Unwind years of struggle. Vanilla self-help books. Endless platitudes of diversion, rehab.

Inhale sweetness, that's all. Can't stop myself. Smoke is solid, spun sugar in my lungs.

Pinned and wriggling, mouth agape, breathing helpless in white delirium. A mind-reeling, spinning cinema, of a scale vastly beyond the human.

Anxiety feels distant, benign awareness of risks behind my pleasurable veneer. Remember, the smoke doesn't kill. It's the ancient things behind. That's what got Elizabeth. Dangers unknowable to us, except by their beautiful creation. The loving smoke.

We just have to remember the music. Our book tells us so. A soundtrack, far away, reminds me. Climb again. Here Elizabeth glows, a slow motion drift. Her smile tells me she knows my thoughts.

I drop to the floor beside the bed, out of range of the smoke. Lying on my back on the polished hardwoods, head clearing as lungs gasp flavorless air.

Bettine leans down, grabs my right hand. "Come on!"

She pulls, but my sweat-slick hands slip loose. She takes my wrist two-handed, pulls.

I'm up again, beneath the skylight, pressing my face into a warm, blissful dessert.

"I want you to see it up close. Not just the outer smoke. Delve inside, to the heart of it."

Together we enter a whirling other-realm, throb with impulses triggering every sense, amplified. A cycle of mad hunger and feeding, only to feel greater need, a desire where attainment merely heightens craving. Everything escalates. There is no limit. I press deeper into the whiteness, sensing power, concentrated and profound. My eyes see a darker core within.

A hand on my shoulder surprises me. I'm still here, tangible. So long since I lost track. I remember, I'm standing in Bettine's bedroom.

Grinning wildly, she shakes me. "Isn't it the utmost?"

"I decided to give in." I'm breathing hard. "Stopped fighting."

She embraces me. "You took the smallest taste, went flying."

The way she holds me feels wrong. Her body pressed against mine, nudging me away from the Victrola.

"What are you doing?" Insinuations flash, a flash recap of memory. Abduction, life on the run, used and objectified too young, exposed to who knows what kind of occult madness? Of course she's damaged. Is that why she came to me? Trembling, I pull back. "Bettine, no."

She grips me by the shoulders, pushes my face into the miasma's seething depths. I try to pull back, against her wrestling my body, half of me wanting to give into whatever she plans. For a moment I stop struggling. That's enough. I've lost control, perspective.

I don't care. All I feel is my wanting.

"Don't fight. Come with me." Her hands release.

I pull back, inhaling fresh air. I want to say something. It's hard to remember.

She looks at me strangely, possessed of some overpowering intention. "That's why I came here, to jump into heaven. Like Mother, like Daddy." Her eyes lit with fervent desire. "These windows are gateways to that infinite paradise where they dwell. I knew you'd want it too."

Bettine lunges, knocks the Victrola off its stand. The record bounces off the platter, shatters on the floor. She turns back and for the first time without music, opens herself to the cloud, arms wide in acceptance. One hand grips my wrist, tugging me along.

"They left me behind," she says. "Then I knew it would be you."

I try to pull away.

Translucent white strands, like ghostly ropes or smoke tentacles, reach into her mouth, penetrate her eyes, her ears, her nose.

Her grip loosens. I pull free, scramble on the floor by the bed, trying to right the Victrola. The record lies shattered, jagged shards of brittle lacquer.

More tendrils lash out from above. A pale cord whips around her neck, and lifts.

Bettine's eyes are wild, anticipating her greatest desire. Lips trying to form words, she pulls the cord free of her neck and rasps, "Don't let me… go alone."

As it lifts her away I pull back, turn to the bed, find an intact record labeled, "Music of Zann." Remember the book's words, Songs of Zann to drive them away.

The white membranous lump fully encompasses my daughter's motionless shape as I place the record on the platter, set it spinning and drop the needle mid-song. I inhale a surge of ecstatic pleasure, a sensation both welcome and horrifying.

There's a visceral tearing as the music bursts forth, shrill in such proximity. Malevolent heat, not the sweet warmth of before. Tangy acidity, the unmistakable smell of burning. No screams. The veil covering my daughter smokes as it lifts her away. Flailing tendrils reach for me, only to withdraw from the music.

The white membranous surface resounds, like a struck drum. The vibration dissipates, leaving only the music. No more struggle, no anguish. I delve my hand into the soft warmth, feel the familiar tingle. Taste the sweetness. My hands grope for anything solid, find nothing.

Clouds thin, particles sucked quickly away, as if the glass is open to the sky.

Alone. Just me, and the jarring music. Bettine's gone, again.

I drop to the floor, watch the record spin. When it's almost over, I start it from the beginning. After some hours, I dare brief outings to check the rest of the house. Calling in anguish, knowing I won't find her. Always I return, start the music again, at the beginning.

The smoke can return, any time, night or day. I know I'll feel more secure in daylight. As long as it remains dark, my resolve may slip. I might decide to jump. What did Bettine say? To leap in, give myself over to bliss. To follow, and never come back up.

All night I sit by the player, starting the record over and over. This Zann's music spinning, spinning. Well past sunrise, I remain within the music. Only when I'm sure I won't break, in a room morning bright and growing warm, I finally stand and leave the Victrola behind. Across the hall, I pack the things I'll carry away from here.

AN IDEAL RETREAT

"There is geometry in the humming of the strings,
there is music in the spacing of the spheres."

—*Pythagoras*

THE FIRST BOOK
ARRIVAL FROM KNOWN INTO UNKNOWN

1. Driving. A playlist of four decades, and surprise on arrival.

When Noone Raddox agreed to make the drive alone into the remote Central Oregon high desert, she wanted her husband Ian to think she was just trying to do him a favor. That wasn't her real motivation.

It was true that fourteen hours a day spent at his office left Ian time for little else, which pretty much ruled out his wasting an entire day driving out to the middle of nowhere. But someone had to make the trip, to check on the old Raddox family getaway, long-forgotten by every Raddox except Ian's brother Jodah, who had recently vacated after more than twenty years occupying the place like a squatter. If Ian couldn't go himself, his sister Callie could just as easily have gone. Callie was a real Raddox. Noone had carried the name half a lifetime, since marrying Ian, but that didn't make her truly part of the clan.

The real reason Noone agreed to drive four hours to visit a little shack she'd probably never see again, was a selfish one. She believed that if she could escape the city, the scrutiny of neighbors, the paralyzing claustrophobia of a too-large home and the sharp pang of uselessness she felt sitting alone while Ian worked hundred-hour weeks, if she could find relief for just a single day, maybe the voice inside her head might finally stop.

Not that she actually believed somebody was speaking to her. Noone certainly wasn't crazy, not the sort of desperate, unhinged type whose inner voices commanded them to do outwardly strange or violent things. No, the voice she heard was her own. Noone's internal monologue offered a litany of complaints both broad and detailed, a bitter catalog of self-recrimination. Endless shrill questions, suggestive of a habit of corrosive doubt. Even though she knew the voice was nothing real, she exhausted herself, forever arguing contrary positions.

Noone needed a break. The question of who might make this trip actually arrived at the perfect time.

The night she decided to go alone, she stayed up late making lists of all she needed to bring. By dawn, most of the entries on her list had been crossed out, and she ended up packing just one small suitcase. Hoping to make the drive enjoyable, she selected a handful of CDs, old college favorites. Billie Holiday and Astrud Gilberto, Joni Mitchell and Kate Bush, one album by each. These women were important to Noone at discrete stages in her earlier life. It seemed funny now, the way youth so clearly divided into these neatly delineated chapters, segments of time marked by teachers, classes, semesters. Later, each epoch was demarcated not by school events, but the arrival and departure of boyfriends. Now that she was married, had been with Ian longer than she'd been alive without him, her life offered no such markers. No classes in school, no beginnings or endings of relationships. Days extended, blurred together, no different from years.

So she drove, listening, reflecting on each recording in turn. It occurred to her that each album exemplified not only a specific era in her own life, but also in the world. The albums were released in consecutive decades:

Songs for Distingue' Lovers in the 1950s.

The Astrud Gilberto Album in the 60s.

The Hissing of the Summer Lawns in the 70s.

Hounds of Love in the 80s.

Was it still common, Noone wondered, for young people to have a selection of personally important favorites from the four decades leading up to their college years? Each album was important at a different stage in her college experience, but this sequence did not correspond to the chronology of when the albums had been created. In fact, the reverse was true. The first to make an impact had been a current release when she'd discovered it. Freshman year, Wilcox dorm, she fell in love with Kate Bush, starting with *Hounds of Love*. From there, without trying, Noone had delved backward through musical history, exploring decades before her own birth. She supposed that was what it meant to develop taste, uncovering newness among the old, things that had always been wonderful, all along, but simply not yet known.

Now in her mid-forties, Noone considered herself an 80s girl. One thing that frustrated her about Ian was his stubborn, inexplicable characterization of himself as a 70s boy. Despite a gap of only four years, an entire cultural generation forever separated wife from husband, a canyon-wide rift splitting their connection.

It didn't really matter. Ian never seemed to consider his own past, at least not that he allowed Noone to see. Lately, the dim, wavering mirage of history obsessed Noone's every moment.

Listening to Joni Mitchell for the first time in years, she pictured a vivid scene, a haunted atmosphere and a delicate, tremulous emotional state. Signing up for figure drawing and painting classes. Haunting the art supply section in the student store's basement. Staying up all night, drinking coffee with amaretto beside an open window as rain misted outside. Working charcoal sketches in a ring-bound drawing pad, feeling fragile and painfully solitary, full of bewildering, objectless love and shuddering desire that came on like a sudden knife wound, left her always prone to sudden tears.

What became of that girl?

The little stack of CDs carried her away from Portland, over Mt. Hood's snow-fraught shoulder, then into the heart of Oregon. Through native reservation lands, then Bend, the last city of any size in Central Oregon. As she left behind the last illuminated hints and traces of scattered human development, Noone turned off the music and drove in silence. Following directions Ian had given, she turned onto Selwyn Road. The world seemed to break apart into pieces of discrete geometry, to simplify into sharp stony ridges and fields sparsely dotted with plants and trees which seemed alien. The landscape looked so different from the green rainforest of Portland and the Willamette Valley. The high desert plateau formed a broad shelf at the center of the state, where everything seemed deprived of oxygen and rain.

Four hours from home, with only a map, an address, a ring of keys. She couldn't believe Ian would send her out somewhere so remote like this, all alone. How could he—

No. She stopped, felt her face redden at her own dishonesty.

"Remember, you wanted to come. Stop lying to yourself, at least."

The odometer indicated nineteen miles since she'd turned off the highway onto Selwyn, and Ian's notes said after about nineteen miles, she should look for number 7117. Just then, a driveway ahead. On the tall concrete mailbox pillar beside it, the number 7117.

Noone slowed the big Expedition and turned onto the gravel drive. The old house had to be way back, behind a row of spindly desert trees. Through barren branches, Noone glimpsed a weathered gray facade with broken windows opening onto vacant darkness. What had Ian called the place? "A dirty little shit-shack." But then, he hadn't been out here since childhood. Thus the point of Noone's visit, to see what remained of the old house in the long decades since Jodah had taken it over. The rest of the Raddox clan had eventually stopped thinking of their desert place, especially after the parents had purchased a nice five-bedroom in Manzanita with partial ocean views. That beach house had become the new gathering spot for every Raddox, even Noone and others who'd married in, for Thanksgivings and July gatherings for old Gavin Raddox's birthday. Then, after the patriarch himself had passed, the summer birthday get-together switched to a June birthday celebration for Gavin's widow Maxine, at least until she passed away last year. Every Raddox had shifted the focus of their attention from Central Oregon to the Pacific Ocean. All but Jodah, who had fully withdrawn in the years since his disinheritance. Nobody had seen or heard from Jodah, who hadn't even attended Gavin's or Maxine's funerals.

So the rough old desert bungalow had faded from mind, as if it had never been something they all shared. Likewise, Jodah had been forgotten, barely ever even mentioned, until this past week. Then Ian had received a FedEx, Jodah's keys to the place, and a lengthy letter handwritten in a loopy, childish scrawl, changing ink color from page to page. Ian had refused to let Noone read it, even to tell her what Jodah had said. He'd assured her it clarified nothing useful about why Jodah had finally abandoned the place.

A wave of nerves came over Noone like a flash of sickness. She looked down, away from the row of trees, and braked. Stopping tires made a *skritch* in the gravel. Maybe she wasn't quite ready to deal with this. Noone squeezed her eyes shut, rubbed them until they watered, then wiped them dry. She grabbed her purse from the passenger seat, dug through the contents until she found the Xanax, and dry-swallowed two.

Then closed her eyes again, but tried not to rub them. Breathed. Waited.

That battery-on-tongue sizzle of anxiety finally began to settle out. Sometimes Noone worried something was wrong with her brain, some kind of chemical problem the doctors couldn't diagnose.

"Come on, Noonie." Her voice trembled. "This can't be all that bad." She could handle it.

The vibration of the idling engine gradually superseded the buzz of her faulty central nervous system. She opened her eyes, put the car into gear and drove onward, up the curve of the long driveway.

Beyond the trees stood a house, but not the one she expected. It was nothing at all like the run-down shack Ian had described, and not even similar to the facade Noone had just glimpsed through the trees a few minutes ago. This was a big place, modern and immaculate. Two stories, with tall front windows that reached to the sky. Amid the rough, stony landscape, the house occupied a beautifully-designed oasis of cultivated trees, sculptured land, and tiered concrete steps and walkways.

Noone hit the brakes again. "This can't be right."

She fumbled out Ian's directions and re-read the note again and again. Her mind replayed everything he'd told her. What aspect had she misunderstood? An old shanty, built of unfinished, rough-sawn wood. Probably five hundred square feet, or maybe six hundred. And he'd said the place had been "ready to fall down," even decades ago.

Was this a mistake? Maybe she'd misread the mailbox number. These might be neighbors, a second house sharing a single driveway. No, the driveway ended here. After curving around the row of trees, it stopped at this house.

Noone kept looking away and looking back again, trying hard to focus. The number beside the front door was the same, 7117. This had to be the right place. Noone shook her head. "You might've gone one pill too far, Noonie."

Clean, planar lines, the exterior newly painted silver-gray. A concrete walkway stepped up through fastidiously maintained landscaping, met the front door and veered left through cinderblock alcoves, tiered planting beds and rock gardens, around the back. This modernism was right up Noone's alley. After college, she'd studied design, and had long dreamed of freelancing as an interior decorator and landscape designer. This place, the style of it all, gave her an immediate twinge of envy. She felt breathless with excitement.

She pulled the Expedition up to the front, parked and climbed out. Already she felt impatient to call Ian, but reminded herself she hadn't come here to stay in constant contact. Better to at least make an attempt at self-reliance. She reminded herself to stay calm, proceed slowly. "Anyway, let's at least see inside before we get too carried away."

2. Entry. Everything newer and better than expected.

B efore she unlocked the front door, Noone whispered aloud, "This can't be real."

The impression already formed outside, of the "curb appeal" of sky-reaching two-story windows, incredible tiered landscaping and the artful arrangement of white concrete walkways, had to be overreaction. A product of fatigue, or maybe the pills she'd popped outside.

Hand on the knob, Noone hesitated. Finally she opened the door, halted and stared inside.

The frontmost room was wide open, ceilings vaulted to at least twenty-four feet. Between the double-height front windows, a natural stone fireplace narrowed to a chimney, crossed horizontally by an elegantly rough black wood beam which served as a mantel on which rested one white candle flanked by a pair of black and white photographs of textural stony desert landscapes framed in black wood. A modern gothic black metal chandelier hung over the center of the room.

Noone shook her head. "Unbelievable." Everything was even better than she'd guessed outside.

Straight ahead, a doorway opened onto a dining area and kitchen. To the right of this door, a hallway led to stairs. Though Noone wasn't ready to venture upstairs quite yet, she guessed that near the top of the stairs must be bedrooms, and that from the upper landing, a catwalk bridge cut back to the left, crossing and overlooking the great room. Noone wanted to delve deeper, to see and touch everything all at once, but only made it a few more steps before she found herself stopping, digging for her cell phone. She dialed Ian at his desk, then froze in indecision, wondering if she shouldn't hang up. Hadn't she just decided to take a little while longer to explore on her own before bringing Ian into it? She stared at the phone, trying to decide, though already the line was ringing.

"Ian Raddox," he answered.

Too late. "I made it." Noone scrambled mentally, trying to cover, so Ian wouldn't guess what she'd been thinking. "Ian, you simply would not believe this place if you saw it."

"Mmm, okay," Ian observed. "So, you're saying there's still four walls and a roof, at least."

"It's all so beautiful," she gushed. "Everything, Ian, listen. It's amazing, seriously."

"All right, Noonie, seriously." He exaggerated this last word in mockery of her breathlessness.

She couldn't really be surprised at Ian defaulting to skepticism. Still, Noone pressed on, letting his dismissiveness bounce off her. She breezed toward the kitchen. "I really mean it, Ian. He's done lots more than upkeep. This place is big, and everything's so new. Zebrawood cabinets, recessed lighting. I saw these barstools in an ad in *Dwell* magazine."

Ian addressed some muffled aside to someone on his end, then his voice came back, louder again. "All I know, Jodah never once left anything better than he found it."

She knelt, opened a cabinet and peeked in. "It's a little smaller than home, but not a lot. And it's so much—" Noone stopped herself, about to say, *so much nicer than our place.* That was true, though she'd decorated their home herself, a five-year project, no expense spared. "I'm just so impressed, even jealous. And I haven't even been upstairs yet."

After a pause, Ian seemed to register what she'd said. "Upstairs? Noonie, don't kid the kidder."

She always reminded herself that Ian's dismissive attitude wasn't really about her. He was always so busy that everything seemed an unwelcome intrusion. Probably something had just gone wrong at work. He worried so much over every detail at that place. She wished he could just relax a little, let his department managers run things. Ownership was hard, he always said. A sliver of attention was all Ian ever managed to give.

Noone found a kitchen window overlooking the rear patio, and beyond that a plateau of rock and dry desert landscape extended until it dropped away into what appeared to be a canyon or narrow valley. "I don't understand why your family stopped coming here, just let Jodah take over." Beside the sink stood a half-dozen unopened bottles of wine, a variety she enjoyed, and two clean glasses. Without thinking, she found a corkscrew, opened a bottle and poured.

"Mom always said the drive was too far. We could get to Manzanita in eighty minutes. Anyway, Callie and I never really loved the desert. Then while I was off at college, Jodah moved in. At first he said it was just for a month, like he needed to get back on his feet after this arrest, or that rehab, some other fuck up. Then he stayed, like he owned the place."

Noone sipped the wine and considered whether she should keep arguing, persist in trying to convey to Ian what this place was like, or let it drop for now.

"To be honest," Ian added, "I doubted you'd want to sleep there. I reserved you a room at this resort in La Pine."

"Oh, no." She returned to the kitchen doorway. Her eyes surveyed the great room. "I don't want to leave."

"Hmm. Either it's the wine talking, or my little decorator's found herself a project."

Noone was accustomed to filtering out Ian's remarks about her drinking. Had he actually heard her pull the cork, or pour, or was he just assuming that if she was awake and upright, she must be drinking? Noone told herself to focus on the fact that he'd at least acknowledged her as a designer. That was something, Ian remembering her aspirations, even if as usual he dismissed them as a cute, childish game. Ian had supported her taking design classes, had always gladly left her alone to spend entire days sketching and rendering, but he'd always firmly drawn a line at allowing her to work for hire. You don't need to grovel for commissions, Ian always said. He was right, they didn't need the money. Noone had gradually realized that the downsides to marrying a man like Ian were often related to the benefits, like security. It was a minor sacrifice. They had a good marriage. She wouldn't allow herself to feel ungrateful for what they had.

"Don't get too carried away, making fix-up plans," Ian continued. "It's possible Callie and I will just want to sell right away, as-is, before Jodah changes his mind." He paused, seemed to start over. "So, you're serious? The place is in decent shape?"

Noone almost launched again into another attempt to convey what a beautiful, unusual piece of property this really was, but she didn't want Ian to start calling realtors immediately. Better if he continued thinking the place might in fact need some repairs and clean-up. In fact, though she kept finding herself resentful about Ian failing to come along, this was better. She wanted time to fully explore, so she changed the subject. "Anyway, you can cancel that hotel reservation."

"If you're sure," Ian said. "If you don't mind sleeping there."

"Don't worry, I'll have fun roughing it a little."

After Noone hung up, she noticed her phone battery was almost dead. It didn't matter. She wasn't going to need it. There was no reason to keep calling Ian over and over, irritating him, when he was busy trying to run his business. This place offered plenty to keep her busy, so many intriguing details of furnishing, decor and accessories. What made it more exciting was that nothing even remotely corresponded with her preconceptions. Even now, having matched the address on the mailbox and beside the front door, and having unlocked the door with Ian's key, Noone still couldn't believe she was where she was meant to be. It seemed impossible. Jodah, the do-nothing brother, who never had a dime to his name. Noone supposed Maxine might have somehow secretly conveyed money to Jodah, without Gavin's knowledge, or after he'd died. Ian always insisted that the changes Gavin had made to the family trust had been irrevocable.

But somehow Jodah had managed this. So much expanded, fixed and reworked, really an astounding level of refinement and polish. Why would Jodah do this, then send away the keys and disappear? A property like this, four thousand square feet, surrounded by at least four acres, but probably many times more, such a package had to be worth near a million, even so far from the nearest town. This amounted to all Jodah had ever possessed, or ever would, yet he'd relinquished all claim and run off without explanation. The more Noone thought about it, the less sense it made.

3. Perimeter. To walk around a place is to measure it.

As Noone reached the bottom of her glass, she turned in the doorway to regard the kitchen. She eyed the wine bottle, trying to decide, and finally settled on waiting for a refill. That kind of restraint felt good, though in fact she surprised herself, how easy it was to decline the possibility of another glass. On the other hand, the idea that she should be congratulating herself over something like that made her feel a little sick. She didn't like Ian criticizing her for drinking too much, but she was often her own worst critic. Better to forget the wine for a bit, maybe look around the rest of the house. That sounded fun. Check outside and walk the perimeter.

First she went out front to her car, grabbed her bag, brought it back to the house and left it just inside the front door. The automatic reflex of a city resident made her think of locking up, but she told herself it should be fine to leave the house unlocked. She wasn't planning to leave the property. Nobody else would be coming. Out here, Noone was alone, would remain alone. She thought the idea of solitude was appealing, but also a little frightening.

Out front, she started back down the concrete walk, but rather than continue straight to where the Expedition was parked below, she veered right to parallel the front of the house. The concrete slabs comprising the walkway lay in flat, level tiers with occasional steps between, not smooth curves or inclines. This seemed an elegant design, this staging of flat surfaces, more precise and geometrically sound than varying up or down slopes, or unbalanced curves. The front corner between the walkway, the parking area and the line of trees was organized into squares, also tiered, maybe twelve feet on a side. These brought to mind the tiered gardens of the Mayans. Some of the beds were soil planted with ground cover, others filled with pea gravel with desert grasses sprouting in evenly-spaced tufts as if aligned on a grid, while most were built up with arrangements of desert rock without flora.

Past the corner, around the side of the house, the landscaping simplified. The narrow walkway widened to a broad, flat patio. A glass brick alcove shielded a sitting area and square fire pit made of black concrete blocks. Beyond this, a row of cultivated trees in pots concealed a grand barbe-cue and outdoor dining area. To Noone it looked like the kind of place a successful Hollywood producer might entertain all her friends, and throw wild, intoxicated cookouts attended by a hundred suntanned movie stars and screenwriters. Wild soirees, overflowing with sun-drowned inebriation and hot, covert sex, completely lacking any overhead of judgment or self-consciousness.

All the way in back, behind the house, a motorized black canvas cover concealed a swimming pool. Its length and narrowness implied a primary intended function of lap swimming, though numbers along the nearer edge indicated greater depth, at least at one end. Adjoining the pool was a square spa with its own white cover, and beside that, a full set of deck furniture, not only folding metal chaises for lying out and suntanning, but tables for drinks, decorative gray wicker chairs, and a broad monument table bearing a baroquely ornamented stone planter from which grew a single instance of broad-leaf vegetation which Noone thought looked prehistoric, thick leaves resembling something a dinosaur might have eaten.

Such a life here. Noone couldn't fathom how anyone could design such a place, surround himself with carefully considered design elements, abun-dant excess of beautiful decorative objects and settings, then willingly de-part. Of course she herself was accustomed to money, having been married to Ian Raddox for twenty-three years, yet somehow the life they shared, their home in Portland and their decreasingly frequent vacations, never quite felt like it amounted anything in the same vicinity of this sort of luxury.

The afternoon was unusually warm for March, especially at four thousand feet of elevation. Noone felt hot, overdressed in what she'd worn. The spa seemed appealing, but that heat might be too much on a day like this.

Maybe the pool? But Noone hadn't brought a swimsuit. She'd expected cooler weather. Now she recalled her absurdly long checklist, made only last night. It seemed foolish now, especially considering all the time she'd spent, and how few of the things listed ended up seeming relevant enough to her trip to justify bringing them along. Anyway, the things she'd left behind were still hers. She'd be back to them soon enough, she imagined.

Anyway, who expected a swimming pool, or a chance to lie out sunbathing for the first time in... how long?

4. Landscape. Surrounded by sage and stone, backed by canyon.

Noone wasn't done exploring. Beyond the rear edge of the patio, designed hardscaping gave way to rough, undesigned rock and dirt. The only identifiable vegetation was sage, which Noone could smell as she ventured out away from the house, into the land. A rough gravel pathway cut across the wide field, which she supposed might be considered the house's back yard, bounded at one extreme by a small canyon. The path became less distinct, until it was no more than a pattern of weathered scuffs and distantly forgotten footfalls through rough soil from which the rocks had been dug loose and cleared into small intermittent piles, like small pyramids. Noone kept to the center, afraid rattlesnakes might lurk just off the path. It wasn't yet summer, but the sun was warm. She imagined snakes and scorpions, slumbering in shade.

As she neared the canyon's edge, she slowed, afraid to approach too near in case the wall might crumble and fall away beneath her feet. Noone found the land disappointing, at least compared to the house itself. The only virtue she could discern in this landscape was emptiness, isolation. Of course, any yard ending in a cliff possessed a sort of drama, didn't it? Noone supposed so. Already her interest was running out.

Even standing back, away from the drop-off, she was able to see up and down the canyon. The floor wasn't far down, maybe twenty or thirty feet, and not nearly so steep as she'd feared from a distance. The walls were gradual enough that she could easily scramble down, if she wished. The central stream was nothing more than a weak trickle. In other seasons, the flow must have come in a great rush. How else could the water have carved out a canyon from soil and stone?

No, she had no interest in scrambling down. Though she didn't know what she'd expected to find, this rough, barren land was comparatively dull. What interested her remained behind, in the house itself, and the designed landscaping immediately surrounding it. Noone wanted to return, thirsted to uncover the next amazing thing.

Standing out here felt exhausting. Maybe it was the heat, but she much preferred the idea of exploring inside. Interiors were more her thing. She turned back, for some reason no longer afraid of whatever might be lurking beneath rocks. Nothing had revealed itself, so she supposed whatever she'd imagined had never really existed in the first place. She walked back without concern, thinking ahead. The outdoors seemed not exotic, merely dull, vacant and dry.

The house called out to her, even at this distance. The soothing whisper carried so many implications.

5. Refrigerator. Survey of desirable food and wine.

Yes, she hadn't imagined it. Inside, everything really was different. The air felt cool. With each inhalation, her brain seemed recharged with concentrated oxygen. This made no sense, considering the elevation.

Noone started in the kitchen. The glass-front commercial SubZero fridge was fully stocked, and all the zebrawood cabinets too. Even the dry pasta and tea containers on the counter were loaded, arranged as if for a magazine photo shoot, or staged for an open house. Many of the foods were items Noone often purchased for herself and Ian at home. This made her wonder if Jodah might've had some idea she and Ian would be coming. At first she guessed this could be a possible explanation, as of course Jodah must've realized that when he sent Ian the keys, Ian himself might come. But why would he take the time and spend the money to set everything up this way, if he'd been planning to abandon it all? Whole Foods Market in Bend must've been at least an hour's drive. Yet here was a deli carton of sesame noodle salad dated two days ago. That would've been the same day Jodah had FedExed the keys. The carton was unopened, exactly as it came from the store. Digging deeper, she found none of the containers, cartons or jars had been opened. A vacuum-sealed package of smoked albacore tuna. A dozen organic Omega-3 eggs. A jar of Bubbie's garlic dill pickles. Fresh local farm salsa with charred tomatillos. None had been disturbed. All were fresh, unspoiled.

Noone wasn't exactly hungry, though she knew she ought to eat. Anyway, when the time came, at least she already had plenty of great options for food and drink. No need to return to town. Now that she knew food was all set, she reconsidered the wine. Enough time had elapsed, she allowed herself another glass, with the understanding that she absolutely had to remember to eat something. If she forgot, and had too much wine on an empty stomach, she'd just end up going and going, and really suffer for it tomorrow.

The wine already open on the counter was excellent, but her eye drifted to the many bottles stored in two free-standing wine cabinets made of heavy, natural wood blocks that were mostly-intact tree trunks. Bottle ends protruded from holes drilled into the upright trunks of magnolia or birch trees stripped of bark, the wood oiled gold, streaked tan and brown. The bottles had been arranged label-up, so Noone was able to survey them all quickly. The selection offered excellent variety, both whites and reds, mostly Oregon wines. Several from Lethe Hills Vineyard, one of her favorites, and a few labels she didn't recognize, including an abundance of Pinot Noir and Pinot Gris from Salix winery.

Best to remember what Ian had told her. Just take an inventory, get some rough idea what was left of the place. Find a handyman for any work needed. Basically, figure out what would be needed to get the place ready to sell. Ian hadn't seemed to consider the possibility of keeping the house in the family. Noone didn't know if Ian had spoken to Callie, or simply assumed she would want to sell. Ian remained trustee of Maxine's estate and the Raddox Living Trust. Maybe he didn't need Callie to sign on. Still, it made sense that Callie and her husband would prefer to cash out, rather than add another family vacation home.

Of course they would want to sell. Jodah must have realized if he left, he'd never be able to return.

This kind of logical consideration of what must have happened, and analysis of what it all must mean, only clarified one central truth. The whole thing was a puzzle. Gavin Raddox had disinherited Jodah long ago, after one too many wasted stints in rehab. Even if Maxine had managed to sneak a little money Jodah's way over the years, which seemed unlikely given Ian's constant insistence there was no way Jodah could be doing more than subsisting, the trust had been set in stone years before, designed by Gavin expressly so that Maxine would be unable to reshape it in his absence. Even Gavin himself would have been unable to change it, in the event of his own diminished capacity or change of heart. No, Jodah Raddox had been truly and completely disinherited, for keeps.

Before Noone had arrived, she'd never really held any clear opinion as to what Ian and Callie should do with the house. On some level, maybe she might've hoped for the opportunity to oversee a major restoration job. That would've been fun, not to mention offering a chance to show Ian her capabilities as a decorator. That might have been the kind of proving ground to convince Ian he should allow her to freelance, back in Portland.

But any such speculation was by the wayside. This house required no work, no repairs. Not inside, not outside, not paint, not landscaping. Already it was perfect. Noone doubted she could improve it in any aspect, even with unlimited time and resources.

So then, where did that leave her? She was still here.

"Just try to relax," Noone said. "Drink your wine. You're good at that."

She planned to continue her survey, take a few pictures, scribble a note or two. Maybe she'd return home tomorrow. This prospect made her feel sad, but she could think of no reason to remain. She stood, refilled her glass to the top, and drifted from the kitchen back toward the living room.

Those tall windows were such an eye-popping sight. Outside, the gravel drive and parking area visible out the left window, then the line of trees continuing to the right, and before these, the terraced stretch of yard, curving around toward the side hardscaping, the outdoor living area, and in back, out of sight, the long pool and thousands of square feet of concrete patio. She could see it all in her mind, even what she couldn't see with her eyes.

And yet she still hadn't been upstairs. To her left, as she stood just inside the living room with the kitchen behind her, the hallway trailed off, past a little deck nook and lamp at the corner of the living room. At the end of the short hall, which was really more of a downstairs landing, the stairs headed up. That was where she would go.

6. Upstairs. Bedroom and bath and nothing to wear.

Noone grabbed her suitcase and climbed. At the top of the stairs was a broad landing, almost a room of its own. To the right were doors to a bedroom and a large bathroom. This rightmost portion of the landing continued around, behind the stairs, toward the bridge-like railed catwalk which crossed the great room and appeared to end in the little sitting area. These destinations to the right did not interest her yet.

To her left, from the landing at the top of the stairs, were double doors signifying a master suite. Noone drifted that way and pushed open the door slowly, reluctant to reveal too soon what she anticipated to be a jackpot of design and decor surprises. She found an oversized bedroom, spacious enough to allow plenty of open floor surrounding the king bed to the left. To the right, just inside the door, was a wall of built-in shelves, penetrated by a tunnel-like doorway to a deep walk-in closet. Along the far wall past the bed were a wide, low dresser with an expansive mirror, to the left of a flat wall-mounted TV, and beyond that a curtained window, then a doorway to the bath. She peeked into the closet, and found a space almost as large as the main room, lined by an uncountable number of open shelves. It was like the wardrobe of a spoiled king or queen, but entirely empty.

The master bath area was just as large. Just inside the inner door, a slate tile walk-in shower stood entirely open on one end, lacking curtain or door, apparently large enough that the spray wouldn't escape. Opposite the shower stood a separate jetted tub of sculpted black concrete, formed into organic, almost human curves, with rounded fixtures of brushed nickel. This first area of the bath, with its own counter and sinks, was separated by another door from a separate room with a toilet and yet another counter and sink. Noone wished she'd done something more like this at home. They certainly had space, but she'd wasted too much with excessive decorative cabinets, what now seemed to her mile upon mile of mirrors. Maybe it wasn't too late to scrap it all and start over. Yes. Make it more like this.

Sunlight pushed through blinds over the foot of the tub. So much light outside, beautiful, and so welcome. Noone couldn't remember exactly what the weather had been like back in Portland, just that she hadn't been outside in a long time. Why? Nothing had been stopping her.

Then she remembered the swimming pool. The idea of water, of swimming, seemed wonderful. She knew her luggage contained nothing suitable. She returned to the bedroom and looked around, wondering if Jodah ever had women around. An old pair of Jodah's shorts would do, and maybe a T-shirt. She checked every dresser drawer, looking for anything left behind she might be able to wear in a pinch. All the drawers were empty, but not merely empty, as if Jodah had just moved out everything he owned. Immaculately clean and untouched, as if the dresser had never been used.

Noone allowed herself to consider going without. Why not? Nobody was around. Nobody would see. It wasn't the kind of thing she would normally do, not at all, certainly not within city limits, with neighbors on all sides. But out here, why the hell not? Ian wasn't here to watch, to scrutinize with that neutral face of his angled, regarding her with his left eye only, his right eye hidden in profile. Of course such a look conveyed judgment.

She'd seen nobody in the fields, had discerned no other houses nearby. Nobody from out on the road could see the pool behind the house. For that matter, from the outer driveway she hadn't even been able to see the front of the house properly, through that row of scrawny desert trees. Here she could have real privacy. This place was fully hidden, isolated. Privacy was a possibility Noone had almost forgotten.

Would she really dare? Noone grinned at the mirror. Why did she have this feeling that to reveal herself would be a disaster, a transgression of all decency, even in the absence of anyone watching? Over the years, her body image had gone badly wrong. Of course, this wasn't exactly new information. She laughed. Body confusion was least among her worries.

Noone stood before the mirror, not looking at herself as she stripped off her clothes. She kicked off her sandals, lifted the tank shirt over her head and unfastened her bra. She unbuckled her belt, slid it free of the loops, unzipped the khaki capris and let them drop, then paused a moment. Maybe it was time to look. She had to look.

Maybe she could do this without ever seeing herself. Go outside, drop her towel and lie there in the sun, eyes closed, pretending she was invisible.

"No."

Noone hooked her thumbs into the waistband of her panties, slid them down her thighs, past her knees. When they dropped to her ankles, she stepped out. Then she forced herself.

Look up. Face the mirror.

What Noone saw shocked her. The sight was both better and worse than expected. She wasn't fat, or wrinkled, or misshapen. In fact, the overall outline and contours of her body surprised her only because it was all so familiar, so much like it had always been before, the way she remembered. This much came as such relief that her fears of how dramatically time must have transformed her turned out to be so bewilderingly inaccurate.

The one aspect that surprised her for the worse, the thing she had never expected, let alone feared, was how terribly white her skin appeared. So pale, almost inhuman, like the belly of a fish. Bluish-white. What was wrong with her, was she dying? Maybe she was already dead. Something must've gone wrong with her skin, at least, if not the meat and bone of her. She had always assumed so many things must have gone terribly wrong, had tried to avert her eyes and forget them all, under the influence of wine and pills and sleep.

How much time had passed since Noone had seen herself in daylight? So long, she couldn't remember.

As much relief as she felt to find herself still woman-shaped, in fact looking better than she could've hoped, her color was that much worse. But the news wasn't bad at all, especially for her age. She smiled, sneaking another look through the fingers of a hand covering her eyes.

7. Poolside. The surprise of water,
and the power of sunlight to make change.

Noone decided not to wrap herself in the plush black towel, and instead carried it as she walked naked down the stairs, up the hallway and into the kitchen. She commanded herself not to hurry, but relax.

As soon as she exited the back door, left the kitchen for the outdoors, felt the concrete patio beneath her feet, she began to rush, to feel anxious. Part of her wanted to run back inside. Now that she couldn't see herself, she tried to believe this meant nobody else could see her either.

Noone selected the first chaise, and wanted to pull it nearer the pool's edge. Out in the sunshine, revealed, she began to feel self-conscious. The feeling was too much, too powerful. Rather than move the chaise, she spread the towel, then took three steps toward the pool and dove.

Eyes closed, disconnected from the ground, her body flying, Noone experienced a flash of doubt. Had she forgotten, or had she remembered to draw back the pool cover before she'd gone inside the last time? So foolish, to dive from poolside without a look, only to crash headfirst into the cover, to hurt herself, or tear through.

Noone's eyes opened. Another instant, shimmering blue reflection. That moment of certainty and balance, her body weightless. She felt the water beneath her, sensed the splash but didn't hear it. Water rushed past her ears. Submerged, her body without mass, the weight of water compressing from without, even as it offered support. She made a perfect diagonal glide, exactly as if she had planned it this way, toward what looked like stairs in the opposite corner. The water felt so cool, but not unpleasantly cold. Already she craved the warmth of the sun.

She stood on the bottom and her foot reached for the first stair. Part of her was rising out of the water, into the world again. As Noone climbed free, she felt her heart hammer in her chest, felt pupils react against the sun's too-great brightness. Her skin constricted into gooseflesh, chilled by wetness in contact with air, even though the day was so warm. She waited for the sun to convey its full heat, knew this would happen soon. Hot concrete beneath her soles. She walked slowly, each step made with purpose, carrying her unhurriedly back toward the chaise. Noone straightened the towel. In such a rush before, she hadn't managed to spread it flat. She laughed at herself with a distant affection, remembering how she'd hurried from the house, feeling the eyes of everyone in the world imposing their scrutiny and judgment, how she'd made a mess of the towel, rushing to lay it out, then dashed to poolside and dived toward what might have been blue water or might have been black covering, without ever looking first to see.

Noone sat, reclined and settled in, urging herself once more to relax. Through eyelids, the sun glowed orange. She felt herself being watched, but knew that wasn't real. Part of her knew this anxiousness was just another aspect of her being unreasonable. She was naked, so what? Nobody was around to see. Besides, she hadn't looked bad in the mirror. Mostly she was still beautiful. She could be that way again. The problem wasn't physical. It was more about learning to see again.

Her skin reacted to the wind, then the wetness dried and her body seemed to cure and tighten in the sunlight, to become firmer and take on healthier color. Not exactly tan, not yet. She turned over, revealed the other half of herself to the sun's light, and soon felt the same on her back, her shoulders, the backs of her legs.

Noone wanted only to lie here forever, to keep soaking it all in. The heat was making her dizzy.

She opened her eyes. Everything outside herself remained exactly like before. That nothing had changed unexpectedly was reassuring.

This time when she sat up and stood, she found it easier to relax, to truly believe nobody was watching her. Her steps toward the pool felt different. She dove again, closed her eyes midair without worrying, or even feeling she should be worrying, though she did remember that jagged onrush of thought before, when she'd wondered midair where she was headed.

The touch of water somehow came as a surprise again, almost as if she'd already forgotten what was coming. Another splash. She surfaced, breathed. This time she spent longer in the water, cutting diagonals across the pool. Heat stored in her body took long minutes to dissipate into the cool water. She swam and when she was ready again, she found herself already at the steps, rail in hand, climbing out.

Now the chill was familiar, expected. A cool flutter of wind, a subconscious reaction of nerves, whatever autonomic reflex caused goosebumps, tiny involuntary shivers. All of it was fine. She was no different from anyone else.

The heat returned. She enjoyed the sun, remembered to turn often so she wouldn't burn. This became a cycle, alternating cool water and hot sun. These sensations left her skin tingling, pleasantly alive. How long since she'd felt so relaxed? She was just a body relaxing, barely a person, not a name. But this made her think of Ian again.

Most winters, Ian took her to Las Vegas or Palm Desert, sometimes both in the same winter. Actually, since he'd been busier lately, it hadn't been two vacations in the same winter for a long time. In fact, Noone realized here she was still thinking of these vacations as something they did every winter, when really it had been quite a few years since they'd gone anywhere at all. Las Vegas, that's where they used to go every anniversary until their tenth, then stopped. What about Palm Desert? She hated thinking about it, didn't want to do the math. What had been Ian's excuses?

Vaguely she recalled him saying it would be okay if she went without him, go on her own vacation. They had enough money, she could go anywhere. She didn't need an occasion. Every winter, Ian had some reason. Business expansion, relocation, a new sales manager, the new Yeon warehouse, Gavin dying, Maxine developing Parkinson's, then her death. And that last, that was years ago. So many winters. These latest, his reasons, she couldn't even remember.

Sun penetrated her skin, deep into overwhelmed flesh. Her head throbbed. Now she was beyond relaxation, and felt anxious again. Angry. She remembered herself.

Noone stood, wobbled on unsteady legs, and dove one last time. Now she kept her eyes open as the water came up to smack her in the face. She remained underwater as long as she could, lungs feeling a tug within, eyes burning. Finally she came up for air, breathed hard and deep a long time, trembling. This was enough, she was done swimming. Noone climbed out, stood teetering right at the edge, dripping onto the porous concrete, feeling it burn the bottoms of her feet but refusing to move.

She found herself startled by the outline of her shadow. The shape was something she barely recognized. Once she realized what it was, and convinced herself that it was actually connected to her, she began to study its contours. Sunlight seemed to have firmed all her softness and slack. She held up one arm, turned it over and examined both sides as she might study a cut of steak at the butcher, looking for the right color, a desirable balance of marbling and lean.

Yes, she did approve of what she saw. Now she felt no need to hurry, no urgency to cover up. She walked, picked up the towel from the chaise but did not wrap herself. Nude and dripping, she walked inside, through the kitchen.

Noone thrilled at a sense of mischief and secret. What would Ian say, if he knew?

8. Kitchen. A plan for dinner, and a second call.

In the shower, Noone took her time, savoring the setting, taking in every detail. Within the three-sided enclosure, effectively a stone-lined acoustic chamber, the hissing water made a reverberant ambiance. All else seemed to be stillness. She felt entirely apart from her past, unaffected by anyone outside herself. Her thoughts were safe.

After a long time, she shut off the water, stepped out and stood in front of the bathroom mirror. Dissipating steam allowed her to fade into view slowly, a materializing ghost. First a vague outline, a hint of person-shape, then a few details. A woman's figure, hips and breasts, her face rich with color, framed by wet dark hair. The pink flush and hint of tan made her look younger, as if infused with life by excess of light, water and steam.

More than twenty years of marriage. She'd missed this body. This girl, this woman. This self. She couldn't remember the last time she'd been comfortable, naked in the daylight. Probably college.

Noone went to the corner window, beside the sink, and pulled up the blinds. An expanse of unimproved desert stretched toward the canyon. Out there amid clumps of wild sage, in the shadow of a gnarled, weatherbleached tree, she saw movement. A shape like a person. Somebody watched from a distance, not far from the path where she'd walked before. She'd seen nobody then. Was it possible someone had approached, after noticing her splashing, then walking around naked? How did that make her feel, after lying there, vulnerable and oblivious, only to dive unhurried into the pool and climb back out again, never knowing someone might have been crouched nearby, trying to get a look at her?

But she had known. That it was possible, at least.

She squinted, trying to see clearly through the screen. Nobody was there. Maybe it was just something she'd like to believe, that somebody might hide behind rocks, crouch behind sagebrush, covertly watching her.

The fear this possibility caused to rise in her was overwhelmed by even greater excitement. Something tightened in her, a sexual clenching, a rush of blood and tightening of internal muscles. Some other version of Noone wanted to lower the blinds and walk away. What she wanted, this Noone, was to stand before the window, to display herself plainly as she was. And if there in fact were someone there, if he stood to reveal himself, she would walk outside. She would find him.

Nobody was out there. Nobody watched. She was alone.

Noone closed the blinds and went into the bedroom. In her bag she found fresh underpants, selected jeans instead of the capris. A clean tank blouse, like the one before, but red instead of black. She regarded herself in the bedroom mirror, this one transparent and clear of mist.

"Hello, Noone." She used a voice, but wasn't sure whose.

She didn't look old, really. Maybe a little older than before. That was true of everyone, but she hadn't aged badly at all. And she wasn't crazy, wasn't sick. Definitely she wasn't someone who deserved to be alone all the time. Something remained still alive inside her, still growing, pulsing. She had plenty of life left. Plenty of blood.

"Somebody would still want you."

Noone's words startled her again. Where did this come from?

"Somebody would want… me."

This was Noone. She was the one speaking. Part of her felt embarrassed, wanted to run away, but she also wanted to continue. Finally she brushed her hair and headed downstairs.

Everything she found in the kitchen was great news. Jodah had left all the ingredients for fish tacos. She didn't feel like messing with the grill outside, at least not now, but she could pan sear the fillets with garlic, pepper and sea salt. All she required was on hand. Corn tortillas, red cabbage, fresh tomatillo salsa. Even a large, perfectly ripe avocado.

Noone filled a bucket with ice and chose a bottle of white wine, a Pinot

Gris. Lethe Hills Vineyard, Yamhill County, Oregon. It was one of her favorites, but she paused to read the label. She couldn't remember if Lethe Hills was a place she and Ian had visited. Maybe she'd just imagined what it might be like, after having emptied a million bottles of the stuff. Probably she only thought she'd visited, and if she ever did actually go, she'd find it not at all similar to what her imagination had constructed. She'd never gone wine tasting alone, and didn't think she ever would. That seemed desperate, somehow, a married woman driving around to tasting rooms, sipping all the vintages alone. Not spitting, but brazenly swallowing, asking for more. Not giving a shit what anybody thought of her. A woman alone. So what?

While the new bottle chilled, she poured herself a glass from the prior bottle.

She wished she wouldn't waste energy imagining what other people might be thinking of her, let alone caring. It shouldn't be necessary. But all the life she'd built around herself, her entire foundation of *I am someone*, had all been eroded from beneath her. What did she have left to build on?

She gulped down half the wine.

So. All the fresh food was ready, but the salmon fillet was still frozen. Noone set it out to thaw. Already she was becoming accustomed to this house, the way she'd found it, rather than what she'd expected it to be. Ian's words already seemed strange, even foolish. His odd, childish recollections of a totally different place. Splintered floorboards, wind blowing in the gaps beneath doors. All the Raddox clan huddled around a single wall heater. Sure.

Her cell phone rang. Ian's number, as if her thoughts had summoned his attention.

"Hello?" Suddenly afraid, she wondered what Ian knew. What had he seen?

"Must be having some kind of adventure, Noonie. Not one call from you since morning."

"You always say I call too much." Noone felt strange certainty Ian must know she'd been naked outside. But would he even care? It seemed sensible to volunteer a partial truth, but not everything. "I swam a bit, actually."

"Swimming? Jodah put in a pool?"

"That's not all." She swirled the remaining wine and took a lesser sip. "Everything's totally different from what you told me to expect."

Ian didn't answer, seeming briefly absent again, then returned. "Sorry. Hey, all the better if the place isn't a shithouse wreck, like I figured. Maybe Ian found other things to screw up instead."

"That's what I don't get," Noone said. "Thirty years, no job. You say he received none of the family money."

"Yeah, but who can guess what he might've been into. I told you about this insane letter. Off to Costa Rica, something like, I'm going somewhere it's never so dark. Is that nuts?"

"So he really didn't explain…" Noone trailed off, unsure what she wanted to know.

"Look, I didn't want to tell you because I didn't want you scared, going there. Ian was pretty far gone."

Noone was about to correct Ian, tell him he'd used his own name instead of Jodah's, but decided to let it go. She tried to picture Jodah, but only saw a wild, longer-haired version of Ian. "Hard to imagine you're brothers."

Ian sniffed. "Biology, that's nothing. It's choices that make a person. You don't know Jodah. He'd meet a meth addict hooker at a bus stop and figure, why not bring her straight home to meet the family? He'd start a business with known criminals. He'd even steal jewelry from Mom." He seemed to be working up to a level of passionate feeling rarely exhibited, at least recently. "You wonder how he paid for a pool? Probably learned to cook drugs, or maybe rented out a room to child pornographers. Something smart like that."

Noone sipped the last of her glass. She'd always guessed it must be hard for Ian, following the directive of his parents to cut out Jodah financially. Now she wondered why this had ever seemed so. Ian sounded like he held nothing but contempt for his brother. She poured the glass full. "Jodah must've had something right, despite his troubles. He created this place. You'll see." As soon as she uttered these words, Noone regretted them. She didn't want Ian to see the house.

"Listen, I might be able to swing it," Ian drawled, in that way he had of offering something he had no intention of fulfilling. "Juggle my schedule, I guess. Is that something I have to do here?"

Irritation surged, made Noone want to lash out. Why had he sent her all this way alone, if he weren't so impossibly busy as he'd said? Of course he really wasn't going to come, but it was just so like Ian to tease the possibility, now that she'd already come all this way alone.

"No," Noone answered. "It's okay, I'm enjoying the quiet. I'm going to make dinner, then maybe watch a movie. If there are no videos, I'll listen to my CDs." By a mile, she'd rather sit alone and listen to Joni Mitchell than have Ian come out here and start issuing directives.

Some crisis flared on Ian's end, which was fine. Noone was done talking. She found her purse, dug for a Xanax and popped the last one. She hoped she'd remembered to bring a refill.

Of course they had a good marriage. She knew she was lucky, didn't want to complain, but Ian always left her so wrung out. Her hands trembled again. Why? Hard words barely ever passed between them. Ian never yelled, certainly never harmed her physically. He didn't even criticize, exactly. Not in so many words. Maybe it was just that way he spoke to her, and looked at her, that made Noone hate herself. Still, it was stupid, getting so edgy about it. Pathetic.

Noone sighed. "Just remember to find more pills."

9. Catwalk. Overseeing below, and stereo without music.

N ow that she'd thought of it, music sounded like a good idea. Listening to those CDs in the car had probably been what nudged her into this mindset, feeling all rebellious and independent. Certainly this house was a pleasant surprise at the end of a long drive, but the truth was, her outlook had improved the moment she'd driven out of Portland to the accompaniment of Billie Holiday. She needed to take her pleasures where she found them. Especially the healthy ones.

Of course she leaned too heavily on wine. Noone wasn't in denial about that, really. A drink helped her reimagine herself, transported to a different place, a new woman living an entirely reinvented life. Like rebirth. At least in that sense, wine was pretty much the best thing in the world, but it did take a toll. Every boost she gained from catching a mellow buzz only made the black cloud thicker, afterward. Today she was starting to see there were other things, other pleasures. Maybe things she'd forgotten.

She went out to the great room and looked around. One thing she didn't recall having seen in the house was a stereo that would play CDs, but she still hadn't checked the second bedroom upstairs or the area at the end of the catwalk bridge. She went upstairs, checked the second bedroom which was very nice, maybe the most plush and spacious guest room she'd ever seen, but contained nothing she couldn't find elsewhere. She returned to the landing, ventured out onto the catwalk and paused to overlook the great room. Not only was the room still amazing when seen from above, it created an entirely different impression. The shape of the room, the layout of the L-shaped sofa and two gray lounge chairs, even the patterned carpet beneath the coffee table. The view out the front windows was entirely new as well.

Noone continued along the bridge to the sitting area, an open perch with bookshelves and lounge chairs and a low table, almost like a small, second living room. On the shelf was a stereo receiver and CD player and a pair of bookshelf speakers. The electronics turned on, their displays lit up and appeared functional, but Noone found no CDs to play.

She pressed the receiver input buttons, switched to CD, heard nothing. AUX, nothing. FM, silence. Noone thought she should go down to the car right now, fetch her own CDs and listen to those. Somehow this seemed too much, an intimidating, even impossible distance. To venture outside now felt like a really bad idea. The car was just down the stairs, out the front door, and down a bit of concrete walkway. What could possibly be out there? Nothing, it was stupid. Noone hated the way her imagination got all crazy. First seeing a man hiding in the desert, watching her from below, trying to convince herself he must've been spying on her beside the pool. There had never been any man. Nobody was anywhere nearby. There was nothing to be afraid of.

In the morning she could go out to the car, or maybe tonight after she had something to eat, if she still felt like it. For now, she switched the receiver to AM radio and swept the dial. The static, a high whoosh, responded to tuning. The sound deepened, became a roar, a growl. She scanned slowly, changed frequencies and listened to the resulting change in what came through the speakers. Noone wondered if this was how Ian had used the stereo, with no CDs to play. She caught herself. She meant Jodah, not Ian. Funny, though, how imagining Jodah was not really any different from thinking about Ian.

One thing she didn't like about the house, now that she thought about it, was all the silence. Soon she'd have to go downstairs again. She really was hungry, needed dinner. More wine, but first something to eat. She preferred not to be down there when everything was so quiet like this. Especially once it was all dark. The present silence, and the idea of night coming later, reminded her how truly alone she was. Sometimes solitude didn't bother her for a while, but her mind always drifted back to thinking about it again.

All the frequencies across the dial hid their own interesting sounds, waiting to be revealed. Some scratchy and harsh, others like animal roars, or
wind, the rest pure white noise. Who could tell if the change in the sound
had something to do with the frequency itself, or if she were simply hearing subtle interference from distant radio stations at the right locations on
the dial? Near the top, around 1600, came a particular sound that reminded Noone of two voices harmonizing together. The voices weren't pretty,
weren't even exactly singing. More like a rising and falling moan, one voice
following the other. Of all the frequencies, the different atmospheres shifting, this was by far her favorite. She imagined a man and woman together,
a scene almost carnal. Not fucking, not like a scene in pornography, just
naked bodies lying together, almost motionless. The slowness of their movements reflected in the gradually oscillating sounds of their cries.

Usually Noone didn't let herself think about how much time had passed
since the last time she'd had sex. Now she wondered.

10. Patio. Pinot Gris and incoming darkness.

One realization she was ready to accept, and didn't argue against, was that she was actually hungry. One thing the house didn't seem to have was a clock, not even on the oven or the microwave. Noone could tell by the changing color of light coming in through windows that the hour might be getting late enough to make the fish tacos she'd been planning, especially since she'd already had two bottles of wine, and no lunch.

Leaving the stereo playing the harmonizing voices, Noone went downstairs and set out everything she needed. She washed and sliced cabbage, peeled and pitted the avocado, and heated three corn tortillas one at a time in a dry skillet. Then she turned on the stove, heated a little oil and cut the salmon filet into thirds, which she pan-fried. At the last minute she decided fresh lime sounded good, and when she found a lime in the fridge she wasn't surprised. Maybe she'd seen it before and just remembered it was in there.

The tacos were amazing and wonderful. She ate them standing at the counter, one hand dripping salsa and lime and salmon juice onto the plate, the other hand kept clean and dry to handle the glass of Pinot Gris. The wine was crisp and brilliant, really perfect. Noone wasn't sure what she was going through emotionally, what it indicated about her life to feel so overcome with gratitude, fighting off tears after nothing more than making herself a dinner of three tacos from scratch. For some reason the meal seemed special, terribly significant, the perfectly right thing for her at that moment. Maybe the difference was that the dinner was hers, planned by her alone, made by her alone, eaten by her alone. No one else. But why should that feel like a victory or a show of strength? She didn't want to be alone.

That was her whole problem.

After, Noone cleaned her hands and went out to the patio to sip the last of the Lethe Hills Pinot Gris. She tried to make it last, both the wine, and the disappearing warmth of the day. The sun rode low on the horizon. Her legs felt rubbery again as she walked slow laps around the pool's perimeter. She decided to sit.

When the sky had gone nearly dark, a trio of heavy planters containing little manicured trees lit up from inside, apparently in response to a light sensor. The sudden illumination where none had been expected was startling to Noone. By day, the planters had resembled boxes of white glass banded with metal, but the glass must have concealed a layer of illumination built around the inner compartment of soil and roots. Now magenta, orange and yellow lights illuminated the concrete wall and competed with the vanishing sun for what light remained on this scene. By this changed light, Noone saw that a line of narrow metal towers, artfully rusted and topped with an angled shape, like a smokestack in square tubing, were not only standing sculptures but torches for nocturnal illumination. She wished for a lighter or matches. Probably some were to be found inside, if she needed them. Everything she needed seemed to be here. But what mattered more than illumination in darkness was that not an hour went by without Noone uncovering some new aspect, some detail previously overlooked and now revealed to be interesting or useful in a way never before realized.

The Pinot Gris had run out. Noone decided a red sounded good for a change. Something really different, not just the Lethe Hills Pinot Noir, good as it was. She headed in, and had to turn on a light in the kitchen for the first time. The place looked so different, the sky outside darkening. Previously unknown lights provided the only illumination, inside and out. She knelt before the two wine cabinets, which resembled still-living trees with the necks of wine bottles barely protruding from smooth, glossy trunks. She selected an unknown wine which had caught her attention earlier, an enticing Australian Malbec. Noone felt pleasure in having dug a little deeper.

She was ready to uncork the bottle, but decided to set it aside to breathe until she'd started running herself a bath. The jetted tub upstairs was large, and would take a long time to fill. She ran upstairs, stopped the drain and started the hot water. As she hurried back downstairs, she caught herself smiling again. Noone felt fortunate, almost happy.

11. Hallway. Red wine, footprints, and a locked door.

Pouring a tall glass of the Malbec, Noone found her mouth watering at the color and body of it. Tart and juicy, ruby-colored. Delicious.

A sound drifted through the doorway from the great room. Her heart leapt, her blood chilled. Someone was here. A whisper. No, not a voice. It was the hiss of radio static left playing when she'd come down for dinner. She'd forgotten. Somehow it sounded different, felt different. The house, which had felt like such a perfect balance of refined architecture and en-lightened interior design, now with the fall of darkness felt like a place where it might be possible to be afraid.

She considered calling Ian, but dismissed the idea in an instant, then felt angry that she'd even thought of it.

In the doorway between kitchen and great room, Noone surveyed the un-occupied space. She was here, she was somebody. This house wasn't empty. It was hers. She went to the nearest lamp, on the desk at the corner of the great room, at the verge of the hallway, and flicked it on. Yellowish light revealed the changed mood of the place.

On the pale hardwood floor of the hallway, she saw marks. Footprints. Had she tracked in dirt from outside, before? No, these were man-sized footprints, centered around an old door. Actually, she couldn't remember if she'd noticed a door in the downstairs hall, before now. Chipped beige paint and an old, tarnished knob, these didn't fit the decor of the rest of the house. Not at all. A door like this, an obvious design mis-step, should've stood out at first sight, not to mention the dirty footprints, like somebody had tracked in coal dust, or soot. Was there a basement, or just a closet?

She tried the door, found it locked. The ancient, worn knob wobbled feebly, as if a hard twist might break it loose. Noone rested her wine on the desk and ran upstairs to find her purse, and the keyring Ian had provided. She came back down, tried the keys one by one. None of them fit in the keyhole, let alone turned the lock.

Noone heard an aquatic thrumming overhead, a sound half-concealed by the whoosh of radio static also floating down from upstairs. Remembering the water running into the tub, she flicked off the desk lamp and ran upstairs.

12. Bathtub. Assessing options from a place too hot to linger.

On her way up, Noone envisioned water gushing over the rim of the tub, but she arrived in time. The water had risen to a perfect level, two inches from the rim. The placid surface emanated steam and water beneath swirled almost imperceptibly.

As she removed her clothes, Noone was aware that the process had become easier this time, her reflexive internal conflict now comparatively subdued. As she stepped into the water, she imagined her body capable of penetrating the surface without disturbing its inner stillness. Either she had found some greater dexterity, a new ability to slip in without disruption, or else in her fatigue and intoxication she had become less aware, blithely unconcerned with the unavoidable ripples that must radiate outward from the trajectory of her arc across the world.

Submerged up to her chin, feeling the water's density and power imposed upon her until she was almost overwhelmed by its smothering heat, she remained, waiting for her mind to slow. Still her nerves remained tense, at the ready. She leaned back, seeking consciously to relax her muscles, but moved too abruptly. The back of her skull struck the rim of the tub behind her with a crack.

Warmth, stillness. Here nothing could disturb, nothing could touch her at all. Whatever encyclopedia of unresolved issues and compromises had diminished her life back home, here in this new unknown, submerged within the biting hot protection of the water, she remained beyond harm, unassailable. She admired the stone tile of the shower across from her, its wide, dark opening seeming like the entry to a black-walled echo chamber. The

Rainshadow showerhead gave forth a perfectly ordered and uniform drizzle of streaming raindrops. Noone had always wanted one of those. She remembered staring at an ad in *Modern Home* magazine, just yesterday or the day before, thinking it would be the perfect showerhead for the master bath at home. If only their enclosure weren't so narrow. To make any changes at home, so many proportions would have to be shifted.

Why couldn't her mind remain quiet for any duration? Problems always remained, questions percolating under the surface. The dark footprints in the downstairs hallway, that was a perfect example. How could she have failed to notice them before, walking back and forth numerous times over that very spot?

Again she thought of the man outside. It had to be a man, watching from a half-concealed crouch. Hadn't she seen him?

No, she trusted her eyesight. She'd looked closely, concentrated, trying to focus. There had never been any man.

Yet this kept bothering her. How was it possible to disprove a concept in memory, to be sure that no threat had ever existed, briefly glimpsed out a window, through a screen, hours before? Probably she hadn't looked closely enough. Now she could never be sure what was out in the field.

After a while, the too-brief respite of relaxed subsidence gave way to twitching anxiety. This was always the way. Noone could never understand how it was possible to become more tense, soaking in a hot bath after Xanax and numerous glasses of wine. Hell, numerous bottles.

He was never there. No man.

Noone stood in the tub, found herself rising from the water without having decided to do so. She reached for her towel, dried herself, then put on jeans, a shirt and shoes. Downstairs, she found the lantern-style flashlight on the floor inside the back door.

She had to know. Outside, across the patio, down the path. She followed to where the trail began to disintegrate, where gravel vanished into the foot-scuffed dust and stone of the wild land. Her flashlight beam showed the way. Things looked so different, brightly lit proximity, quickly fading away to darkness.

Footprints, probably her own. At first she followed, but then she began to wonder. If the path hadn't shown her the correct way before, how could she expect anything different now? Her only possibility was to venture off. Fear overwhelmed curiosity, and she stopped. Why did she need to go further? There was nothing more to find. She'd already found a place to stay, with ample comforts and pleasures. Inside she would be safe.

"I'm not afraid," she said, unsure who might listen.

The truth was, she remained fearful of the canyon. Also the open space, and the darkness and solitude.

"There was never any man."

Even if somebody had been hiding in the field, watching as she paraded naked and oblivious at the poolside, what did she have to fear? No, she wasn't afraid. Only curious. Where had he managed to hide? Maybe the canyon provided shelter, some opening in the rock wall. A tiny, hidden camp, invisible from above. Of course, nobody would go down there, searching. Someone could remain there, hidden forever. Probably the entire time Jodah had lived here, he'd never once gone down to the canyon.

Such dark. Noone imagined fire, smoke rising from a little cave. Shimmering light of subdued flames. It was possible someone might survive there, though maybe not in winter. Then, snow might accumulate, months at a time, but people could become accustomed to such hardship. No condition was too inhospitable, especially if we acclimated gradually. Comforts we once believed intrinsic to survival actually weren't necessary at all, but were only the sort of luxuries that pampered the entitled into lives of soft enfeeblement.

"I have nothing to worry about here," Noone said into the dark sky. "The door is locked, and there's no key."

She turned back toward the house, where a light upstairs remained lit for her.

13. Television. The only story is already old and broken.

Noone filled a glass to carry up to the bedroom, certain it would be her last wine for the night.

By the time she reached the top of the stairs, she wondered what she'd been thinking, going outside alone, after dark, in the middle of nowhere. Too much sun earlier, maybe that was it. Though if she were honest with herself, something lately she'd really been trying to do, the problem seemed more likely connected to excess of pills and wine. Everything she'd been through today, and all she'd consumed, topped off with a lengthy soak in a bath so hot, it had left her boneless and dizzy.

She snatched up the TV remote from the dresser top and flopped onto the bed, careful not to spill. Lying back and still holding the wine, she undressed one-handed, first slipping down her pants a little at a time, then pulling up her tank shirt, switching the wine hand-to-hand so she could lift her top overhead. Slowly, as if surrendering to an impulse long resisted, she fully reclined on top of the covers, wearing only panties, legs sprawled, each bare foot pointing at one corner of the bed. She propped herself up on one elbow and thumbed the power button on the remote. The big wall-mounted flatscreen came alive, screen turning from black to blue. No cable box or satellite dish control was visible in the room, and the only remote to be found was this one for the TV. Not even a DVD or BluRay player was apparent.

Imagining there mustn't be anything available to watch after all, Noone was ready to give up, when the blue screen flickered to dim, grainy black and gray. At first she thought it was only static, the kind of snow old-fashioned televisions made when tuned to dead channels. But the picture moved. She blinked, and figures clarified. Characters in motion. Some kind of story.

A bearded, long-haired priest in full robes led a slow procession down the aisle of a candlelit church. The man's features were deeply creased with marks like black painted lines. Walls and ceiling were heavy with thick, sculpted ornaments whose convoluted shapes cast baroque shadows.

From within his robe, the priest produced a heavy sword. He turned to face the others, which the camera eye revealed to be a row of nuns. They regarded the priest with cautious expectation.

The priest raised the sword. The blade flashed reflected candlelight powerful enough to blind the others.

The first nun stepped forward, squinting, eyes averted. The other nuns followed in a line.

The priest rushed to meet them, swinging his sword in wild, violent arcs. The blade cut away the garments of the nuns, who did not resist, but seemed bewildered, unable to fathom what was happening. The priest stopped. All the nuns, confused but unharmed, were left nude but for their head coverings.

At the edges of the screen lurked blurry shapes, vaguely human, moving closer now that the priest had stopped his sword. These shapes were like men only in outline, their faces churning in the discord of peripheral darkness. All appeared the same, interchangeable.

The priest offered his sword to the foremost nun, the first who had dared to come forward. She accepted his sword, then took his place leading the procession out of the church. The priest fell in among the nuns who followed, and after them, last in line, came the faceless shapes.

Outside, they approached a circus, marching in the opposite direction down the moonlit village street. Once all members of the circus had passed, they turned, reversed direction and fell in behind the church's procession. The two groups merged without a word, fire-eater beside priest, lion tamer beside nun, all of them commingling with starving wild beasts to travel slowly through the bomb-ravaged town.

Fade to black, credits run. Music obscured by static. Everything old-fashioned. Titles on the screen motionless.

The movie started again, the scenario changed. Some of the characters seemed the same.

A ragged parade marched beyond the edge of civilization, and passed into desert land pocked with black tar pits rimmed with white powder, like chalk or lime. The flat sand began to rise before them, first a slope, then a great dune. They pressed on, though their feet kept slipping back down the steeply inclining sand. Some fell, struggled to regain their feet, and tried to catch up. None turned back. All continued climbing, increasingly stained by tar from the pits below, the black marks sprinkled with powdery white.

The incline firmed. The sand became intermingled with rocks. A mountain.

Along the difficult climb, some tried to speak, but their words came in some foreign language, nothing Noone could comprehend. The subtitles were gibberish, seeming out of correspondence with even the timing or duration of the spoken dialogue.

A summit.

The group found an opening, a tunnel mouth. Lonely points of illumination blinked within deepest dark. No individuals could be discerned, but as the camera's point of view proceeded down, the pinpoint lights in the background were occasionally occluded by blacker shapes.

Finally, a cavernous theater yawned. A destination. Aisles, seats, all vacant. A broad wooden stage, lights overhead.

Some of the actors changed costumes, or applied fresh makeup. Others took seats, forming an audience.

The camera panned across a mirror in a grand theater lobby to reveal the reflected scene from an opposite angle. Though the camera itself passed fully in front of the entire length of the broad mirror, and in the reverse shot all of the room stood revealed, the camera itself was never seen. No reflection of filmmakers or crew ever appeared. They and their camera passed without notice.

The screen displayed a printed placard fastened to the wall outside a door. The card stated the name of the party within the closed chamber. This name was a code word for admittance, but remained illegible, seeming to wobble, dimly lit and out of focus.

The stage. Dark marionettes pranced around white nude statues, both female and male. The statues were in motion, not statues after all. But their movements were slow, barely enough to prove they were living beings, not inert or dead.

So dizzy. Noone imagined sleep, but the idea repelled her. Maybe this was already a dream.

The room darkened, a switch thrown. But which room? Out of blackness, the screen flared and strobed as the lighting operator tried to keep everyone awake. From loudspeakers issued subliminal hiss, voices lost amid static. Somebody trying to convey an encoded message.

A man and woman in surrealist masks stood alone in a library, browsing books. The shelves were empty, all the books stacked on the floor in tall piles, or heaped on tabletops. The man demonstrated to the woman an open page, an offering of words. Her face creased and froze. Conversation resumed, the language altered yet still untranslatable.

The underlying hissing cracked and burst into fury. The soundtrack gave way to spiral death chatter.

The actress froze, indecisive.

The actor removed his mask, turned to directly regard the camera. He looked at Noone. At first she believed the actor was her husband, Ian. But under the hot, intense lighting, his face appeared rougher, more care-worn, deeply lined with age and worry. She'd never seen Jodah before. Was this him?

The Malbec tingled, hot in her gut, the acid dangerous. Vines grew wild throughout the room, threatened to overrun—

THE SECOND BOOK

NIGHT OF A WOMAN'S FIRST DREAMING

14. Stairs. Wake and descend, stumble and fall.

—a nd something started, then she was awake. A cold body, lying amid wetness, ears full of static, everything in the world hissing gray.

What was this place?

Noone sat up, looked around without recognition. She couldn't remember how or why or where. Her wine glass lay overturned, now empty. This explained the spreading damp in which she lay. A pinched nerve made her neck ache. Her stomach lurched as if in answer to poison. What time was it? She squinted, sought backward, looking for any connection. One thing she remembered, this place had no clocks.

Terribly thirsty, her mouth so dry it felt cracked inside, sticky. What sounded good was cold sparkling water, which reminded her, there were still the bottles of Pellegrino in the fridge. Her mind reassembled the shape of the house, the relationship of all the rooms. The kitchen, that was all the way downstairs. As she thought about it, didn't the situation seem odd, the way she recalled it? A refrigerator fully stocked, with exactly everything she wanted or required. All she recollected now seemed open to question. Nobody would abandon their kitchen that way. This house was somebody else's vacant home, wasn't it? So that made her just a squatter, in a strange, lost version of nowhere.

Noone swung her legs over the side of the bed, feeling unbalanced, as if still drugged. Her feet found the floor. All she needed was something to drink. Cold water, nothing else. Atop the dresser she found her iPhone, but no amount of button pushing or screen swiping would make the display light up. This seemed ominous, as if distantly connected to a movie she'd seen, or maybe dreamed she'd seen. That screen too had gone black, both screens disconnected from the world, too far gone beyond all boundaries to have any hope of—

"No, stop it." What did that kind of nonsense even mean? The phone's battery was dead, that was all. Sometimes Noone found herself pursuing insane thoughts, digressing off into self-defeating craziness. It had to stop.

She remembered to take along the empty wine glass, and staggered toward the door of the bedroom, then out to the landing. The open stairwell was a black void, lacking any indication of objects or boundaries below. She stepped off the edge into the dark, not seeing, only hoping something would catch her. That first step met a stair below. She stepped again. Her right hand clutched the rail in desperation, as if everything might give way utterly at any moment. By this halting process, she descended most of the way. Near the bottom, she began to believe everything might end up okay after all. She might be safe.

Only a few more steps might have remained when she decided to release her grip on the rail. Her body tilted toward where she thought the next step must be, her weight shifted. She hesitated, then overcorrected and started to fall. Too late she tried to catch herself, felt her body launched beyond balance or control. Forward, flung outward toward space, no longer tethered to anything solid. She lost touch, went weightless into the dark, and realized she was unsure how much farther she really had to fall before she landed. Her mind fled to the moment outside, when she'd dived for the swimming pool and in midair begun to doubt, to wonder if what awaited her was only the water she expected, or something less forgiving.

Noone struck the hardwood floor. The wine glass broke in her hand, and shards scattered across hardwoods. As her weight came down, jagged glass punctured her palm. She lay stunned, unable to breathe. After a moment, she gasped as if resuscitated, and writhed in an ineffectual attempt to right herself and stand again.

It's all just another dream.

Listen, she told herself. Her eyes were no help, everything was far too dark. At least if she had to stumble, the fall had been only the last few steps.

Though she remained unable to see, she imagined her face must have come to rest precisely in the center of those unexplained footsteps she'd seen on the hallway floor. She remembered all that clearly now, with such detail and precision she was tempted to doubt any of it could be real, almost preferring to attribute the matter of the footsteps to a vague, dark motion picture only barely recalled. What persuaded her to believe was one certainty, that if she were to end up in a place, it must be somewhere she most feared. Further, a smell, something like an engine. Old, black grease. Her other senses could explain where she was, even if she couldn't see. A rhythmic thrumming emanated from the door, just beside her, within reach. That was something she didn't need to see in order to know. Sound alone was adequate to create a sense of direction, of dimension. That, or maybe the machine existed only in her imagination, and she merely listened to her own heartbeat pulsing within her ears.

Noone found herself moving, reorienting, starting to rise. Though everything ached, she rose to her knees amid all the broken glass. She tried to stand, wavered, almost fell. Even in what had seemed utter darkness, she now believed she could discern some visual hint of the sharpest edges of the broken glass surrounding her. These blades glittered against footprints glossy black, a filthy dance-lesson diagram. Her hand groped, testing the void, until she found something. The edge of the little desk, its surface. Then the lamp.

She pressed the switch. Everything changed.

Though she wanted to look around in the light, to confirm the existence of all the things she had imagined she perceived without sight, she now felt more afraid than when she had been unable to see anything at all.

Maybe if she found her way into the kitchen and gulped down enough cold water to clear her head and calm her beleaguered heart, she might be able to forget everything until she woke again the next morning. She might be allowed to return to a reality in which none of this had ever happened. Sometimes that was how life worked, and avoidance of some painful or threatening truth allowed things to shift enough that she could back away from worrying and gradually forget, as if the problem had never existed. Even the most sickening fear might end up being unfounded after all.

"I never fell," Noone whispered. "There are no footprints."

As her body moved, perspective shifted. She took steps, waiting for her feet to be pierced by glass, but was able to walk without pain. The next thing she saw was the open, bright refrigerator, and her hands doing exactly as she'd envisioned, twisting the cap off a luminous green San Pellegrino bottle. She recognized the insignia, was able to read the label, see every detail. The bottle was real. She drank, then poured the rest into the remaining wine glass by the sink. When the glass was empty, she refilled it. Two glasses, topped off, consumed the entire bottle, the same as her experience with bottles of wine. A full pour meant only two glasses per bottle. Ian always repeated this, saying a bottle of wine was not two glasses, but really five. He insisted on this concept of "true drinks," as if some measures were straightforward and honest, while others revealed self-deception.

Noone found the corkscrew and opened another bottle of the Malbec without cutting off the foil. She'd been cheated of the last of the prior bottle, which had spilled all over the bed when she fell asleep. It was still night, nowhere near morning. It wasn't difficult to yank the cork through, then she poured to within a half-inch of the rim. She wanted to drink fast and deep, but instead lifted the glass, held it before her face, and tried to see through it. The wine was too dark. Opaque purple-red.

One sip would be enough.

She allowed herself a taste, savored and swallowed. That was something she always tried and failed to convey to Ian, at times when he complained about her drinking too much or too early. He didn't understand how much she enjoyed the taste of wine. It wasn't just about intoxication. Noone didn't drink only to forget, or to soften sharp edges, but because she enjoyed wine itself. Ian claimed to understand the matter more clearly than she did, but Noone believed it was a subject Ian barely gave any real thought. He merely repeated ideas he'd read, or things he'd heard from Gavin, who had spent his final half-century sober after surviving various nebulous and secret troubles in his twenties. Most likely, these words Ian used were catch phrases the family had directed at Jodah, whose own lengthy slide into unassailable addiction had turned every other Raddox into an expert.

The wine glass was empty, so she refilled it. The bottle fit perfectly into two pours. Noone found comfort in the perfection of this even measure. One into two. She drank some of the second glass so she wouldn't need to worry about spilling on her way back upstairs. In the doorway to the great room, she lingered, surveying the room, but without looking at the spot where she had fallen. The desk lamp remained lit, dispersing feeble illumination, most of which spilled dim yellow over that spot, the one place she didn't want to see. Noone took in the arrangements of objects around the room, confirmed the floor plan without obsessing on details.

She shrugged off the danger of jagged glass, the threat of inexplicable footprints, and ran toward the stairs. As her foot touched the bottom step, a thought came to her. She imagined someone else was inside the house. But she was running, and that was safety, freedom. Her destination was set in mind, and nobody could prevent it. She would be able to close the door, shut her eyes, sleep the rest of the night. Panic drove her up the stairs by twos. Her feet crossed, she stumbled, but caught herself. No wine spilled. Her knee ached where it struck the edge of a stair, but that sensation was distant. Up again, lifted by fear and intensity of focus to the landing, where blithe shadows moved in tangible darkness.

What was happening here? Noone wondered what was solid, which senses could be trusted. She flailed arms, trying to disperse some congregation she doubted truly existed, like a swarm of gnats that disappeared under scrutiny.

Once inside, she slammed the bedroom door. Compartmentalized, safe. No more hurrying. Now she could put away the fear.

Noone sat hunched on the edge of the bed, breathing so hard she was afraid to drink the wine yet, lest it spill. She caught the smell, wanted a taste. Steadying with two hands, determined, she raised the glass. A single deep swallow took the wine down halfway. Remedy for a racing heartbeat. Her mind slowed. The contents of her psyche seemed to back off a short distance, and politely turn to face the wall.

The television remained off, black and quiet. No static. She couldn't remember how she had left it.

So stupid, always being afraid, seeing things that weren't even there. After such a nice day, why did she have to spin out like this? She hated herself, ruining a good thing. It had been so long since she'd had a perfect day, and this day had really been perfect. Hadn't it?

Noone wanted to call Ian, and she didn't want to call. Some part of her had formed a resolution that to call would be a surrender to the status quo, something she could no longer tolerate. Anyway, her phone was dead. The charger was out in the car. If she wanted it, she'd have to go back downstairs. What was there to say to Ian, really? If she called, the moment she dialed, her mind would begin racing in anticipation of a million predictable recriminations about glasses of wine consumed.

No, thanks.

Her mouth was still dry, sticky, as if glue had dried behind her lips. She rubbed her eyes. Too much sun, that was all. Now she couldn't walk without tripping. This house, she didn't really know her way around yet. It wasn't second nature, the way a person could walk around and dodge obstacles in the dark, in a place where they'd lived long enough. Didn't people fall more often on unfamiliar stairs? She thought so. Fall down, fall up. Noone couldn't remember which.

She really didn't want to drop off asleep with a full glass again, so finished the wine and placed the glass carefully on the table. Her eyes closed. Somewhere, she couldn't recall exactly, something had broken. The problem was when, and where. Just had to remember not to step in whatever it was, had to look out. Don't step—

15. Sleep. Late visit, indistinguishable from a film half-forgotten.

When he came to her bed, his weight shifted the mattress. They lay front to back, both on top of the covers. Ian's shape, his familiar smell. Though he said nothing, she knew. His hand squeezed her hip, then slid down her panties.

So dark in here.

She'd been right before, she hadn't needed to call. Ian must've known he ought to be here, despite their plan that she come alone. All resentment vanished. She felt glad, relieved. A small offering of care could unwind years of neglect.

His skin, so hot. His breath.

Noone pressed back against him, felt his firmness. After everything, their endless complications and so many disappointments, the two of them still fit. Their shapes corresponded, like a lock with a key.

He pulled her up, onto her knees. His dark outline loomed over and behind her. His thrusts pressed her away even as his hands, low on her waist, pulled her back again. Insistent, forceful. She moved with him, giving in, yet resisting. Here, to force back against his pressure felt cooperative, not contrary. It was exactly the way her body ought to move. So many things fell loose and floated away, already forgotten. Problems became distant. She might never remember her past.

The force he exerted against her resembled an expression of anger, but in this context, it was exactly what she wanted and required. He said nothing, only moved. He slapped her ass, tugged her hair, pulled her head sideways. She contorted, twisted around, turned back almost far enough to see his

185

face, even as her body continued working hard against him. She wanted to see, but straightened and forgot. Her nails clutched behind, dug into his thigh, scratched and tore flesh.

He never relented, seemed he might never stop, only continue harder, harder.

She couldn't remember the last—

The air so thin here, she couldn't breathe. Lungs rasped, gulping in desperate need of oxygen. They were both carried away, slick with sweat. Pleasure ached within the center of her. Was it really pain? Muscles clenched in heightening urgency, bound together with all the hatred she felt, and the forlorn wish to be relieved of it.

She saw something, a vision of another time. A memory. She recognized the scene, Ian's place in it, but sought to deny the recollection from her own mind. Ian striving behind someone, was it Noone herself? Their positions were exactly like now. Had she changed so much, lost so much of herself? That woman was not her.

Flash of an idea: She had to disappear, find a life of her own. This notion gasped within her, lightheaded.

What if she had known it must come to this? Everything she'd once wanted, the life she always dreamed for herself. The woman she'd become was in no way connected to the girl. Though no single detail of her now could be reasonably complained over, the convoluted arrangement in its entirety was a bundle she'd give anything to dismantle.

Without a sound, only pressure and hot insistence, he reached culmination. She felt the change in his rhythm, a trembling pause, then a forceful heat beyond words or reason.

He stood and shifted away, a silhouette outlined against a wall of churning noise. That static again.

"Where are you going?" She didn't mean to ask anything of him, had resolved to demand nothing at all, but couldn't help herself. Her question arose automatically, just as he had arrived without any plan, or time to form intention.

Noone sprawled, panting, alone on the bed. Her breath returned as her heart slowed, and the drying sweat cooled her skin. She turned her face toward the pillow's softness and drifted within mind.

"Ian?" He should return to her, lie down. If not talk, at least sleep.

The bed remained empty. She alone had remained here, but nothing else, no one. No footsteps, no sounds, no inference of presence. Only darkness too thick to breathe. Solitude made tangible, thick enough to choke.

What if her life could still change? This thought rode in on a wave of anguish, a gut surge not unlike the burning of clenched muscle and seething anger that arose during sex. Despair surged, then departed into lassitude and slow breath.

She decided.

"I'm drunk, that's all this is."

There was one thing she knew she could make happen.

"Just forget it, Noonie. Forget everything."

THE THIRD BOOK

PAST VANISHES BEFORE
FUTURE COMES INTO VIEW

16. Wake. Interruption of daylight, an ebb and flow of sickness.

S unlight penetrated curtains. Noone's eyes opened and she tried to speak
Ian's name, but her tongue stuck in her mouth. The door was shut, the
room far too hot. That explained what was wrong here. Why hadn't she
opened a door? Her mouth was so dry, her head throbbing, like fever sickness, a pain more immediate than she had ever felt

Last night was a blur, memory an eradicated smear. Nothing had happened. All she possessed from that time was this strange, transformed place
in which she now lay, sweaty and trembling. A universe sickened, stained
antique yellow and dead orange. Alone, without a clock. Nothing connected her with the outside world.

Her stomach burned. Hadn't she gone downstairs for sparkling water, trying to ease an acid stomach? She thought she remembered wanting to get
up for a drink. Had something gone wrong on her way down? That must've
been part of a dream. She definitely remembered waking up, feeling afraid,
then telling herself to go back to sleep and in the morning everything would
be fine. But it wasn't fine. Maybe it was worse than ever. If she had gotten water, at least she wouldn't feel like this. Why was it always so hard to
remember what she ought to do, in order to avoid this awfulness the next
morning? It always seemed perfectly clear later on, but in the moment,
when she needed to make right choices, options always seemed confusing,
almost impossible to narrow down.

Life used to be so much easier. When had every decision become so hard?

She threw off damp sheets, tried to stand. Her panties were pulled down
around one ankle. Pain spiked her forehead. Ian, she remembered. He'd

been here. She looked around for proof, but saw no trace. Where had he gone? No, that must've been another part of her dreams. Vaguely she recalled sex, but that seemed least likely of all. That was something she'd definitely remember. It had been way too long. This realization made her feel pathetic, an adult woman married yet so painfully neglected, so detached and physically isolated from every living person, that her last resort had become the confused adolescent's thigh-clenching dreams of ravishment.

Yes, she was alone.

Everything else could wait. She had to get something for this headache. Water, some kind of pills. Noone wobbled from the room, across the landing to the top of the stairs. As her hand clutched the rail, an image shot to mind, a kind of dark flash. Running up and down stairs. Tiptoeing through broken glass. Smeared footprints. Yes, that last was real. This much, she knew to be true. Last night, she'd discovered tracks in the hallway. Some events seemed real and definite, while others shifted into uncertainty, taunting psychological echoes from that weird movie.

On the lower stairs, a puddle of wine had dried dark, blood black. In the hallway below, glass shards were scattered everywhere, encircling a cluster of dark, shuffling footprints outside the door. Noone approached, still barefoot, cautious, and reached to pick up a triangle of broken glass. As her hand extended, she noticed a scabbed wound on her palm. Pain returned the moment she saw the puncture. Then she remembered falling. Being tripped.

"Ian?" She tried to project her voice to fill the entire house. "Weren't you here?"

No answer. She could always phone, a casual *Just checking in*, to make sure. She didn't have to admit her uncertainty as to whether he'd visited in the middle of the night, unannounced, and left again. But how would she ask?

Honey, did you maybe just drive four hours in the middle of the night to fuck me while I was sleeping, then immediately drive home? It's okay if you did, I just need—

No. She wasn't making that call.

In the fridge she found the cold Pellegrino she'd craved last night, the bottle still unopened. Trembling hands twisted off the cap. Bubbles imme- diately relieved the acid burn in the pit of her stomach.

What time was it?

The microwave blinked 88:88. The LCD display on the range said the same. Noone didn't know why she couldn't seem to remember that none of the clocks here worked. At least, they'd never been set. Either she needed to keep her phone charged, or check the time once, then set these clocks. After that, she'd have some reliable, steady frame of reference.

She finished the water as she staggered upstairs, and grabbed her keys. Even if she didn't want to call Ian now, if she ever did want to call, she needed to charge her phone in the car. Why hadn't she brought a wall charger? Maybe she'd been too preoccupied selecting CDs for the Noone's Greatest Hits jukebox.

She opened the front door, stepped out, and faced the brightness of the day. Fear pulsed, an electric twinge. She felt exposed, dangerously suscep- tible. To what, exactly?

Noone tried to hurry down the walk, stepped gingerly across the gravel parking area, and unlocked the car. The console clock read 1:23. Had she really slept that late? She couldn't remember the last time she'd slept past ten, let alone into afternoon. Jesus, her head ached. Her eyes seemed in- capable of adjusting to this stabbing sun. The light penetrated to sensitive hollows within her brain, behind her eyes and below her ears, acid-filled vacancies where her mind ought to reside, but which had been overrun, breeding grounds for throbbing disease, or merely the chemical breakdown of a mind completely—

Fuck, she was so hungry. That was all.

She climbed out of the car, slammed the door, and staggered up the walk- way. Even the view out front didn't impress her much right now. It seemed like a different life, that first moment she'd seen this place. At a time like now, who cared about architecture or design? She needed breakfast. Medi- cine.

In the kitchen, she quickly discarded any pressure to create a complicated breakfast, and simply slow-fried two eggs in yellow-green olive oil. The idea had sounded good, but the smell made her sick and she had to turn away.

She decided to grind some coffee while the eggs finished cooking. On the back counter, to the left of the sink, was a commercial grade espresso machine. This she could handle. While two shots drizzled into a squat Barum double-walled glass, she turned off the stove and slid her eggs onto a plate, trying not to break the yolks. Caffeine shot straight up her spine and into her brain. Her headache lessened, but not the nausea. Faced with the eggs, her stomach refused. She set them aside, hoping they might seem tolerable in a little while. Of course she needed to eat. Many times, she'd gotten into bad trouble, forgetting to feed herself while she chased other sustenance.

Her ankle throbbed hard. Now that constricted blood vessels in her battered and swollen brain had begun to dilate with caffeine, the stabbing pain in the joint rose to the surface of awareness. She must've fallen, rolled the ankle on the stairs.

She needed a pill, but couldn't remember where she'd left her purse. She seemed to vaguely remember seeing pill bottles in one of the kitchen cabinets. The first door she checked brightened her state of mind, revealing the stash Jodah had left behind. Vicoden, Percocet, Oxy, even more Xanax.

Two Percs made the prospect of a shower vastly more tolerable. After chasing down the pills, before the drugs could even begin to have an effect, Noone went out to the hallway and cleaned up the broken glass. Then she limped back to the kitchen, washed her hands, and made a sandwich, two eggs sunny side up on sourdough with her favorite artisanal mayonnaise, the stuff in the jar wrapped with blue twine, plus Irish cheddar and a blanket of pink Himalayan sea salt. Everything was already getting better again. She could tell things had begun changing, because she was able to imagine pleasures again, at least small ones.

Noone put her plate in the sink, ran hot water over it, and breathed. She was going to get through this. The terrifying black cloud had begun to drift off, and thinned enough to allow the passage of a little sunlight. What she needed next was a shower.

17. Landing. A room from memory, objects from pictures.

At the top of the stairs, something caught Noone's eye, like the flitting of a butterfly at the edge of peripheral vision. But nothing had moved. At first she wasn't sure what had changed, and just stood staring, doubting her perceptions.

Then she saw it, right in front of her. A new doorway, straight ahead, directly in the middle of the light gray wall, where before no door had existed.

Her blood chilled. Goosebumps tingled up her arms to her shoulders. This wasn't right, it didn't fit.

She'd always categorized this flat, unadorned wall as one of the house's few architectural shortcomings. Why not at least a window, to overlook the view outside? But this wasn't an exterior wall, it turned out. At least, not any more.

Noone hated herself for doubting both what she saw now, and what she remembered having seen before. This wasn't similar to the locked door at the bottom of the stairs, with its cracking paint and wobbling antique knob, so badly out of sync with the design of the rest of the house.

This upstairs door was different because it was slightly open. Beyond the narrow gap was another space, a sunlit room she'd never seen. Her assumptions about the shape of all the rooms, the placement of every door, wall and window around her, now seemed questionable. Hadn't it seemed the least bit strange before, a house nearly four thousand square feet, but with only two bedrooms? True, both upstairs rooms were enormous, in fact the entire place seemed to have been designed with a respect for open spaces, broad hallways and high ceilings, rather than a larger number of enclosed rooms. That was part of what she'd liked about it from the first. Besides, she'd always assumed the place was a remodel, with—

No, she'd never assumed that. She had to remember to start being honest with herself, always, no matter what. A beautiful show home like this had never been a falling-down shack, or whatever term Ian had used.

A whole new space, not a dozen steps in front of her. A sunlit room, never before seen by anyone.

Noone hesitated, trembling with fright, and also perverse excitement. She wanted to back away, close her eyes and descend the stairs. She wanted to avoid thinking about this. But also, she needed to see what was here, inside. Not only desired to know. Needed.

Three steps closer. She paused, then moved again. Close enough to reach out, push the door open a little more.

The room was still under construction, a smell of raw wood and drying interior latex paint. The narrow section of wall visible from outside appeared half-finished. Bare studs to the left, then taped, unfinished sheetrock, then to the right, textured and painted walls, ready to show.

Closer. Almost near enough to poke her head inside.

The floor ranged from open beams, to rough plywood, and to the extreme right, was finished in the same glossy bamboo flooring as the rest of the upstairs.

New construction overnight? No, she would've heard, and anyway, nobody built this way. An entire room gradually fading into solidity, like an inexplicable dream. Real construction was a sequence of discrete processes, each stage finished before the next was undertaken. Not like this, a kind of magic that drifted cloud-like, bringing a vague unfinished conception from the left into complete, finished reality to the right.

Noone backed up slowly until she felt the drop-off behind her, the stairs too close, then turned and fled into the master bedroom. Who was she fucking kidding? She had to get out of here, now. She flung her suitcase onto the bed, and frantically threw in every loose item in a wide-eyed, heart-thudding rush. This manic surge peaked, and began to trail off.

What else? Nothing was left, back home. She was still afraid, that hadn't changed, but she didn't really want to run. Not home. Not a return to the way things were.

"Calm, Noonie." Her voice remained low and steady, one corner of her mind trying to talk the rest down from the brink of panic.

She just had to make sense of this, that was all. Another day exactly like yesterday, that was all she wanted. Solitary pleasure, a quiet mind. Stability, that feeling of residing within her own boundaries. She pulled aside the curtains, drew up the blinds. Intense sun, just like yesterday afternoon, beside the pool. Brilliant light eradicated the bland yellow sickness that had filled the room since she woke.

"Just look, take another look." She moved her face nearer the window, and the overpowering sun. She remembered yesterday, outside. So bright. "This is it. What you wanted."

Noone turned back to regard the disorganized mess of her open suitcase. This was the way her mind worked, always overreacting, like a skittish cat. Anything that bothered her, any obstacle she encountered, anything unknown, she flung aside everything around her and scattered in mad hyperpanic. No wonder she could never make any kind of progress. She was always too busy picking up broken pieces of the night before, spending time resetting all life's fragments into their proper places. Always trying to make up for the last crack-up.

She moved the suitcase from the bed, back to the top of the dresser, and stopped dead. Whatever recognition she'd achieved, or momentary peace she'd found, any hope for a return to calm, vanished as her heart thudded anew. Sweat trickled cold down the side of her head, and dripped down her neck. She didn't want to look directly at what she saw, but it was right here in front of her.

The bedding was a black and white grid pattern accented with a few red Jackson Pollock spatters. Yesterday, the bedding had been different. She remembered it clearly, dark gray with light gray circles. But the problem wasn't just that it had changed, or that the stain of red wine spilled in the night was no longer visible. What was so much worse, more upsetting, was a particularity of this new design.

She dug through the suitcase, beneath the tangle of clothes, looking for the new *Dwell* magazine she'd been reading two days ago. Madly she flipped through pages, frantic in her search for a specific photo spread.

Here. This pictorial had stuck in her mind, some artist's home in Barcelona. All white-stained structural concrete, glass brick and square aluminum tubing. And the artist's bed, identical to this one. Now that she looked more carefully around the room, she saw it wasn't just the bed covers. The headboard too was different, exactly like the one in this magazine. And in another photograph, the shower was a slate tile enclosure and a Rainshadow spray head.

Things were changing. She might have sensed it before, but had believed the problem resided not out in the world external to herself, but derived from some glitch of mind or failure in the mechanism of memory. Easier to believe it was only pills, or too much drinking, or that she had simply been taught by desperation and loneliness to imagine the world around her different from how it was objectively. But this magazine, the specific details of this pattern. Solid things couldn't just transform, remake themselves to conform to daydreams, or wishes, or photographs of ideal lives in magazines.

Something was shifting, something true, and maybe not only within her. Something inside wanted out.

18. Inventory. A catalog of measurements, and a drawn key.

N ot yet ready to venture out, Noone retreated to a safe place. The stone-
tiled shower, though it stood completely open on the side nearest the
soaking tub, had the feel of an enclosed compartment. When she stood
beneath the hot drizzle, steam rising around her, she felt embraced within a
warm haven, an anechoic chamber safe for dangerous thoughts. The water
burned, sensitized her skin. She liked it. Everything seemed clarified, the
future becoming ever more possible.

She could not decide which possibility seemed more agreeable to her,
apart from the less relevant question of what might be actually true. Could
solid objects transform themselves while she wasn't looking, or were her
memory and perception utterly failing?

Her mind tended to reject any explanation reliant upon the impossible,
however preferable. She couldn't dismiss the chance that slippage occurred
within a subjective system. If she needed to know what was truly happening, she had to rule out distortions of sense and mind. She formulated an
intention to sketch floor plans, and take a detailed inventory of every room
in the house. No more wondering whether a bed covering had actually
changed. No more wasting time wondering whether a new room had appeared overnight, of if she'd failed to notice a new door.

Time to rule out uncertainty.

One way to improve her situation right away, she decided, was to stop
averting her eyes every time she encountered something that frightened her.
Time to stop running away, and start confronting reality as it truly existed,
no matter how uncomfortable. Nobody enjoyed fear, but far better to face

individual fears head on, try to deal with them without evasion. That reflex of avoidance had gotten her into this tangle, the mess her life had become. She wasn't going to start blaming her marriage to Ian, but she should at least own up to the reality that both of them had begun ignoring major problems over the years. The arrangement no longer worked for her at all, yet instead of confronting the issues, she'd practiced avoidance and denial. This only made the fear and tension extend forever, and gradually multiply. A lifetime worth of problems, trailing behind, like cans tied to a string.

Now she would fix this. To start, she needed something to write and sketch with.

She shut off the shower, toweled off and dressed. On her way down to the desk for pen and paper, Noone reflexively averted her eyes, but this time, she caught herself. She forced herself to look at what she feared. When she stopped, she didn't just turn her head to see, but stood straight and open, facing the door. She glared at it, like an enemy. After a moment, the fearful expectation faded. The door wasn't anything to worry about.

In the desk, she found an ultra-fine black Sharpie and a yellow pad. On the pad's top sheet, a shape remained visible from what had been drawn on the page before, since torn away. The outline was clear, an old-fashioned key. It resembled none of the keys Ian had given her, which were all modern. An old key like this was the kind that she expected would fit this antique knob. But why a drawing of a key, and not the key itself?

Noone reached for her purse, looking for her phone, planning to call Ian. But the purse remained upstairs, and her phone was still charging out in the car. Anyway, why should she call Ian? He'd only ask about the usual. Lately Ian had become exclusively interested in the twin subjects, pills and wine. She wished Ian might somehow become able to accept her again, and not only judge. Like last night when he—

She caught herself.

"He was never here." She recalled Ian's smell, and the way he touched her. She missed how it had felt to be with him, or at least be with someone. Her hands trembled, and she wasn't sure why.

Noone went into the kitchen and headed for the cupboard full of Jodah's leftover medication.

"Careful there, Noonie," she warned in a deep voice, intended to sound like Ian.

This was all she needed, two more of the little ovals and a gulp of water. Swallowed, forgotten. A clean slate.

There in the kitchen, she began her all-encompassing inventory. Her project required nothing more than the Sharpie and legal pad. She was able to measure distances by pacing barefoot, heel to toe. Every object, every room. She sketched, wrote detailed lists. Downstairs alone took over three hours.

She took a break to eat something, proud of herself for what she'd accomplished, and for remembering to eat before falling into confused desperation. She felt no temptation to open any wine before she was finished.

One thing she was learning was that every place was the same, fundamentally. Just doors and walls, floors and ceilings. Sometimes a window. Every interior space in the world was assembled from these same parts. One room, one house, was no different in kind from the rest, really. Just differently arranged.

By the time she began upstairs, the fears that had driven her downstairs had drifted far away, like the clouds of another day's storm. Everything felt weightless. Even the new upstairs room, which she realized now she might have actually noticed upon arrival but only forgotten, had become merely another set of details to document and measure. One indulgence she denied herself, at least for now, was to waste energy trying to decide whether the room had become still more complete, more nearly final and solidified, in the hours since its discovery.

When she had finished with the entire house, every page in the writing pad was filled. The house, its contents, and the number of sheets of paper available had been a perfect match.

Some time before, without her noticing, the sky outside had gone dark. Noone felt proud of her accomplishment, but her psyche also had begun to fray around the edges. The problem was more than just worry about the details of the house. Her accustomed balance of pills and wine had shifted, probably too much. A little wine would help.

She went down, poured a familiar Pinot Noir.

Last night had been such a nightmare, a nasty disappointment after such a beautiful, revelatory day. In and out of sleep, black shapes floating in the darkness, and falling every time she took the stairs. Now it was time to leave fear and panic behind. She was lucky, Xanax softened everything, especially on top of whatever else it was she'd taken earlier. And wine was a key ingredient in a tolerable life.

Her predicament, which had before been a direct and immediately confrontational threat, now sat quiet, at a discreet distance. She glared back at it, unblinking, with no more anxiety, just calm regard, and perfect willingness to accept scrutiny. Noone barely recalled what anxiety was even supposed to feel like. Already it seemed foolish, all her earlier worry, and that jittering nervousness, dormant now. The whole story of her life, all her bound-together worries, how could that be of interest to anyone? She stood in the hallway downstairs, looking at the desk, the floor, the doorway, and wondered how she had ever felt afraid. This sensation was like reading someone else's case study. Facts on the page conveyed no emotion. This was the relief the pills were capable of granting her.

Speaking of pills, enough time had passed. She slipped into the kitchen, opened the Xanax bottle and shook out two more ovals. She chased these down with a slug of Pinot Noir from the bottle. She laughed. Her back and shoulders had begun to ache, more with fatigue than tension.

But not for long.

19. Spa. Night sunbathing, cold darkness with closed eyes.

Waiting for the pills to kick in, Noone wasn't quite sure what to do with herself. Warmth was something she still craved. She could take another shower, or maybe go outside, try the hot tub. Really, the idea that was stuck in her mind was this desire to revisit the way she'd felt yesterday afternoon. She'd set aside her fears, dared to unclothe herself and venture out. Not that she needed to swim and sunbathe naked again. Anyway, now that the sun had set, yesterday's plan couldn't be repeated, at least not until tomorrow.

Why couldn't she go outside? Tonight, in the dark, she'd have more privacy than under yesterday's direct, hot sunlight. It was probably cold now, but somehow, that didn't matter. She couldn't stop thinking about it. Lying there, feeling her body transform, anxieties diminish. None of that had anything to do with the sun. The point was that she had forced herself to relax, to remain still, eyes closed.

Though she hadn't forgotten the central problem with this idea, the inevitable cooling with the fall of darkness, Noone went upstairs for a bath towel. She returned downstairs still dressed, carrying the towel, determined though unsure what would happen outside. From the kitchen, out the back of the house. The patio surrounding the pool was not entirely dark. The three planters glowed green. Last night, the colors had been different, at least that was how she remembered it. But outside hadn't been part of her inventory, so she wasn't sure. Also, there was another feature she hadn't noticed before, accentuated by the sidelong shadow cast by the green lights. A triangular cantilever step, or a low bench, which jutted from the concrete retaining wall halfway between pool and spa, about six inches off the ground.

Instead of seeking the chaise at the corner of the pool nearest the house, Noone continued past the pool, toward the spa. She spread her towel on the last of the lounges, and almost removed her clothes, but hesitated. The night was far too cold outside, even colder than she would have guessed.

She knelt beside the spa, intending to check the water temperature, but the cover was fastened so firmly she couldn't even lift the edge. No lock was visible, let alone any means to open it. Strange that the pool cover opened and closed automatically with the press of a plainly visible button, but the hot tub remained off limits, secured by some secret.

Still, she knew what she wanted. The concept remained fixed in her mind, impossible to dismiss. Hurriedly she undressed. Her skin constricted at the touch of cold. She lay on the towel and closed her eyes. This wasn't going to work. She wrapped arms around herself, turned on her side and drew knees up in a fetal position.

Just think of warmth, she thought. Remember the way it felt.

The shivering began as a reflex. Noone told herself to ignore it. All she needed was to convince her body to relax, eyes closed. The human mind could find a way past anything.

"Lie here. Imagine the sun."

The only impressions made upon closed eyes were abstract patterns in the darkness. Maybe this was feedback from inside her eyelids, or an attempt by her mind to make sense of null inputs. Eyes closed in the dark. Why not open them? Noone pressed her knuckles into her eyes and auras flashed green and purple, shot through with white pinpoints.

The movie last night, like nothing she'd ever seen. Noone had no idea of the title, and hadn't really comprehended a single word spoken, at least in any way she could explain verbally. Was it possible, inexplicable images and sounds glimpsed in the dreamy haze of night, might have the power to redirect her life?

Noone imagined how it must feel to die. Would she become afraid, as inevitability grew nearer, and wish she might rush backward in time, change her mind, reverse decisions lost past? It would be easier to face, with the right pills and enough wine. That combination made everything seem easier. Probably she was already full of more than enough pills. She could make the final summit climb, and finish things with just one more.

She wanted to will her mind into transformation, put into motion a constructive force. When the time came to open her eyes, she wanted to feel stronger, full of certainty. Not just a warm, tan body, but an entirely new person inside. The woman she'd always meant to become. Someone who could handle Ian, make things right between them, or decide to do without him.

Other women had done it.

Imagine the sun. Feel it warm your skin. It's possible.

Noone opened her eyes, and her mind returned to a body already shivering uncontrollably. The night was so cold. She stood, grabbed her towel and clothes and ran back to the house.

20. Shower. Unquenchable cold, and listening to static.

Noone had never really enjoyed liquor. Ian always accused her of only sticking to wine because she believed that dislike for the hard stuff proved her drinking wasn't really problematic. This moment she returned to the house, feeling chilled to the core, if she'd found any whiskey at hand, Noone would've gulped down mouthful upon mouthful.

Instead she jogged upstairs, ran the water hot in the shower, and stood under it, eyes closed, remembering how she had felt outside. At first her teeth chattered and her body shivered, with the occasional convulsive twitch. Even when this stopped, her skin felt bitten by cold. Hands and feet were the worst, as if the blood refused to circulate in these parts of her, which ached as if pierced by cold nails, despite the steaming spray. Her extremities belonged to another different person, aspects to some strange, dislocated body.

Something had to change.

Noone reached down, touched herself between the legs. Xanax usually reduced the need, or at least her sense of desire, until it all became so pent-up and tangled, she stumbled over it. She felt on the verge of tears, so ridiculously, foolishly overrun with undefined need and wrenched by physical wanting. Two different women, at odds within one body. Her hand acted upon herself as if possessed by another's intention. This moment, as she gave in to the furious desire to touch, and the hungry need to be touched, she felt none of the romantic longing supposed to drive feminine desire, at least for women considered textbook normal. What she felt in its place was more like nausea or despair. This awareness did not make her less determined or frantic. She couldn't stop, driven by a kind of inwardly-directed anger, a furious urgency toward bodily punishment or harm. She pushed fingers deep inside, not the way she normally touched herself. Noone imagined someone else's hands. Someone's body, their force and weight—

Yes, this. She bit her lip too hard. So hungry, so full of pain and unmet desire. Most of the time she couldn't admit to herself how much she lacked. Now touching this way, hard and hurtful. Using her body the way she wished someone would use it. A stranger. Muscles of her thighs rigid, pelvis clenched, one part of herself resisting another. She pushed back, both sides of a struggle, grinding hand against body, body against hand. She threw back her head, took the hot spray full in the face, eyes open, mouth wide. Breathing hard, inhaling the spray that threatened to choke her.

"Yes, this. This." Someone else.

That burning ember, acid-hot seething in her gut, trying to burst, to explode outward.

"I need." Another's voice, speaking nearby. "Need, finally."

The fierce clenching culminated, then lessened. She leaned forward, coughed out what she'd inhaled, still breathing hard, but slowing, returning to normal.

Noone turned the hot water down to lukewarm. She began to see again. It was as if her mind had been absent from her body for years. Now yesterday and today, she was experiencing what it was like to be herself, to reside within her own body and feel awareness of it rather than detachment. Noone hadn't felt guilty or ashamed about masturbating since her early teens, but this was different from usual. Most often, it was something done without thinking, quickly and without investing much of herself. She'd never really considered it exactly sexual, and most often managed to fall short of feeling satisfied in the moment itself. A poor substitute, but better than nothing.

She toweled off inside the shower enclosure before she stepped out.

Yes, this was new. Different. She felt giddy, astonished, as if she'd accidentally stumbled upon some important secret, long hidden until now. So much frustration had boiled over, risen in a kind of deranged lust born out of ferocious, hostile need. She hadn't felt that way in so long, she couldn't remember if it was the first time. This aftermath seemed strange, at once triumphant and shameful, as if she'd finally been unfaithful to Ian. Her hands trembled, not only from fatigue. Already she knew this was something she wanted to do again. With somebody else next time, or at least soon. This realization was a massive new presence, a proximate planet around which she now orbited and could not escape.

As she pulled on white jeans and a gray T-shirt, Noone heard something outside the room. Maybe she'd been hearing it all along, but had managed not to notice for a while. Yes, it was the stereo, the detuned radio. A howling, windswept landscape of static emitting from speakers on the other end of the upstairs. She followed the sound out of the bedroom, around the landing and along the railed bridge of the catwalk. The sitting area at the end was open, not really hidden from the rest of the house, but easy to put out of mind. Noone kept forgetting she'd left this static playing since yesterday. This background noise was issuing from speakers, and wasn't a surreal ambience inherent to this place.

She knelt on the leather ottoman, closed her eyes and leaned into the left speaker. Yes, she could envision the place. A road swirling with wine, people climbing a mountain slope. What was this place?

Enveloped in the wash of static, like the hot water of the shower, or the piercing light of the sun on the patio, Noone recalled a dream. Had it been last night, or maybe before she'd come here? A dream world of hissing noise, just like this. She'd found a black box barely concealed, hidden in plain sight. Within the box, a folio of secrets, sketches and diagrams. Exact measurements, geometric studies, descriptions of hypothetical spaces. The key to this house, output of a mind obsessed with relationships between spaces of habitation and their occupants.

Noone's hand brushed against something hard, unexpected between ottoman and shelves. She opened her eyes.

A black box made of wood. No lock. The lid came off easily.

Inside was a folio of papers, as in the very dream recalled just moments ago. Although she had remembered the dream, opening the box, leafing through pages, she retained no recollection of exactly what she'd found inside.

Now she could see. So many pages.

In one, a white-robed figure stood in a flat field, staring across a gap of distance at a large house. The significance of the gap between observer and structure was clarified by a geometrical drawing in that intervening space. A triangle overhead, too high to reach, but significant. The lower corners of the simple equilateral were marked B and C, while the triangle's peak was A, and connected via vertical line to point far overhead. That lofty ideal was marked D. The figure's identity could not be seen because she was facing away, toward the building, the object of her desire. The loose white robe covered her body and her head. Only a small gap allowed her to peer out from eyes which remained hidden.

In the next, a bridge of stone blocks arched across a gap, over a narrow, dark river. As in the other image, geometric figures were superimposed over vacant space, giving ratios and measurements to tangible objects below. This geometry was more complex, the angles not symmetrical. A larger triangle encompassed a central square, corner points labeled E, F, G and H. Each of the component parts of the larger triangle that were not the inner square were themselves smaller triangles, with their own corners marked.

So much truth. The geometry explained everything, proved what Noone believed, had always believed. Everything around us, every structure and aspect of decor, including the natural world, was comprised of complex shapes interacting. Geometry was all. Beauty itself was only an appealing balance of ratios. Empty space could be altered and transformed by non-existent objects. When a bedspread changed its pattern, or an arrangement of rooms altered overnight, that wasn't impossibility. That was nothing but how the universe had always been made.

21. Bedroom. Whispers outside, possible dark shapes.

This line of thinking, Noone realized, was the very thing that had always gotten her into trouble. Such philosophical digressions made her head throb like a concussion, and worse, initiated these never-ending lines of speculation, which she continued chasing even long after recognizing the problem's basic inscrutability, meandering and spinning in mind, until the next thing she knew, the sun would be rising again and she'd crash, sick and angry, wanting to die. Ian wasn't here to force her to eat, or take her pills. At least she usually remembered the pills on her own.

She shut the folio of drawings inside the box and hid it away. With the intention of turning off the stereo, she reached for the switch, but decided to leave it playing. The static noise soothed her, like a song. Didn't people listen to white noise machines to help them sleep? That meant the sound conveyed beneficial properties.

Downstairs she ate four mouthfuls of sesame noodle salad, as if taking medicine, then swallowed another pill and poured a fat Pinot Noir. On her way back upstairs, carrying the glass with special care to avoid spilling, she admired the wine's color and body. She preferred dark wine, saturated ruby red, too opaque to see through. Thick as blood.

Noone settled onto the bed, feeling loose-limbed and pleasantly foggy. She attributed this state of relaxation to what she'd done in the shower, and smiled with contentment and a kind of joy at her secret. "Best fuck you've had in ten years, at least," she whispered playfully, and almost laughed, then stumbled over an unexpectedly jagged twinge of sorrow. Not only was the joke probably literally true, but those ten years didn't remotely cover the full extent of her problem. Times like this, she found herself counterbalancing reality with platitudes. *It's a good marriage*, she might have said, or *I'm lucky to have a man like Ian*. These thoughts always managed to dead-end whatever line of thinking she might've been itching to pursue. Some part of her always wanted to believe their marriage to be a good one, though it actually wasn't.

Savoring a mouthful of wine, she reached for the remote. The TV clicked on and the screen resolved as it had the night before, from blue to black, then coarse, busy static. She allowed herself to consider the movie, though she'd been trying to avoid thinking about it. Probably that dark, weird narrative explained her nightmares. She would've slept better if she'd shut it off, even if it had seemed interesting enough to grab her attention, at the time.

Noone raised the remote, thinking maybe she ought to shut the TV off and sleep, rather than getting started with another movie. Her hand wavered, skewed sideways, back and forth, out of control. The remote dropped from her hand, bounced off the bed and clattered to the hardwood floor. The room spun. She tried to reach down for the remote and almost fell off the bed.

"Whoa, shit Noonie."

Two-handed she steadied the wine glass, then slurped several mouthfuls, trying to lower the level so she'd be less likely to spill. At once she felt badly out of control, wildly drugged. Hadn't she eaten something? The glass was below half-full now, so she slowly maneuvered it toward the side table, and placed it there.

Lately, everything was flailing and smashing. She'd been fine on her way upstairs, and before that, in the shower. But she'd lost track of time, listening to the static, and looking through the folio of old pictures. Definitely better to sleep now, shut everything down. She didn't want another night of upheaval.

The television's monochrome noise brightened. The sizzle reminded Noone of radio static, though the effect upon her mind was contrary. Rather than relaxing, the wildly churning visuals ratcheted up her anxiety. Her surroundings felt threatening, as if danger had rushed up and poised nearby. Her hands twitched, and her heart fluttered, weak as a dying bird.

Beyond the bedroom's double doors, something rustled.

Even more than fear, Noone felt anger. She was only trying to relax, to self-reflect and maybe learn to better cope with her problems. Why did everything have to be so difficult?

She tried to stand, wobbled and crashed sidelong across the dresser top. Her shoulder slammed the mirror so hard it cracked, and her head struck the corner of the TV. Dazed, she tried to straighten, to regain her feet. In her disorientation, she almost eased back onto the bed, but decided she had to know what was making that sound. She eased toward the doors, still not trusting her balance, One steadying hand slid along the bed's footboard, and she shuffled her feet until she was near enough to almost lunge toward the closed doors.

The hinge creaked as Noone eased one of the doors open.

Dim light floated up from below, some downstairs lamp left on. Against the dark background of the landing, darker shapes, tar-black outlines of men, drifted up and down the stairs, circulating weightlessly in silent, organized rows. The house moaned as if shifting on its foundation, settling into some newly-changed shape.

Noone's heart thumped painfully. Was she hallucinating, or crazy? She tried to breathe but felt paralyzed, lungs unwilling to expand to intake air. Her entire body resisted movement or action.

One of the black outlines veered from its drifting echelon and flitted toward her, hissing an airy sound.

Wishhhhhh.

Not a human voice, not even distant static, but wind howling at the gap of a window not quite shut.

Noone didn't want this, but couldn't move. How could she possibly just turn back, try to sleep this away? She couldn't hide. A closed door wasn't adequate protection to allow her to pretend this wasn't happening.

Then she remembered a promise she'd just made herself, to face things, no matter how difficult. Anger at her inward timidity overwhelmed any outward fear. She flung the door fully open. Illumination of TV static filled the landing. Dark shapes broke around their edges, became vague, less similar to men. Gaps between the forms widened. Noone was already less certain what she had seen. It was like watching a cloud shaped exactly like something familiar, transformed beyond recognition as individual clouds shifted in the migrant wind. No individuals remained outside, no traces of threat, just wisps of indefinite shadow.

Noone was alone on the empty landing. Her head felt clearer, her body returned to her control. Already she doubted she'd ever really seen shapes, and wondered at the way imagination acted upon emptiness and darkness, conjured solid things out of blind fear. This was always her way, doubting what she knew, questioning all she saw or felt. She refused to run. This house was precisely where she belonged, exactly what she wanted, a place of her own. She could learn to manage obstacles, find ways around them. Even this overwhelming fear had lasted only a moment. It had been broken down by nothing more than an accident of light.

Of course in the morning, everything would be better again.

Before she shut the door and went to be, one thing remained. The desk lamp downstairs remained lit. Noone wanted to turn it off, but still didn't quite trust her coordination, even though she felt better now. What had gone wrong? Too tired, and yes, she admitted, probably too much wine, too many pills. The lamp bothered her, an unfinished matter. She could make it to the rail, then hold on, ease her way down. One foot after another, pausing between steps. Her vision wasn't entirely clear yet, but she could handle this much, if she took it slow.

Carefully she stepped down, gripping the rail. Whenever she started to feel actually afraid, really in trouble, she stepped up to a level of extra care that allowed her to get by. The real problem was the other moments, after caution ended.

One more step, and she was there, the bottom of the stairs. The desk, the lamp.

Something she saw arrested her reach. On the surface of the otherwise empty desk was a tarnished silver key, exactly the same shape as the outline she'd found on the legal pad. The key certainly hadn't been there before.

Noone reached. At the moment her fingertip touched the key, three forceful knocks sounded.

She jumped. Already fully within the grip of fear again, she spun to face the hallway door.

The knocks repeated, not from beside her, but the front door, across the room. Someone had arrived.

22. Arrival. A knock, a door, a visitor.

Without having solidified any intention to move, Noone found herself in motion, skewing diagonally across the living room in the direction of the sound. Her legs weren't exactly under her control, so she veered, and rather than reach the door, she ended up at the right-most window. She was still near enough to reach the door in a few steps, but paused to look out the window. Nothing revealed itself in the tangible darkness outside. No head-lights below. Nobody standing on the porch.

Noone wanted to say something, hoped to trigger some answer which might help clarify the situation. She hesitated, afraid her voice might reveal fear or vulnerability, but she had to speak. "Who's here?"

"Me." A man's voice, familiar and impatient. "It's just me."

Noone sidled away from the window, found the door's outer edge, reached for the knob and gripped it. "You wanted this," she whispered to herself, try-ing to convince herself. Anyone could be out there.

She turned the knob and pulled the door open. Outside was very dark. Ian stood there on the porch, face barely visible. He side-stepped past her, into the house. It occurred to Noone she hadn't managed a clear enough look to be sure it was him. Already he was inside. It was too late to change her plan. Anyway, who else could it be? This was Ian. He was here.

"You really gave me a jolt." Noone's jackhammer pulse began to slow. She tried to convince herself the fear was behind her, now that she knew who had arrived, but her palm was slick on the doorknob as she shut the door.

By the time she turned, Ian had already crossed the room to stand before the desk, where Noone had been at the moment of his knock.

"Ian, what are you doing here?" Noone squinted, eyes straining. She started toward him. "What are you—"

His hand shot to the lamp and clicked it off.

Noone perceived only blackness, no shapes or movement. Where was he? The only trace of light was a tangent of dim glow from the kitchen. This had to be the uncalibrated LED clocks on the stove and microwave, she guessed, barely reaching around the corner into this room.

A shuffle of movement in the hall. Had he stepped closer, or away, toward the stairs?

She held up the old key with fingers so sweat-slick, she thought she might drop it. "Turn on the light, look what I found."

"Let me," he rasped.

Suddenly Ian was much closer, hand extended, palm up. The hand was just an outline, only vaguely connected to a faceless man-shape. It was strange, feeling this direct, immediate threat from Ian. She preferred him this way. At least, part of her did. Noone took a few steps, but stopped short of reaching him. She held the key outstretched, still beyond his grasp. He lunged, snatched away the key, then moved to the old door a few steps away. His broad back concealed his hands, which began to work the key in the lock. She didn't need to see. The click and rattle of loose metal created enough clarity.

"Don't!" Noone's voice quavered. Of course she was afraid. Why had she ever tried to believe she wasn't? "Leave it locked. Let's go home." This suggestion felt worse than surrender, more like giving up completely, but despite any dejection at failing to take a stand in her marriage, the prospect of a return to safety seemed enticing now. Better to endure the trickle of low-level misery than remain locked in the grasp of panic, in the face of this outsized unknown.

The lock made a solid click, the key turned, and the door swung open. Old hinges creaked. Fragments of rust cracked loose and fluttered to the floor, making minuscule ticking sounds like grains of sand on wood. His shape slipped past the threshold and stepped down. He disappeared.

"Ian?" Noone saw nothing, could find no solid point of external reference. She felt herself spin, as if whirling in a tire swing on a long rope. Her stomach heaved. It would be better to see, even to be faced with something terrible. So much better than imagining.

She remembered the desk lamp. Her hand groped beside her and found the switch. The rebirth of that dull orange glow changed her immediate sphere, but barely seemed to affect what lay beyond the doorway. Only the topmost descending stairs stood revealed. Worn steps of plain wood faded down into black. Everything Noone could see, she could deal with. Whatever came, she would force herself to face. No more looking away. No more hiding.

"Iii-aaan!" Noone's cry extended, and trailed into raggedness until her voice cut off, broken by a fit of hyperventilation. Gasping in panic, she leaned back against the wall, trying to stay calm, then let herself slide to the floor. Had it been long enough for another pill? She squeezed eyes shut, covered them with unsteady hands. "He'll be back," she moaned. Why didn't he at least say something, let her know he was okay? She tried to hold her breath.

Noone, stop. She lowered her hands, but didn't open her eyes. Her arms dangled so her fingertips brushed the floor. The boards felt rough, not the smooth, gleaming hardwoods she recalled. A memory returned, one of the stories Ian had told about coming here as a kid. The ragged, splintered floorboards always snagged their socks and left slivers in their feet.

She breathed.

Imagination was her real enemy. Especially when she was alone, it only made things worse, constantly wondering what might have just disintegrated, or come into existence the very moment she looked away. It was better to see than to wonder, she kept telling herself this, repeated it so many times, but the idea always passed through her, immaterial as a nagging ghost. This time, Noone needed to listen. She had to learn what was below, if she ever wanted to understand this place. This was her home. If anybody should be exploring, she should.

Fingertips stroked the floorboards, feeling for the texture. The floor was smoothly polished, even glossy, exactly the way she remembered it looking from the moment she'd arrived. Exactly as she wanted it to be.

23. Downstairs. Unmeasurable unknown, and answers to questions.

The perfect smoothness of the bamboo floor was reassuring. Nothing had really changed.

Noone stood, opened her eyes, and before she allowed herself time to venture again toward apprehension, she turned. The door remained open right beside her, where it had been all along. A half-step took her to the edge of the stairs down. She reached, found the rail and gripped it. With a last reminder to breathe deep and slow, she ventured that first step. Weak light from the desk lamp behind her already dwindled. Darkness below was a pool of ink.

Another step. Her foot probed below, then her weight settled. Again, and again.

Down and to the left, around an invisible corner, a tiny light flickered like a wind-blown candle. This small presence encouraged her. A few more steps brought Noone to a landing, from which stairs angled left. The next step in this new direction creaked under her weight.

She saw him below, huddled near the candle, searching a shelf of books. He seemed to notice her sound, but didn't turn.

Though Noone couldn't yet see enough to understand what was happening, she felt relieved. This was something, at least. She reached the bottom, a floor of stone or concrete, and paused until she was able to make herself speak.

"What did you find?"

He turned, though his face remained shadowed, impossible to read. His hands held an offering, an open book, as if he wanted her to look within.

Rather than the book, she noticed his hands. They were nothing she recognized, skin dry and rough, unlike Ian's. This man was nobody she'd ever known. With this realization, Noone admitted that she'd always perceived him as a stranger, and only pretended to imagine familiarity.

"Old stories." His rough voice, a hacksaw on metal. "All about every life that ever brushed against yours, or mine."

Noone bit her lip hard, hoping pain might shock her back to clarity. Her eyes kept closing, as if she were terribly tired, yet her mind was brilliantly awake. She wanted to run away, but forced herself to remain and to watch. "You tell me the stories." Blood flowed, salt and iron slick on her tongue.

Without hesitation, he spoke as if reading, though he still held out the book as if for her to read. "A weak and insecure husband, whose ego manifests in cruelty." The man gestured with the book, beckoning her nearer. "His heart all coldness and spite, disguised by soft hands, gentle manners and superficial care-taking."

Motionless before her eyes, words steady enough to read, yet she refused. The candle yielded enough light, now that her eyes had adjusted. She knew she could easily accept what he offered, in fact to avoid seeing the plain words required an effort of will.

He shrugged, seeming tired of waiting, and flipped pages. "Here, a story of Noone's avoided child. Never solid enough to be person, only a ghost of the flesh or a might-have-been, shrugged loose before she ever grew in."

Noone gasped, wanted to shrink and hide, but remembered what she'd promised. She remained.

"This unspoken name could have become a woman," he continued. "Not here, but only in another life, one you never let yourself to make real, or even try."

The candle hissed, sputtered. Light fled, replaced by eye-burning smoke.

His voice continued, disconnected from any shape. Without his familiar profile, which had suggested identity, the voice now seemed nothing at all like Ian's. "Chapters of faithlessness, and all the many lies that flowed downstream. The neighbor Ian fucked while Noone was pregnant. The woman he swore he'd finished with, said the woman had moved to Seattle. Noone believed, but look in these pages. Or later, the time Ian came home to tell

Noone about the photocopier saleswoman he planned to run off with, only to return in the morning and insist Noone had only misunderstood, that Ian had never planned to leave." He paused, cleared his throat. "See how many more pages?"

Noone couldn't see anything at all. Couldn't he tell? All she could do was listen, choose to believe or not believe, or possibly forget. None of these stories were unfamiliar. Only some details were new, but to hear certain aspects spoken aloud was shocking. She felt the man's angled scrutiny, a trait she recognized, like his smell. This sense blended the long-term familiarity of Ian's characteristics with more a more recent introduction. A smell redolent of intimacy, the recollection of which brought her to heightened sensitivity. That mingling of flesh, one with another, seizing pleasure both surface and internal.

Something she hadn't guessed before, she now realized might be possible. "Jodah? Are you Jodah?"

She assumed that to ask would be enough, that he would reveal himself one way or another, but he said nothing. Her certainty faltered.

"What is this place?" Noone's voice cracked to reveal a remnant of fear still active. "Can you explain…" Eyes adjusted, fed by feeble strands of sourceless light, something new. His scent faded. Certain she was alone again, Noone left that place beside the standing desk, flanked by tall library shelves near the base of the stairs. She ventured away, into the dark, arms outstretched, hoping for what she was unable to see. The time for exploration had come.

Openness became aisles and hallways, which diverged at angles which could be measured. Velvet drop-cloths lifted to reveal broken mirrors. The atmosphere vibrated with the smell of ferment, centuries old. A cobwebbed ring of ancient keys hung on a spike crusted with blood. Lanterns burdened by the dust and grease of age. Beyond such familiar artifacts, she found mechanisms barely recognized, connected to corners, bolted to the ground underfoot, and extending to the ceiling, attached by hinged brackets. Here also were tools of measurement, made for obscure increments. Copper surveyor's sights, tripods of stained oak, and white chalked plumb lines. Alembics resembling glass bird heads on patinaed copper stands, some seething with the remnants of subtle, pale flames made by absent alchemists, whose own eyes burned their own shelves of books, in pursuit of the timeless chemistry of power, of life without end, and insight without end.

"Can I stay here?" Noone asked, aware no answer would come. Nobody was near.

Overhead, unseen timbers creaked, gears ticked, and delicately arranged machine components made subtle adjustments to the rust-seized geometries underpinning the house. So much more remained buried, and would always remain hidden from sight, no matter how long she searched.

24. Ascent. Return to the surface, with knowledge.

The strongest impulse Noone had ever felt was this need to explore. She was driven by the hope of discovering some transformative impetus, though she was also aware there could be no hope of gaining solace without an equal measure of anguish. To find meaningful connection would require first a penance of solitude. Even the best outcome would mean to wade through a river of pain, hoping to emerge transformed. What if this suffering were beyond her capacity to process and absorb? The prospect of successful emergence seemed unlikely, too distant.

Noone turned back, retraced her steps, delved down paths that seemed vaguely familiar.

After a long, solitary walk through quiet darkness, she rediscovered the flickering candle. That small fire was burning again, or had never really died. The flame was low, but offered light sufficient to convince Noone that she stood again in the same place as before, near library shelves of books and the high counter at which the man had stood flipping pages. He'd revealed part of her story, and what had that helped? Whatever book he'd discovered must now be replaced, too similar to all the rest for Noone to discern which one it had been. For the first time, she saw the existence of far more books than fit on the shelves. Tall stacks teetered on the ground, and on the surface of a broad work table behind. Noone recognized this scene.

What she really wanted was time of her own.

"You can't make me leave!" Noone shouted, for whoever might hear. Ian, Jodah, she didn't care. Anyone.

No response came.

She searched memory, retraced her life's progression in reverse, past milestones like the loss of ideals, the death of love and breakdown of marriage, and that invisible tipping point beyond which more life lay behind than ahead. All such markers were in the rear view, if they had ever truly existed as discrete, identifiable moments. Such events in her life had been so poorly marked, she'd never recognized them in passing, and now the woman she'd become was too far removed from the concept she imagined herself to be. Noone Raddox was a stranger, a realization which set her adrift, not only detached from any fixed base, but also free from restraint or responsibility. To acknowledge this gap within her was actualization, not betrayal of self. The important thing now was to reconnect, to merge the person she saw in the mirror with the body she carried around, and her internal concept of what she was meant to become. Future must connect to past, or future died in obsolescence.

Noone scanned the shelves and stacks. It was all too much, the stories too painful to retain in mind, too numerous to stow, the dismal betrayals too bitter to swallow and digest. All that was left was to walk away. She turned, faced the stairs, and started up. What she should hope to find above was uncertain, though she knew there would be no trace of Ian's presence. No silver Maybach sedan parked outside, no other visitor's car. To remain in solitude was the best she could hope for. What alternatives existed?

She could return to Portland, ignore Ian's expectations, disregard his demands, fully aware of the limit to how long this would be tolerated.

She could file for divorce, move to their Mt. Hood condo, and start her own decorating business. Winters on the mountain would be snowbound, and what clientele could she possibly hope to gain in such a small town? Once, she and Ian had hoped to retire there, but when had they last even visited?

Prospects for business would be better in Portland, but how would that work? Any hope of taking advantage of existing contacts would mean remaining in proximity to Ian through their common friends. Another dead-end. Her aspirations still twitched as if living, yet she could envision no path to all she required. Decades of secure marriage, which Noone had always tried to believe offered stability and comfort, really only held her back, stifled her spirit, and sanded off the rough edges of character which might have allowed her to become something.

Summarized this way, these limits clarified the reasons Noone had remained so long with Ian, despite feeling constantly starved, aching every moment with disappointment and sadness and the pang of undefinable loss.

Ian was welcome to what remained of their Portland life. What had she left of any value? Nothing.

All she needed was here. Nearing the top of the stairs, Noone envisioned the broader world, far from here, eradicated in a clamor of noise and static. Clouds blotted sun, except here. Only this house would survive.

She reached the hallway, where the desk lamp remained lit, dimmed almost to nothing, as if its fuel had burned away like the candle in the basement. The floor creaked beneath her feet. She flicked off the light, no longer worried what might reside alongside her in the dark. The only remaining fear was that she might see clearly now, without the filter of denial, the disintegration that had always resided beneath the skin of everything, including herself. If she were to close her eyes, her fingers would feel the true, degraded roughness and decay, the age beneath the appealing facade of deception. Every person and thing looked best from one angle, or in a specific light, as compared to the many other truer possibilities. Noone hoped never again to stumble into that point of view from which all appearances cracked, and perfection dissolved.

So many pleasures dwelled here, waiting to be discovered. Diverse luxuries, abundant beauties and delights which increased in count and variety faster than she could consciously invent newer objects to desire. This was enough to offset her fear of what whispers might come in the night. Those voices had always derived from within herself, not only here, but always. Shades flitting in the dark were welcome to sing her to sleep, with their hissing, static breath. Each morning, she would find a world made bright again, redesigned and expansive.

In this dark hallway, Noone could not see the ground beneath her feet, but knew she must have tracked in a black dust from the basement. The dead powder of ancient wood, fine metal grindings from the disintegrating undercarriage, and the grease of subtle mechanisms, all slowly rattling toward decrepitude. This place would outlive her. That was enough.

When she woke in the morning, she would wipe away these last, dirty traces. After that, she would have no need for the basement, or anything outside this part of the house which was under her control.

Noone pulled the door shut and locked it. The key vanished from her hand, as if it had never existed. She walked toward the kitchen and did not need to look back, already certain the door too had disappeared.

ENDURE WITHIN
A DYING FRAME

Mazlo sat invisible in the dark window at the front of the old farmhouse, watching, waiting for her to come. The driveway, likewise dark, was no more than twin dirt tracks through acres of overgrown weeds and dying grass. No street lamps, no glow of civilization, because there were no streets, no neighborhoods anywhere near. Within this neglected estate, just a few ancient oaks survived, gnarled branches pointing in contradictory angles.

Despite the true darkness, the front of his home seemed illuminated by Mazlo's intensely focused anticipation, which increased the instant her headlights approached. As she parked, Mazlo swallowed a pang of shame at his ragged, disintegrating home. Gray boards warped and split, leaving gaps penetrated by wind and weather. The construction no longer carried the strict, linear geometry by which it had been built. All now bent with the entropy of age, sagging and misaligned.

The car door slammed shut. Front steps creaked.

Mazlo peered out, knowing she couldn't perceive him through the glass. From out of obscurity into the brightness of his expectation, a woman ascended toward the dimly lit porch. Long black wool coat, red-auburn hair tied under a scarf. The sight triggered in Mazlo something like recognition, though all he knew of this woman was the description offered him by the service. Her arrival birthed a complex of desires, mostly reflexive echoes he'd felt repeatedly over decades. The ache of regret. A lustful and impatient hunger for insights he hoped she might deliver. Tangled memories of previous women who had arrived and departed in sequence. Mazlo did not distinguish. All he possessed was this place, and his hoped-for future. His heart thudded. Beyond anxiousness, a reaction more like panic. It rose in him again, the sickening blend of regret and wanting. To desire with such intensity felt desperate, even painful.

Fear, too. Fear for himself. Mostly for her.

Mazlo had asked the agency to send a woman of a type similar to Sandra, whom he'd described in terms of height, build, hair color and age. Sandra had been latest. Such approximate familiarity, even mere similarity in superficial details, sometimes allowed him to derive more from first encounters. A good start was key, picking up where he'd left off, one companion leading to the next, no backtracking to repeat ground already covered. He needed to overlook the jarring aspects of transition, to conceive of them not as distinct persons, but chapters in one book.

Awaiting the knock, Mazlo froze. He didn't want to startle her by opening prematurely. No ring came. Seconds ticked away. Had she become afraid, somehow retreated unseen in the dark? Certainly her car hadn't moved, but it had been too long. He leaned, squinted out the window.

Knock, knock.

Mazlo jumped. Tension flickered in his chest. Soon a new face, a different name. She was here.

Another knock.

What could he hope for? He told himself, as always at these times, she might be the last. One to bear him the rest of the way. If she couldn't be his final companion, at least she might deliver him nearer what he sought. How close? Impossible to guess. Not even Mazlo's unique knowledge could measure infinity with precision.

A thrill surged. That anxious jitter in his gut, a wild flutter of interior muscles. Trickle of sweat beneath his suit. Mazlo composed himself, switched on the brighter second porch light, and creaked open the front door.

The woman squinted into the sudden light. "I thought you weren't home.

Everything here is so dark."

Thin and pretty, about thirty-five, with green eyes and prominent Hepburn cheekbones. Just as described.

Mazlo flicked off both switches and gestured her inside. "I find it unsettling, too much of the wrong light." He held out a hand to accept her coat. "Miss Lenora."

She pulled off the scarf first, metallic green fabric patterned with tiny silver stars. Hair released from confinement expanded, took on new shape. "Just Lenora." A scarlet smile brightened her face.

Always hungry to seek order within patterns, Mazlo's eyes followed the scarf, tried to count the stars and arrange them, even as Lenora put it in her pocket. Never mind, he thought. Their alignment probably lacked significance. Likely random, like most everything.

The corners of Lenora's eyes crinkled as she pulled off her coat. Some fragrance reached him. Was the scent actually present in the room, or another echo of stagnant memory? Mazlo took her coat, and his other hand reached to touch Lenora's arm, skin newly bare in the sleeveless dress. He stopped, hesitant. She offered an accepting look, acquiescence implicit with a lift of her chin. He touched her. The warm skin of a woman. How long? At least since the last month before Sandra's departure. She'd changed by the end. Become something else entirely.

"You have so much privacy," Lenora said. "Far from everything."

As if noticing his surroundings for the first time, Mazlo looked around. "I never think about this place, almost don't perceive it at all. But unfortunately the tangible still envelops and binds me, against my will."

Mazlo removed the jacket of his suit, a very specific and rare herringbone. Seen close up, black and white shapes interlocked into a simple repetition, while from a few feet distance, the pattern resolved to a dazzlingly shimmery silver moire. The fabric possessed both qualities at once, depending upon perspective. Beneath the jacket, Mazlo wore a black dress shirt, buttoned all the way to the collar, without a necktie.

"I'm so pleased, seeing you in a suit for my visit, Mister..." Lenora waited.

"Mazlo."

"Is that a first or last name?" she asked.

Mazlo had the impression she already knew, just a suggestion of confidence in the angle from which she regarded him. He smiled, took one step toward the hallway, and stopped to have another look at her. A lone candle on the bookshelf glowed. The two of them, a man and woman standing together close, encompassed for that moment within a gently luminous sphere, like a pair of fireside storytellers huddled for comfort against encroaching dark.

Like the living room, Mazlo's bedroom was lit by a single handmade candle, red and scented of copal, a resin incense imported from South America.

Mazlo indicated the bench at the bed's footboard. "Mind that sharp corner."

The room's unadorned, bachelor's quality belied the near-constant presence of women, one after another, over a quarter century. But within the first week or two after their arrival, each of these women become too distracted to care about decor. Mazlo himself was interested in pursuing a philosophy of numbers, all the lofty possibilities that implied. Why bother decorating a world so mundane, and soon to be left behind?

"Tell me about yourself, Mr. Mazlo," Lenora asked. "What do you want me to know about you?"

Mazlo considered. It was the first time he'd been asked this way. Not what she wanted to know, but what he desired her to know. "I'm a mathematician. Retired."

Lenora looked impressed. "So young for retirement."

Mazlo was forty-nine, knew he looked older. "I'm still interested in theory, but can no longer tolerate the university, the social aspect. My focus was hypothetical geometry. Ordered symmetry."

"Symmetry. I know what that is." Lenora's eyes lowered, then lifted again. She made a self-deprecating face. "Probably it means something different than what I think it means."

Mazlo shook his head. "No, tenth-dimensional symmetry shares qualities with any 2D symmetry you might sketch on scratch paper." He gestured at a geometric ink drawing which hung framed on the wall. "Even difficult spacial isometries can be reduced to points, lines, triangles."

"I know better than to ask about a man's income, but I wonder how a mathematician survives out here, alone in a country farmhouse."

"Isolation is beautiful," Mazlo observed. "Isolation is poisonous."

Lenora kept watching, didn't look away.

"I don't have to work," he continued. "I won a prize once. A major prize. When I was young."

"You're still a young man. It can't have been so long ago."

"Winners of this prize are always too ridiculously young to handle the award. Can you imagine, a prize sufficiently grand that recipients find their lives destroyed by twenty-five?"

"Sometimes you get sugar and poison together, the very same pill." Lenora smiled pleasantly, as if she perceived no contradiction in this. "How did you win?"

"For insights relating to branching systems. Specifically, for formulating predictions in unfolding fractal patterns via modeling prevalence of hierarchical complexities."

Lenora whistled a single, descending tone.

"The key was predicting upstream causation via granular retro-convergence," Mazlo said. "I imagine that sounds like nonsense."

"Not nonsense, exactly. More like it might drive you crazy, if you let yourself think on it too long."

Mazlo considered unbuttoning his shirt's top button. "Certainly did the trick for me."

"Branching patterns, like rivers and streams?" Lenora sat down on the edge of the bed. "Or veins and capillaries? It doesn't seem like branching things would be symmetrical."

Surprised, Mazlo laughed and clapped his hands. Even the mathematically naive sometimes offered fine insights into deep matters. "A good instinct. I like you already, Miss Lenora."

"It's much better if we like each other."

Mazlo draped Lenora's coat and his own jacket across an armchair in the corner, then sat on the sharp-cornered bench to remove his shoes. "I'll lie on my side. You'll please recline here." He indicated the side of the bed nearer the door. That bedside table was empty.

She reached behind herself, started unzipping her dress.

Surprised, Mazlo raised a hand. "I should have explained. You don't have to—"

"I understand, sweetie. A man's wife leaves, he's lonely." Half out of her open dress, she leaned back on one elbow. "I can figure out what you need without you having to tell me."

She found his hand where it rested on his knee. Her fingertips traced delicate arcs on his skin. In a room so nearly lightless, she was only an outline, a vague suggestion of human form. Her touch could be anyone's.

Mazlo withdrew his hand. "Sandra was never my wife." Still fully dressed, having removed only jacket and shoes, he settled back atop the covers and gestured to indicate she should do the same. "It only takes a few seconds of quiet. Be still."

Lenora smiled gamely and lay back. After a moment she looked toward him, expectant and playful.

Mazlo was impatient, hungry. It had been so long. The thousandth time. "Please lie motionless," he whispered.

Mazlo held himself still. Lenora reclined fully, gazing at the ceiling. Gradually her limbs went slack and her slow breathing made the only sound, Mazlo having taught himself to breathe in silence. In that frozen interval, Mazlo glimpsed a flash through time, a flicker of memory like an image projected onscreen, extinguished before it could be savored.

His marriage, in the time before awareness had come, the only time he'd shared his life in any lasting sense. Even as he'd possessed her, Mazlo recalled wanting more. Something grander, more distant.

Mazlo snapped back to the present as a gap opened in the air above them, a luminous slit wavering in darkness. From this unfolded a cloud, spinning particles gently glowing like silver dust. This light was subtle, not enough to read by. Lenora seemed unsure what she was seeing, but to Mazlo it was unmistakable, familiar as a loved one's face. The rift opened, a knife wound in space, a small, silent fireworks spilling into the room from a distant time and place.

"Here she is." Mazlo lifted one hand, moved it in a gesture like conducting music. The particles swirled around his fingers without touching his skin, like metal shavings vibrating in proximity to a magnet. He lowered toward

Lenora's neck, stopped just short of contact where collarbones met at her vulnerable throat. The light, as if understanding and intelligently following his intentions, drifted onto her. Though the particles had maintained a gap of separation from Mazlo's skin even as they were led by his movement, they immediately clung to Lenora. Their brightness moved quickly, cast light over her face, spreading down her neck and chest to encompass her entire body.

So quickly, Lenora became entangled.

The body-shaped aura only imperfectly fit the solid woman within, as if wavering undecided between her actual shape, and the slightly different forms of other bodies no longer present.

Lenora gasped.

"Don't be afraid," Mazlo said. "I'm sorry I couldn't tell you what to expect. How she'd make you feel."

"She?" Lenora trembled minutely, then her whole body spasmed. Her eyes darted.

Mazlo thought she might shriek, bolt for the door. At this stage, many fled. But if she remained still, accepted the sensation a few seconds more, she would recognize that pain was no part of this. Mazlo wouldn't need to explain. Her natural unease would give way, replaced by a hunger for more.

Lenora's tremors lessened. She sat up halfway and eyed the door, as if openly contemplating escape.

"Will you lie back?" Mazlo whispered, trying to soothe with breathy words. "Her outline is nothing tangible, it can't harm you." He slid away, careful no part of himself should accidentally touch her.

Lenora's expression softened, wide-eyed and wondering. Watching her own hand, she raised it slowly, as if sudden movement might disturb the phantom aura. Her mouth hung open. "What is this?"

Mazlo wanted to tell her of equations, of calculations perfected in cracked midnights, decades ago. He said nothing, only savored the knowledge of coming transformations.

Like a projection sharpening into focus upon a screen, the apparition resolved, became more coherent. Lenora's chest rose and fell in a breathing rhythm slightly offset from the movement of the aura, until the two synchronized. Lenora arched her back in response to some unseen stimulus. It was happening. Vast distances were narrowing.

Again Mazlo found himself doubting the very thoughts that appeared within his mind, wondering if they truly arose from him, or were imposed from elsewhere. What if all his beliefs and desires were being fed to him? Even now, he no longer really believed the presence to be some kind of female spirit, as he once had. The mind was so stubborn, even when it knew better.

The very air seemed charged with an alien electricity. Objects in the room were spaced at very precise intervals, measurements knowable, angles perfectly incremented and arranged. Every measurement adhered to the symmetric principles Mazlo himself had calculated in isolation, in those long-ago years just after the prize. At this moment, the ancient house felt newly made, the atmosphere not stale with dust and rot, but alive with the hum of possibility. Dull surfaces were beautiful once again. Even the twin specters of aging and death could be ignored. Mazlo didn't care whether such perceptions indicated slippage within his mind. He didn't want to return to the outer world, cared nothing for the scrutiny or judgments of dim people. Life had been nothing but an extended exercise in auto-explication of truths incomprehensible to any mind but his own. For this he'd been first rewarded, then shunned.

Even if others could be taught to perceive, if they could peer alongside him into the infinitely vast dimensions of that sublime place beyond, they couldn't possibly grasp what meaning it held.

Mazlo caught himself drifting, drawn bodily nearer Lenora. Again he forced himself away, toward the edge of the bed. He'd learned he might accidentally reach out in his excitement. Touch her too soon.

Eyes lightly closed, Lenora shook her head and moaned, slow and deep. Her tongue swirled within her mouth, as if savoring some potent liquor. Another long moan trailed off into hitching, gasping breaths, then she laughed in delight. Her eyes flicked open and she looked around, as if caught in some embarrassing public act.

"Is that me, those sounds?" Lenora giggled and shifted a hand to cover an abashed grin. "I'm sorry, I—" Some further distraction interrupted. Her eyes rolled back, her neck lolled, sweat trickling down her skin.

Urgency increased within Mazlo. He wanted to press forward, had to restrain himself. Stay calm, patient. Lenora felt familiar, but this was new to her. She wasn't ready to continue where Sandra had left off.

"Don't apologize," Mazlo said. "Tell me everything you're feeling, no matter how intimate. Sensations on the surface of you, or inside."

"Hmmm…" Lenora writhed and her body shifted within the open dress. Another moan built, resonant in her chest, and grew louder as her mouth fell open again. "I'm reaching toward you." Her lips formed the words, but the voice sounded not at all like her own.

"You can come through," Mazlo urged. "This is the one."

"Last barriers." Lenora looked side to side, eyes focusing on nothing. "Almost cracked. So near."

"This way." He reached, unthinking, almost touched. He caught himself, jerked away his hand.

"Tell me how to find you," she huffed.

"I don't know how. You have to—"

"Your name. A beacon."

Mazlo too breathed faster, compelled by the quickening rhythm. Unable to help himself, he leaned in, hovered close. He savored the tingle of proximity to Lenora's sweat-drenched skin. Nerves cried out for touch. Terrible to be so near, yet remain apart.

"I can't," he cried. "Tell me how!"

Though driven by a sickening intensity, he remained mindful enough to fight the urge to overreach. This stage was delicate, not a time for passionate clutching, or easy release. Remain focused, eyes open, receptive. Breathe slowly, not too intense. Listen and learn.

As Lenora flailed, the bed rocked beneath them. Mazlo leaned, too eager, shifted close. His touch penetrated the glow, brushed Lenora's arm, slippery with sweat. Immediately his palm felt the sizzle of contact.

At once she stilled, quieted. The light dimmed.

"Wait," Mazlo gasped, breathing hard. "Not yet."

The colors comprising the light died away, chromatic layers diminishing one at a time until the last of the unearthly implication had drained out of the room. Mazlo tried to remember, to grasp hold of that sense of meaning, but already it seemed alien. He closed his eyes, pressed knuckles into his eyelids, desperate for an afterimage. Any flash of color, a prismatic spark. A hint of new realms.

The room was merely dark again, indistinct from all the bland, colorless rooms of the world.

Lenora's breathing slowed. Her hair, darkened with dampness, stuck to her forehead and neck. Sweat soaked her dress. "I saw..." She sighed, slumped in exhaustion. "For a minute, I understood everything."

Mazlo fought the urge to try again, to compel her to push on. The risk was too great to disregard. Already once tonight his eagerness had ended things prematurely. Sometimes his objective seemed near enough to grasp. He had to remember patience. This plan had evolved through decades. Sketched diagrams, maps for a new universe. Once the way was clarified, convoluted structures could finally be grasped, the system proven by equations first glimpsed in amphetamine-fueled waking dreams.

It was the same for Mazlo as for the women. As soon as he'd become aware of his desire, the impulse had already been too great to ignore.

For tonight, the resumption of pursuit would have to suffice. A single step. Lenora could only bear so much. Her body, mind. The force of Mazlo's need wasn't sufficient to carry her through.

Mazlo and Lenora rested together, breathing, clarifying impressions of what had transpired. He wondered how her interpretation might differ from his own. Although the glow had vanished, a coppery tingle remained in his nostrils, like ozone after a lightning strike.

Lenora's eyes evaded his. Had she already begun to change? Her skin appeared still vital and smooth, barely freckled at the cheekbones. He wanted to reach out, touch her again. He searched her eyes for signs of distress, failure to process what had happened, and found only the flush of pleasure's aftermath. She would be unable to resist, but a small, weak part of Mazlo feared she might leave and not return.

Lenora sat up, straightened, reached to zip her dress. "It's a little hard to understand."

Hearing her uncertainty, he felt in control again. "Profound truths are never transparent at first glance."

At this her eyes narrowed, as if in defensiveness. "I might have a better idea than you think. What happened, I mean."

Mazlo ignored his urge to explain her error. Better to hear what she believed. "Really? What?" He leaned forward, hoping to appear not skeptical but receptive.

The corner of her mouth lifted. "I've always been interested in metaphysics. My uncle was a spiritist, used to include us in his shows. Lanny, my cousin, told me it was never really ghosts in those seances. Not fake, but not ghosts either, not spirits. Something else. Something not from here."

Maybe she possessed a small insight or two, understood that what many called ghosts or spirits had never been human, nothing so local as that. But there remained so much she couldn't possibly know. Mazlo battled the impulse to inform, to build upon her small understanding, explain the rest. He couldn't, yet. He needed to be certain he possessed her. Let her leave and return, drawn by her own desire. This would make her willing to test her own capabilities. How much stamina in such a slight body?

"Many are afraid, driven off by it." Mazlo didn't mention what happened to those who weren't driven away. The ones who stayed.

"You don't really believe it's some woman's spirit," Lenora said.

Again Mazlo restrained himself. So often he couldn't say the words that came to mind.

"You know it's no human thing," Lenora added. "Not from here."

Mazlo was surprised, but more than that, felt possessive of this world of his. Her presumption surprised him, made him want to lash out. She couldn't possibly have gained such a quick understanding of what had entered the room, where it had come from. He calmed himself before he spoke. "What do you think it is?"

Lenora looked at him straight on. "Something formless, without a name." Then she looked away. "Cold, and so distant. It barely realizes what we are."

"Maybe," Mazlo mused. "Anyway, we're finished. That's all for tonight."

She stood, straightened her dress, and started toward the hallway. She turned back, smiled as if embarrassed at the circumstances, and looked at the floor. "That was… everything you wanted?"

Mazlo conceived of ever-growing complexities, invisible and convoluted matrix sets. Distant, that much was true. Intangible, but knowable. Some day.

He nodded. "Yes."

Lenora retrieved her coat from the corner, started out and again stopped. She seemed reluctant to leave.

Mazlo stood. He hated to let her go, but knew her return must be volitional. The only way. Experience told him Lenora remained unaware what had been taken from her. She might feel an intangible absence, impossible to name. Even the most essential, intrinsic aspects of a person were insubstantial enough, they might not immediately be missed. Just such an ephemerality ruled Mazlo's every waking thought. A thief had left behind something else, a placeholder for what had been stolen. A sliver of tomorrow, to offset a trace of yesterday. Anyway, what was the point in hoarding all this life, this pettiness and mundane striving? Better instead to gamble on the chance to glimpse the numinous.

Lenora went out to the living room and stopped just inside the front door. Mazlo leaned close enough to smell whatever perfume scented her, mixed with the pleasing earthiness of drying sweat and lingering hint of ozone. Better than a kiss. Lenora pulled on her overcoat and Mazlo handed her an amount of cash. The agreed fee, plus a generous tip. She began to refuse, trying to articulate something. Couldn't possibly, after how things… He insisted.

Mazlo knew, she would never forget, would revisit obsessively those minutes, would return not for him but desperate for another straining connection, a stimulus utilizing every nerve.

"Goodbye." She went out into the indifferent cold.

Mazlo wanted to call after, tell her she might as well stay. He closed the door.

This plan, he'd worked so long toward understanding. So many years. Now that he'd brought Lenora in, made her part of it, he hoped she might endure. That was the precise word: hope. Through all Mazlo's despair, he'd always kept hoping. Moments of sharpest pain, deepest anguish, those were the very moments hope seemed most important, most keenly possibly if momentarily out of reach.

The important thing to recognize was that the past was hopeless. Had always been. Would always be.

There was only the future.

Mazlo had felt himself driven to extremes, every day, compelled toward things he otherwise couldn't have imagined. Where were such impulses born? Certainly not within. He believed there existed some free-ranging waves of energy or force invisibly permeating the universe, like gravity and the illusion of time, giving shape to thoughts, influencing the human mind to considering undertaking the otherwise unthinkable.

Why not? If only.

At these extremes of abject weakness, the mind became most susceptible to this influence. Driven to desperation, trembling in feverish wanting. Rationalizing that somehow, hope would prevail.

Mazlo tried telling himself the future had already been designed, built of shapes cut from ancient patterns. He had only to find his place. Vivid, eternal dreams awaited. A blossom dripping honey to the tongue. Tastes surging like electric shock. Unearthly scents, carriers of arcane secrets encoded in beguiling patterns, like occult songs. An ecstatic surging of blood. The coming of pleasure. A clenching fury.

Waiting, hoping for a brush with godhead.

"You'll return," Mazlo whispered. "I'll welcome you."

He was alone again. Ever closer.

Alone, all perspective retreated. Mazlo suffered in fear, despair and uncertainty, despite the previously certain knowledge of what he must soon attain. The certainty of her return, proven by many past repetitions, did nothing to prevent a persistent ache in his gut, urgent as a burst appendix. His desire for Lenora, or what she might convey to him, retreated into the distance, a barely-recalled vision already fading.

Why this lack of hope? Such fear, every time he became alone. Why couldn't he remember this was only desperation, fear of solitude? Of course she would return.

What if she didn't? What if Lenora was gone forever, and nobody would ever replace her?

Mazlo imagined the fear he experienced was far greater than most people. Probably it arose from guilt. He didn't deserve a lofty future, or anyone to share it with him, not when all the damage was taken into account. The truths he'd learned had value, but at what price?

All truths derived from the primary cause. From the fundamental, all else emerged.

Once, a younger Mazlo had determined mathematics to be a dead end, and instead sought truths within the written word. Religion, philosophy, the occult, endeavors directly aimed at enabling a personal experience of the cosmic. These offered insights, amplified by psychedelic drugs, which clarified that nothing important was happening *HERE* or *NOW*, not when compared to the cosmic scale. Profound distances, deep time. What connection did *TODAY* have to ancient history, or the distant future?

As to the cyclical and connected nature of all things, Mazlo had sought explication, but found philosophers, magickians and theologians gave only hints.

Mathematics had always drawn him back. It covered the full spectrum of possibilities.

Plane reduced to line, line to point. Quanta vibrant with intent conveyed infinite possibility.

The strange actions of baryons disproved false notions like distance and proximity. Mazlo was neither physicist nor astronomer, but could see even that was connected. Vast helical galaxies, subatomic microuniverses, all forms of arrayed information. Confusion spun toward toward clarification faster than light, birth and death on a collision course, ending and beginning, a cycle of repetition faster and faster throughout the infinite history of this universe and all those prior.

Fear of death, hunger for pleasure. By these words, timeless beings spoke from far realms, into ours. This way, everything could be understood.

From a university, to a prize granted. Finally, to this house, which had once seemed appropriately humble and non-distracting. Now it seemed to be gruesomely dying, flesh disintegrating, falling off its bones. But this place was a hub, had been granted significance by the towering structure of Mazlo's cumulative knowledge.

Yet he was only a man, made of flesh. A home made of wood, failing.

Mazlo snapped back to his room, eyes aching at the window, seeking Lenora in the vacant dark. Would she return? His mind spun. Fractal geometry, branching principles. What did those mean? One woman, but… Every individual resembled all others. One, same as many. Natural laws derived from the ontological first mover. All accounts were to be settled, the end would become a new beginning.

On one extreme, infinite expansion worked in ceaseless opposition to entropy. On the opposing side were the insistent illusion of linear time, and the dull finitude of human existence. The sublime, the terrible.

Mazlo counted on the possibility of leaving behind these aspects he despised. That was the only way he could convince himself to go on. Lenora could carry him closer. Maybe she would be the last. He hoped, but he'd hoped before. Most died never knowing, never having glimpsed even the first hint. Spirals, recursion, the golden section, Fibonacci numbers, secret primes. All men and women were numbers arrayed in space, a recipe for multiverses. The language of children conveyed seeds of prior knowledge, lingering hints, genetic memories of prior realms, to which we might return.

Lenora's desire must be unimaginable. Much as he ached, her suffering must be worse. She must be dying to return. Dying. He laughed.

How had he survived two months after Sandra left? Those weeks had passed in delirium of sleep and fevered dreams. Now, a single night alone left him tormented. He drew curtains against daylight, leaned close against the fireplace until the heat obliterated the unbearable chill.

Still he waited, rocking in the dark room. A voice within spoke of guilt, self-recrimination. How many had he allowed to disintegrate?

"Everyone disappears," Mazlo explained.

So many consumed, devoured by his selfish needs.

"They had desires, too. Autonomy."

No one was listening. Only himself.

This was the cost of isolation, remoteness from humanity's coursing. A dead home surrounded by dying trees in a comatose, insane world. He had to break through, before the veil fell.

Doubt had always before been erased. Second thoughts, fears he shouldn't go so far, should turn back, had always been quelled upon the woman's return. And she would. She understood the danger, knew that if something else didn't consume her, death still waited.

Delirious in a swirl of desire, Mazlo glimpsed red hair glinting under the dim light. Lenora. His heart leapt from despair to hope. He hadn't heard the car park, the door shut. But here, a knock at the door.

He stood, crossed to let her in, imagining all she'd endured. Sleepless nights fighting against desire. Fever dreams, somehow aware of the threat. Shut inside all day, like Mazlo himself, shuddering behind blanket-darkened windows.

Another knock. Lenora.

Mazlo tried to sustain hope for her, but knew that like others before, she couldn't forestall disintegration. She would become hollow, a dreamless amnesiac, then either slink off into the brittle gray fields while he slept, or die in bed beside him, consumed. Those who hadn't escaped left no trace but white dust like baker's sugar, a few wisps of hair, and dry shards of marrowless bone. Better they made it out alive, that some instinct for self-preservation broke through hedonistic delirium in time. That wasn't something he could influence, even if he wanted, and lately they seemed not to last as long. Maybe his desire was nearly manifest.

He imagined her on the other side of this door, mind seized in a struggle to hold onto sanity, only vaguely aware of the nameless controlling force. Lenora, blended with an intelligence which lacked its own flesh and visited in borrowed gaps, devoured pinched fragments until slowly mind turned to ash.

Mazlo gripped the knob, turned, and opened.

On Lenora's face shone the doom he surmised. A melancholy smile, vacancies behind eyes burned away by memories of pleasure, skin split by subtle cracks where her beauty rent apart and liquid substrate leaked through.

Something else beneath the sadness, some secret, guarded. Mazlo tried to read those eyes, gazing back golden green, some midway between the need he was accustomed to seeing, and a confident readiness he couldn't explain.

"My love," he whispered, wondering if this pattern might be less certain than he assumed. Could some extraordinary woman alter his trajectory?

Lenora leaned back in their embrace to look at him. "Love, you called me?" In her eyes something flashed. "Is that what this is?"

What did she want him to say? Yes, Mazlo had sacrificed others, but always hoped one would continue with him, survive as he'd managed. Sometimes this distinction seemed a feeble excuse, but it was true. He hoped. For now, Lenora remained beautiful. When that diminished, as it must, Mazlo would focus on other qualities. Most valued were the capacities of perseverance and stamina. Like a living work of art, the ability to endure within a dying frame. To find pleasures, to enjoy without diminishment, to ignore the onrushing inevitability.

"Until we shed this carapace," he whispered, "and wear only infinite space."

Hair vivid red, warmth of her body against his. Aspects tangible, objective, if transitory. Her longbow smile, that hint of knowing.

Already in this embrace, she'd begun to fade, the scent of her to change. Smell of decay blended with the copal candles, intended to attract the sublime.

Lenora sighed. "These past days, I've been through so much." Light, almost teasing.

Fear nettled. What if he'd misjudged, if Lenora was different, not only stronger than the others, but himself? The insights he'd struggled decades to gain, another might apprehend more easily. Maybe she would survive, and he would decay? Uncertainty nagged him. Something about her fed this murmur of doubt.

"Would you ever have told me?" she asked.

He felt judged, accused.

She leaned close, whispered so her breath tickled his ear. "Now I understand you."

Now Mazlo felt afraid. What if she outlasted him, if the cosmos would be unfolded as he'd conceptualized, but not by himself. Lenora, transcendent in his stead, after he'd faded to ash and bones. No, that wasn't possible. The thing wasn't just intuition, but complex mathematics, both theory and computation, the arena of his indisputably great achievement. This universe couldn't be seen directly except through the veil of complex number sets. "What do you mean?"

"You noticed my fair skin, so white?" She ran fingers through red hair strands. "I've spent all my time in dark rooms. Since I was little."

Mazlo began to tremble. This abstract future goal didn't matter, if he couldn't survive the here and now. "Please, you can help me. I'm only trying. That's all."

"Only trying. Trying seems hard for you." Lenora's voice was strange. "It's easy for me."

"Please, we can help each other." He considered. "I can help you too."

"You'll help me?" Her lip curled, mocking.

"Yes, both of us," Mazlo insisted, desperate. "I'm only trying to survive. To stay intact long enough to find a way out of his hateful, devouring—"

"Devouring?" She shrugged, took a step back. "I don't see it."

"You will." He breathed, feeling dizzy. "Just look around. Always watching. Judging."

Something in her smile, not sadness, not decay. A secret. Mazlo couldn't quite read those eyes, green speckled gold. Certainly they didn't convey the powerless need he expected. More like confidence, an inexplicable readiness. He'd always wondered if his pattern might break. If some woman, possessed of unprecedented knowledge or strength, might reach past him.

"What is this?" he asked. "What's happening?"

"All those summers, cousin Lanny and me, staring at dark ceilings. Counting the things Uncle called down, before they flitted away. Each one a number."

He'd convinced himself Lenora had already begun to disintegrate, that he'd smelled the sour hint of her imminent doom. Horror overtook him as he realized he was wrong. The smell was his own failing body, already falling apart. Mortal terror rose from his subconscious, grabbed hold of him. Very soon he would be gone. Lenora would awaken one morning in bed beside his ashes, wisps of sickly hair, and chips of parched bone. She would be the one to finish what he'd begun, long ago.

Something in her aspect had in fact changed, but not what Mazlo expected. Not disintegration, not fear or entropy, but new depth. An increased complexity revealed itself in her eyes. A hint of the very same eternity Mazlo had always sought. Now it was near, contained within Lenora. Under her control.

He wondered at the odd smile on her lips. Already it was too late.

THE ONLY WAY OUT
IS DOWN

The truth I had come to fear, that my life did not rest upon a firm foundation, but shifted upon a dangerous lack of solidity, was confirmed by the handyman's casual words. As I handed over payment for his services, he told me the unexpected problem he'd found. He'd just come up from below the house.

"You've got standing water, down in the crawlspace there." At this, he must've seen my look of shock. "It's nothing too bad. Toward the front of the house, that corner there."

At that, he set aside the subject of this worrying discovery, and returned to why he was here.

We stood beside the cooktop on the granite kitchen island. The handyman tried every switch in turn, demonstrating that function had been restored to the burners and ventilation fan. He'd gone below to diagnose and repair the electrical problem, wires that exited the bottom of the island and came loose, while I'd remained above, blithely unaware of the depth of my life's complications.

There was this other matter now, this terrible surprise. Water, where none ought to be.

The handyman sketched an H-shaped outline, marking an X near the right front of the house. "Just here."

"Underneath," I said, recognizing the shape. "It's exactly like it is above ground."

"Sure. The house matches the foundation, fits on it real close." The way he looked at me, my reaction must have made him believe I doubted this. "The shape has to be the same, above and below."

I'd mentioned the fact that my wife and I were putting the house up for sale this weekend, but hadn't revealed the reason for the special urgency I felt to escape not just this house, but the neighborhood. I planned never to return, even to pass through. A year had passed since the events that worried me. My wife, Ilene, remained unaware. In fact, even if we remained here forever, I thought she'd probably never find out. The neighbor with whom I'd betrayed my wife was as eager as I was to keep the matter hidden. She was keeping a secret of her own.

My concern, more than fear of discovery, was the ongoing burden of guilt. The anxiety seemed never to decrease with time, which I believed was due to remaining so near where it happened. The constant reminders. When Ilene wasn't with me in the car, I entered and left the neighborhood by a circuitous path of avoidance, but we drove together often enough. That meant driving past the place several times every week.

Ilene had never seemed to sense anything wrong. Her own desire to move was more straightforward, a wish to be nearer her job, closer to Portland, and free of these bland outer suburbs. I carried this constant pressure of concealment, the subliminal throb of guilt and fear of discovery. Trying to cope, I refused to allow myself any thought of the transgression. I never thought her name, never visualized her or remembered our time together, and of course avoided looking at her house whenever I was forced to drive by. Force of will had eradicated events from my mind. Now was my time to escape the reminders. I couldn't wait to move across town, to another house in a place very unlike this one. The ache might lessen. The last tethers of memory might finally loosen, at least enough to allow me to move beyond this constant, fretful repression.

After weeks spent packing boxes, emptying rooms and cleaning carpets, it was almost time.

Though the handyman considered himself a generalist and not specifically an electrician, drainage and water mitigation were beyond his expertise. On his way out, he suggested I might go down myself and bail it out.

I chose a quart Pyrex measuring cup to scoop water from the puddle he'd described as shallow and narrow, and a five-gallon utility bucket to carry out the water. The handyman had estimated the standing water might be twenty gallons, might be fifty. An hour's hard work ought to take care of it.

The opening that led down to the crawlspace, hidden in a small closet under the stairs, was covered by a carpeted wood rectangle which fit the opening. The handyman had left it open, uncovered. My flashlight beam illuminated a circle below. The crawlspace floor was lined with heavy black plastic sheeting, lying smooth in flatter areas, elsewhere bunched around obstacles I couldn't make out from above.

I was about to climb down, but decided first to tell Ilene, still at a meeting with our realtor, what I planned. I took my cell phone from my pocket and sent two quick text messages.

Handyman saw water in crawlspace.

Going down to start bailing.

No more delay. I pocketed the phone and sat on the edge of the opening, legs dangling a moment, then lowered myself the short drop. The crawlspace was so shallow that standing in the hole, the closet floor came to the middle of my chest. I knelt, aiming the flashlight toward the right corner. The space was unexpectedly large, but full of obstacles. Round concrete piers every ten feet formed bases for stout vertical columns which ran up to joists extending the width of the house, in turn supporting floor beams spaced about a foot and a half apart. In the underground version of our house, these beams were effectively the "ceiling."

The "floor" was the plastic vapor barrier, beneath which smooth, packed soil alternated with sections of rounded stones the size of golf balls. I tried crawling on all fours, but my knees ached after a short distance traversing the rocks. I shifted to a hunched, head-forward squatting position and shuffled sideways, flashlight aimed ahead, orange bucket trailing. The light revealed tiny footprints of an opossum or raccoon, a dry, apparently old, trail of mud tracks.

The discovery of this place felt strange. An alternate version of home, foreign and inhospitable, yet possessing the same outline within which I'd lived ten years. The cold air smelled faintly of mold and damp.

Rather than proceeding diagonally to the corner, which would have meant crawling over piers and ducking under joists, I stayed parallel to the row of support columns until I neared the side of the house. There the big joist to my left ended and turned ninety degrees toward the front, making one riser of the H shape. Despite slow progress with each crab-like step, already I found myself within ten feet of the spot the handyman had indicated. I paused, aiming the flashlight ahead.

In that corner up against the foundation, the vapor barrier was rumpled, even tangled. In a flat section before me, light glistened off a stretch of water smaller and shallower than I'd expected. This puddle couldn't have been a gallon of water. Was this all the handyman had seen?

I told myself not to jump to conclusions until I had a closer look. Setting aside the bucket, I held the flashlight in my left hand and probed the water with my right. It was very cold, but clear and apparently clean, like rainwater runoff. This was hardly the swampy disaster I'd feared. The water at this end was maybe an inch deep atop the plastic, though it appeared deeper ahead. I edged forward and found I was able to press the plastic down. Not rock or soil beneath, but water, or at least wet mud. Here was the low spot. I reached back, grabbed the bucket and started bailing into it using the Pyrex cup. This seemed an absurd solution, taking only a cup or two at a time, but there was no way to get more of the shallow water.

I stopped short of filling the bucket completely, unsure I'd be able to haul it out if it weighed too much. Even this partial bucket, which took at least five minutes to fill, seemed to weigh at least thirty pounds. Crawling while holding both bucket and flashlight would be impossible, so I decided to leave the flashlight, balanced on its base and aiming up. This created an aura of moderate illumination, enough to guide me most of the way back to where similarly dispersed light streamed down from the opening above.

I was barely able to lift the bucket before it struck the beams. Each lurching squat-step, carrying the sloshing weight, was awkward and difficult. I might be able to fill the next bucket a little higher than this, but not much. The heavy burden made the way out seem much longer than the way in.

When at last I stood in the opening in the closet, I found there was no way to climb out while still holding the bucket. I lifted it inside, across the carpet, and set it on the stone tile in the hallway just beyond. I lifted myself to ground level, arms and shoulders already tired. As I stood, my knees ached. I carried the bucket out the sliding back door to the patio and dumped three gallons of perfectly clear water into the grass.

Heading down for another try, I wondered how long this had taken. At least fifteen minutes, probably more like twenty, for a single bucket. I felt at once assured, having found the problem less terrible than I'd feared, and also daunted by the time and effort expended in just barely getting started.

This time I knew where I was headed. The sideways creeping motion came more easily. When I returned to the flashlight, the amount of water on the vapor barrier seemed no less than before. I pushed open a seam where two sheets of plastic met and found more water beneath. The pool atop of the plastic wasn't the whole story. Underneath was more, hidden and mingling with smooth rocks and muddy ground.

Still, the puddle was shallow, and no larger in area than the outline of a person lying down. I just needed to establish a routine, some kind of rhythm. Scoop water, fill the bucket, haul it out. Keep going.

The second was easier than the first. By the third, I fell into a kind of groove. Becoming accustomed to the difficulty of the labor, I guessed I should be able to keep going like this until the job was finished.

As I carried out the fourth bucket, I did some mental math. Five-gallon bucket, maybe four gallons of water. At this rate, a bucket every ten minutes at best, I was removing less than twenty-five gallons per hour.

Worrying wouldn't do me any good. I forced myself to stop counting, stop thinking, and pushed on.

At some point after many cycles, preparing to go down again with yet another emptied bucket, I wondered why Ilene wasn't home yet. I paused to breathe, my shirt soaked with sweat, my knees wobbling as I started to lower myself to sit on the edge of the opening. So exhausted, I needed a break. Though I tried to buoy my spirits by imagining I'd carried out fifteen buckets, I knew it was probably only eleven or twelve.

I decided to wait for Ilene, and tell her what was happening. Maybe she could help. She could stand above the opening and carry the buckets from there to outside, saving me having to climb up and down, and giving me a brief rest between buckets.

Damp with sweat, streaked with gritty mud, I staggered outside to lie on my back on the concrete patio. It was hard to believe my night had turned out this way. A visit from the handyman, a last-minute wiring repair before the house went on the market, and somehow I'd ended up in this sorry state. I decided to call the handyman and tell him I was having trouble solving the problem. Maybe he had suggestions.

My cell phone was still in my pocket. If I'd known how wet and dirty the work would be, I might've left it inside, but I was glad not to have to crawl back inside for it now.

I redialed his number from my recent calls list.

"Pollin Brothers," he answered.

"It's Parker Davis." I was surprised at the effort it took, just to speak. "From today."

"Sure, I recall," the handyman said. "Everything good, electrical-wise? Got your cooktop cooking?"

"Mmm-hmm," I affirmed. "I'm calling about that standing water. You remember?"

"Sure, of course I do. That was, what, just three hours ago?"

Three hours, already? No wonder I felt so exhausted. I'd begun working as soon as he'd gone, planning to continue until Ilene returned. She still wasn't home. It must be almost nine, more than four hours since she'd gone out to meet the realtor.

"I hauled quite a bit of water," I continued, "but under the plastic, the level still seems to be rising."

"I can imagine. Sometimes the quick jobs end up anything but quick."

"So I've been working pretty hard, and wonder if I might have taken on too much, you know. Just one guy with a bucket and a measuring cup." I held out hope for some kind of assistance. "You mentioned you might know an irrigation guy?"

The handyman inhaled and didn't exhale right away. When he did exhale, it sounded like a sigh. "Right, irrigation guy. I did call him, soon as I left your place, just making sure. He's booked solid, two months. You believe that? I told him I'm in the wrong business, trying to fill my days with run-and-fix-its. Guess everybody's got problems with water in the ground below 'em. Water going every which way."

"Two months?" Irritation came through in my voice. I breathed, trying to calm myself.

"Don't worry too much," he said. "This is Oregon, it's November, raining real bad. Bit of water in someone's crawlspace, that's not too unusual."

I wanted to remind him the house was going on the market tomorrow. He didn't seem to realize how important this was to me. It wasn't his fault, I knew. He was trying to help as much as he could. Just because he'd discovered the water didn't mean I could expect him to drive back again and fix it himself. Besides, the way he was talking now, maybe I shouldn't worry too much. Just try to relax.

"It's just," I began. "I'm worried what a buyer might think if their home inspector sees it."

"Can't lie. You've got yourself a problem to solve." The handyman offered nothing more.

I tried to think of some other approach, some alternate tack in search of any kind of help. Of course there was nothing. I thanked him and hung up.

At that moment, I heard the door from the garage open and shut inside the house.

"Hello-o?" Ilene called.

"Here." I started to sit up, intending to stand. Every muscle resisted, so I lay back. "Out here."

"Park?" She came to the screen door and flicked on the patio light. "What are you doing, lying outside in the cold? You're muddy. You're all muddy, Park."

She stood there, tall and narrow behind the screen, not at all muddy or wet. Her outfit was the kind of suit she wore to work. Her brown hair spilled to her shoulders, loose curls messy as if she'd just climbed out of bed.

"I was..." I gestured vaguely toward the house, too tired to explain. "Didn't you see my messages?"

Ilene shook her head and ran a hand through her hair, as if she'd just remembered the disorder of it. "I was meeting with Diane, Park, don't you remember?"

I wanted to ask how meeting our realtor could take four hours, but lacked the energy for an argument.

She pulled her phone from her purse. When she read my messages, her face changed. "Just what we need. Tomorrow's the agent's preview. Tomorrow, the listing goes live."

I sat up and told her the rest. The handyman, the standing water, the bailing and carrying out buckets.

"But tomorrow's the agent's preview," Ilene repeated. "Park, tomorrow our house will be officially listed for sale."

I was tempted then to reveal to her why I so desperately wanted the house to be sold. "I know."

"The house must be perfect, Diane said and said. You never know which person coming through our front door could actually be the buyer who'll want this house to be theirs. It has to be perfect, Park."

Ilene suggested we should start again right away, continue bailing like I was before. Two of us working together, one below to fill buckets, one above to empty them, it would go faster. She said she was going upstairs to change into "rough clothes," but paused, waiting for me to agree.

I told her I was too tired to continue tonight. I needed a shower and some sleep. "First thing in the morning," I promised.

She was still buzzing with nervous energy from all that was going on, but agreed we could start in the morning, very early. We needed to finish and clean up before the agent's preview at eleven.

"We have that deadline, Park," she reminded me. The way she appended my name made it sound like this was all my fault, but she was willing to help me solve it because we had no time for any other option.

That night, Ilene slept easily while I lay there, looking up at the dark. I was trying to remember when she'd started calling me Park instead of Parker, as she had at first.

In the morning I woke early, and found Ilene already up. She showed me the fluorescent work lamp and long extension cord she'd found in the garage. The lamp was far more powerful than my weak flashlight.

I guzzled coffee and climbed down. Ilene remained above, wearing new white jeans and red leather loafers.

"What if we get a day-one offer?" she asked with giddy, wild energy as we readied to start. "A first-day offer is possible in this market. But what if they inspect below and find a swamp down there? Ugh."

I went to work. My arms and back were still sore, but I remembered our deadline. Eleven o'clock.

The level of the water hadn't diminished overnight, but remained shallow enough I had difficulty scooping more than a little bit at once. Venturing farther into the corner, I pulled back plastic, searching for a lower point to scoop from.

"What's happening?" Ilene shouted, far away.

I gave no answer, just set to work filling the first bucket to the usual level, then lugged it out. At the opening, I stood and lifted the bucket.

"It takes so long," Ilene said, clearly trying to suppress disappointment. "Why not fill to the top?"

"Take it," I said. "You'll see how heavy."

Though slight of build, Ilene was as tall as me, and strong from five gym visits per week. The bucket jerked her forward when she accepted the weight. "Oh!" She seemed ready to say more, but focused on getting her burden out the back door.

I was already sweating, but relieved not to be climbing up and out and back down again. Remaining below should be easier.

"Four hours," Ilene said when she came back with the empty bucket. "We have four hours, so we can do at least thirty buckets. More if we have to."

I estimated that was more than seven buckets per hour, under nine minutes each. Now that I knew the routine and could focus my energy below, it seemed possible. Thirty buckets, four gallons each, that was still only a hundred and twenty gallons. It didn't seem like much, until I visualized it as two or three barrels full. Last night, I'd done forty or fifty gallons. This should be enough. I allowed myself to feel cheered by the possibility that we might finish before our deadline.

The next five or six, Ilene and I worked without speaking. Each time, she raced back to me, carrying the empty bucket. I could see she wanted to urge me to hurry, but didn't.

In the spot where I'd been working last night, the water level was down to muddy rocks. This was encouraging at first, until I discovered I'd been mistaken again about the low point, which was actually still nearer the corner of the house. I pulled back a large section of black plastic and found more water, clear and undisturbed. The puddle wasn't too much larger than it had first seemed, but went deeper.

At least the depth enabled me to dip the cup fully under, and scoop nearly a quart at a time. My bucket filled quickly.

The next time I returned to Ilene, having shaved a couple minutes off the time to bring the previous bucket, I didn't reveal what I'd discovered. I enjoyed her wordless surprise.

I returned below to discover a sharper smell. Water in the hole was nearly a foot below the level of the crawlspace floor. An oily sheen glistened on the surface. I lowered the scoop and it came up tangled in thin, pale roots or strands. I couldn't guess what this plant might be, just kept scooping as fast as I could. When the water reached bottom, I pulled out loose rocks and found more water.

That bucket was the quickest yet.

Ilene spoke her first words in a long while. "Good, that's good."

I went back under. The hole penetrated the topmost layer of rocks into loose mud. I reached in, pleased to see how far down the water had gone, yet still surprised not to have found the last of it. My hand on the rim slipped into the muck, and came up tingling, covered with fizzy bubbles like root beer foam, which quickly dispersed. I scooped through slimy vegetation that looked like a muddy tangle of white lace.

Another bucket. The cycle repeated, each trip back and forth seeming identical.

"This makes thirty-one," Ilene said as she accepted the bucket. She hesitated to ask what she was clearly dying to know. "Is it working?"

"Thirty-one?" I straightened, hands on hips. "The water's going down, but we're not finished."

"A few more." Ilene looked at her watch. "Nearly clean-up time."

I went down into the dark and filled the bucket, pulling water through strange leaves that seemed now like thin, flexible bones. I took care to avoid slipping, braced on the mud-slick rim. Faster, always faster. No end to the water below. Another bucket. Another.

The water had subsided almost too far below ground level to reach. It no longer seemed like part of the house anymore, so far beneath it all. No time remained for another trip. I pushed stones piled around the rim back down to the bottom, then pulled the edges of the vapor barrier across, covering it.

When I came up, giving Ilene the last bucket, my arms trembled with fatigue. "It's not done."

"We have to stop," she said. "There's no time. We have to clean up."

While I'd been working below, Ilene had been carefully cleaning anything that spilled on the closet carpet, on the stone tiles of the kitchen and dining room, or even on the concrete patio. The house remained perfect, show-ready from floor to ceiling, but Ilene and I need to shower and change so we could get out of here before our realtor arrived to welcome her competitors and colleagues for a preview.

"I've got blisters, and my shoulders ache," Ilene said, looking down at her white pants, still pristine. "And I'm filthy. But I can't imagine how you must feel. We'll get through this. Our house is going to sell."

My wet, muddy T-shirt and jeans stuck to my skin. I felt grit in my hair, in my eyes, under my fingernails. Before climbing up to the closet, I removed shoes, socks and shirt, still standing below, the top half of me rising through the opening. My legs and back were so stiff I could barely pull off my jeans. Ilene deposited the filthy clothes in a plastic bag. Wearing only my boxers, I climbed up to the closet and accepted the towel Ilene offered.

"This is still going to happen," she said, her tone less confident than the words themselves.

"We can't call it off." I felt no great certainty, but bore in mind that events were already in motion, too late to be postponed. "Our house is officially for sale. We just have to shower and clear out."

I toweled off, shivering, almost naked. Ilene took the wet, dirty towel and gave me a clean, dry one.

"I'll go first," she said, headed upstairs, toward our master suite shower.

I felt I should describe for her everything I'd seen, all I'd experienced, but there was no time. The problem remained less than fully solved, but the real estate agents or their clients wouldn't be looking below, not yet. When they came, they would be looking at the house as a place for people to live, focusing on rooms with carpet and paint and windows. Overall impression counted most, and our house exhibited great appeal.

More than simply telling Ilene that a quantity of water remained below, I craved to talk about what it had felt like. Textures, smells. Those lacy white leaves below ground. She deserved to understand what had been beneath us all this time, even if it might seem strange, or at first upsetting.

But we had no time, so I forced the notion from my mind. Anyway, I was afraid to start revealing secrets. Afraid once I started, I might be unable to stop.

Ilene kept the door shut until she was dry and almost fully dressed.

"They'll be gone by three," I said to myself, when it was my turn to shower. "We can come back and keep working then."

Over lunch at the bistro a few miles from home, we didn't talk about what might be going on at the house, but that was all I thought about. This created a sensation of living in two realities at once, overlapping in certain details but completely distinct in others. Again and again, I nearly gave voice to some thought that came to mind, only to catch myself, realizing this wasn't at all what Ilene and I were thinking about.

Only me.

Ilene's buzzing energy was gone. She looked at me directly, seeming to actually see me without distraction. "We're doing this." Her voice was flat, neither overenthusiastic nor critical. "We are, right?"

She was just exhausted and stressed, but this still surprised me.

"We never talk about what we want," she added. "Both of us do things, and I guess later we must figure it had to have been the right thing, because it's already done."

"I've certainly…" I trailed off, realizing I almost admitted something big, almost let slip a terrible truth, the very one that had been weighing on me this whole time. Hoping for relief from this new concern, daring to believe it might all soon be over, I nearly let out the other thing. I was tired too. "I guess so much seems overwhelming, and that changes how we both think."

It was a pretty thin statement of philosophy, certainly not worthy of what she'd said first. I just wanted us to make it through this, get away, then it would be easier. Still I couldn't ignore what was revealed by this brief interaction. How different we'd become, and how insincere. Two people once inseparable, now veering apart. The gap was so wide.

As the waiter cleared our table, I told him we needed to stay away from home, so though we'd finished eating, we might sit around a while.

"You have all the time you need," he said, as if we should have known this.

After he left, Ilene looked at me strangely, head tilted, seeming determined to break through in some way. Just as she started to speak, she was interrupted by the chirp of a text message.

"It's Diane," she said, looking at her phone, then added, "our realtor."

I wanted to know right away what Diane had to say, but as I'd started doing so often lately, forced myself to behave instead in direct opposition to my natural impulse.

Ilene read from the screen. *"Might have something to report soon.* What could that mean?" She smiled, having decided to take this as signifying some promise of good fortune. She beckoned the waiter. Without looking at a menu, she named a bottle of wine I'd never heard of.

I allowed myself to consider the house, the realtor, and possibilities. I made no attempt to shield what I was thinking, and permitted everything to show on my face. "Wow," I began. "This really might change."

Ilene stopped looking at me, either because she'd failed to notice what I was trying to reveal, or because she couldn't stand to see it.

The wine arrived, a Pinot Gris in a black bottle with a flying silver bird on the label.

"Too expensive, but who cares, this once," Ilene said, pouring. "It's my favorite."

I wanted to know why her favorite wine was something I'd never seen her drink.

"To better luck," she said, her glass inclined toward me.

I touched my glass to hers and sipped, mind buzzing with too many thoughts. The smell was bright citrus, a perfume of sharp grapefruit.

The wine disappeared so quickly, I was afraid that might indicate a bad omen for our real estate luck. My head spun with possibilities, with imagined futures, almost enough to override my physical fatigue. A second bottle was out of the question. It wasn't yet one o'clock.

We settled the check and went slowly outside, carrying so much invisible weight. In the parking lot I told Ilene I wanted to be certain nothing might give potential buyers any reason to avoid our house. She understood what I meant.

I drove us to Home Depot. We bought a portable electric sump pump and a fifty-foot garden hose.

"We'll be able to use the hose at our next house," I said, justifying the expenditure, though Ilene hadn't said anything against it.

We drove out Marine Drive along the Columbia River, killing time, first east toward Troutdale, then west again, past PDX and back toward I5. For a while, a hawk glided over the water beside us, perfectly matching the speed of the car. This must've been an accident. The bird was looking not at us, but for some shape it hoped to pluck from the river. It felt like an indication of something, but I wasn't sure exactly what.

Though neither of us said so, both Ilene and I must have anticipated another text or call from Diane, after the preview finished. No such contact ever came. At three o'clock Ilene called Diane and, getting no answer, left a message saying we were returning to the house, we hoped things had gone well, and that we'd talk later.

Everything at home looked exactly as it had before we left, with the addition of business cards from sixteen realtors on the edge of the counter, beside the newly-repaired cooktop.

I went upstairs and changed into work clothes,. When I came back down, Ilene was standing at the back patio door, looking out.

"I won't celebrate again until I'm sure we have a reason," I said, trying not to say what I'd been thinking, which is that the bottle of wine at the restaurant had been premature.

Ilene muttered something, offering to help.

"With the pump, neither of us should need to do much," I said. "In a few minutes you can help me get the hose out through of the vent, into the yard. Run it to the back so the water can run down the hill."

I lowered the pump and hose, then the utility lamp and extension cord, into the opening, and climbed down. Below, I switched on the light. Such sharp illumination didn't make the below feel anything more like the above. White glare only heightened an alien quality, like living on the surface of another planet.

As I began to move, I found the optimal posture and supported my weight evenly distributed among hands and feet. My body was becoming accustomed to this, like a subterranean creature who lived an entire life hunched and crawling on hands and knees.

The familiar smell was stronger than before, less an actual scent, and more a sharp horseradish tingle in my sinuses. I wondered if I might be coming down with a cold from all the damp, chilly overexertion.

In the front corner, beneath a cover of plastic, I hoped to find what I'd been wondering about all afternoon. Would the water fill in again, or finally recede now that so much had been removed?

I pulled back the plastic to see water had begun to fill in. It wasn't as high as last night, but certainly up since this morning. Our house was situated a few blocks below the top of the hill, far enough that ground water must've been drifting down to settle here, in this low point. The volume wasn't much, and might evaporate when hot, dry weather returned, but in the damp rain of a Portland autumn, the water wasn't going away. The puddle didn't spread atop the plastic as it had before, but found its way into this deeper hole.

Further pulling back the vapor barrier revealed more dense, clay-like mud. Across the smooth surface spread a pattern of white speckles, a fungus like delicate lace. I didn't know enough to identify what it was, not exactly. Just some weird mold or spore, entirely out of place.

I attached the pump output to the female end of the garden hose and ran the other end to the rear corner, where Ilene had said she'd wait to help. She didn't appear to be out there, until I heard something beyond the vent. I shifted closer, listening. A near sound, shuffling in the bark mulch. A subdued murmur, as if two people were talking, whispering, trying to converse without being heard.

"Is that you?" I asked through the screened vent. "Ilene?"

No answer came. The weird sensation I briefly entertained, that this presence outside was not my wife but some stranger, or two, passed in a moment. I focused on the ventilation screen, trying to pry open the corner. The shuffling movement outside increased, became a greater commotion, until I felt other hands working from outside to pry and pull as I pushed from within. When the corner opened, I was able to press the hose through, widening the gap. The hose began to slip through my hands, pulled faster than I could feed it out. It ran across the back yard to where Ilene and I had discussed. At the back fence, the hill began to slope away, so from there, water could run down and dissipate into the hillside weeds and brush before it reached the flat portion of our rear neighbor's yard.

I returned to the pump while the hose kept hissing and slipping past, until it stopped, apparently pulled far enough. The instant I plugged the pump into the cord's second outlet, the motor began to buzz and churn. I set the base of it into the hole, and as water fed through, the sound quieted. The water's surface vibrated and shimmered, but gave no indication of any quantity being pumped away. Reflected light from the work lamp close by dazzled my eyes.

Though I believed water must be flowing, I couldn't be sure. The hose seemed to move slightly, but then earth and water alike vibrated in what seemed a general state of imminent transmutation. With nothing else to do, as the pump took over my work I'd done before, I returned to peer out the vent.

Ilene's outline stood against the back fence, appearing focused, holding the end of the hose. She bent strangely, as if talking through the fence, then pausing to sniff at a trickle of water. Maybe drinking from it.

"Ilene!" I shouted above the churn of the pump, half-submerged twenty feet behind me.

If she heard, she gave no sign.

I kept calling her name through the vent. Finally she started toward me, her attention still focused on that rear corner of the yard. She approached from an oblique angle and stopped to one side of the small opening, out of my view.

"It's working," came a whisper, then a sigh, almost disappointment. "Water coming. It flows out."

I set aside my worry about Ilene's behavior. The pump was working. Based on rated capacity, the pump was removing a volume of water equivalent to three of those orange utility buckets every minute. No need to bail or carry or climb up and down. In even the most pessimistic scenario, the last remainder of our problem would be drained away. Less than an hour's work, using tools that cost just over a hundred dollars.

"We're going to make it," I said, knowing Ilene was too far away to hear.

I was exhausted, still sore from last night and this morning. We were going to make it. I could finally get away. Though I'd done something irrevocable, something that threatened to break my marriage, I could now hope to move before Ilene found the truth. This last, unexpected disaster, the only thing that could have prevented me finally being free of the weight of this place, would be repaired.

"I'm going inside to check my phone." The voice sounded like Ilene's. It seemed like something she would say, but she always kept her phone with her.

The pump was still running, with only the base of it touching the water. I lowered it until it was fully submerged. It felt strange, dropping an electrical motor into the water, but the pump was designed to be used this way. The instructions said this was not only safe; it was the way the pump was built to be used. I kept reorienting it so the opening in the base, through which water entered, remained unblocked.

After a while, distracted by thoughts that this might all finally be over soon, I allowed the water level to drop below these intake ports. The pump screeched until I shifted it again. As the terrible chatter faded back to the usual churn, I heard shouting from inside the house, through the opening into the closet.

"What's wrong?" I shouted, and held quiet in case Ilene answered.

Getting no response, I moved that direction, straining to see anything inside the house.

Nothing to see, nothing to hear. No movement, but I couldn't climb out. I crawled back to the pump, back to the water. The level had fallen lower in the hole than I'd guessed possible. I had to keep clearing rocks, making room for the pump to descend. Though before I'd worried only about the presence of water, now I became concerned about the vacancy left behind. A rock-filled pit at least two feet deep, probably more.

As I sat near the edge, looking down, I was afraid I might slip. I teetered, swaying, afraid to go away, and afraid to approach too near.

Another sound from inside the house. Not laughter, not a conversation. I was certain I recognized the thump of a phonograph needle dropped onto a record, the careless way Ilene does when she plays my vinyl, rather than lowering the tonearm smoothly with the lever. A rhythmic chatter came through, a hint of melody. What was it? I couldn't recognize the song, but closed my eyes, straining to hear enough hints to help me guess. Was she having her own little party up there? Maybe she was trying to send me a message, assuming I could hear the song and recognize the lyrics.

"What are you playing?" I shouted, knowing there was no way she could hear. I was too far from the opening to the house. "Ilene?"

No answer, or none that I could detect.

I nudged the pump still lower in the water, then crawled back to the opening. The music came clearer, but still wasn't recognizable. Strange, because all the records were mine. Ilene listened to CDs.

Another sound, Ilene laughing. Then quieter, a murmur beneath the music. Was the song nothing but a cover for secret conversation? A blanket of words, a breathy hush shared, barely above whispers. I couldn't make out any specifics, but had a general sense of the exchange. Ilene wasn't talking to herself, but someone else. If someone was with her up there, who was it?

Not ready to call out, or climb up and confront her, I decided instead to stay hidden, listening.

Then I must've fallen asleep.

A lifelike dream, a nightmare cascade of accumulating problems. One disaster led to another. What started the avalanche was my first mistake. The one slip I should never have made, and wished I could erase. But to make it truly right would mean to tell her, which I couldn't do. Better to carry my own suffering, and not give in to the compulsion to unburden myself at her expense.

My body jerked as my mind jolted unpleasantly awake. How long had I been slumped here, leaning against the support pier? My shoulder ached.

The pump, somewhere, still ran. I crawled over to check, but couldn't see the pump itself, just the cable running down, which I jerked sideways until the weight shifted and the line went slack.

I crawled back to the opening to the house, ready to climb out this time, but was surprised to find Ilene standing near, or if not her, then at least the shadow of her, leaning against the edge of the kitchen island. She was facing away, toward the back patio, talking into her phone, laughing at something.

"Ilene?" I asked, half afraid to interrupt.

She didn't turn toward me, instead took two steps nearer the sliding door. Where the living room met the dining room, concealed behind a pillar, she stopped. Then she shifted and I saw her face, a bright sudden smile.

"We already have an offer!"

"What?" I shouted. "Are you talking to me?"

"Diane said..." Her mouth kept moving, but the sound trailed off. She seemed at the same time excited and worried, as if wonderful and terrible outcomes might occur, both at once.

The next words I heard: "...buyer offering above asking price..."

Then a mechanical clicking which came not from the pump below, but from above, inside the house. Something like the record stuck in the runout groove.

"They're quite particular," she said, and, "...complications."

"What does that mean?" I asked. "Ilene, is Diane saying she thinks the house is sold?"

A long time passed with no answer spoken, just a series of affirmative nods and contrary head-shakes, one after another, an intricate code I was meant to understand. The only actual sound, aside from the clicking of that played-out record, was the steady churn of the pump running somewhere far off, a cyclic whirr of water being removed.

"Aren't we dry yet?" she asked.

I tried telling Ilene, unsure she could hear, that it ran much deeper than I thought, that the longer the pump ran, the more water came out, water without end, and the deeper the hole was revealed to be. The problem was worse than we'd believed. My words spilled out in a rush to make up for all I hadn't said before.

"A limit," she said. "There's a limit."

"Right," I agreed, nodding. "It can't go on forever, filling, emptying and refilling. All the rest of the crawlspace, the ground is dry. There's nowhere for so much water to keep coming from."

Even as I said this, I realized the water could be coming from below. I understood it within myself, but didn't want to suggest it. That piece of knowledge seemed dangerous, a clue to revealing secrets I hoped to keep. It seemed there was no way to tell truth, only to hide.

My vision shifted, and I no longer saw my wife. When I'd looked away, she must've moved elsewhere, maybe within the house, maybe back out to check the hose, or talk on her phone where I couldn't hear.

There was nowhere to go, not for me. I had to remain near in case the pump needed to be moved or lowered. I decided to remain below, keeping watch over the ever-deepening hole.

Time passed, not a smooth line, but a series of jumps.

Where was I? What was this place? A dark home, with such a low ceiling. Beside me, a harsh light, but everything outside the circle was dark. Right here, a space in the ground, something at the bottom.

Then I remembered, I was below my house. My wife was upstairs.

"Ilene," I said, hoarse and weak.

I hurried back toward her, wanting to hear news, dragging myself across the dirty plastic.

"Diane says…" It was her voice, it had to be. She told me things.

Our buyer wasn't a U.S. national. He had "banking issues," so was willing to pay a higher price. This sounded like good news, until the next caveat, "you'll need to remain extremely open-minded."

I ducked away, returned to find the water almost too low to reach from above. I kept lowering the pump, as I'd done, loosening the cord wrapped around the nearest post, letting it out a few inches, then snugging the loop around the wood.

My routine developed, a back-and-forth, first minding and adjusting the pump, then returning to crouch in the opening to the house above, the real world, where I might search for Ilene. Sometimes I found her. If she was there, she might feed me bits of information, remaining always hidden from my view. The news, difficult to piece together, seemed to derive from Diane's emails, calls and text messages. Maybe Diane was actually up there with her.

The buyer was a U.S. citizen after all, in fact, earlier confusion was due to his employment being government-related, Top Secret, impossible to document. Unable to provide proof of income. "You see, he might have difficulty with financing." We were advised of danger, but told not to back away.

I escaped to the dark. From within my hole in the mud I heard an urgent slipping and splashing, as if something below had seen me and wanted to remain hidden. Who was she? For a moment I wondered, what if there was a whole different world down there, other people, new lives? I remained quiet, hoping to tune out the churn of the pump and determine if I'd actually heard something.

In Ilene's next report, the deal was back on. All parties agreed to the earliest possible closing date. Great news. The buyer's financing shouldn't be an issue. He'd filed tax returns after all, only, "some of the numbers don't appear to add up."

My old life above, the other world below. I had both, at least for a while.

Near the top of the hole, where the water had long ago drained away, visible layers of strange white leaves hung, wraith-like strata long supported by the water now subsided. This naked, pale vegetation gave off a smell that burned my lungs and made my vision shimmer.

Another return. The opening, my wife, illumination and proximity to the clean, odorless air of a well-kept interior. These were things I knew I should seek, but standing below, I received none of them. I breathed the air down where I was now, not what was above. Ilene remained beyond view, always leaning around corners, lurking in ways that seemed suspicious, even paranoid, gathering information for her running commentary, an implausible play-by-play in a real estate melodrama.

And back to the water, where I could set aside worry over whether or not to tell Ilene how bad it truly was, how deeply the hole penetrated the earth beneath the house. How could I possibly have found words to tell her we'd been living all these years above such a vacancy? Not only water, but this mud-slimed structure of rocks, soil permeated by a mesh of white stuff that hung loose in places and at other levels remained rooted to the earth. Everywhere, all around, white spores spun in fractal patterns, stinging my nose, choking me, bending my mind, deadening my lungs. I breathed it all in. What choice did I have?

The next I heard, our buyer required the house sooner. He wanted it tomorrow, simply had to have it tonight. His offer might contain escalation clauses, rewarding us for getting out sooner. A higher price still, if we agreed to forego the usual protections of law. We'd accept responsibility for his tax issues, for his bank problems, for any legal repercussions from wire fraud or money laundering. We must accept funds in unknown currencies, from sources all involved parties knew to be less than perfectly clean.

After all, who was actually clean, here? I wasn't. Even Ilene, I couldn't be sure. Not any more.

He'd pay more, if we accepted liability for his future happiness, for his physical safety. Of course we'd sign special documents. Proceeds from sale would be held in escrow for an indeterminate period. We might never be permitted to spend the money, in case the buyer ever decided the deal should be unwound.

I would need to stipulate that the house had always been sinking, had been built atop a bottomless, aching passage to unknown places. Certainly we must have known.

Not only divulge to the buyer. I would have to tell Ilene the truth.

Our house was not a house, could not be sold, could never be vacated. The house was nothing but a cover for all the water that constantly flowed underneath. Water soothing the emptiness.

Fear above, and relentless worry. Below, cool and peaceful quiet. I preferred to remain here, head down, where everything was dark.

So much water, such unexpected depths. I could never remove it all, could never possibly measure all that had been taken out, drained away. If I'd ever known, I'd forgotten. For so long this had accumulated. How many years had I avoided truth, living a life of dwindling honesty, of greater and deeper betrayal?

I leaned down into the hole, reaching, straining to grasp the sides, afraid I might fall. The pump was too far below to see. Where was that cord?

Reality had begun to dawn on me. Selling this house might be more trouble than it was worth. All the conditions and compromises weighed on me. I'd been hoping to finally escape, but might never be free. This new awareness settled in.

By the time I'd begun to accept what might never be possible, that I may not be able to shrug off what had been holding me here, I was shocked to realize a more immediate danger.

I was hanging upside down, deep in the hole, head toward the bottom, my body so far beneath the surface I was surrounded by nothing but slippery mud and darkness. My fingers clutched into rock and clay walls, dense enough to support me, wet enough that my grasp could penetrate. Without realizing, I'd gone below, following the same instinct that had driven me before, seeking without reason or plan to move lower, always lower. My feet and knees braced against the walls near ground level, while arms strained downward, probing.

The pump vibrated and hummed before me, just below the cold surface, straining against the limit of the cord. I no longer wanted to take the water away. All of it should remain here. I should bring in a new flood, enough to replace all that had gone, enough to last forever. Everything should remain wet and hidden.

I could stay here, pressing down to where the smell was pungent, tangy with varieties of life newly discovered. I might thrust my face into it and finally breathe.

This place had always been here, a mirror of the house above. Only now I saw the way things had been arranged. Below where we'd lived, eaten, breathed and slept, on the opposite side of a floor that was a ceiling here. All this had accumulated, evolving to conform to lives acted out above. Now that I saw it from so close up, was able to smell and almost taste, I knew what I needed. To go deeper, to put my face in the water. To smell the cold, hidden life. Meet new, strange faces, learn their names.

I yanked hard against the pump until the plug came loose above. Released, finally quiet, it drifted away, out of sight. I wanted never to drown, but to reach a place where I might find something deep to breathe. My life had been over a long time. The only way out was down.

I strained forward, hungry mouth gaping near the cold, black surface, so close to what I desired that I no longer had to pretend. I gave in, and finally allowed myself to taste.

THE INSOMNIAC
WHO SLEPT FOREVER

T he sleep research facility hides among the trees in the hills west of town, a squat cylinder of graphite metal rusting at riveted seams, resembling an abandoned water tank. At Conrad's approach, black doors of opaque glass slide apart to reveal an inner hallway. The strangeness heightens his anxiety and uncertainty, but he can't go back. He has nothing left.

His intake interview occurs in a windowless room at the end of the entry hall. A large video panel reflects Conrad's diseased face back at him, a barrier between himself and the interviewing nurse. He failed to get a look at her as he entered, so now he's talking to someone he's supposed to call Nurse V, and has no idea what she looks like. Conrad knows this shouldn't bother him, but many things bother him that shouldn't.

"Conrad W. Snow."

He stares without recognition into bloodshot eyes, sunken into deathly pale skin lost in greasepaint shadows. The mouth moves in sync with Conrad's mumbled words.

"Thirty-nine. Forty next… Next Thursday? Anyway, next week."

That must be him, that face. Pale cadaverousness was a desirable look, in his younger Goth days. Now it's evidence of sickness.

"2722 N. Diagonal Road, Portland, 97203. That's in St. Johns, near the theater."

Nurse V seems to be writing, rather than typing, Conrad's replies.

"Diagnosis was PTSD. About a year ago."

Nurse V, that's not even a name. Just a letter.

"Yes, my primary physician, a couple different shrinks. No help."

Such predictable questions give no hint of the clinic's renowned unortho-doxy.

"Not just mainstream. I tried hypnosis, naturopathy, traditional Chinese. Later tried alcohol, ecstasy, sleeping pills, over-the-counter, prescription. Even meditation and yoga. Nothing helped. I need something else."

Attention subsides, replaced by rising impatience. Conrad isn't bothered by the questions, but the notorious doctor's refusal to show himself. Many scoff at the methods of Doctor Zyz, characterize him as occultist or char-latan. Others insist he possesses an unmatched understanding of the ways and mechanisms of sleep.

"At first I was dealing with grief, so I didn't notice the insomnia until months later. I realize I'm making it worse. My own mind, nothing exter-nal. Physical fatigue, depression, cyclical panic attacks. Anxiety becomes a feedback loop. Inability to exercise, to work. I never go out except to buy food."

The intake room's dramatic lighting casts sharp-edged black polygon shadows on walls. Conrad can't discern which objects in the room create which shadows. He raises a hand, and in vain searches the glaring surround-ings.

Nothing moves. The shadows are painted on the walls.

Focused on this oddity of decor, Conrad realizes he's missed Nurse V's latest question. She repeats herself.

"How would I characterize my experience? Like drowning in black pitch. My body disintegrating, being digested in the belly of some monster. And that monster is the entire world outside my own head."

Every elevator Conrad's seen, in hotels, offices or hospitals, has been brushed stainless steel and wood paneling. This one resembles a gray stone box, slightly larger than an upright coffin. He enters the compartment alone while Nurse V remains outside. The door slides shut.

Only two buttons, impossible to mistake.

Above.

Below.

Mind clouded with fatigue, Conrad doubts his first, obvious assumption, that this indicates a simple, two-story structure. The elevator starts down, and continues so long, Conrad realizes he must discard all preconceptions, simply wait and accept whatever comes. After a while, he no longer feels a sense of downward movement, begins wondering if he's ever been moving at all.

He presses the "Below" button again. When the car finally slows, stops, gravity seems briefly increased.

"Below" illuminates. How long did the ride take? How far down has he gone?

The door opens, revealing vacant darkness. Strange, this extreme contrast, from brutal luminosity above to this endless, quiet black openness.

Out of the dark, a voice. "I'm Doctor Zyz." The name rhymes with *fizz.* That's one of Conrad's questions answered.

The old doctor steps into the light spilling from the elevator. His hair is an explosion of white cotton. He wears white gloves and pants, with a wrap-style gray jacket more suited to practice of martial arts than medicine. He holds a monocle to his left eye with a pearl and silver handle. Conrad's unsure whether it's still called a monocle, mounted to a handle this way.

The doctor gestures behind. "Let us sit."

Conrad can't stop wondering how far below ground he's descended. The appellation "underground" to this research facility is both metaphoric and literal, then. No matter. Conrad is ready to accept the strange, the unexpected. His mind has reached a point of such disintegration, he's prepared to try anything.

Two chrome and black Barcelona chairs face across a Le Corbusier coffee table. Conrad tries to formulate some comment of appreciation for the doctor's Bauhaus furnishings, but thoughts won't cohere.

"Please." Doctor Zyz takes the right chair, gestures at the left. "Conrad Snow. Describe your trouble."

"I just finished describing—"

The doctor interrupts. "Yes, your interview with Nurse V. I need to hear your words, unmediated. Often the story is told differently, this way. Down here."

"My trouble. It's complicated. A life ruined by trauma. Or maybe it's simple, my sleep mechanism's broken. My mind's stuck, an unbreakable loop. A wrecked machine."

"I will fix the machine."

Surprised to feel himself encouraged, Conrad recounts details of a year of hell. Agony of mind, a body failing.

Doctor Zyz nods. "Cerebrospinal fluid flushes toxic byproducts of consciousness. Waste material of thought, of life. This occurs only during sleep. In the insomniac, poisons accumulate, adding to misery. Eventually the wretch finds a point of no return, too sick and traumatized to relax. The only possibility that might forestall death, sleep itself, remains out of reach."

"Maybe I try too hard. Intentions end up running wild. I become overly focused—"

"Overly focused, on what are you focused? On whom?"

"You already know."

"Again I say, you must become willing to name your difficulty. Restate it, again, again. You may believe your answer repeats identically, but in my experience, answers shift. So. Please name this object of your excessive focus."

"Hanna." Conrad exhales, almost deflates. "Hanna."

Doctor Zyz mouths the name silently, as if trying it out before he speaks. "You are focused on Hanna. What aspect of her? What is it about Hanna?"

Again, Conrad's first impulse is to protest. "What happened… is hard to think about. Let alone tell."

"You must tell. Must relive. Face your memories until it becomes second nature."

"Must relive, you say. That's practically all I've done. That's my entire problem. I want to stop reliving. Not start."

"You misperceive psychological mechanisms crucial to your cure. You must relive, to transcend this state of trauma victim. This you will be able to do, under my guidance, influenced by medications of my design, and physically manipulated by my constructs." Doctor Zyz presses a button on a tiny remote. Lights flicker on. Convoluted machinery, chromium arrays like perverse jungle gyms covered with white cushions, entangled with black straps. Tools for sadism. For torture.

Conrad refuses to reveal fear, even reservation. "Why is this room so large?" he asks, instead of what he's thinking.

"Is the room in fact large? Or merely so dark, your eyes mistake its measure?" Doctor Zyz leans forward, flicks the monocle away from his eye. "Our work requires open space. You will dream with ferocious intensity. With violence. Such summonings of mind are impossible to restrain. They require room to fly."

Conrad fumbles for a response, uncertain whether Doctor Zyz is joking.

The doctor gestures dismissal. "Enough evasion. Describe her to me now. Describe Hanna, not in detail. How would you evoke her in a few simple sentences, to a friend who has never met her?"

"Hanna was…" Conrad subsides into memory, lets himself sink into waters both painful and comforting. "She's like this place. At once brilliant, blinding to the eyes, also dark, with deep, hidden aspects. When we met, Hanna called herself Onyx. She wore only black, and her skin was powder white, like alabaster. In darkness, in night, she felt most comfortable. She considered the dark sensuous, beautiful. Onyx modeled for magazines, and for record labels. She managed Goth nightclubs, the Batcave and the Vogue. Later she became a photographer herself. When she discovered poetry, she became Hanna. She began to wear colors, not just black. Hanna wrote stories, books of erotica. Called them perverse romances."

"Yes. Now I picture her." Doctor Zyz turns. "See my machines. My therapy is a brute medicine. A mechanistic hypnosis. You will be strapped down while metal braces adjust, by subtle hydraulics, flaws in your alignment. Attitude and posture, manipulated as you sleep. Body-mounted sensors give feedback from your organic machine."

Sweat dampens Conrad's skin, and tension pulls in his chest. Change is exactly what he wants, what he's come seeking, yet still he resists. Is this fear of the unknown, or resistance to relinquishing some final, perverse closeness with Hanna?

"We will discern your future," the doctor says, "if we stare sharply enough at your past."

Conrad refuses to see the racks, gears and engines. "It's my future that interests you?"

"Future should interest you, as well. It's the only thing you may hope to change."

Conrad is prepared to stay as long as necessary. Overnight, at least. Probably longer. Nothing waits for him at home. Here in the clinic, everything he requires will be dispensed.

After a period of psychotherapeutic preparation, and injection of medicines, Conrad reclines. He feels ready to be bound to the curved platform of chromium steel, undergirded by a mechanism of oiled gears ready to churn and pull. Hydraulic motors hum, idling. He tastes burnt sour cherries, an artifact of the drug cocktail already trickling in his blood.

Doctor Zyz stands over Conrad. "I will deprive you of sleep before finally I grant it. You may be impatient to give in, impelled by medicine and latent physical need, yet I keep you teetering on the edge, escalating your hunger for rest." The doctor pauses as if he anticipates objection.

Conrad says nothing. He feels his mind soften and deform.

"Observe within yourself an increase of urgency, as inner proportions shift. Mind, muscle and viscera. Blood, hormone and aether. All these combine into yearning for the other world. Your thought slows to a stillness. Physicality trembles with wanting, as on the cliff's edge before a dive, or the verge of penetrating a new lover for the first time. Desire so great finally will become irresistible."

"If I do fall asleep..." Conrad steadies his breathing. "Will you let me remain there?"

"Of course, in this first instance at least. Crucial at this stage is repair, recovery. Our primary goal is to restore basic function to compromised systems."

Doctor Zyz works alone, fastening cuffs around wrists and ankles, wrapping heavy bands around chest and waist, until Conrad is so tightly bound to this articulated platform of armatures and mechanisms, he feels he might be instantly torn to pieces at the whim of some unseen controller. But of course Doctor Zyz will be in charge.

The brute engineering force of heavy welded components purrs beneath him. Smells of oil and subtle smoke. High-contrast light overwhelms Conrad's vision, so his surroundings resemble some grainy, flickering silent film, a perverse documentary of sadism.

The doctor turns, makes some adjustment. Pinpoint spotlights die.

Conrad needs only lie still, eyes shut against the outsized gravity of the room's immaculate lightlessness, and hope the doctor achieves his intended effect. As Doctor Zyz murmurs final instructions, Conrad wonders when sleep might come. The possibility seems beyond all hope. If it does arrive, will the reunion be wrenching, traumatic rather than restful? It's been so long. He needs help to relearn the practice of peaceful sleep, and put behind him the blood-soaked visions of murder. Why does he feel so terrified, just facing the possibility of dreaming?

He sees the knife swing, hears the cutting of flesh. The cries. Dripping of blood.

Sees. Feels.

Hanna's breath hisses out, through a hole cut in his own chest. This is different. A vision imposed, forcible intrusion from without. Like watching a movie of his own life. The light flickers, unreal.

Relive:

Leather bonds constrict my wrists. Fingers pulse, hands tingle without circulation. How can I grip, cut? How am I supposed to cook? Have to finish dinner. Hanna's coming—

Bound hands can never untie themselves. My eyes shut against the world, my past. See myself waiting anxious in the kitchen. Quartered red potatoes boiling, olive oil at hand, green onions sliced. Smashing cloves of garlic, pulling each from dry skin.

Eye meets the chef's knife, resting on the board, the blade's angle threatening—

Hanna, what time?

Premonition rises to mind, heaves with force. Is that what it is? Ache of worry, impossible to place.

I've handled things badly, given Hanna less than she deserves. Twelve years. Made her wait too long for a future. Finally ready to move in. Finally to marry. A new kind of foundation.

I blame myself, guilt ever-present. Try to stop, it's fine, we're fine, what matters is the future. Don't let the past be a curse. Don't carry it any more. Have to move forward.

No, this feeling isn't that. Not regret for past wrongs. What nags is agony to come. Tragedy looming.

Do we give birth to trouble just by imagining? Worry creates the very problem it fears, wishes to prevent. A harm made manifest in mind, like a jinx. But real.

A new input, a sensation. Vision from without. A hint of light.

A voice. "You slept." Doctor Zyz.

Eyes open. "I did? Already?"

"Quickly now, recount your dreams."

Conrad seeks to assemble fragments into sensible narrative. "I found a child on the street. Murdered. Maybe I killed her myself? No, I wouldn't. Maybe the child is my symbolic self. I remember when life was simple. But it was a girl, I think. Could be a version of Hanna, young, innocent?" He tries to sit up, can't move against restraints.

"The dreaming mind rarely generates such obvious symbolism," the doctor insists.

"If I'm both dreamer and murderer, how can I also be the victim?" Conrad wonders. Does this make any sense?

Doctor Zyz shakes his head, looks into Conrad's eyes. "Stop trying to analyze. Relive. Describe the child."

"A girl. I'm sure she was a girl now. Maybe nine or ten. She wore her mother's shoes, too large, and an overlarge black shirt. It went to her ankles, like a dress. She lay in a pool of blood, blinking as if sightless, mouth making a kissing motion, like a fish suffocating in the air. I couldn't see her body under that black silk. Couldn't see where she was cut. But the blood kept running. It could only come from her. Where else could it—"

Doctor Zyz turns, reaches for a control panel. No more light.

Relive:

Memory of screams. I hear the shrieking before the sound makes any sense. Then I know. Familiar, it's her. Hanna.

It can't be her. I tell myself I'm only associating that sound of screaming with Hanna because it echoes my paranoid, idle thoughts while preparing our dinner, waiting for her arrival just moments earlier. But I'm not in my kitchen, back then. I'm in the dark below—

Another scream. A thump, someone falling to the ground.

I run outside, downstairs. Dusk sky, streetlights no help. Not a single car on the street.

Run slow-motion, flickering on a screen.

Do I see a shape flit away, not huddling over the body but slipping free? He's decorated to blend perfectly into the background, shadows painted across his form, matching shadows cast from trees overhead. Black paint slashes on the sidewalk. Pattern of his clothing, asphalt camouflage invisible against the street.

I reach the gate barely moving, as if reality is a film cut again and again, edited to move me forever further away—

This fleeing man, an impossibility. It's me, another Conrad, visiting from a future which becomes this present dream. Intruding upon worries of a lost moment, a futile wish to change his past. Her past, theirs together. Ours.

The present instant must not unravel.

Obsessive in heartbreak, drowning in unceasing remembrances, doomed forever to haunt this scene. Hanna lying there. It's her, must be her. Recognition twists. Blood trickles from her gut, gurgling breath. Hanna. Is she already lost?

Stay with me, stay with—

I kneel, afraid before I reach her she'll be pulled away, vanish from my grasp. Slipping, impossible to hold. So much blood. Touch her face, say her name. Her eyes remain open, but does she see? I'm here, she must know I'm here. I believe I see through her eyes, see her perspective from where she lies sprawled there, it's Conrad leaning in, meaning to diminish her fear of the onrushing cold.

It's me.

Is this my own perspective, my future mind coping with what happened before, or is it Hanna's final moment, impressions of a fading mind? A twinge of regret for the heartbreak cut across my face. I impose this upon her, something she never felt.

Cycles pass, including brief interludes in which Conrad sips water from a straw, or strains to clarify his mind sufficiently to respond to Doctor Zyz's efforts at talking therapy. Sometimes his eyes are open. His body is never unbound.

"This is the stage," the doctor intones, "at which the course of your future will be set."

How many cycles? Conrad doesn't care. He desires only rest, to never again relinquish the embrace of emptiness.

This morning, if it is morning, his eyes open wide. His voice comes forcefully. "Music is restored to me," he proclaims. At length and with passion he digresses upon the recovery of a pleasure almost forgotten, or at least believed forever lost. For some reason the rougher music of his twenties remains at a distance, but he has somehow regained the restrained music of his thirties. ECM minimalism, David Darling's honey-thick cello atmospheres, the ecstatic and infinitely varied piano improvisation of Keith Jarrett, Terje Rypdal's glittering blue-black guitar clouds. Conrad expounds upon the enigmatic structures, the glorious delicacy and balance. Music formed like a painting. At last he recalls how it felt to listen. It's like awakening to find a missing sense miraculously restored. He loves to listen, with a glass of port, in a room dark but for a single candle. It's not necessary to hear the music now. He remembers, knows he will listen again.

But the doctor seems displeased. "Come."

Conrad realizes his harnesses have been unfastened as he spoke. His mind is clearer, the concentration of medicine in his bloodstream diminished enough that he can keep his eyes open. He sits up.

When he stands, Conrad sees he isn't naked, as he believed himself to be, but wearing a skin-tight black bodysuit. He feels neither warm nor cold, merely relaxed and comfortable. Everything is changed. "I'm not fully rested," he says. "But almost. A bit more sleep is all I need. You did it. You fixed my broken machine. There's hope for me."

"Come, we must talk. Not here. This is for sleeping only."

The doctor leads Conrad away from the sleep machinery, the interview chairs. They pass beyond a barrier wall of black panels into a rectangular room. The ceiling is so high and so dark, it can't be seen. One wall is an enormous aquarium, ten feet deep and twice as wide, yet front to back no more than six inches. Conrad sees a black fish swimming alone, seeking somewhere to hide from the penetrating scrutiny of these new arrivals.

"We must revisit your earlier dream," the doctor begins.

"A dream of mine?" Conrad asks. "Which?"

"About the girl. A young girl, you said. In a black shirt, too long."

Conrad tries to remember. "How long ago has that been?"

"That was your first dream here," the doctor insists, urgent. "Do you remember anything?"

"Remember more?" In the process of searching, Conrad realizes this involves not only memory, but invention. "I was a small boy, wearing my mother's black silk blouse. It was long on me, like a dress. I kept tripping over the bottom."

"Yourself?" the doctor asks. "You said before, a girl."

"In my dream, I bled on the sidewalk." Conrad wonders what this signifies, the changing of a dream.

"A girl was murdered," the doctor sputters. "In reality, just as you dreamed. How did you know?"

Conrad shrugs, uncertain what he actually dreamed, and what changed since then.

"A young girl," Doctor Zyz continues. "She was discovered wearing a long black silk blouse, and her mother's shoes, much too large, as you said." The doctor is not merely curious at the coincidence. He's upset, angry, afraid. "Found stabbed to death, on a sidewalk. Not in front of your house, not exactly. But very near."

"Did my dream murder the child? Or did I foresee a murder that was inevitable?" Conrad pauses. "Do you think, if you or I had reported my dream to the police, they could have done anything to prevent it?"

The doctor rubs his eyes, as if very tired. "No. But don't you feel culpability, that your dream became actual?"

"Can you imagine, if we had called the police, their all-points bulletin? All officers, be on the lookout for nine-year-old female wearing her mother's black shirt and too-large shoes. The young girl may be real, or only merely the psychic projection of an insane thirty-nine-year-old white male."

The room is supernaturally quiet. Conrad wonders why Doctor Zyz selected this place for these questions. In the gap between the illuminated back wall and thick glass front of the aquarium, water seems to churn and swirl, though the water's motion itself can't be seen. Sometimes the fish swims straight, and other times its trajectory is disturbed by currents. It fights against invisible motion. Only by the perturbation in the line of the black fish can this be observed. Aether affects Conrad the same way. The room's air appears to present a neutral environment in which to move, yet Conrad feels himself pulled, affected by subtle drafts. No sound. Dead atmosphere full of dead thoughts. The universe's inherent matrix seethes, working against him.

"I'm concerned," the doctor says. "This may be a step back."

"I feel we're on a path to success," Conrad says. "I came to you, Doctor Zyz, for magic. For dangerous, illegal drugs. For insane props that resemble torture mechanisms. I needed your willingness to break me down, burn me to ash, then plant me in the ground to grow again. That's why I came. I lack the nerve to do this for myself."

As he speaks, Conrad is trying to find where the fish has gone. Maybe the water has always been empty.

Relive:

What if my house were located somewhere else? If I lived farther away, she might have driven, not walked. I might have chosen some other city, or safer neighborhood.

Do I deserve blame for these decisions?

There's so much in this world I might have changed. Any time before that night, I might have shared my home with her, not made her walk to it. Then she would never have been seen by the wrong eyes, on the wrong night, on that sidewalk.

The doctor is giving me a chance to relive that night, not only to see again, but to encode into myself forever Hanna's process of dying. I'll suffer, but unlike before. I'll break through. End the cycle.

What could I have done, from my kitchen, failing to look out in time? Any change in timing, or shift in luck. So many things might have gone differently.

Too late.

I want to die as Hanna died, not as I saw firsthand, or imagined later. To wade into her trauma, reach a culmination of suffering adequate to supersede my own. If I'm ever to have any chance of coming through this, of walking open-eyed in the world, I have to accept what happened. Face the reality, and move past.

As I come to her side, is she still present? Does she feel my fingers grasping her arm, slick with blood? I tell myself I know her eyes well enough, ought to see the difference, to discern presence within them. What if I miss the moment she vanishes? I know my fiancée like I know myself, believe I recognize what's behind her eyes. I take measure of her fears. But now I live this nightmare of self-blame and endless wondering.

Only a week until we finally would have married. After all our directionless time, just before that threshold, that was when I lost her. My Hanna, already gone. A vacant body cooling in a pool of relinquished blood by the time I arrive.

Darkness narrows, an iris closing on a scene.

Conrad comes awake in the blackness.

"What more have you recovered?" the doctor asks, invisible.

"*Three times before*," Conrad gasps, bound so tight he can barely breathe, "I stopped death from taking her."

"Please describe."

Eyes closed, Conrad sees clearly as a dream. "One, at a rooftop party, when she was still Onyx, tightrope walking a ledge under moonlight. I tried to hold her hand from below, but she wanted to walk alone, so I let go, and followed along. She made it to the corner, then stepped on a loose brick. She wobbled, started to fall, not inward toward the roof, but away. Her arms pinwheeled. I grabbed her hand, almost missed it, and pulled her back from falling. She climbed down and we held each other. Her sudden sweat, mixed with tears, and relief, heart pounding at what was avoided. Fear for what almost was. She still looked invulnerable, perfect, but the rest of the night, her hands trembled. Trembled."

"Yes. And the next?

The scene changes. "Two, below ground, at an illegal rave, an abandoned subway, before we moved to Portland. We drifted away from the heat, the sweaty crowd. Wandered down black tunnels, seeking cool air, and a quiet place. Privacy to have sex, I remember. Her idea. We found a heavy door stopped open, stumbled through. Into a room. There was light, and someone screamed. Four men surrounded one on his knees. Blood sprayed from his throat, just cut. Onyx laughed, must not have understood what this was. When they turned, then she saw. They started for us."

Only as Conrad recounts this freshly recovered memory does he recall another presence at the scene: Doctor Zyz. This can't be possible, yet there he is. Insane white hair, gloves, monocle. Even the gray jacket.

"I pull Hanna back," Conrad recalls. "We rush out, the door latches behind. Up the tunnel, everything passing in a blur. Then we're back among the crowd. We push through, leave the rave. Out into the night. Drive, and drive."

How is Conrad to know for certain whether Doctor Zyz was actually present in that room? He couldn't have recognized the doctor at that time. They wouldn't meet for another decade.

"And number three?"

Conrad is confused. "Three?" Then he recalls having said, three times before. Were there really? He can't imagine why he would've said so, would have felt prepared to describe three instances supporting his theory, only now fail to recall.

The doctor inhales noisily through nostrils. "Why do you suppose your mind made this error? What it signifies?"

Conrad is less concerned with his mistake, occupied instead with the image of Doctor Zyz superimposed upon his past. "What do you think might explain it?"

"Perhaps Hanna was meant for death."

Conrad feels relief. Someone finally said it. "Maybe I helped her cheat mortality." For a while, at least.

"If so, what do you believe was pursuing her?"

"I don't know." Pursuing her, because death remained inevitable for her. It was always following.

"Please speculate. What entity tracks such debts? Who follows one in Hanna's situation?"

Conrad doesn't know. He's tired of saying he doesn't know.

Relive:

I step outside, lock the door behind. Execute a mental checklist of superstitious routines, OCD efforts at differentiating this present day from *that day*. It's the only way I can force myself down the stairs, to the sidewalk. My armpits drip sweat, hands tremble, but less than before. I think it's less. Everything feels strained and desperate, until I reach the sidewalk and turn left. Then for a while, all that is left behind.

The store is only three blocks away. In that interval, I plan the groceries I'll buy. It's never much. I make the trip every day, but only this far.

When I approach, the automatic door slides open. The light inside is garish, yellow.

He stands there, waiting like a greeter. Doctor Zyz.

I almost walk past, so accustomed to seeing him everywhere. I remember how much worse things were for me, before I drove up the hill, to that place among the trees.

This time, I stop.

"My dreams are changing," I tell him.

The doctor seems unsure how to respond.

"Everywhere I go, I see you," I say. "I know you're beside me while I sleep. Helping me."

"I tried," the doctor says.

"But when will we know…" I begin, tentative, afraid to seem ungrateful.

The doctor tilts his head, as if trying to puzzle me out.

I need to make sure he understands I'm grateful, and I won't presume to decide for him when my treatment should be over. But I can't help wondering. It feels like years I've been sleeping underground, motionless in the dark, with Doctor Zyz standing by. It's better than the way I lived before. I just want to know there will be an end. "I'm sleeping. Dreaming."

Doctor Zyz nods, seems about to speak.

"I wonder when you can unbind me. When I can stand up. Leave therapy." It's frustrating, getting no response. "When will I be able to stop sleeping in your lab, and go home?"

The doctor's face slackens. "You're no longer in therapy."

"I…"

"You left my facility, years ago. You drove home, resumed your life, only filtered through this interpretive layer."

What he's saying terrifies me. I'm not dreaming from the safety of a quiet, dark sanctuary, deep below ground. Not monitored and protected by Doctor Zyz. I'm out in the world, walking around, but not seeing.

"Why would you release me?" I demand, furious and afraid. "Let me go home, like this?"

"You sought release from pain," he says. "And you sought dreams."

He's right, I found these things. I have everything I asked for. If there's anything more worth wanting, I don't recall.

THE HUMAN ALCHEMY

T he first time Aurye saw the home of Reysa and Magnus Berg, she thought it resembled a castle that must have stood for centuries, fixed to the rock of the snowy mountainside. Though she'd often imagined what the place might be like, she couldn't believe the grandeur, all towering stone walls and high windows. Pale streaks of cloud behind gleamed against the sky's darkening background, trailing off the shoulder of the sloping ridge.

Reysa at the wheel, the gray Range Rover climbed the snowy drive, and veered toward the high peaked entryway. The amber glow of interior light made stone and ice appear golden. Snow covered a roof broken by two chimneys, and at the very summit of the place, an angled square of clear glass, something like an enormous skylight, stood clear of snow.

Likewise at ground level, a rectangle of textured concrete outside the front door, sheltered beneath the peak of the gabled entry, was bare of snow. Reysa parked, explaining, "There are heating coils underneath."

"Such a beautiful setting," Aurye said. Impressive lodges and chalets weren't rare up on the mountain, even million-dollar places that sat empty all but a weekend or two per year. Even compared to such homes as those, the Berg place was beyond Aurye's expectations.

"Magnus will love hearing our home made an impression. He was worried you'd take it wrong, him staying behind while I drove down to pick you up. I told him not to worry. He was so excited, I left him arranging his new stereo setup."

288 · MICHAEL GRIFFIN

"A stereo?" Aurye wasn't sure why this should be surprising. She felt overwhelmed, almost breathless about it all.

"The old-fashioned kind, only two speakers. Just for music, Magnus said, not surround sound. I think he's trying to impress you." Reysa winked, looking bright and glamorous as a 1950s movie star. She killed the ignition. "Come on."

It seemed crazy to Aurye, this suggestion that either Berg might wish to impress her. She was the one who'd been nervous all evening, wondering how this would go, what they'd think of her outside the familiar setting of Midgard bar. Both were older, Reysa a youthful thirty-six and Magnus a decade older, both successful physicians, so worldly compared to herself. Aurye knew them from her role behind the bar at Midgard, the mid-mountain restaurant where the Bergs frequently dined and drank. Midgard was the only restaurant in the village frequented by people like them, the rest catering to the burgers and brews crowd, snowboarders in winter and mountain bikers in summer.

Upon climbing out, the scope of the landscape struck Aurye. Beyond the dry, bare section, a frozen sheet sloped away. "Your place. I just can't believe..." She ventured onto the ice, careful to keep her feet under her center of gravity. "When you said, come up, see our lodge, I didn't picture..."

Reysa remained back, nearer the house. "What did you picture?"

"Nothing as grand as this. It's like a castle from an old movie."

"That was the idea," Reysa said. "Of course, there were no actual Gothic castles existent on the mountain. Magnus and I decided to build one."

As impressive as the house was the setting. The broad white expanse fell away into darkening mist until it reached an abrupt edge. Aurye felt herself drawn nearer the cliff overlook. Wind etched the ice into jagged coarseness, edges glistening like blades of polished diamond. Everything was pristine, so unlike the dirty, snowplowed village below, where she lived and worked. Soon Aurye stood near the edge of a precipice, swaying there, afraid to move. The gaping openness exerted a pull. Beyond the initial steep drop, the canyon flattened into a convex snow field and rose again to the next ridge. Behind that, the lowering sun glared white, emanating wild, swirling tendrils of mist, backgrounded by a sky diminishing blue to black.

"Let's go inside," Reysa called.

Her words broke the spell. Aurye turned, found Reysa standing well up the slope, clutching her narrow frame in an exaggerated show of shivering. She looked tiny, waiflike in her dark green cloak-style coat with oversized monk's hood. A thick zipper cut diagonally across her chest like a scar. Aurye hurried back up, too aware of the deadly attraction below.

They stamped snow off their boots on the spiral-patterned coir entry mat inside the double doors.

"You know the hardest thing, living on the mountain full-time?" Reysa took Aurye's black peacoat and green and grey patchwork scarf and hung them on a branch of their coat rack, a leafless silver metal tree. "Wearing clothes that feel pretty, when outside it's all freezing wind, icy roads and snowfields."

"Layers are the thing." Aurye indicated her own dress, thin and white with antique lace trim. "I could never wear this alone, but with tights and boots… not thin yoga pants either. These are fleece."

"That's what I meant. It's tricky, managing to look like a girl up here, but you do." Reysa pulled off her boots, left them beside the mat.

Aurye's face flushed with pleasure at the compliment. She'd always found Reysa so elegant and stylish. "You need waterproof boots, with a good sole. Like you said, the trick is finding some you feel good in." Aurye lifted one foot, modeled her knee-high boots, shiny black leather with a diamond quilt pattern. She untied laces, slid off one boot at a time, and left hers beside Reysa's. "When I came back from school, all I had were red suede Fluevogs with three-inch stacked heels. They looked really cute around campus, but hopeless up here."

Her own exit from college was a subject Aurye wished she hadn't opened, hoped Reysa wouldn't want to talk about. Reysa let it pass, flipped back her hood to reveal mid-length blond curls which bounced as if they'd just been styled, and never held down under the hood. Beneath the coat, Reysa wore a white wool long-sleeved dress over charcoal leggings, barely lighter than Aurye's. "You always look feminine, but mountain-appropriate," Reysa resumed. "I just wanted you to know I got some great ideas, watching you at Midgard."

Though flattered, Aurye couldn't quite accept the idea. Had she really provided fashion inspiration to someone as polished and glamorous as Reysa? The Bergs had been regulars long enough to strike up a sort of friendship with Aurye, but the relationship was unequal. Their conversations ended in Reysa or Magnus handing an Amex across the bar, then calculating Aurye's tip.

The entry floor was slate tile, and from a black ceiling hung a sculpture of clear and frosted glass, within which orange-glowing elements radiated heat and light. A single piece of framed art dominated each side wall. The silver-framed square to the left was an extreme close-up of a woman's face draped in black fishnet. Her skin was unnaturally white, eyes gem-blue, lips vivid red and hair intense yellow-gold. The colors were saturated to such a rich, exaggerated degree, Aurye first took this for a painting. "Who is she?" she asked, and only then realized it was a photograph.

Reysa seemed surprised. "She… was me."

Aurye thought the image looked nothing like Reysa, but didn't say so. Maybe the picture was old. All women aged; it would happen to Aurye. But the woman in the picture wasn't merely younger. Reysa Berg was every bit as beautiful and striking as the woman in the photograph. Thinner now, with prominent cheekbones, more natural coloring. Reysa's face had not so much aged as shifted, taken on a very different character.

Aurye's attention shifted to the opposite wall. The mural there, in contrast to the photograph, was a grid combining four pieces of very old symbolic art, subtly colored ink linework. Most of the arcane signs were unrecognizable, though a few were traditional, symbols for male or female. Others reminded Aurye of astrology.

"Engravings by Jakob Bohme," Reysa explained. "A very interesting mind. He believed Adam, the Adam of Christian myth, was both man and woman at once, able to birth his own children by parthenogenesis. Can you imagine? No need for Eve."

No response came to mind, so Aurye changed the subject. "Thank you for inviting me up. And for driving down to get me. It sounded fun, spending time with you and Magnus. I haven't seen you much at Midgard, lately."

"Oh yes. About that." Reysa seemed uncharacteristically flustered. "The truth is, we bought the Midgard. We were afraid it was failing. I mean, imagine if the only nice place in the village went under, just as we shifted our lives up here."

So, the Bergs were her employers. The news was a shock, but she knew better than to voice the many questions that spun to mind. "That explains about Tolliver, at least."

Reysa looked confused.

"When I asked for tonight off, at first, Tolliver said no. Then I mentioned you'd invited me up here. His face got all red, and he couldn't look at me. He just said, of course you can go."

From inside the house came footsteps. Aurye and Reysa turned.

Magnus approached from the next room, shoeless in jeans, grey wool socks, and a form-fitting black sweater with diagonal white slashes across the front. His salt and pepper hair, long on top, was closely undercut on the sides. Aurye almost commented on how different Magnus looked, but caught herself. Better not to say. Probably the difference was that he was more casual at home.

"Aurye." Magnus came to embrace her, moving as if about to kiss her mouth. Aurye felt a flash of surprise, and in that instant decided to accept it, as if nothing were strange. But Magnus shifted, kissed her on the cheek. He was inches taller than she remembered, even shoeless.

"Why that look?" Magnus touched the frames of his eyeglasses near the hinges. "Is it these? They're new."

Aurye looked around for Reysa, just approaching with two glasses of ruby dark wine.

"We love the same things," Reysa said, "so I know you won't turn down a good Pinot Noir. This one is excellent. A gift from a client of Magnus's."

Strange, a doctor saying "client" to describe a patient, but the Bergs were unusual in many ways, despite their taste and easy elegance. They did things their own way. Smiling, Aurye accepted the glass. "Impossible to refuse."

"From Switzerland, believe it or not," Magnus added.

The taste was startling. After three years working at Midgard bar, Aurye knew hundreds of wines, but mostly from Pacific Coast winemakers. This Pinot was unusually full-bodied, complex. "Wow. Almost gamey. Smoked meat, black raspberry and pomegranate." Aurye struggled to articulate the rest of what the wine conveyed. More than just flavor. A suggestion of exoticism, of deep time and distant locales, worldly pleasures Aurye had never known. In fact, she'd never really spent much time anywhere but this mountain, other than trips to Portland, and a year and a half in college in Eugene. Aurye could imagine nothing so suggestive of a better life, altered potentialities and pleasurable indulgences, than a strange, excellent wine. The taste of age and memory, of earthy desires. Even lust. Her powers of description fell short here. If anything, the taste reminded her of the Bergs. She wondered what Reysa and Magnus thought, watching her sip. How did they perceive the wine? Maybe such spicy, exotic flavor had become routine to their tastes.

All three looked at each other, unspeaking. Aurye was first to turn away.

The enormous central room was more open hall or great room than living room. To the left upon entering was an open dining area and chef's kitchen, then an unused fireplace and a wide curving staircase up. On the opposite wall, between two large windows, a heap of wood burned in a second fireplace.

"We're still decorating," Reysa said, as if to explain the mostly empty room.

Magnus headed toward the kitchen. "I'll get myself a glass."

Reysa showed Aurye toward the windows.

"Like *Citizen Kane*." Aurye indicated the stone fireplace. "You could stand inside there."

Even twenty feet away, the fire radiated intense heat.

"Might be a little warm." Reysa guided Aurye toward the rightmost window. The extraordinary view overlooked a different drop-off and canyon opposite the one Aurye had seen outside. The grade swooped away steeply, flattened and rose again across the canyon. Tips of evergreens barely penetrated the deep snow.

Before the window was a heavy black book on a stand, like an old bible or dictionary, open near the beginning. The pages drew Aurye's curiosity. What did the Bergs feel important enough to display? She leaned in, read aloud. "Of all created things, the condition whereof is transitory and frail…" Aurye stopped, feeling someone approaching behind. She glanced up to find Magnus standing back, looking out the window, sipping from his glass.

Magnus began to recite. "The common matter of all things is the Great Mystery, which no certain essence and prefigured or formed idea could comprehend, nor could it comply with any property, it being altogether void of color and elementary nature." He paused, seeming to look for Aurye's reaction.

"Are you reading from this?" she asked.

He continued. "The scope of this Great Mystery is as large as the firmament. And this Great Mystery was the mother of all the elements, and Grandmother of all the stars, trees and carnal creatures."

Reysa approached from the other side, stood so the Bergs flanked Aurye.

"As children are born of a mother," Magnus went on, "so all created things whether sensible or insensible, all things whatsoever, were uniformly brought out of the Great Mystery."

Aurye twitched reflexively, half-aware of a kind of spell being cast. More likely it was the wine than Magnus's incantation. She glanced again at the page, recognized words he'd recited from memory. The mystery fascinated her. The Bergs had never seemed religious types, not the least dogmatic.

"It's Paracelsus, from *Liber Primus*," Reysa said. "You know Paracelsus, the Renaissance alchemist and mystic?"

"Alchemist?" Aurye asked. "Isn't that turning lead into gold?"

"Alchemy is creation by combination." Magnus gestured down the wall to their left. "I'll show you."

In such a large room, each section felt vastly separate. Magnus proceeded along the outer wall, past windows, toward the arrangement of stereo equipment. Two tower speakers flanked an aluminum stand upon which electronic components stood ranked, facing a trio of low-slung black leather chairs. Magnus gestured Aurye into the middle chair.

She sat, wondering why three seats, and tried to read the nameplate on the two identical black metal slabs beneath the stand. Each was the size of a small coffee table, with finned heatsinks along the left side. "Krell." Amplifiers, each connected to one speaker with a white cable thick as a garden hose. Aurye was tempted to mention she'd dated an audiophile in college, but didn't want to talk about him. Anyway, she'd never learned much about the equipment.

Magnus selected a CD from a small stack and inserted the disk into the tray of a player with a glossy white faceplate. He pressed a button, adjusted a volume knob on the walnut and brushed stainless steel box on the shelf, and handed Aurye the CD case. He sat to her left.

The sound began, an intricate flurry of violin gestures repeating in varied agitation. Culmination and pause, then a piano took over. The effect was quieting. Aurye and Magnus leaned forward in their chairs, Reysa standing beside Aurye. At the edge of this cavernous room, not far from windows overlooking the grandest view, this hushed music narrowed the atmosphere. A feeling of closeness verging on intimacy.

On the CD cover, the words *Arvo Pärt / Tabula Rasa* hovered over snow fields wind-blown into sculptural shapes.

"It's incredible," Aurye said, still listening. "These hunks of steel, all glowing tubes and fat copper cables, making such delicate sound. So pure."

Reysa took the seat to Aurye's right.

"Blank slate," Aurye said, and at once regretted it. The Bergs didn't need her help translating basic Latin.

Magnus looked nothing but pleased. "*Tabula Rasa* is one of my favorite things."

"I never noticed before, your eyes are mismatched," Aurye told him, before she could stop herself. Aurye wondered how she'd never noticed. Not only different colors. Irises of different sizes. Like two people watching her. Two minds.

"Tell about Aurye Feuer," Reysa said. "We know a few details. Tell us something new."

Aurye felt an ache of infatuation. She wanted to know Reysa better, to let Reysa know her. Magnus, too. Why did she feel so strongly that being closer to the Bergs might remedy her problems? In the course of their dining and drinking at Midgard, Aurye had mentioned her intention to return to college, try to rediscover herself. This had seemed to intrigue them, for some reason. More than anything, she hoped to learn what they found so interesting about her. Aurye felt a sense of auditioning, but didn't resent their attention. She was willing, even glad to reveal herself.

"I'll tell you whatever you want," Aurye said. "I like you both so much, and this is the best wine I've ever tasted. Probably the best I ever will."

"I doubt that," Reysa said. "You'll have greater pleasures ahead, I'm sure."

Aurye wondered where to begin. "You know I was in college."

"It's rumored you were pre-med." Magnus paused. "I think Reysa and I would both tell you medicine is a field to avoid, if you possibly can. We couldn't." He smiled, as if implying something more.

Aurye knew she'd mentioned college, but never pre-med. "I never got that far, just lots of Bio and Chem, before I flamed out. That's why I didn't mention it. What's the point of bragging about my two years? You're successful surgeons."

Magnus grinned at Reysa. "You hear that? She thinks we're successful."

"Don't tease." Reysa touched Aurye's arm. "Why not go back, finish?"

Aurye felt a twinge of pain in her side. Her hand moved toward that spot, but she commanded herself not to draw attention. "I'm saving up, most of what I earn, but it's hard. Since I came crawling home, I live at my mom's. She stays with her boyfriend in Rhododendron, so I have the place to myself, for free. Maybe I'll save enough, go back. Not U of O, but somewhere." She sighed. Being honest felt good, but she should stop. "The truth is, it's hard to imagine starting again."

Reysa leaned in, looked close, as if some key were to be found in Aurye's face. "Shame to quit, once you started."

"It was stupid, embarrassing." Aurye looked away. "Just… a boy."

Reysa looked at Magnus. "Isn't it always a boy?"

"Except when it's a girl," Magnus replied.

"Well." Reysa stood, straightened her dress. "I'm sure we're not finished talking about boys and girls tonight."

Reysa herded them toward the dining area and kitchen. Magnus followed, after raising the music's volume. A large, circular gray wood dining table was surrounded by eleven black bucket chairs. Six wine bottles and three glasses rested on a central black spinner.

Magnus pulled out three chairs. Reysa ran her fingers through her hair.

The blond waves were longer than Aurye had realized. How much time had passed since she'd seen the Bergs? Both seemed indefinably changed.

Reysa selected two bottles. "Which do you prefer, the Swiss or Argentinian?"

Magnus offered his glass, conveying his preference to Reysa without words. She poured from the left hand bottle, then held up both for Aurye to choose from.

Aurye shrugged. "Either for me."

"Ever flexible and accommodating." Reysa's mouth angled in suppressed amusement. "You're not at work tonight. You're with friends. You must speak your true mind." She poured Aurye brim-full, then finished the bottle herself.

Aurye tasted. "This one's peppery. Leather, coriander and tobacco leaf."

Reysa sat on the table edge. "Aren't you nimble with the tasting notes."

"Everybody at Midgard seems to appreciate quick reference points to help them choose."

"I find," Magnus pronounced, "most people prefer being told what to do."

Aurye wondered if agreement might reveal too much of her own inclination. "Me, too."

Reysa held up two empty bottles and peered into the openings like binoculars. "Only two? I thought we had more."

"Three." Magnus indicated another empty hidden among full bottles. He stepped nearer the women, and leaned against the table. "That's enough for Aurye to tell why she dropped out. Talk about the boy."

Reysa bit her lip. "He cheated?"

Aurye couldn't move, or think of what to say.

"Don't be embarrassed." Magnus turned, as if sparing Aurye his scrutiny. "We've both been hurt that way."

"As an idea, love is glorious, but we're cynical. These human vessels are unfortunately flawed." Reysa adjusted her sleeves, as if some vulnerable part of herself might be exposed at the wrists. She crossed arms, angled her head.

Aurye wondered what she was hiding. Scars? "Infidelity wasn't the whole story. It was complicated."

"It always is." Reysa selected another bottle, started opening.

"I'm not giving up," Aurye insisted. "It's not hopeless. You two seem happy. So, your cynicism surprises me."

Reysa eyed Magnus, then refilled glasses. "We are happy. Well matched, truly in love. We're even faithful. But that isn't how we're made. Human nature is laziness, dishonesty."

Magnus's eyebrows lifted. "People take the most crucial things for granted."

"No." Aurye protested, though she couldn't say they were wrong. The Bergs were so attractive, so successful, so appealing in every aspect, she couldn't understand how their prior partners could have rejected them. But she realized the very same thing had happened to her. "It wasn't the cheating. He pulled away. First I was beautiful, everything he wanted. Then he got to know me, and discovered... things that disgusted him. About me."

"Aurye, no," Reysa said. "There's nothing about you less than beautiful. Not one single imperfection."

Aurye squirmed. They didn't know. She wanted to tell them, wanted to show—

"Actually," Magnus interrupted loudly, seeming to sense Aurye's discomfort, "for both of us, what triggered the final breakdown of prior marriages was a crisis."

"Crisis?" Aurye asked, relieved her turn for storytelling seemed to have passed.

"For me, a car crash," Reysa said. "Tearing metal, cutting glass. My face was disfigured, my neck, one of my breasts. This was before Magnus and I. We were married to others, all working in the same hospital. After the crash, Magnus was my surgeon. He created this face. My own husband, he did not love this face. Or more likely, he'd already fallen out of love with me. This face was only his excuse."

Aurye scanned Reysa's skin, looking for scars. She was smooth, symmetrical. "What about you, Magnus?"

"My crisis? It was something I made. A creation of my own." He looked away, distant.

Aurye looked to Reysa for elaboration.

Reysa stood. "We're going to fall over, drinking so much without food." She slipped away to the kitchen.

Aurye felt herself swaying, affected by the wine.

"People hurt by rejection become pathologically terrified of it," Magnus said. "I was driven mad by fear. It's something I admit. There's no shame in having suffered. My first wife abandoned me in my moment of greatest need."

Reysa returned with two gold leaf platters, each bearing three black plates. "Steamed and chilled mussels with black lava salt, half-shell oysters, and aged gouda. And here, wild mushroom truffle tarts, kalamata tapenade, and the best fucking baguette I've ever had. All from Portland, this morning."

"See, Aurye?" Magnus said. "We might try to rescue ourselves, but more likely someone else does it for us."

"You weren't kidding, I really will fall down if I don't eat something." Aurye took some food. This intoxication was hard to distinguish from excitement, but she knew she might crash if she drank too much without eating.

"There are great advantages to marriage," Reysa said. "Partnership. Not just one fling after another, but a bond that can last for life. But if we remain with a single type, no variety, always the same body shape, the same face, same color of skin, we get bored. Overfamiliarity creates temptation to revisit the new."

"I don't have energy for that," Aurye protested. "Constantly shuffling through different boyfriends. My friends who do that, they end up with nothing to rely on."

"That's what she's saying," Magnus said. "We've known polyamorists. It's a term that most often seems to mean indiscriminate openness, as you said. Constant shuffling. I believe, we believe, a person is meant to be with one other."

"But you said—"

"That is," Magnus continued, "if we do something to remedy that inborn need."

"Humans require a variety of stimulus," Reysa added. "We're prone to boredom. By we, I don't mean myself and Magnus. Everyone. You. Human nature, like it or not."

Aurye saw their point, understood it derived from personal experience. In fact, it fit what she knew from her own small bank of relationship data. The problem was, she preferred not to think that way, even if it might be true.

"I see that look," Reysa said. "We won't push. But one thing we share is willingness to question received wisdom."

Aurye smiled. "I count myself an atheist, rebel and deviant."

Reysa laughed. Magnus joined in.

"Ours is a transgressive philosophy," Reysa said carefully. "Desire is important. Lust."

"But what does that mean?" Aurye asked, heart pounding.

"Come. We'll show you." Reysa took Aurye's hand, and she stood.

As they walked toward the stairs, Magnus took Aurye's other hand. Aurye wanted to ask what was happening, though she thought she knew.

When they reached the cold, unused fireplace, Reysa surged ahead, pulling Aurye by the arm, trying to run. Aurye in turn dragged Magnus along, all of them laughing in a chain linked by hands.

"I think I'm drunk," Reysa shouted.

Magnus jogged to keep up. "I think you are, too."

"Aurye too," Reysa said.

"All of us!" Aurye wailed laughter.

Reysa veered away from the foot of the stairs. The three gained speed, all running together, none resisting. Reysa's laughter infected the others, as they played an energetic game of whiplash momentum, pulling and swinging against one another, whirling and gaining speed. Reysa led their circuit of the room, between stereo and chairs, past picture windows and the great hot fireplace, the entryway, kitchen and dining table, and finally back to the cold fireplace and the sweeping curve of the staircase. With a shriek Reysa fell. Aurye tried to jump over, but tripped and crashed. Magnus stumbled, almost regained footing, only to sprawl at the foot of the stairs. He lay on his back, moaning. Reysa still laughed madly.

Aurye tried to find herself. Was she in pain? She felt joy, the excitement of belonging, not fear. It occurred to her, breathing hard, looking at the high ceiling, that she may have an advantage after all. She'd felt disadvantaged ever since Reysa picked her up. Clearly the Bergs held some agreed-upon plan, which Aurye didn't know. But maybe she had a clearer idea than they realized. Was it possible they believed her completely unaware, when in fact she understood all but the details? Reysa and Magnus expected her to be cautious, but she was a woman of experience beyond her years. She was tired of playing by imposed rules. If an opportunity came to jump to a new realm of experience, she'd take the chance. What better fix for stagnant life than to destroy it?

Still she wondered. Was their secret as simple as she guessed, some of experiment in transgressive intimacy, or something weirder? She kept thinking of three new chairs by the stereo. Maybe they wanted to invite her in. Of course this was presumptuous, but they didn't need to know what guesses played in her mind.

Aurye looked up, found both Reysa and Magnus watching, clearly guessing at her thoughts. She looked between them, intending to convey understanding and acceptance. "I have to admit something," she began, feigning confidence, trying to bluster through. "I think I've guessed why you invited me up. Were my assumptions wrong?"

Reysa looked amused. "I could probably guess your guess."

Magnus popped himself up on his elbows. "Yet still you came." His glasses having fallen off, the difference between his eyes was more pronounced.

Aurye looked away, covered her mouth, then realized she was only playing coy and girlish. She didn't want to convey anything but what she actually felt. In fact, she hadn't realized how receptive she actually was until that moment. Though nervous, she was unafraid. "I don't know exactly what, not specifically. But I assume there's some kind of proposition. I just don't understand how it fits with what you said about faithfulness." She sat nearer Reysa than Magnus, and Reysa was the one most focused upon her. "Whenever you look at me, both of you but especially Reysa, I feel you trying to figure me out. Studying me."

"So that was it?" Reysa asked. "We convince the comely twenty-two-year-old to frolic with one of us, or both?"

Magnus looked amused. Reysa laughed, leaning against her husband, sprawled comfortably against him in the languor of intoxication.

"Isn't that it?" Aurye asked. Any frustration or confusion dispersed as she joined their ridiculous laughter. She felt both relief and disappointment at once. "Well, then what?"

"You're almost completely wrong," Magnus said.

"We do have something in mind," Reysa clarified. "An offer. An arrangement we'll explain soon enough."

"Sorry, I just thought I'd try being blunt, or direct." Aurye felt slightly embarrassed, but couldn't help noticing the Bergs still looked at her with the same eager curiosity. "At least our game doesn't seem to have ended."

"No," Magnus said. "And your flexibility of mind comes as a relief."

"Blunt directness is a virtue," Reysa said.

"Sorry. I shouldn't have had so much to drink," Aurye said. "Not my first time here."

"I'm the one who poured gallons of wine, and led us around the room like a madwoman," Reysa said. "Anyway, when the time comes for us to be blunt and direct with you, I hope you'll keep that open mind."

"You plan to be direct with me," Aurye noted. "Just not yet?"

"Not quite," Reysa said.

"So then." Aurye looked again at the staircase. "What were you going to show me?"

Reysa was first to stand. The trio gathered at the bottom of the stairs, each seeming to ponder the eventuality of going up. Such a prospect seemed momentous, at least to Aurye. All the answers must wait above.

"Are you sure you want this, to know more?" Reysa asked Aurye. "Such things we could show you."

"You know I sort of idolize you both. You have so much figured out. Just, seem to be living exactly right."

"But you don't know everything," Magnus cautioned.

Aurye nodded. "That's true, I really only know a little. And we all tend to idealize people based on too little information. But you have each other. This incredible home, and property. And success in your careers."

"Success, that's nothing solid." Reysa shook her head. "It's a cloud. Not something you attach to."

"Past failures weigh me down," Magnus said, "so much more than successes have ever lifted me."

"I don't even know what kind of medicine you practice, but I think you're being over-modest." Aurye looked between the two of them. The Bergs possessed so many pleasures, not just luxuries and money, but simple things.

Reysa stepped to the first stair as if prepared to climb, but stopped, turned. "If anyone understands the way people judge by appearances, you do, Aurye. They assume you must be a certain way, without knowing your mind, how it feels to be you. People notice your appearance right away, see the confident way you hold forth behind the bar, and what do they think? That girl, she's beautiful. Confident, has this killer body. Aurye's perfect. She possesses everything. Lacks nothing."

Aurye was stunned, wanted to protest. There was so much they didn't—

"That's what people think," Magnus added. "But is that you?"

"I know how people regard me, their assumptions. You're right, of course I hear it. Pretty face, that body, and she's supposedly smart, too. What's she doing in this shitty little village? At her age, why doesn't she get out, go into the world and… What? I don't know. Life is complicated. I want more from…" Aurye didn't know what. She wanted Reysa and Magnus to tell her what to do. The way they acted toward her, alternately flirtatious and protective, as if they held some secret they might tell, or something to ask. Now they'd invited her to their home, filled her with wine, unfurled this unorthodox philosophy.

She still wasn't sure what they wanted to offer, or to take. When Aurye had dressed to come up here tonight, she'd believed anything might happen. Now she didn't know, wished she understood. The pain in her gut burned anew, a pain Aurye knew wasn't really present. At least it didn't have to be. The ache came and went, depending on her mind.

Aurye took the first step. Reysa climbed ahead, paused at the first half-landing, and lifted the bottom of her smooth cream-white dress, peeled it up over her head. Underneath she wasn't naked, still wearing the grey tights, and on top an ornamented silver brocade camisole or tunic, with white and black beads in a sort of constellation. In this reduced attire, Reysa led Aurye and Magnus the rest of the way.

The upper landing mirrored the square entry below, one side open to the great room, art displayed on two side walls. The broad double doors on the fourth wall must open on something, not the snowy outdoors, like below. What lay behind them? Instead of a coat rack, here the lone accessory was an antique divan, covered in a silky light gray. Reysa reclined, like a Norse goddess adorned in her strange ceremonial top, like a chainmail camisole. Aurye thought it was a little surprising, Reysa pulling off her dress, but she wasn't naked. Layers, that was the word Aurye had used. She was still clothed.

Aurye looked down, taking in the entire lower hall at once. Magnus stood to one side. Clearly he and Reysa wanted to show Aurye their art.

"Prometheus," Reysa announced.

In the painting, a large man, naked beneath a dramatically flowing gold wrap, reclined on a rock. Prometheus was not relaxing, but in agony. A giant eagle loomed, eating from a gaping wound in his belly.

"Prometheus created mankind from clay," Magnus said. "Formed a shape from mud and water, and bestowed life. We are his creations. While other gods and titans warred in their struggle for power, Prometheus opted out."

Aurye had to look away. The wound, open to the world. Why were they showing her this? What did they know about her?

"Prometheus stole fire from the gods," Reysa said. "Made it a gift to mortals."

Aurye vaguely remembered the myth from school. "It's striking, but I…" She guessed she might be missing the point, too distracted by the gory mess. The guts of a god on display.

Magnus gripped Aurye's shoulder. "Prometheus disregarded the law. He created men and women, and gave us fire. Others didn't. He dared. And because he dared, he was punished, the eagle feasting on his liver, forever."

Aurye knew they wanted her to see, but she couldn't bear to look at the painting any more. She wasn't squeamish about most things. The wound was too specific, too familiar. She turned to the opposite wall.

"Pandora?" Aurye asked.

"Yes," Magnus said.

Reysa sat up, watching Aurye's reaction before the second painting.

A woman knelt, barefoot in a wild forest, leaning over a small container. A hand concealed one of her eyes. She bent forward, mouth open, on the verge of discovery.

"What connects Pandora with Prometheus?" Aurye asked. "I'm sorry, I don't remember."

"We all learn, then forget," Reysa said. "If we're lucky, we learn again. Pandora was the gods' punishment for Prometheus's gift of fire. Pandora was the first human woman, created to bestow suffering, which would spread forever. She opened her jar, and our weaknesses flowed. Jealousy. Vanity."

"She's the reason we take for granted any good we ever gain," Magnus said. "Our punishment for Prometheus."

Reysa stood, came to Aurye's side. "You can't forestall death, but you can fight the poisoning of love."

Aurye turned. "But how?"

"We shift our minds. Transform language, every way we speak or relate. Alter habits, remake every routine. Constantly change places we go, foods we eat. We constantly trick one another into thinking we are both someone new."

"Is that all?" Aurye asked. "That simple?"

"Not entirely," Reysa said. "Other means exist to transform the self, means abandoned by the science of our age. So we look to the past for various powers that have been forgotten, or suppressed."

"A blend of science, alchemy and occult magic," Magnus said. "For radical self-transformation."

"In a couple, the partner is our second self. Do you understand, Aurye?"

"Yes, some," Aurye said. "But you're making my head spin."

"How far would you go, to create an entirely new self?" Reysa asked.

"I wish I could. It sounds…" Aurye trailed off, overwhelmed by how appealing it sounded. Was this possible?

"I hope you don't think we're deranged," Magnus said.

"Deranged?" Aurye laughed before she could stop herself.

Reysa looked at Magnus.

"No, don't worry," Aurye assured them. She felt the wine again. "Hell, I'm the one who's deranged. What I think is you might be, just maybe, more than the usual amount detached from the mainstream."

Reysa smiled. "Detached from the…" she began, seeming to taste the words as she spoke. "Actually, I like that."

"That means it's a good thing, then?" Magnus asked.

"You must not know me very well yet," Aurye said.

"We're getting there," Reysa said. "We're all learning. All of us."

"What I started saying was, it sounds incredible." Aurye spoke slowly, with reverence. "The possibility of building a new self."

"Almost anything's possible," Magnus said with assurance.

"Speaking of medicine," Aurye asked, "how can you still practice, living sixty miles out of town?"

Reysa blinked at the reversal. "I keep a condo outside Southeast Portland, ten miles from the hospital."

"What do you specialize in?" Aurye turned to Magnus. "I heard you're a plastic surgeon."

"You heard?" He appraised Aurye over his wine glass. "So, it's not just Reysa asking around about you?"

Aurye considered whether she should just tell them now about her situation. Her hand twitched as she consciously prevented it from moving, giving her away. Of course they didn't know, couldn't possibly assume. Only if she told them.

Magnus smiled. "It's true, I specialize in reconstructive plastic surgery. Burn victims, disfigurements, birth defects. I have no interest in working on the insecure, those who only want to eradicate distinctiveness, to look more like some bland ideal. Beauty matters, but more important is to believe oneself appealing. I wish we didn't always seek beauty of the most mundane, unchallenging variety. Trimming down an interesting nose, making it less noticeable. How boring."

Aurye understood his ideal, but felt confused. "But if you're a plastic surgeon and don't believe in making people more beautiful, then what?"

"I'm willing to rebuild, to sculpt. Form reveals character. Personage manifests not only in personality, but arrangement of body and face."

"You said you made errors," Aurye said. "Had some kind of problem."

Reysa spoke up. "Failure, he said."

"I made an aesthetic error. Disfigured someone, apparently." Magnus shrugged, as if everything had been told.

Reysa elaborated. "He repaired the arm of a teenage girl. The limb was mangled. The way Magnus rebuilt it was more aesthetic, functional. Magnus believed it matched the other limb. The problem was, it looked different than before."

"My patient was displeased," Magnus resumed. "Her family claimed to be shocked. To be fair, probably were shocked. The girl herself became suicidal. Her parents sued."

"What happened?" Aurye asked. "It must have worked out. You're still practicing."

Neither Magnus nor Reysa answered.

"You lost the lawsuit?"

"Lost, no," Reysa said.

"My malpractice insurer settled," Magnus said. "The limb was superior. Functionally better, more interesting." He stood, went to the rail and looked over. He leaned out over the edge, as if pulled. Aurye remembered this feeling, outside, at the cliff.

"But you're fine," Aurye insisted. "You can still practice."

"He could," Reysa said. "Malpractice insurance is vastly expensive now."

Magnus turned to face the women. "I learned a lesson, the need to rein myself in. No more idealism. It's not my place to make limbs more interesting, to sculpt intriguing shapes. If I want a mainstream practice, it can't be to please myself. The person I must please is the customer, the owner of the limb, or face, whatever. The path forward was obvious. I could do the uncreative work of restoring bodies and faces to the way they used to look. Give people what they expected. Creative sculpture was something I needed to keep to myself. Hush hush. I'm lucky I have a woman like Reysa."

Reysa stood, went to his side. "Lately he's moving from standard clientele to more of a niche. Clients willing to pay extra for flexibility and discretion."

"Openness of mind is valuable," Magnus added. "One piece of outside work earns more than a year in the clinic."

"Many clients come to stay with us here," Reysa explained, "to avoid any risk of being seen while healing. We're so isolated, often snowbound, it's perfect."

"What about your specialty?" Aurye asked Reysa.

"Orthopedic surgery."

"If I'm mostly face, hands and skin," Magnus said, "Reysa is the real meat and bone."

Reysa shrugged. "I keep a body upright. Able to stand, flex, move."

"She's too modest," Magnus insisted. "Reysa's a respected authority in limb reattachment. She hasn't achieved as many surgeries as some older surgeons, not yet, but her success is unrivaled. Limbs may seem clumsy, mechanical chunks of meat, but they're all fine detail. Nervous and vascular systems are intricate, complicated puzzles. Surgeons effective at reattachment and transplant must connect an array of interlocking parts, impossible to design in advance."

"Most cases are emergencies," Reysa said, though she seemed more comfortable letting Magnus explain.

"Donor and recipient interfaces must fit, be made to synchronize, exchange fluids and electricity, the prime movers of life. It's a magical power, almost godlike." Magnus seemed genuinely proud, awed by his wife.

This seemed to please Reysa more than embarrass her. "Working on athletes and accident victims doesn't afford me Magnus's freedom to exit the mainstream. I can't opt out, at least not yet. I'm looking for ways."

"We do collaborate well," Magnus said. "Our skills are complementary."

"And we're seeking others who are sympathetic," Reysa added.

"She has a recent story," Magnus said, as if just remembering. "Pretty dramatic. You might find it interesting."

Reysa looked to Magnus. "The legs?"

Magnus nodded.

"A car accident," Reysa began with slow caution, as if telling the story were as fraught with potential missteps as one of her surgeries. "Well, before that. From nowhere, this young man approached me, while eating lunch. He'd learned my name, sought me out. A great athlete, a sprinter, Olympic hopeful at 400 meters. He asked about Paralympic athletes, who compete on artificial limbs. You've seen those, flexible carbon fiber blades?"

Aurye nodded.

"I spoke with him on a Thursday afternoon. That Saturday night, he was rushed to the hospital. His car had been totaled. The legs, I judged, could not be saved." Reysa paused, watching Aurye's response.

Aurye couldn't believe what she'd heard. "That's terrible."

"Why is it terrible?" Magnus asked.

"For this young man, the sprinter, it was not terrible," Reysa said. "It was exactly what he wanted. The athletic advantage of ultra-light limbs. More than that, to be noteworthy. Not just win races."

Aurye tried to process all she was saying. "He wanted?"

"It was arranged, scheduled," Reysa said. "I was ready at the hospital."

Though Aurye believed she understood the first impulse, another aspect troubled her. "But he had a gift. I'm not sure he should destroy such a capable body."

"We destroy to create," Reysa said. "He wanted to be an inspiration. To remake his life."

"But he could have died, if things had…"

"Died?" Reysa looked puzzled, then understood. "No, the accident wasn't much. The legs weren't destroyed, barely damaged really. I told him in advance, just make sure there's lots of blood. Enough to be convincing."

"Told him… In advance?" Aurye looked back and forth between Reysa and Magnus.

"No reason to risk his life. We decided I should take his legs, for Magnus. The sprinter wanted to become an inspiration, and that's what he became. He has a book deal now. Some producer wants to create a movie, his life story."

"He found what he wanted," Magnus added. "And I have new, athletic legs." He stepped away from the rail, took a stride and turned, as if modeling.

Aurye wondered, could this be true? Even now, it seemed more likely the Bergs just wanted to shock her.

Reysa watched, appraising her husband's movements. "It was my first chance to contribute to our plan in a major way. I showed Magnus I was ready to help remake him, the way he was already changing me."

"The way he was…" Aurye looked at Reysa. "Both of you?"

"Come closer." Reysa rotated her hands to show off her wrists. Around each ran a line, which Aurye first took to be suicide scars, but the lines continued all the way around. "Magnus left the seams visible, by design. We wanted to accentuate them, to clarify what we are. Assemblages of varied parts."

"What?" Part of Aurye was shocked, the rest couldn't believe it was possible. "Who are you made of?"

Reysa looked into Aurye's eyes, held her gaze steady so Aurye wouldn't doubt. "I won't tell you the names, not yet. But these hands of mine, they aren't the same I was born with."

Magnus unbuttoned his jeans, pulled them down and stepped out. "Here, see?" He demonstrated the clear delineation, mid-thigh, just below where his boxer briefs ended. Both legs were slightly mismatched above and below the line. "We love the contrast, where skin joins skin."

Aurye considered. Reysa's wrists, Magnus's legs. Each body exhibited a sharp transition between shapes, colors and textures. Where differences met, how could one even be sure which was the original? Distinctions blurred.

Magnus picked up his jeans, reached in the pocket and produced photographs. "Look, see? Don't worry, nothing graphic."

The photos showed a teenage girl, blond and vigorously athletic.

"I could show you the torn-up mess of pulped meat I had to work with. But look. Reysa and I collaborated. She reattached, kept flesh alive, restored limb function. I made it look new. Better than new."

Aurye wasn't sure how to react. The girl's arm displayed nothing like the jarring transition of Reysa's or Magnus's transplants. She was a normal girl, skin the radiant, buttery tan of healthful youth.

"Do you see what I meant to achieve? Never mind that it didn't work, I mean, we try, sometimes fail. Do you see my intention?"

One arm tapered differently than the other. The imbalance was slight, reminding Aurye of tennis players, whose racquet arms often developed more muscle. She looked strong, poised, if slightly asymmetrical.

"The girl didn't like it, I can't deny that. I was going to lose a malpractice lawsuit. So I learned to paint by numbers. Until I found another way to practice my art."

"This isn't just Magnus." Aurye's statement to Reysa contained a question.

"No," Magnus corrected. "We've developed our philosophy together, over time. And we never harm. Never anything the client doesn't want."

This aspect Aurye found inspiring. The Bergs weren't in competition, Reysa wasn't merely in support of Magnus. The two collaborated. "But are you sure it's safe, legal? I mean, of course you are." If she knew anything about the Bergs, it was their precision about everything.

"They sign waivers, agree not contact medical boards or authorities," Magnus said. "Informed adults of sound mind. That doesn't preclude eccentricity, or strange desires."

"What do you think?" Reysa asked cautiously.

Aurye considered. "It's surprising, disconcerting. My initial gut reaction was fear, to be honest."

"Understandable," Reysa said. "And do be honest."

"But I get it. You're looking to make lives that work for you. Sometimes that's not easy, or takes stepping over some lines." What line would Aurye be willing to cross? To be able to take control of herself, she would give anything.

"Yes, I admit it," Reysa said with a smirk. "We do things others might consider perverted, disgusting and wrong."

"You want to hear the true revelation?" Magnus looked pleased, self-contained and satisfied, as if he had a beneficial secret to share. "I couldn't become myself until I severed all ties, went underground. My vision became clearer. And I was shocked what people will pay for unorthodox services. The majority may be appalled by willful disfigurement, but those who desire it might happily pay millions."

Aurye almost repeated the word. Millions. She didn't want the Bergs to think her too interested in money. Really that wasn't the first thing they possessed that appealed to her. She wanted help eradicating herself.

"Thus the mountaintop castle," Reysa said lightly.

"Money is freedom." Magnus shrugged. "At least it helps. The rest is not giving a damn what anyone thinks."

Aurye couldn't believe this was real. She felt inspired, impressed by Magnus's uncompromising transformation, and more, she desired something like it for herself. Though her hands trembled at what they'd revealed to her, Aurye admired them more than ever.

"Exiting the mainstream wasn't exile," Magnus said, "though at first, I thought it was."

"I still commute into Portland on Tuesdays and Wednesdays," Reysa said.

"I do good work. Sometimes I take weeks off to travel with Magnus. He's free. I'm still becoming free."

Magnus turned and went to open the double doors. "Time to go in."

Though the room had been shut, the dry warmth from the fireplace downstairs reached even here. Moonlight fell through the skylight, making the operating theater almost day-bright. A central surgical table was surrounded by carts and stands of medical gear, and less recognizable industrial equipment. In two far corners, white curtains drew back to reveal vacant hospital beds. Against the rightmost wall, metal racks stood far enough out of the light that whatever they stored was obscured in shadow.

Aurye stepped toward that darkness, lured by the unknown. Light glinted off glass. The shelves held jars, or tanks.

Sudden light flashed above, jarringly bright. An instant later, thunder crashed. Brilliance illuminated everything stored in the glass containers, suspended in emerald liquid. Body parts small as fingers, hands and eyes, and larger. Heads, limbs, torsos.

"In death, they leave behind much that remains useful," Reysa said. "But living flesh is easier to work with."

Aurye swallowed. "You didn't bring me here to take—"

"No," Reysa answered quickly, then giggled in a manner that put Aurye's fears to rest. "You're not new flesh to us. We value more than youth, which counts for nothing in the end. Magnus excels at cosmetic shaping, so if the point were only to constantly tighten, well. We could forever remake ourselves into younger-looking versions of the same people. We're physically fit, healthy. Younger than our years."

"What, then? What do you want from me that you don't already have?" Aurye looked to Magnus.

"Varieties of personhood, within the same partner," he answered. "Reysa gave me the eye of a very tall and thin Kenyan immigrant, who died aged twenty-nine from severe burns to legs and torso. His eyes were undamaged. I took only one, afraid to change my vision too much at once."

Aurye leaned close, looked again at Magnus's eyes. Her first impression had been correct. The eyes of two different men. "And you?" she asked Reysa. "What else? Your wrist seams. How could a surgeon cut off her own hands?"

"It's not necessary to cut through to bone, though that's what we did with Magnus's legs. My new hands are what you might call a veneer, like most of my changes so far." Reysa gestured to demonstrate the flexibility of her hands, then lifted off the decorative camisole to reveal a patchwork torso. Her flesh was a beautiful puzzle. Not deformity, not feeble grasping for youth's shallow appeal. She was more beautiful than anyone Aurye knew. A sculpture of contrasting parts.

Magnus moved to Reysa's side. "Can you see how I love my wife even more, this way?"

Aurye understood. She'd always thought Reysa striking, at least as conventionally attractive as Aurye herself, but less ordinary, eyes and mouth far more interesting.

Magnus pulled his sweater over his head. He and Reysa stood revealed, proof of their convictions offered in varied surprising details. Thick scars, proportions which might seem wrong at first glance, but which careful appraisal revealed more pleasing, by some perspective of aesthetic judgment Aurye found hard to articulate. She heard it inside her, a voice speaking for the first time. Felt the pull of unorthodox attraction, of weird possibility and strange desire.

What Aurye wondered was, could they do this to her? Fix what was broken, remake her to become more strange, even perversely beautiful? She imagined her future self, someone as yet unknown.

"It's true, we objectify you," Reysa said. "But we've always objectified ourselves, and one another. Everyone."

"So you're not asking me to swap legs?" She laughed, nervous despite the enticement. "Anything like that?"

Magnus answered. "We don't want to consume you."

"Then what?"

"Our plan is long. Eventually, you should finish college, med school. But first, help us broaden our circle."

"You want others?" Aurye tried to assemble pieces of this offer. "Not just me? Who?"

"We don't know. You'll help us find them. You're attractive, likable. You work in a visible spot, the coolest bar on the mountain, with a clientele of active mountain types. Snowboarders, climbers, travelers staying at Timberline."

Aurye nodded.

Magnus continued where Reysa left off. "Young athletic men and women, decadent, pleasure-seeking. Accustomed to living outside the lines. Yes, our ideas are transgressive. They require a certain willingness to step past boundaries, where others stop. For some, life's thrills may have worn thin. They might be receptive to dramatic transformation."

"If we wanted to be promiscuous, we could," Reysa said. "Creative living is all the perversion we need. You know, if a universal maker existed, she'd be the most perverse being imaginable." She shot her husband a look and a wink.

Magnus smirked. "Reysa determinedly postulates this notion of a female creator. I think we need more wine."

"This is a lot to understand," Aurye said. "Explain it to me a different way."

"We want a larger menu," Magnus said.

"Friends," Reysa said. "We'll take from more. Give to more."

"I think I see, and understand." Aurye wanted to sit. All the tension had left her. She felt no more apprehension, no more wondering what the Bergs intended. "Also, I think you're right about more wine."

"I'll go for a bottle." Magnus started for the stairs.

"Bring two," Reysa called. After he was gone, she turned to Aurye. "Do you think he could've carried three?"

Aurye laughed, head still spinning with everything their suggestions entailed. Some aspects seemed shocking, but when she weighed her personal affection for the Bergs, their desire to help her, along with the resources at their disposal, and balanced these against her otherwise dismal options, gravity seemed to draw her inexorably nearer their orbit. They were so vibrant, more engaging and attractive than any couple Aurye knew. Even more so, now that she knew the degree to which they'd become who they were by their own uncompromising efforts. This unorthodox approach formed the core of what kept them energetic, vibrant and youthful in mind and body.

Could this be true, could her own life transform, broken parts be replaced? Everything would be easier without so many limitations. A life of energy and health, clarity of mind, leisure, physical elegance. She loved how the Bergs offset each other, beautiful balanced within themselves and counterpoised against one another. It all felt so seductive.

"So, have we shocked you?" Reysa ventured. "Exceeded your boundaries?"

Aurye considered. The contrary was true, but she hesitated to let them think her too desperately willing, lacking any restraint at all. "I'm afraid actually you'd be shocked, if you knew what I'd give if I could just…" She gestured, but was afraid it came across as nihilistic rejection of everything in life, rather than willingness to obtain something better, and optimism Reysa and Magnus could help. She wasn't sure how to explain her predicament, afraid they might see her differently if they knew everything, could see all her hidden flaws laid bare. But of course they would see, eventually.

"You're tempted," Reysa guessed. "We could take you such places."

Magnus entered with two uncorked bottles. "Away from the humdrum, toward the beautiful strange." He poured.

Reysa lifted her glass. "To possibility."

The three toasted, and drank as though thirsty.

"If it seems strange, my lack of shock at your… surprising suggestions, there are reasons," Aurye ventured. "I think once we hit bottom, and face what seems like the impossibility of going on, if we do come out the other side, it's freeing. So I'm probably open to alternatives most would reject."

"I'm the same," Reysa assured her. "Broken down by trauma. For me, three times. First, as I was leaving for college, my stepfather tried to prevent me. Made threats against my mother, broke my arm, then my nose. When these didn't deter me, he escalated. Emotional, sexual. It nearly broke me, but I left, never returned. Never again considered that place home."

"Horrible," Aurye said.

Magnus kept his eyes on the floor, motionless except to sip from his wine. Reysa continued.

"Next, my first husband, another surgeon, and yes I realize how that sounds, marrying one surgeon after another. He rejected me for a woman less accomplished, less challenging to him, after my accident. He even said,

She may not be as hot as you, but at least she's not so fucking familiar. I didn't think I'd make it, but I did. I found Magnus."

"And third?" Aurye couldn't help looking at Magnus, fearing the possibility he may once have harmed Reysa in ways similar to the two prior stories. That seemed impossible, but they were always talking about inevitable betrayal.

"Magnus, but not something he did to me. The lawsuit, seeing the toll it took on him. That devouring fear. Both sleepless, afraid of losing our home, his career, which he believed to be everything. When I saw Magnus break, something in me broke." Reysa looked away, gulped her wine, then seemed to remember she wasn't alone. "I became willing to cross any line, to protect this. The only life I'll ever have."

"You seem very strong to me," Aurye told her. "Both of you."

"Do you understand now?" Magnus asked. "This is how anything becomes possible."

"I'm younger, but I've faced my share," Aurye said. "But to have an ally against the world, willing to do anything to protect me. I want it. I used to believe I'd find a man like that, but it's rare."

"You will," Reysa said.

"How do I know when I have it?" Aurye asked. "I mean, that I've found perfect, faithful devotion, someone willing to die for me, kill for me, and not just another weak, betraying bastard?"

Magnus moved between Aurye and Reysa. "Find someone whose desire to remain close to you doesn't decrease when trouble comes. Who stays closer by your side when you need them."

"That's right." Reysa took Magnus's hand. Aurye could see them squeeze.

Reysa knelt on the bare stone, then sat and lay back. "Lie down. Look up. The clouds are coming again."

Magnus did the same, so Aurye followed suit. The skylight revealed a thin crescent moon against pure black sky.

"Clouds?" Aurye asked. "Are you sure it's—"

She was interrupted by a flash, not so bright and proximate as what had first revealed the storage tanks. Soon, thunder followed, then wispy clouds moved across until the moon was nothing but hidden backlight.

"Tell me again," Aurye said. "Tell me what you want us to do together."

Magnus answered. "We want to widen our circle. To share with others, just one at first, then another. A few more, not many. Wider variety of personhood. That's what we crave."

"If we can't transcend personal death," Reysa said, "we can create an immortality of relationship. Mutual support."

"What do you think of what we've said?" Magnus asked, hesitant. "Maybe we frightened you."

"In all our talks at Midgard, you seemed receptive," Reysa said. "Not to this idea exactly, but our various strange hypotheticals. You always seemed to get it."

"If you want to go home, you can," Magnus said. "We'll consider you a friend, even if—"

"It isn't that you've frightened me," Aurye interrupted.

Reysa rolled over, touched Aurye's arm. "What then?"

"Something troubles you," Magnus said. "You still seem afraid."

"I am afraid. Not of you." Aurye stood. She reached for the lace hem of her dress, lifted it over her head. Still she wore the black fleece tights and white long-sleeved sweater. She lifted the bottom of the sweater, raised it enough to start revealing her bare belly, then hesitated.

"You don't need to—" Reysa stood, approached almost close enough to touch Aurye, but held back.

Magnus sat up, seeming mortified, certain Aurye had misunderstood. "We didn't mean you should have to—"

The glow through the skylight diminished as clouds advanced. Nothing remained of moonlight. Snow swirled, barely visible.

Aurye didn't cover herself. "I understood. I just have to show myself." She stepped back, leaned against the operating table.

"I don't…" Magnus trailed off.

Aurye lifted the under-sweater to reveal her naked torso. A six-inch strip of surgical tape ran vertically up the side of her abdomen, below her left breast. Her hands wanted to cover, but she fought the impulse. Now was time to reveal. Against her will, fingers flitted nearer the wound.

Lightning struck, filled the room with ultimate brightness. For a flash, nothing was hidden. Electricity surged through the strange machinery behind the surgical table. Static popped and invisible power filled the air with a living hum.

"I used to cover it with thick adhesive gauze," Aurye said. "It's something I've gotten better at."

"Wound care?" Reysa asked.

"Concealment. Hiding a wound that will never heal." She pinched the top end of the tape, pulled up, then down. She shuddered as the tape came free. Flaps of skin opened, pulled apart. The wound wasn't bloody, or even wet. It was an open vacancy, not a recent injury. Something had always been missing. "No matter what, people end up seeing."

Magnus stood, came to Reysa's side. Both approached.

"This is me." Aurye expected inquiries about doctors, diagnoses, how parents could have allowed the wound to remain. Why hadn't someone cut out the disease, sewn her shut?

The Bergs said nothing, only regarded Aurye gently, seeming afraid their scrutiny might inflict further damage. The room had become so dark. Aurye could barely see Reysa and Magnus, knew she too must be almost invisible.

Lightning flashed, and for another instant everything was perfect white. Thunder followed.

"It's rare," Aurye whispered. "Thundersnow."

Reysa knelt, did not touch, but looked unflinchingly at the opening in Aurye's side. It led not into her gut, to some vital inner aspect of her. It led away, like a pit in the ground, vanishing into the dark. Aurye hated it so much. It had always been with her. "It's like your painting," Aurye said. "Prometheus with the giant eagle, devouring."

"If you want to change," Magnus said, "we'll help."

"I've always wanted to," Aurye said, "just didn't believe it."

"You can change yourself as little as you like," Reysa said.

"More." Aurye felt emotion surging. She couldn't let herself cry. "Change as much as I can."

"You don't have to," Reysa cautioned.

"Let me give something back," Aurye suggested. "Something small. First to Reysa, then when I heal, to Magnus."

"Not yet, and don't worry," Reysa said. "We have plenty of donor parts."

"There's always meat," Magnus added lightly. "More than we could ever use."

"What I want is for my body to be always torn apart," Aurye insisted. "Again and again, forever. I might age, but never become old. I'll constantly be something new. Cut apart, and sewn back into some fresh unknown shape."

Reysa touched her shoulder gently. "Dare try, or never know."

Aurye felt it for the first time, believed it was true. Acceptance, the first she could remember. She felt no desire to return home. "To be my new self, I want to give away pieces of the old one."

Magnus nodded. "We have only one life each. One chance."

"So we endlessly role-play, speculate on every possible ending," Reysa said. "Betrayals, murder-suicide pacts, feeble dissolutions. We plan for any eventuality, solve each in advance and thus avoid them all. Along the way, replace parts of ourselves. Someday we'll die, but first we can be entirely new."

"All our work is to ensure this never ends." Magnus gestured not outwardly, around the room, at the grand house or the mountain, but between himself and Reysa. He expanded the gesture to include Aurye.

Clouds thinned, glowing at the moon's insistence, and latent energy carried within atmosphere ozone-rich after penetration by lightning.

"None of this should ever have to end," Aurye said. "None of us."

Lightning flashed again, cut the sky as if in agreement.

PUBLICATION HISTORY

"Firedancing" appeared in *The Children of Old Leech*

"The Smoke Lodge" appeared in *Autumn Cthulhu*

"Everyone Gathers at Haystack Rock" appeared in *Walk on the Weird Side*

"The Slipping of Stones" appeared in *Strange Aeons*

"The Tidal Pull of Salt and Sand" appeared in *Xnoybis 1*

"Delirium Sings at the Maelstrom Window" appeared in *Cthulhu Fhtagn!*

"An Ideal Retreat" was first published in a stand-alone limited edition by Dim Shores

"Endure Within a Dying Frame" appeared in *Lovecraft eZine*

"The Carnival Arrives in Darkness" appeared in *Nightscript 2*

"The Insomniac Who Slept Forever" appeared in *The Madness of Dr. Caligari*

"The Human Alchemy" appeared in *Eternal Frankenstein*

"The Only Way Out Is Down" appears here for the first time.

"If you live and breathe both black metal and literary horror, this book is a gift." –*CVLT Nation*

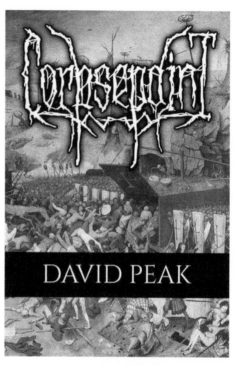

It's been years since the groundbreaking debut of black metal band Angelus Mortis, and that first album, *Henosis,* has become a classic of the genre, a harrowing primal scream of rage and anger. With the next two albums, *Fields of Punishment* and *Telos,* Angelus Mortis cemented a reputation for uncompromising, aggressive music, impressing critics and fans alike. But the road to success is littered with temptation, and over the next decade, Angelus Mortis's leader, Max, better known as Strigoi, became infamous for bad associations and worse behavior, burning through side-men and alienating fans.

Today, at the request of their record label, Max and new drummer Roland are traveling to Ukraine to record a comeback album with the famously reclusive cult act Wisdom of Silenus. What they discover when they get there will go far deeper than the aesthetics of the genre, and the music they create–antihuman, antilife–ultimately becomes a weapon unto itself.

Trade Paperback, 240 pp, $15.99

ISBN-13: 978-1-939905-38-3

http://www.wordhorde.com

From the earliest depictions of winged goddesses to the delicate, paper-winged fairies of the Victorians, from valiant Valkyries to cliff-dwelling harpies, from record-setting pilots to fearless astronauts, women have long since claimed their place in the skies, among the clouds and beyond.

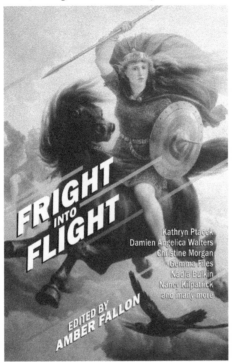

Word Horde presents *Fright Into Flight*, the debut anthology from Amber Fallon (*The Terminal*, *The Warblers*), in which women take wing. In these stories connected by the unifying thread of flight, authors including Damien Angelica Walters, Christine Morgan, and Nadia Bulkin have spread their wings and created terrifying visions of real life angels, mystical journeys, and the demons that lurk inside us all. Whether you like your horror quiet and chilling or more in-your-face and terrifying, there's something here for every horror fan to enjoy.

You're in for a bumpy ride..So fasten your seatbelt, take note of the emergency exits, hold on to your airsick bag, and remember that this book may be used as a flotation device in the event of a crash landing.

Format: Trade Paperback, 258 pp, $16.99

ISBN-13: 978-1-939905-44-4

http://www.wordhorde.com

ABOUT THE AUTHOR

Michael Griffin has released a novel, *Hieroglyphs of Blood and Bone* (Journalstone, 2017) and a short fiction collection, *The Lure of Devouring Light* (Word Horde, 2016). His stories have appeared in magazines like *Apex* and *Black Static*, and the anthologies *Looming Low*, *Eternal Frankenstein*, *The Children of Old Leech* and the Shirley Jackson Award winner *The Grimscribe's Puppets*.

He's also an ambient musician and founder of Hypnos Recordings, an ambient record label he operates with his wife in Portland, Oregon. Michael's blog is at griffinwords.com and on Twitter, he posts as @mgsoundvisions.